BIRDY CLEARY

BIRDY CLEARY

A NOVEL

CATHERINE BUSCH

CERULEAN
PRESS

To Tom, my corner man for life.

If you can learn a simple trick, Scout, you'll get along a lot better with all kinds of folks. You never really understand a person until you consider things from his point of view—until you climb inside his skin and walk around in it.

    —To Kill a Mockingbird, Harper Lee

She knew!
Love.
That was what she had that IT did not have.
She had Mrs. Whatsit's love, and her father's, and her mother's, and the real Charles Wallace's love, and the twins', and Aunt Beast's.
And she had her love for them.
But how could she use it? What was she meant to do?

    —A Wrinkle in Time, Madeleine L'Engle

Fall 2007

1

BIRDY CLEARY DUG HER left thumbnail into the soft wood of the pew. The choir was awful, but it was persistent. Its ancient members warbled the responsorial psalm. "God, in your goodness, you have made a home for the poor." The few congregants repeated the line cautiously, unable to decipher the intended melody. Birdy kept digging and composed her own psalm. *God, in your goodness, make them sing better.*

Mr. Doppelski, star lector of St. Ann's Catholic Parish, had given the church a facelift a few weeks earlier. Birdy studied the back of the pew in front of her, which he'd slapped with shiny white paint. The seats remained their original faded walnut stain. Mr. Doppelski had also conjured a thick, ugly carpet from somewhere, and now it ran up the center aisle, its dark swirls of color clashing with the Ordinary Time green adorning the altar. Mom nudged Birdy in the ribs and pointed to the lone pot of Easter lilies rotting in the back left corner of the church.

"I just can't believe no one's gotten those poor flowers yet!" she whispered. Birdy nodded, as she did every week when the flowers remained in place and Mom remained indignant. The odor of candles, wood, and old lady perfume mixed with the paint smell and made Birdy's nose itch. She swallowed a sneeze and amended her prayer.

Sorry for being mean about the choir. The choir ladies were already middle-aged during Vatican II, an event that had left them salty, and their voices had withered in the intervening decades. Mom turned back to Birdy.

"You know, I was a wonderful singer when I was young. I just don't have the time to do it now," she sighed.

Birdy nodded again, the picture of empathy for her mother's many burdens. Mom took a long sip from the straw of her giant water jug. Seven years previously, Mom had landed in the hospital for heat stroke and came home with this medical-grade water receptacle. Now she believed in hydration as firmly as she believed in God. On Mom's other side, Dad was concentrating on the second reading with his head bowed and his eyes shut tight. He stirred to scrawl something in his journal and then resumed his listening position.

On the pulpit, Mr. Doppelski read a passage from Hebrews with reverent diction, abandoning his weekday twang.

"God is treating you as his children. For what children are not disciplined by their father?" Mr. Doppelski broke character for a moment to wink at his not-quite-two-year-old daughter, Hannah, who was standing up on her seat saying "Hi, Daddy!" A giggle rippled through the congregation. Mr. Doppelski's wiggling mass of children filled the first two pews on the left side of the church. Mr. Doppelski's brother Abe and his family filled the first two pews on the right.

Abe permitted himself a full bark of laughter at his brother's little joke, but Mr. Doppelski had already moved on. He finished the reading, genuflected slowly, and returned to his seat. Mrs. Fitzgerald, the cantor, belted the Gospel acclamation, making Birdy and her brothers wince as they stood. Father Bill droned the greeting, droned through the reading and then began droning his homily.

Birdy's real name was Bernadette. Family accounts of how she had acquired her nickname varied wildly. Mom said she had picked it because Birdy was so tiny, but so strong, and sang so beautifully, and was destined to fly. Dad said Birdy had liked when he sang "Mockingbird" and would request it by asking for "the birdy song." Birdy's brothers had less touching accounts. Peter said they started calling her that after a bird pooped on her, while Patrick said it was because when she was born, she looked like something that hatched out of an egg. Chris was too young to remember the truth, so he of-fered various inventions, such as that it was because of her shrill call or the feathers she secretly had growing on her butt.

Birdy had always felt that being named Bernadette was like being designated as a poster child for the Catholic Church, fated to die young from tuberculosis or some other medieval ailment. Wishing to avoid an untimely demise, she embraced her avian moniker, no matter how poetic or disgusting its origin.

On the opposite end of the pew from Dad, Patrick sat watching Father Bill deliver his message. Patrick was seventeen and looked alert, but he was drumming his fingers against his knees as though typing the words he was really thinking. When Father Bill said, "the Lord wants to warsh us in his grace," Patrick's eyes swiveled to Birdy's. She smirked and looked away.

Patrick and Birdy had an unspoken agreement to not crack each other up in church, but their foil was sandwiched between them. Chris was sixteen and chomping at the bit. He was doing his best to catch Birdy's eye, and she was doing her best to avoid him. Chris shared her dislike of the choir, but did not share her guilt about this or any other feeling. Instead, he tried Sunday after Sunday to make her and Patrick laugh.

The Cleary kids were arranged in birth order, but they were incomplete. Peter should have been the one on the far end of the pew. If he was there, he would have been sitting perfectly still, singing along in his clear voice without cracking a smile. All the while he would be absorbing and computing the inputs of a Sunday morning, preparing an amusing but nonetheless thoughtful commentary for the car ride home. But Peter didn't live with them anymore.

The next day, Birdy would start high school. She wished she was going with Chris and Patrick. They were starting 11th and 12th grades at Don Bosco Catholic Prep, a private all-boys school 30 minutes south of Conrad, if there was no traffic. There was always traffic. Birdy's father was ideologically opposed to being beholden to other commuters, so the Bosco-bound Clearys were guaranteed an hour-long survey of winding back roads instead of an hour-long crawl along the interstate. Dad taught history at Bosco, so Chris and Patrick attended the school on scholarship. Thanks to her noticeable lack of a Y chromosome, Birdy did not have this same privilege. Instead, she was fated to pioneer a new educational institution.

Father Bill had been sermoning for several minutes when Mr. Doppelski stood once again. The parish jerked to life at this breach of Mass protocol, but Father Bill looked relieved.

"Yes, and that reminds me, we've got an announcement from Jude Doppelski." Father Bill sat down fast, and Mr. Doppelski reclaimed his position up front. He gripped the pulpit with scarred, calloused hands and grinned out at the congregation.

"Morning folks, I don't want to take up too much of your time this morning, but like Father Bill said I just wanted a quick word. I know Abe and I have been talking your ear off about Divine Mercy for months now—mostly Abe—" a pause for laughter "—but tomorrow's our first day.

"Some of you have known me since I went to school here at St. Ann's, and Lord knows those empty halls could use some life in them. Divine Mercy's really gonna fill a need in Conrad, and we've got a lot of interest so far. Gosh, we got the Clearys just about as soon as they moved in!" he said, sweeping an arm in their direction. Mom giggled and Chris muttered, "Oh, Jesus Christ," which nearly cracked Patrick in half, but Birdy kept quiet.

The Clearys had moved, again, during Christmas vacation. After Dad landed the job at Bosco, the family searched for housing in the school's 30-mile radius. The only affordable slice of that pie was Conrad, an old Maryland town cut off from all the other old Maryland towns by a wide river and a misplaced sense of pride. Mom considered their entry into the Bosco sphere to be a miracle, leaving Birdy wondering why no divine intervention had occurred on her part. Oh, but it had, Mom would have said. Because the Clearys moved to Victoria Street.

When Mom and Dad got the keys to their new house, they had assured the kids it was spacious and had a big yard. These things were true, but not in an appealing way. The yard was a carpet of dead, mighty weeds, and the house's high ceilings and dark corners swallowed light and heat. Birdy was unloading the U-Haul and trying not to cry when a crew of neighbors showed up ready to help. There were two men around her dad's age and a handful of boys around hers. The tallest one smiled at her like they were already friends and asked, "Are you going to be at Conrad Middle?"

Mom and Dad hadn't wanted to squander Birdy's brains or soul on the local public schools, which they assumed would be both academically and morally bankrupt. They'd floundered to an unconventional placeholder while they figured out what to do with her.

"I'm actually homeschooled right now," she choked out, hating the way the words felt in her mouth.

To her surprise, the boy broke into a delighted smile. "No way!" he nearly yelled. "Me too!"

The boy was Dominic Doppelski, and he was sitting up on the altar now, listening to his dad advertise. They lived just up Victoria Street from the Clearys, next door to Abe and his family.

To the Clearys' great surprise, the remote and decrepit Conrad was availed of an intense flock of Catholics, most of whom were taking great pains not to utilize public education. There were private schools like Bosco to the south and the flailing St. Monica's High School right there in Conrad, but the real Catholics educated their children at home. Real Catholics did not make the amateur mistake of tolerating the four horsemen of the secular apocalypse— abortion, birth control, homosexuality, and welfare queens. To avoid exposure to these horrors and their champions, the homeschoolers organized themselves under a group called Catholic Homeschoolers of Conrad, or CHOC. This acronym was supposed to evoke a vague academic flavor, but it made Birdy think of trying to clear phlegm from one's throat.

Based on previous encounters, Birdy had always thought of homeschoolers as unsocialized weirdos who lurked on farms and wore saint t-shirts, long skirts and chapel veils. Her bias was only partly accurate. The people of CHOC were abundantly socialized within the bounds of a short and intense feedback loop, and the

Doppelskis pulled Birdy right into it. There were farms aplenty, but there was no shortage of activities to draw the homeschoolers away from them, to the point that Birdy didn't understand when the schooling happened. As for the clothes, there were some frumpy skirts, but the t-shirts skewed less to saints and more to slogans such as "Cool to be Catholic," "Pro-Life," "Catholic to the Max," and "Modest is Hottest." This last was worn only by girls and implied they were desirable future wives because they didn't flaunt their female appendages.

Mom considered the discovery of their house down the street from these two large, Catholic, patriotic families to be another miracle. Birdy knew this because Mom had said so at least once a day for months. While Birdy didn't think their living quarters met the qualifications for a miracle, it did feel significant and comforting to have so quickly fallen in with a tribe.

And it had provided the answer to the question of Birdy's education. Like the Clearys, the Doppelskis and some of their friends wanted the benefits of the traditional classroom while avoiding such pitfalls as non-Catholics and bad Catholics. After mulling it over for years, the CHOC parents had recently cooked up a courseload, filed some paperwork, and founded Divine Mercy School.

Bosco was elite and expensive. Divine Mercy was a bargain and a bit more slapdash. It was founded on the conviction that the evils of the world could be rectified by creating an insular community of like-minded children, who would in turn grow up to use their knowledge of saints, Latin, and the American Revolution to overturn Roe v. Wade. Mr. Doppelski, a self-proclaimed ideas guy, had pointed out that the St. Ann's population was mostly octogenarians, and as such was dwindling. Practically speaking, St. Ann's needed an income stream to survive, and it had an empty school building right there on its grounds.

"Anyway," Mr. Doppelski was saying now, "This morning we're taking a second collection to benefit the school, so if you have an extra bill in your wallet today, think about giving it to the kids. God bless." Mr. Doppelski sat down and Abe Doppelski sprang up, wicker collection basket at the ready. An upsetting, greasy cologne wafted from his tan suit as he approached the Clearys' pew. Dad jerked from his meditation, took out his wallet, and placed a ten-dollar bill in the basket. Mr. Abe mouthed, "Thanks man, thanks so much," and Dad nodded back into contemplation.

Conrad had developed its own nomenclature to classify the two sets of Doppelskis. Dominic's parents, Jude and Tammy, were generally known as Mr. and Mrs. Doppelski. They and all their children had dark hair, so when referring to the whole family, people called them The Dark Doppelskis. Abe Doppelski was great with people, something people knew about him because he mentioned it whenever he got the chance. In keeping with his genial image, he was quick to urge people to call him by his first name. Kids called him and his wife Mr. Abe and Ms. Karen. Abe and his family had fair hair, so their family unit was dubbed The Light Doppelskis.

After surviving a disturbing rendition of "Be Not Afraid," the Clearys genuflected their way out of the pew into the post-Mass bottleneck, where Mom ran right into Mrs. Doppelski.

"Tammy! How was your trip? Can you believe school starts tomorrow? Thank you again for letting Birdy carpool with you this year! She'll help you out with anything you need!" Mom gushed and Birdy stood behind her, watching her smooth blond ponytail wagging on the back of her head. Mrs. Doppelski's hair was loose and long. She balanced Hannah in one arm and jiggled the potato-like Rebecca in the other.

"We don't mind at all! We love Birdy! The kids have so much fun when she comes over!"

Ms. Karen and Mrs. Doppelski's general strategy was to combine their 16 walking children to entertain each other. Birdy was a helpful facilitator of this tactic and had been an especially frequent visitor around Rebecca's birth. Between the two houses, there was always a game to play, a picture to paint, or a doll to rescue from a dog. But both families had been out of town for the past few weeks visiting yet another set of Doppelskis (of unknown coloring), and Birdy had returned to relative loneliness.

"I'm just really swamped right now," said Mom as Hannah lunged for Rebecca, pincers ready. Mrs. Doppelski giggled sympathetically. Mrs. Doppelski deployed her giggle in many situations that Birdy found odd.

"Can I see you?" Birdy reached for Hannah, who immediately gathered fistfuls of Birdy's brown hair and launched into a hard-to-follow story about the horses at her uncle Max's house. Meanwhile, Ms. Karen clutched Mom's arm.

"Maggie! When's our next walk? I've been dying without them!" said Ms. Karen.

"Let's do it soon," sighed Mrs. Doppelski. The three mothers cherished their walks with a fervor that made Birdy nervous about someday having children.

"Oh my God," muttered Chris. At St. Ann's, the pews were fused on one side to the walls, which meant the ladies' reunion was blocking his only escape route down the center aisle. Birdy felt his claustrophobia vicariously, but as she was now holding Hannah, she wasn't trying to leave anymore. She looked around the church and spotted Dominic genuflecting by the altar. He turned and squared his shoulders before joining the crowd. Dominic always seemed to wear the beginnings of a smile, and he turned one up at Birdy as he approached.

"Birdy! It's been so long!"

He gave her a huge hug, which she returned gladly around the squirming Hannah. Behind Dominic's back, Chris smiled psychotically at Birdy, as he always did when she spoke to a male of her own age and species. Patrick, on Chris's flank, made a heart with his hands and batted his eyelashes.

Maybe it was okay she wouldn't be at school with her brothers.

"Ready to be carpool buddies?" Dominic said expansively. "Wow, you got really tan since last time I saw you."

"Yes I am! And yeah, I did a lot of yard work the last few weeks."

"Why didn't your brothers do that?"

At this, Patrick scratched the bridge of his nose with his middle finger.

"Uhhuum, well, they did some, but they also have jobs, so... and anyway, I like it." *Good way to get out of the house.*

"Have you seen Mary lately?" Dominic asked casually.

Birdy smirked pointedly before saying "No, actually, she was gone visiting her cousins in New Hampshire at the same time you guys were gone."

"Wow, is it cousins month or something?"

"Apparently! She's supposed to be back tomorrow though. I think she's going to come to the back-to-school picnic."

Dominic straightened at this. "She's coming to Divine Mercy?"

"No, no. That would be so fun! But no, she's just coming to the picnic to hang out with everyone."

"Oh. Well. That will be nice to see her. And everyone else."

Birdy nodded with exaggerated cheeriness as Dominic pretended to be embarrassed. Then Hannah lunged for him, and he accepted her with a smile. She bubbled with laughter as he tickled her tummy. Dominic looked back at Birdy mischievously. "Well, Isaac is going to be ticked off that he missed you. He's been missing you for weeks."

"I'm sure he'll live. Where is he, anyway?"

"Probably helping Uncle Abe—but why do you want to know?"

Her retort was drowned out by a sudden nauseating riff from the organ. Mrs. Fitzgerald was already practicing for next week.

"We need to go, Birdy," Mom said, grabbing her wrist. With her free hand, Birdy waved at Dominic, who flashed another smile at her as he swept little Hannah up on his shoulders and turned to talk to his mom.

Chris and Patrick made to follow them out, but then Ms. Karen said, "Oh, Maggie, I forgot!" and the two of them started an urgent new conversation. Birdy dove through a narrow gap behind Mom, pausing only to shoot a gloating smile back at Chris. Patrick itched his nose again.

The concrete steps beyond the doors were hosting another post-Mass conference. Mr. Doppelski and Mr. Abe were fond of cornering Dad after church. Birdy kept her head down as she continued her flight.

"Miss Birdy! Are you going to run off without saying hello?" called Mr. Doppelski.

That was the goal. Birdy looked at Dad, who wore a resigned expression. She stood close beside him.

"Hi," said Birdy.

"Ready for school? Better study hard to keep up with Isaac!" said Mr. Abe. Isaac was Dominic's cousin, the oldest of Abe's brood.

"Yeah," said Birdy, which seemed to vaguely address both of Abe's statements.

"Isaac!" Abe called over Birdy's head to where a skinny kid was balancing on the wrought iron railing. "Cut that out and get over here!" Isaac hopped down and got over there.

"Hey," he said to Birdy. His hair was bleached almost white by the sun. "Long time no see."

"Hi!" she smiled back. "How was Colorado?"

Isaac started to answer, but Mr. Abe interrupted. "I was just telling her, she better study hard to keep up with you in Algebra!"

Birdy was blushing and trying to figure out her response when Dad looked down at her, puzzled. "I thought you took that last year."

Isaac grinned while Birdy nodded with relief. "Yeah, I did, I'll be in Geometry."

"Oho, so you'll be with Dominic!" said Mr. Doppelski.

"I guess," said Birdy, though she had known this for weeks.

Abe crossed his arms. "Well, you know, Isaac's real good at math, he's actually going to have a tutor coming from the community college to enrich him because that curriculum Mrs. Hart picked is a little weak. I taught him really well, you know, I'm real good with numbers, I graduated from the Smith School of Business at Maryland, that's why our business is so strong year after year."

The Doppelski brothers owned and maintained multiple rental properties together under their creatively named company,

Doppelski Brother's Company, and they also did under-the-table car repairs from their vast shared garage. Their flexible self-employment made them available to assist with both the education and transportation of their progeny. For this, they were considered very "involved dads," and were unsubtly coveted by the CHOC moms.

Mr. Abe continued blabbing. "I can't just leave him to that weaker curriculum, I can't settle for second best, you know, I'm a bit of an alpha." Dad maintained his composure and Birdy clung to his example, but Isaac acted out her sudden, visceral embarrassment by instantly pivoting and kicking a stray rock out into the parking lot.

"Right, don't mess with alpha dog over here," said Mr. Doppelski.

The consequences of Mom's hydration saved them all. "Arthur, let's go, I really need to go to the—" she said desperately from behind Birdy, but she stopped when she saw the Doppelski brothers.

"Let's get out of here, honey," said Dad. He offered Mom his arm and marched for the parking lot, Birdy, Chris and Patrick hard on his tail.

"You're going to have such a good year, Birdy!" said Mom. "Are you excited? Don't you think it'll be so amazing?"

Birdy tried to be both honest and nice. "Well, I don't know, I haven't started yet!" she said with a smile.

Mom wilted, then said "Sweetie, everyone's been working so hard to make this happen for you kids, you have no idea how wonderful it's going to be!"

Squashing her irritation, Birdy recited, "You're right Mom, I'm so thankful for everything. You're the best. Thanks. I can't wait."

The Cleary kids' footsteps accelerated as they approached their green minivan. In one seamless motion, Chris shoved Birdy into Patrick, wrenched open the sliding door, and vaulted himself into the back row of seats so he could spread his long legs out on the bench. The losers of the weekly battle got in the middle section, vying for the seat without the weird buckle. Dad opened Mom's door for her, then got in himself.

They drove home in silence for a few minutes, until Mom said "Well, what did everyone think of church today?"

"It was heavenly," said Patrick solemnly.

"I feel sanctified," said Chris.

"Guys!" said Mom.

"No really, I feel sanctified after suffering through that music. God must be crying right now, oh, sweet baby Jesus, it was so bad!" Chris went on as Birdy and Patrick laughed.

"They're trying their best!" said Mom defensively. "More people should be that dedicated! God has a calling for everyone, and it's really admirable when people listen to what He tells them, even if other people don't understand!"

"Like Peter," said Chris. These words held a barb that no one in the car missed. Birdy chewed a nail.

Dad glanced in the rearview mirror. "Son." Chris looked at Dad's reflection and fell silent, looking out the window from his lounge.

A few minutes later, Patrick said, "She really does sound like broken bagpipes though," and Mom snorted.

"Those are the woods where George Washington camped," said Dad, pointing out the window to a patch of forest.

"We still need to go see the cabin," said Mom, referring to a minor museum that had been erected in honor of this colonial incident.

"Yeah, where the father of our nation once froze his nuts off, there now stands a cabin full of historical knickknacks! Let's go see it!" said Chris.

"Chris!" said Mom, crossing her arms. "You're lucky to be living somewhere so interesting and rural!"

No one had anything to say to this. Mom was fond of describing Conrad as rural, but Birdy thought of it as wispy, more gaseous than solid. In seven more minutes they were back home, where Chris opened the fridge looking for food.

"Hmmm" he said, "Supplies are running a little low. I thought Dad went to the store yesterday."

Birdy had awoken in time for breakfast and had already noticed the barren fridge. She had gotten the last bowl of cereal, but the milk had gone bad, which she had discovered on her first and only mouthful. Her stomach rumbled.

Mom tapped her foot. "He went to print some things for me at Staples instead." Mom had recently been hired as a secretary at a dentist's office and had been scrambling to compile all her scattered personal documents.

Chris gripped the handle of the fridge. "Okaaaay... well, it sure would have been nice if they sold lunch meat at Staples, because there's none in here."

"We have all that leftover spaghetti!"

"What— this? Are we all sharing this?" Chris cracked open an aged Tupperware to reveal a limp serving of spaghetti.

"You'll figure something out!" said Mom. Chris stared at her in disbelief. "But we have school tomorrow! Is no one going to the grocery store before tomorrow? What are we supposed to bring for lunch? Air?"

"We have all that chicken in there!"

Chris leaned in to investigate. "It expired last week." He unearthed some ancient salsa, peered inside, and recoiled. "Moldy," he accused.

Mom tensed. "You always act like it's so easy to take care of a family, but you have no idea what your father and I have been dealing with!"

Patrick spoke up. "Mom, why don't I take Chris and Birdy to Food Lion with me? I'll get the things we need for our lunches this week."

Mom brightened. "Okay. I also need you to pick up some toilet paper and some more printer ink."

There was a loaded silence. Chris looked at Birdy and she widened her eyes, begging him not to say it.

"But... what are we having for lunch *today*?"

Mom inhaled, ready to blow, but Birdy interjected, "We'll just get something while we're out. We can go to Chipotle!"

Mom and Chris both exhaled, satisfied. They spent a few minutes taking down Mom's burrito bowl order and establishing that Dad would eat the leftovers. Chris called shotgun as soon as his hand touched the screen door handle, and they headed out to Patrick's Dodge Spirit. Birdy cranked down her window. The wind made enough noise to almost shield her from the sound of Chris ranting about how there was never food in the house.

As they drove up Victoria Street, they passed Dominic and Isaac's brother, Joseph, on their skateboards. Birdy waved, and Dominic did some jump and flip with his board in response. Then he waved back. Chris's outrage at the contents of their fridge temporarily abated and he rounded on Birdy.

"Sooooo," he said.

"Shut up." Birdy said. "I don't like him!"

"That kid is such a tool," said Chris. "Oh my god, he loves it up there on the altar. And what the hell was that about how me and Patrick should have done the yardwork? Sorry I don't have a million free hours to ride around on my stupid skateboard! I was working! So I could afford to buy my own fucking food!" His rant was transitioning from molten anger to humorous theatrics. Birdy settled back to listen.

Somehow their parents had never worked out how to keep food entering and exiting the house in any sort of predictable fashion. Birdy knew it was theoretically possible. She had been a guest in homes where the cabinets were stuffed with granola bars, crackers, and cookies, where fridges overflowed with apples and pre-sliced cheese and individual yogurt cups. But with their perennial lack of money and energy, food always seemed to be an afterthought to Birdy's parents. It was irritating, but Birdy didn't mind the occasions when she and the boys got out of the house to get their own stuff. It tasted a lot better than aged spaghetti.

2

CONRAD WAS NESTLED ABOUT an hour each from DC and Baltimore. This location enabled some residents to commute and the rest to occasionally visit the cities on day trips and then flee home to their wholesome country refuge. To get in and out of town, drivers had to cross the Hickory River via a half-mile long steel bridge. The bridge was constructed during the town's brighter days, and thus was uncomfortably narrow for modern vans, pickups, and SUVs. Patrick made for Conrad's tiny downtown, which was marked with a weathered sign declaring "Conrad: Not Your Ordinary Place." It was hard to argue with that.

A stone Gothic church with stained glass windows rose from the crumbling sidewalk. Patrick deepened his voice and rounded his vowels in imitation of their father.

"Now kids, over here we have St. Paul's Church, which an old racist guy once said looked just like his plantation." Most of the CHOC families attended St. Paul's, Conrad's flagship Catholic parish. Despite its suspicious volume of female Eucharistic ministers, it was thriving, and as such could not lease its gathering spaces to Divine Mercy. Just as Washington had once camped in the nearby woods, Robert E. Lee had once ridden through downtown Conrad and remarked upon the beauty of St. Paul's. A plaque relaying the incident now hung on the outside of the church. That the hero of the confederacy had found the church noteworthy was an outsized point of pride to the locals.

Every time the family moved somewhere new, Dad delved into its history, which he then shared with his children. Last winter, he had descended upon Conrad Library's archival newspapers and asked their neighbors to fill in some of the information gaps. He soon learned that Conrad was not always so wispy. The downtown was peppered with empty buildings that had bustled just decades ago. Through them wound a wide and unkempt creek that trickled into the woods at one end of the city and emptied into the Hickory River at the other. The Hickory fed into the Potomac and had once been a key player in Conrad's prosperity. Now it was full of trash and the fish who ate it. A crow took flight from the vacant smokestack of a huge, dirty building near the water's edge.

"Look kids," said Chris, "There's the factory where that guy jumped off the top and ruined everyone's lives. His guts are still on the pavement today and they're the most interesting thing in town!"

"Gross," said Patrick.

The Conrad Steel Mill used to employ hundreds of workers. Its owner, Robert Grouse, had also been the head of the St. Ann's school board. St. Ann's was built in 1966— the year of Abe Doppelski's birth, as Abe told Dad smugly—on the stretch of land beside the existing Catholic cemetery, so the headstones of dead St. Paul's parishioners from centuries bygone lent an aura of dignity to the newer building. Back then, it was considered the modern and wealthy parish.

In 1975, the Doppelski brothers showed up to school and learned the nuns who taught them were being transferred, their parish priest was being transferred somewhere else, and the school would be imploding presently. Conrad's remaining Catholics were rabid defenders of their institution and didn't much like to talk about this incident. Jude Doppelski was a loyalist himself, but he was not shy.

"I'll tell you, man," he had told Dad one day, "People don't like to say it, but all the kids knew it and all the adults did too. Something was going on between Father Gerard and one of the nuns. Just awful." Dad's face had drawn shut as Mr. Doppelski leaned in closer. "I actually heard one of the St. Ann's kids walked in on them."

Two weeks after the school closed, Robert Grouse jumped off the roof of his mill. While still in their funeral suits, his colleagues checked the books and discovered their portfolios were in deep shit. To salvage what remained, they sold the mill at a loss to "some Baltimore bigwig," as he was still known to the locals. The mill stood empty while dozens of smaller buildings collapsed around it and families hemorrhaged from town. St. Paul's school closed, the local public schools consolidated, and St. Monica's High School declined.

People who stayed in Conrad were left to scrape together their own methods of making an honest or dishonest living. The river that once connected them to the world now cut them off from it.

Beyond the downtown, Conrad had a few shopping centers separated by pockmarked roads and empty fields. The Cleary kids ended their journey at a stronghold of newer establishments, which included an 8-screen movie theater, a Chipotle, and an ice cream shop. The county government had recently gambled that Woods Crossing Shops would entice more people move to town, but so far it hadn't worked. Visitors came for their cheap movies, ate their big burritos, and went right back to wherever they came from.

With provisions in hand and in their stomachs, the Clearys returned to their miracle home at 3819 Victoria Street. It looked like a historic colonial, but it was built in 1974 and consequently had bad bones. Birdy walked through the door with an armload of grocery bags and heard her mom talking

"Oh, hi, Mary, hold on, she just walked in!"

Birdy dropped her groceries and grabbed the phone. "Mary?"

"Hi Birdy!" said the warm voice on the other end.

Days after the Clearys had moved in, Ms. Karen had invited Birdy to join them at a popular CHOC custom called a barn dance. Birdy soon found herself bouncing beside Dominic in the Light Doppelskis' fifteen passenger van, studying the shredded cuffs of her jeans. The turbulent carriage had not helped the feeling in her stomach. *What if no one likes me?* Isaac had looked back at Birdy from the passenger seat and smiled, reading her skepticism and nerves correctly.

"Don't worry, Birdy," he said, "I can tell you right now you're cooler than everyone else who will be there." This made her laugh, but it rearranged rather than quelled her anxieties. *What if I don't like anyone?*

The van stopped after twenty rural minutes, and she trailed the Doppelskis to an industrial grey barn. A girl wearing a long blue skirt and a baggy pink turtleneck squeezed the daylights out of Dominic and waved merrily to Isaac before looking curiously at Birdy. Isaac opened his mouth and gestured to Birdy, but the girl didn't need him.

"Hi!" she said, bouncing her corkscrew blond curls out of her lively green eyes, "I'm Mary Vespa! What's your name?"

Mary had swept Birdy into her care, complimenting her outfit and introducing her to the entire party. They bonded over their mutual appreciation for Cheetos and their sneakers that almost matched. Despite feeling like she would die if she had to do one more square dance under the watchful eyes of two goats and a cow, Birdy had fun.

In the following week, Mary had called Birdy four times, sent her a letter in the mail, and invited her to something called Praise Night. They soon had a loud and goofy friendship that involved frequent updates from Mary about what was exciting in her life and lots of listening by Birdy, whose life updates were never as ripe for discussion.

"How was your trip? How have you been?" Birdy asked now, putting away the new milk.

"I've been so good, New Hampshire was amazing and then oh gosh, Father Tom told the funniest joke during the homily—oh wait, have you been to church yet today? Was—"

"Yes," said Birdy, laughing. She checked to make sure Mom had left the kitchen. "And he asked about you."

The first and most crucial secret that Mary had entrusted to Birdy was that she had romantic, everlasting, and unquenchable feelings for Dominic Doppelski. Mary and Dominic were both strictly forbidden to date anyone, but they had flirted outrageously for years, and every time they saw each other there was always some noteworthy exchange that needed to be dissected later.

Mary did not have an email address, instant messaging, or Facebook. She could use the phone, which she did, frequently, but she could not be seen calling a boy. Birdy had accidentally become the solution to this problem. She was now a liaison between Dominic and Mary, a helpful means by which their forbidden relationship could proliferate under the noses of the adults.

"He did? Oh my gosh, what did he say?" Mary pleaded. "Wait actually, first, I've been DYING to tell you what happened at the August Praise Night!"

"You did tell me," said Birdy, laughing, "*at* the August Praise Night!"

"I know I told you the best part, but now I have to tell you *everything*! Okay, before you got there, Dominic gave me just this huge smile, and the best hug, it lasted for like ten seconds. He always hugs me like that. And we pulled away and he smiled, and he said, 'Wow, Mare, your hair looks stunning today.' And he kinda tucked it behind my ear. And then I said, 'Wow, Dom, your hair looks stunning too!' And so we start cracking up and then we were holding hands, and he asked if I wanted to go for a walk. So we went walking and we let go of our hands for a minute, but then we held them again as soon as we were back behind the house. And then we looked up at the clouds and I told him what I saw, and he told me what he saw, and then we blew on dandelions and he asked if I made a wish and I said yes! And then he asked what it was and— we *kissed*!"

It sounded romantic, a little cheesy, cute. Birdy squealed at the appropriate intervals and said, "Well, it's about time!"

"Oh my gosh, I know! It was just the best feeling, he's the best guy in the world! So what did he say today?" said Mary.

"Well, he asked if I'd seen you lately, and I said you were probably coming to the picnic, and—" Chris was walking back out the door in his Pizza Hut uniform, holding Patrick's keys. "Oh, shoot, Mary, I need to go, can you call me back in like ten minutes? Chris is leaving for work, and I need to get some stuff out of the car first."

"Yes! I need to hear the rest of this story! Love you!" Mary hung up and Birdy rushed back outside.

"Wait, Chris," she yelled, sprinting to the car. He stood beside it as she grabbed her purse. "Is today your last day?"

"Yup," said Chris. "I got hired at the Harris Teeter by school so I'm quitting today." He looked beyond Birdy's shoulder. "Oh, God."

Birdy turned around and saw Dominic and Isaac walking down the street. Isaac wore a burgundy Sean Taylor jersey, and Dominic, for some reason, wore no shirt at all.

At first Birdy had assumed Dominic and Isaac would be more friends with Chris and Patrick, but it didn't turn out that way. Her brothers were so heavily involved at their school and worked so much that they were never home when Birdy went over to the Doppelskis'. While Birdy had spent hours playing soccer in their yards and Monopoly in their houses, the Doppelski and Cleary boys had spent barely any time together.

More importantly, they just didn't click. Patrick was ambivalent, but Chris found Dominic actively annoying. At various times, Chris had said that he didn't like how Dominic sucked up to him, that his reverence at church was an act, and that the way he talked to Birdy was just weird. Chris's Spidey Sense had proven robust in the past, but Birdy thought it was clouded in this case by his resentment about the move. Still, she couldn't deny there was some truth to his points.

"Chris, what's up buddy!" said Dominic.

"Hey," said Chris, drumming his fingers on the roof of Patrick's car.

"Heading to work?" said Dominic.

"Yeah, just want to squeeze out a few more dollars so I can get some new cleats."

"Oh, gotcha man, how's preseason training?" said Dominic.

"Pretty good," said Chris, chafing. He was a benchwarmer on Bosco's JV soccer team, but full dedication was expected from everyone on the deep roster. He looked over at Isaac, who he found less irritating. "Nice jersey, man."

"Oh, thanks," Isaac said, his voice ascending in a catastrophic crack. His face immediately turned the exact hue of his jersey. Chris said a hasty goodbye and fled into the car. Birdy knew he was trying not to let them see him laugh.

After he pulled away, Dominic raised a quizzical eyebrow at Isaac. "Awkward much?"

"I get it, it's hard to talk to boys," Birdy teased.

"Shut up," said Isaac, an uncharacteristic edge to his voice.

"He was probably just nervous because Chris looks just like you," Dominic crooned, slinging an arm around Birdy.

"Not really, he's like a foot taller than her," said Isaac.

"I like her this way," said Dominic, giving her a squeeze.

"Can we stop talking about me like I'm not here?" said Birdy, stepping out of Dominic's grasp.

"Aw, you're so cute when you get all annoyed," said Dominic, still singsongy.

Birdy revisited the conversation later as she got ready for bed. It kept snagging her thoughts like a hangnail.

It was true that the Clearys had a family look. When Chris was in elementary school, a boy had walked up to him and said, "When I look at you, the first thing I think is 'eyebrows.'" Like any good bully, this boy had chosen material that was both hurtful and accurate. Chris had since grown into his dark and heavy features, but the story was now a family legend. Peter, Patrick and Birdy had also gotten their dad's face. Mom had naturally sleek blond hair, restless blue eyes, and a small, energetic frame. Birdy had her mom's negligible height and would have happily taken the nice hair, but the brown poof she ended up with perplexed them both. After seeing a picture of Dad as a curly haired toddler, she suspected he was to blame.

At Birdy's last school, a girl named Kelsey had walked up to her and said, "You know, I heard Mark say he likes you, but I also heard him say that he thinks you're cute but not hot." When she brought this story home to her family, she had acted indignant and bothered only by the banality of the comment, verbally dissecting the meaning of the word "hot" and how accurately it could even be applied to seventh graders.

But like Chris's bully of yore, Kelsey had plucked up one of Birdy's silent insecurities and driven it right into her psyche for eternity. She feared that she was likable but not preferable, would always be outshined by girls who had something she didn't. However, she couldn't bring herself to try to get whatever it was they had. That seemed time consuming. She still wanted to look like herself, just magically better.

Why did Dominic say she was *cute,* anyway?

Probably no reason, she thought, turning her face this way and that in the grimy bathroom mirror. *He was just goofing around. He always tells Mary she's gorgeous. Which she is.*

3

THE NEXT MORNING, BIRDY woke to the sound of Chris slamming the front door behind him. The two cars grumbled in the driveway as she dragged herself to the bathroom. She ate breakfast in silence and started some coffee for Mom. Then she put on her khaki pants and white polo shirt, attempted a hairstyle, and went back downstairs to hug Mom, who was now standing in a fog in front of the coffee maker.

Birdy's favorite part of her uniform was her shoes, which she'd found on clearance at the mall near Bosco. On the outside, they were standard brown boat shoes, but on the inside, they were pink with white polka dots. She slipped them on and went outside.

The sun was already hot, but Birdy always welcomed a chance to breathe fresh air alone. She took *And Then There Were None* out of her bag and read until she saw the Dark Doppelskis' gray, 15-passenger van pull up in front of her house.

"Hey guys," said Birdy, finding a spot next to Hannah's carseat. Kids from both Doppelski families were scattered throughout the four rows of seats. Mrs. Doppelski was bringing them to a playgroup after she dropped the older kids at school. Isaac had picked the back row, and Birdy waved to him.

"Long time no see," he said.

"What?" she said. "You're so far away I can't hear you!" He grinned and looked down. She smiled too and turned back around to see Dominic wiggling his eyebrows at her from the passenger's seat. She rolled her eyes.

"You look so nice, Birdy!" said Mrs. Doppelski.

"Thanks!" said Birdy, smiling more than she'd meant to at the polite comment.

"Yeah, I love that shirt," said Dominic.

Birdy smiled even more and felt like a fool.

"Mom, you need to turn your blinker on," said Dominic authoritatively. Mrs. Doppelski turned on her blinker. Mrs. Doppelski's ready obedience to others' commands had earned her a reputation of saintliness in CHOC. She was the serene support to Mr. Doppelski's dynamism and seemed endlessly accommodating of the lively personalities of her husband and kids, even of her brother-in-law and *his* kids. Ms. Karen would not have bossed Mrs. Doppelski, but she wouldn't have listened to Dominic, either. She was more peppy than serene and was always leading some project for CHOC. This morning, she was already at the playgroup, preparing an Ordinary Time craft for 40 elementary schoolers.

"High five!" said Hannah. Birdy reached over to give her one and noticed one of the buckles in her car seat was not attached properly. Birdy tried to fix it but couldn't make it click.

"Um, could someone help me with this buckle?"

"Okay, you're clearly the youngest," said Dominic. "Even Sarah can buckle the little kids in. She did it this morning."

Well, obviously she doesn't know how to do it either, Birdy thought, but she didn't want to be rude. He unbuckled and climbed back to their row to fix the harness. She scooched over to give him more room, but he somehow expanded, filling the space she had created so their arms touched. After the buckle clicked into place, he gave her a comfortable smile. She looked out the window, feeling her face get hot.

Mrs. Doppelski turned left—blinker on—into the lot. At Birdy's previous schools, the parking lots had been packed with mini vans. At Divine Mercy, the lot wasn't as packed, but the vans were full sized. Birdy, Dominic, Isaac, and Joseph said goodbye to Mrs. Doppelski and climbed down from the van. The school building jutted off the back of the church building, attached by an enclosed breezeway. It was squat and industrial, all low dark windows and gray cinder blocks, double doors yawning wide open.

Inside, the building smelled like old bread. The floor tiles were light beige, the walls were dark beige, and the ceiling tiles were medium beige. Down the long hallway stretched the classrooms that would host 30 students from 12 families. One small classroom was what they called the locker room, though it contained only cubbies, which the adults had ordered the children to distribute them amongst themselves in a Christian manner. Birdy pulled a tattered schedule from her pocket and consulted it, but this was just a way to look busy. She'd spent the last two weeks memorizing her schedule. Her first stop was Religion class, taught by Mrs. Amon.

Staffing Divine Mercy had been difficult, requiring several homeschooling parents, including Mrs. Amon, to try classroom teaching for the first time. All the families paid a tiny tuition, but none of them could afford much, so the school was small and had no extras to offer its students. It would be educating 6th through 10th graders during its maiden voyage.

Some of the classrooms had desks, but Room Four had four folding tables arranged in two lines. Birdy grabbed a seat next to Isaac. Because the school was so small and the staffing so scant, grades were combined for several classes. Dominic, Polly Hart, and Olivia Strabinski were in 10th, and Isaac, Birdy, Josh Hart, Margaret Amon, and Fred Michaelson were in 9th. Birdy knew all the other kids, but hadn't seen them since the August Praise Night.

According to most of her classmates, Praise Night was the best night of the month. Which it was, if you enjoyed suffering. Suffering was essential to salvation, however, and salvation was rumored to be a good time. Praise Night was made possible by the generosity of Mrs. Amon's 24-year-old son, Kyle. The late-arriving Margaret provided Mrs. Amon with ample opportunity to preach that women should be open to life at every age, but Kyle was her next youngest and was considered a CHOC success story. He had started classes at Conrad Community College while still in high school, earned his AA in five years, and now devoted himself to evangelizing his fellow Wal-Mart cashiers.

At her first Praise Night back in the winter, Birdy had stood with Mary, feeling uncomfortable. Kyle strummed his guitar softly.

"Now, friends," he said, "open your hearts to the Lord. Commit your hearts to him, commit your chastity to him, commit your lives to him. He loves us, he loves us. Oh, he loves us. Oh, Jesus, Jesus." Birdy imagined Chris's reaction to Kyle's euphoria and stuffed down a burble of laughter. Kyle broke from the meditation to drag them through a worship song. Kyle's voice was reedy and Mary's was angelic, but Margaret's was aggressive. Margaret bit, chewed, and spat her words, scanning the perimeter to see who might be watching her. Mary kept nudging Birdy and asking, "Isn't this beautiful?"

The truth was that although she had no serious training in the subject, music was the place where Birdy felt closest to God. Well-placed violin set her cautious heart free; poetic lyrics rearranged her questions into convictions. Music was a life raft during gut-wrenching moments—abundant, lately—providing reassurance that no matter how bad it got down here, somewhere there was a creator who wanted magnificent things for his creatures. But all that felt private, and Praise Night didn't. People kept stealing glances from beneath reverent eyelids, gauging everyone else's reactions and altering theirs as necessary. It felt more like competition than communion. Standing unmoved in a sea of her smitten peers, Birdy felt crushed by a new type of loneliness that would soon be familiar.

In the months since, Birdy had learned that while knowledge of general culture was seen as frivolous, if not abhorrent, enthusiasm for the Christian music scene was practically a requirement of entry in CHOC. The Christian artists seemed convinced that if they only peppered their compositions with enough repetitions of His Holy Name, they were not required to otherwise exert any creative efforts. The other lyrics would fall into place, probably, and the melody could be anything, really. Artists who really wanted to inspire the youth employed tepid electric guitar. Fast songs were a race to see who could look most ecstatic; slow songs were a race to see who could dissolve into tears fastest. Birdy believed Jesus had died for them and was grateful and all, but not enough to be moved to immediate and copious sobs in a crowded basement every first Friday of the month.

At the August Praise Night, Birdy had kept a firm grip on her song book so she wouldn't have to raise her hands in praise, like Margaret was doing. Margaret was singing so intensely that she looked like she might faint. Birdy glanced at her in annoyance at the very moment that Dominic opened his own eyes and looked at Birdy. She started, worried she'd been caught doing something offensive. Dominic flicked his eyes at Margaret and then raised bemused eyebrows at Birdy. While she was still registering her surprise, he smiled and winked. Then he shut his eyes again, so he didn't see the way she smiled back.

Birdy set her pencil and notebook in front of her and flipped through her Religion textbook. It was copyrighted in 1923 and had strange pockets of focus, including a paragraph on how dueling was not morally permissible. Mrs. Amon led the class in a passionate Hail Mary, then turned to the board, her denim skirt stiffly framing the brown tops of her boots. She wrote "Love" on the chipped blackboard and turned back to the class. She itched beneath her cream turtleneck and cleared her throat. "God gave us two great commandments. The first is to love God with all your heart, soul, mind, and strength. The second is to love your neighbor as yourself. Now, who can tell me someone they know who follows the first of these commandments?"

Fred Michaelson raised his hand solemnly. "Pope John Paul the Second was a wonderful example of the first commandment."

"Wonderful example, yes, Fred," praised Mrs. Amon. Fred nodded humbly.

Dominic shot his hand in the air. "Isaac is probably the best person I know at loving his neighbor. He loves his neighbor much, much more than his neighbor loves him."

There were some nervous titters. Isaac sighed and looked at the ceiling. Margaret was obviously caught between wanting to show

Dominic she was laughing at his joke and annoyance she wasn't in on it. Birdy didn't react. There was no reason to bring the adults into this.

"Well, that's... lovely to hear'" said Mrs. Amon, who wasn't sure if she was being punked or not. She adjusted her small wire glasses and frowned at Birdy. From the corner of her eye, Birdy saw Dominic lean over and beam at her. Birdy glanced at him and shook her head as Margaret watched indignantly.

After class, she pounced.

"Does Isaac *like you*?" she said, standing in Birdy's way. A large bow, patterned with pink rosaries, quivered atop her braided bun.

"Oh, uh, no, I think Dominic just likes to say that."

"Why?" she demanded.

Isaac's alleged unrequited love for Birdy was high entertainment to Dominic. Sometimes Isaac even played along, issuing pick-up lines so cheesy they seemed facetious. Normally, Birdy responded by bringing up Mary. Sometimes she thought Dominic joked about Isaac just so he could hear Mary's name. But she didn't think that information would appease Margaret.

"I guess he just thinks it's funny." Margaret scowled and stalked off to Biology class, where Birdy grudgingly followed.

In the afternoon, Mr. Doppelski drove them home, arriving in his for some reason prized Ford Escort. He was on a work call, so they were spared his interrogation about their first day. The car was already pulling away as Birdy trudged up her driveway. She fished her keys out of her backpack, unlocked and unbolted the door, and entered to darkness.

The first thing she did was open the living room shades. Mom was worried about the sunlight fading the furniture, about the electricity bill being too high, and about strangers looking into their house and learning their behavioral patterns. Thus, the shades were kept down unless they needed to appear prosperous and non-neurotic to visitors. Birdy's private rebellion was to let sunlight in during the hours she spent alone. The living room was carpeted with graying acrylic, its walls papered with columns of sunhatted geese marching on blue backgrounds. The couches bore scratches from their dead dog, their rehomed dog, their rehomed cat, and the time Peter and Patrick had played Crusaders and Infidels with their pocketknives. On the wall across from the window hung a collection of framed photos, paintings of saints, and baptismal certificates. Many more frames cluttered the floor in front of this wall, waiting for the day when Mr. Cleary would crouch down with his hammer and nails and hang them. Three tall bookshelves overflowed with novels, poetry anthologies, history books, comics, saint biographies, and children's science books.

Birdy went to the kitchen and opened the curtains covering the big window over the sink. She looked in the cupboard, decided against the stale tortilla chips that lurked within, and set a timer to remind herself to make frozen pizza later. Then she went up the kitchen staircase.

The stairs opened just in front of Chris and Patrick's bedroom. Birdy's bedroom was next to theirs. Mom and Dad's room was beside hers, and across from their room was Peter's room. Or it would have been, if Peter had come with them. Chris had never complained about having to share a room with Patrick even though there was an extra. None of the kids liked thinking about that aggressively unoccupied bedroom.

Next to Peter's not-bedroom was the bathroom all the kids shared, and finally, across from Chris and Patrick's room was what Mom loved to call "the nook" and what Patrick liked to call "the oubliette." This was a tiny room where the computer desk sat among teetering piles of boxes. Every time Birdy emailed or IMed one of her old friends, she could feel the weight of her family's chaotic nomadism stalking her.

Birdy dropped her backpack on her bedroom floor and flopped onto her purple comforter. When they'd arrived in Conrad, she'd purchased her own bedding set from Walmart, sick of the Little Mermaid blanket that had come into the family's possession via Goodwill long ago. Next to her bed was a small table for her nightstand, upon which she had balanced a pile of books and a lamp.

Above that was a bulletin board where she'd tacked movie tickets and pictures of her friends from her old schools. After a minute she went to her closet, where her clothes sat folded in a plastic dresser. She changed into shorts and a once-oversized t-shirt from the soccer team she had played on in fifth grade.

Birdy pulled a spiral notebook from her loaded bookshelf and flipped it open to find Peter's precise handwriting. Of all Birdy's brothers, Peter had been the one who played make-believe games with her the best and longest. As they'd aged, they had transitioned from acting out their stories to verbally imagining various ludicrous and entertaining scenarios. Two years ago, their collaboration took on yet another expression when Peter began a creative writing class at school and started overflowing with ideas. He'd recruited Birdy and they'd started writing a comedic fantasy tale together in the note-book. One of them would write a chapter and then leave it for the other with notes of siblingly affection such as "here you go you piece of scum!!!" The story was just getting to the good part when things went sideways at home and Peter stopped writing.

The doorbell rang. Birdy shut the notebook and rushed down the front stairs. She stood on tiptoe to look through the peephole and found Dominic, Isaac, and Joseph standing outside.

"I see you ditched the uniform," said Dominic when she opened the door.

"Well, yeah so did you," said Birdy, gesturing at their normal clothes.

"I liked your uniform," said Isaac.

"Ew," said Birdy. Isaac laughed.

Dominic inspected the quiet house. "So is it just gonna be you alone here? Every afternoon?"

"Yeah."

"What do you do?"

"Uh... homework. And then I read or see if anyone's online. And then make dinner."

Dominic looked intrigued. Birdy supposed such solitude was rare in his house.

"Don't you get lonely?" asked Joseph.

Birdy tilted her head, trying to phrase her complicated answer, but Dominic interrupted.

"Can we see your room?" said Dominic.

"Uh... sure," said Birdy. She had been to their houses probably fifty times apiece at this point, but they had crossed her threshold only a handful of times and had never been in her bedroom. For some reason, the thought of them seeing it made her nervous. She hoped they would like it, but that seemed like a silly thing to care about.

Upstairs, Dominic's eyes swept over everything and landed on the notebook she had left on the desk. He started reaching for it, but Birdy plucked it away and tossed it back on the bookshelf.

"What's that?" said Dominic.

"Just something my brother and I did together a while ago."

"Chris or Patrick?" said Joseph.

Birdy's lips felt wrong. "Peter."

Joseph looked confused and started to say, "Who's Peter?" but Isaac coughed loudly and shook his head at him. There was a churning silence as Birdy and Joseph mutually struggled to find a new topic. After a second he came up with, "This is me and Isaac's room at home."

"Oh, yeah, I know," said Birdy, relieved.

"Oh, do you now?" said Dominic, stepping close to her and flicking his eyes between her and Isaac. "It's so sweet that you know that!"

Birdy shoved him. "Yeah, and your room is where my family keeps junk! How fitting!" He laughed and parked himself on her bed, looking annoyingly at ease.

"So, I heard Mary might come over here sometimes to hang out," he said.

"Yeah, her brother has a class on Wednesdays at CCC, so she was thinking she might be able to hang out with me while he does that."

"Hm. Well," said Dominic, turning up a winning smile. Birdy knew what he was after, but she liked teasing him.

"Yeah, so funny how Mary will be so nearby, huh?"

"You know, that is funny!"

"Well, if you ever wanted to stop by for a visit on Wednesdays at 3:45, you know, that might be good."

Isaac had been examining the titles on her bookshelf, and he looked up at them. "You could come too," Birdy said, but Dominic interjected.

"Isaac's going to have his math tutor on Wednesdays. Right Isaac?" Isaac raised an eyebrow.

"Yeah. Not sure how you knew that."

"I could come!" said Joseph.

"No," said Dominic. Joseph sighed but didn't argue.

After they left, Birdy went to the oubliette, clicked the AOL icon on the desktop, and spun in the chair while listening to the dial-up symphony. Once it was loaded, she saw she had a new email. *Peter.*

4

From: icanseeclearynow@aol.com
To: bluebirdy@aol.com
Hey Birdy,
How was your first day? Chris said it might be kind of a weird school.
How does it compare to St. Francis?
Love,
Peter

WITH SHAKING HANDS, she rushed to respond.

Hi Peter,
My first day of school was fine. Chris is right, it might be kind of weird. It's very different from St. Francis. It's tiny, for one thing. My biology teacher is the uncle of one of the sixth graders and he works

at a real lab that's kind of far away, so he can only make it here on Mondays and Wednesdays. The other days of the week we're going to watch a recorded lecture. So that's kind of weird. And most of my classes are combined with 10ᵗʰ grade. Some of the kids are kind of annoying, but I have some friends too.

Birdy paused, wondering what to say next. Should she ask him a question now? Mention Mom and Dad? She decided to tell him a story she knew would have made him laugh, if he was home.

One of the annoying kids is named Fred. At the beginning of biology, Mr. Murry (my bio teacher) asked us if we knew what an organelle was. We were supposed to have done some reading over the summer, but I also knew the answer already because of that one Usborne book we have. So I raised my hand, and this kid Fred just called out "it's things like your liver, appendix, and other such things." Mr. Murry said "Not quite—what do you think?" pointing at me, and so I said the answer. Fred was shaking his head no, until he heard Mr. Murry say I was correct. So now Fred hates me—but don't worry, moments later, I found out he's my lab partner! Should be a fun year.

Oh, and I got a cell phone!!!

Patrick had recently found a cunning way to secure a cell phone for Birdy and upgrade himself and Chris to better ones. "Mom," he said, "Birdy's going to be home alone a lot, and she'll need the internet for her homework sometimes, but if she's online, she won't be able to call anyone in an emergency... I just really think she should have a cell phone."

Patrick went in for the kill by presenting Mom with a pamphlet for a family plan that would be cheaper than their current pay-as-you-go phones. They had to be stingy with their texts, but overall it was a convenient means for Chris and Patrick to manage their developing social lives. Birdy still mainly used IMing and emails to keep in touch with her old friends. Of her friends in Conrad, only the Doppelskis had cell phones so far, and she already saw them every day.

On the way home Friday afternoon, Dominic turned around in his seat. "So you're coming later, right?"

"Yes!" said Birdy. "For the tenth time!"

Dominic laughed. "Sorry, I just want to make sure it's going to be fun. You know some of the other kids are a little..."

"Dominic," chided Mrs. Doppelski.

"...wonderful and so, so, cool and my favorite people ever!" Dominic finished.

Birdy laughed. "Yeah, they're my favorite too."

"Aw, I thought I was your favorite," said Dominic.

Not knowing how to respond to this, Birdy ignored it completely. "Should I bring anything?" Birdy knew exactly what she was supposed to bring. She'd read the email four times.

"Mmmm, no, I don't think so, Mom?"

Birdy's insides itched. She knew she was supposed to bring a snack. She'd already purchased chips.

"Oh, anything," said Mrs. Doppelski dreamily. *A snack! I bought chips!*

"But we're going to play soccer and capture the flag and maybe ghosts in the graveyard when it gets dark."

"Oh, Mary will be happy. She loves ghosts in the graveyard," said Birdy slyly.

"Oh, interesting," said Dominic as they pulled up next to Birdy's house.

Birdy went inside and watched TV until Dad and Patrick got home. Chris had Patrick's car at work. She went upstairs to get ready and glanced once more at the email Mom had printed and left on her desk:

You're invited to the Back to School Picnic in the Doppelski's back yards! The dads are handling this one—Dads, feel free to stay and hang out—Enjoy It!! Come join your schoolmates and friends to celebrate the start of the year with prayer and fun! Wear you're

Divine Mercy shirt or a cool Catholic tee! Arrive at 6, stay till 9!! Guys bring a soda, girls bring a snack!

Ms. Karen was the obvious author of the email. Birdy didn't have any cool Catholic tees, nor did she ever intend to, so with a grim heart she put on her white polo and some soccer shorts. On her way out the door, Patrick informed her that she looked like a gym teacher. She made sure Dad wasn't looking before she flipped him off and left.

Someone's maroon van rolled past her as she rounded the curve to the Doppelskis' houses. Both homes had identical layouts to each other and to the Clearys'. In Dominic's yard, a flagpole stood front and center, flying an American flag, a Maryland flag, and the eagle, globe and anchor of the Marine Corps. Birdy sighed. Dad's friendship with the Doppelski men was awkward for many reasons, some of which were related to the scarlet and gold banner flapping in the breeze.

Dad was a proud graduate of the Naval Academy. After commissioning as a Marine officer, he had gone to training at The Basic School in Quantico, Virginia. Three weeks into the program, Dad was the designated driver in a car full of his friends when he was hit by the drunk driver of another carload of Marines. Everyone else involved was okay, but the steering column wrecked Dad's knees. After a few months it was apparent that he would not be in fighting shape anytime soon, and he was honorably discharged.

Dad never betrayed any sadness about the story, but it was a specter that haunted their family. Dad's intelligence, virtue, and imposing physicality made him a born leader. He had longed to devote his life to protecting his country, but the accident snatched away his dream. And though Dad remained devoted to the weight bench and pullup bar in their garage, the pain had never really left his knees. One day after they got home from a hike, Birdy had heard Dad alone in the kitchen, getting out food for dinner and whispering "Ouch. Ouch. Ouch."

Jude Doppelski had enlisted in the Marines after high school and had enjoyed four years of shooting things and travelling. He went to college on the Montgomery GI bill and returned to Conrad with his new wife upon graduating. Dad was excited when he first discovered Jude was a Marine, but whenever they discussed the topic it seemed like they were speaking different languages. Dad loved discussing military history, leadership philosophy and training ideas, while Jude preferred telling stories about drunk adventures and exploding objects. Dad also had a certain affection for exploding objects, and used this shared interest to construct a shaky middle ground of conversation. Mr. Doppelski seemed satisfied with these exchanges, but Dad always looked pained and disappointed when they were over.

Mr. Abe added yet another piece to this uncomfortable puzzle. A native speaker in the language of tricky family dynamics, Birdy had recognized early on that Abe's primary motivation in life was a desperation to measure up to his brother. Abe had spent four years in the Army, a fact he mentioned with obnoxious frequency. When all three dads got to discussing their military service, it was unbearable.

Many of these conversations had taken place in front of the huge garage that stood between the two Doppelski houses. Abe and Jude had built it to hold work supplies, freeing their homes' garages to be packed with bikes, scooters, skateboards, skates, and even a unicycle. The flowerbed in front of Dominic's house overflowed with sunflowers that were taller than Birdy. On the front door, one of the little kids had left a sign that said "PARTY HERE, COM IN!" but another kid had scribbled over it and written "KEEP OWT."

Birdy opened it to find Hannah and Bobby crouched above a pile of dog poop, about to pick it up. "Whoa, whoa, whoa," said Birdy, swooping in.

Hannah had a roll of paper towels and a container of Clorox wipes beside her. "I was going to cwean it up," she whined.

"Well," said Birdy, "I'll just take care of it for you, and you can put away this stuff when I'm done. Deal?"

"No," said Hannah, pouting.

"Don't worry, we'll take care of it," Bobby said in a man-to-man tone, even as Birdy worked. She brought her disgusting trash pile to the outside trashcan and returned to find the kids and cleaning supplies gone. She stopped in the hall bathroom to wash hands.

All the houses on Victoria Street opened to a wide front hallway that had a big staircase in the center, a bathroom and a bedroom to the right, and entries to the living room and kitchen on the left. The Clearys' front hall was occupied by piles of boxes, which served as a place for everyone to lay their junk when they came inside. The Dark Doppelskis' front hall had row upon row of coat hooks and 15 baskets of shoes. There was also a huge gun cabinet for hunting supplies. "And self-defense," Frankie had explained the first time Birdy came over.

Birdy walked through the living room. It was bright and loud, messily organized. The floors were hardwood, which expedited the cleaning of constant messes. A careful arrangement of DUPLOs stood on a table right beside the doorframe. Ten sets of tiny briefs were for some reason lined up in front of the couch. A stuffed lion, a balding doll, and a GI Joe sat at another little table, none willing to claim responsibility for the sticky orange juice dripping from their upended teakettle. Sarah Doppelski and Fred's little brothers pounded past Birdy and out the front door. Sunlight streamed through the windows. There were no blinds on any of them.

In the kitchen she found the Doppelski brothers, Mr. Amon, and Fred's father. Birdy supposed this was the group of dads who had opted to stay and handle things, which looked a lot like sitting around the table drinking beer. The CHOC dads were generally slouchy with mustaches and dark hair. The Doppelskis broke the mold by being clean shaven, and Mr. Abe further distinguished himself by being blond.

Her biology teacher, Mr. Murry, sat at the close end of the table. Though not a CHOC dad, he also had a dark mustache. His face lit up when he saw her. "Birdy Cleary! Nice to see you again!"

"Hi, Mr. Murry," said Birdy, putting her chips on the table.

"You know, I wanted to tell you I'm really glad you're in my class? You ask questions like someone who actually did the reading."

"Thanks!" said Birdy, thrilled. "It's really interesting."

Mr. Doppelski's face twitched at this exchange. He leaned toward Birdy over his Budweiser, brown eyes glinting in the bright evening sun. "Heard Gunner left you a gift."

"Yeah, it was really thoughtful of him," said Birdy, as her canine benefactor rushed up to sniff her.

"Hannah's pretty mad you took over her job!" Mr. Doppelski cackled. Then he got more serious and pointed at Birdy. "Let her clean it up next time." Birdy nodded uncertainly. *Not sure why you want the girl who still wears diapers to clean up the dog poop but okay.*

"Welcome, little lady," said Mr. Abe, who was drinking Bud Light. On Sundays, Mr. Abe favored three-piece suits, but during the week he curated an everyman look. Today he sported a Redskins cap and an Army t-shirt. He looked at her for a beat too long without speaking, then said, "You've really done a number on our poor boys!"

Stunned, Birdy could only say "...huh?"

"Oh, don't act like you don't know," he roared, like she was the biggest joker in the world. "Going around with your little school uniform and breaking their hearts!"

Birdy had never considered the possibility that anyone, let alone someone's father, would speak to her this way. She stared at Mr. Abe trying to respond, not wanting to honor it with a response. She'd thought her school clothes were boring at best—she had thought that was the whole point of the uniform. But Mr. Abe was acting like she was some sort of temptress.

The other dads did not seem to notice anything wrong, except for Mr. Murry, who had paused mid-sip to stare at Mr. Abe. Mr. Abe was done guffawing, and done smiling, too.

"Get on outside now," he said, jerking his head toward the back door. "That's where all your boyfriends are."

Red in the face, she did as she was told.

She crossed the lawn, the smell of freshly cut grass hanging in the air. Little kids sprinted around the wide backyard, while the older kids stood in an awkward-looking clump. Birdy spotted Mary and Dominic in the clump and waved. Mary, whose Modest is Hottest T-shirt stretched tightly across her chest, squealed in excitement and hugged Birdy when she got up close. Dominic watched them coolly.

"Oh, you made it," he said to Birdy's shoulder, betraying nothing of his earlier enthusiasm. He swept his eyes down her body, brows contracting, then turned away. *What did that mean?* Dominic wasn't wearing a cool Catholic tee or a school polo. He had just worn a regular t-shirt, and evidently, no one cared. Why hadn't she thought of that?

"Okay, now that Birdy's here, does anyone want to play soccer?" Isaac said.

"Me!" said Birdy. Olivia raised her hand too, but Fred intervened.

"I'm not sure we should be encouraging something so intense right now when it's almost rosary time."

There were some noises of dissent and Isaac opened his mouth in protest, but Dominic interrupted.

"That's right," he said. "We need to get into a more prayerful mindset."

At this abject betrayal, Mary looked at Dominic with stars in her eyes. No one argued. Dominic, apparently, held more sway in the group than Fred.

Isaac said, "Well, I'm gonna play a little." Birdy joined, but no one else did. They passed the ball back and forth, trying to look like they were having fun. After a few minutes, Isaac motioned to Birdy.

"Watch this," he mouthed. Then he wound up and beaned the soccer ball right into the back of Dominic's head.

Dominic clutched his skull as he spun to face them. "What the fu—heck! Isaac!"

Isaac slapped a hand to his cheek in exaggerated concern. "Sorry!"

Birdy turned away from Dominic, grinning.

After Mr. Doppelski paused handling things to lead them in the rosary, fun was formally authorized. True to Birdy's prediction, Mary squealed in delight when Dominic announced ghosts in the graveyard. From her hiding spot, Birdy saw them stealing off together, holding hands.

The next day Mary called Birdy with the news that during ghosts in the graveyard, she and Dominic had made out for twenty seconds behind the shed. Then she bemoaned the fact that she didn't get to see Dominic every day like Birdy did. "I would hate going to school though. They just correct all your spelling and make you write papers all the time, like that really matters."

Birdy took offense to this, but didn't know how to explain that when she was sure Mary should already know Birdy would be offended. Instead, she focused on Mary's interests.

"Well, speaking of Dominic, he mentioned that he'd heard you might come over on Wednesdays so..."

"Is he gonna come too?" gasped Mary.

"Exactly!" said Birdy.

"Yes! That would be so amazing! I can bring schoolwork or whatever to do. We can all hang out and work and have snacks together!"

Hope you like stale tortilla chips, Birdy thought, but her heart warmed at the idea. It would be nice to have company after school and give Mary and Dominic a chance to see each other more. She was nothing if not sympathetic to having parents whose standards felt insane, and she was happy to help them out.

5

ON THURSDAY, BIRDY SAT on the front steps, tying the laces of her cleats. After their umpteenth game of pickup soccer that summer, the Doppelskis had invited Birdy to join the local rec league.

"You should sign up for Conrad Rec League. Our friend Mel's signing up for the girls' 12 and up team. I know you two would get along great," said Dominic, eyes animated.

"Oh, well, I'd love to. I just..." Birdy ached to join, but could think of several barriers. She latched onto the least personal one. "Why is it a 12 and up team? Is that high school and middle school all together?"

"There's not enough interest for each age group to have its own team," explained Isaac.

"So does Joseph play too? Or Coz and Damian?"

"Coz and Damian are eleven," said Dominic.

"And we don't let Joseph come," said Isaac.

"Aww, why not?" said Birdy.

"Because then Coz and Damian would have to come," said Isaac.

"Come on, Birdy!" Dominic said. "The boys and girls have to scrimmage half the time because no one shows up. It'd be so much more fun with you there."

"I'm just not sure if... my parents don't get home till late..."

"I'll walk you over! It's the same fields we always go on!"

"It's just I don't know about the money." Birdy was ready to feel embarrassed, but Isaac and Dominic seemed to get it. "But I'll see. I really do want to."

That evening, Birdy had found her dad sitting at the kitchen table, hunched in front of a mountain of books and planning the upcoming school year. Patrick stood by the fridge, eating jelly off a spoon.

"Dad?" she said.

He looked up. "Hi honey."

"Dad, um..." Birdy hesitated. "Well, I found out that there's this soccer team, and it meets right over on the elementary school fields, so you wouldn't have to drive me. It's for ages 12 and up. I mean I'm wanting to join it, I mean. But it's $75 to sign up but I have a lot of money saved up so I could pay for some of it or all of it if you needed me to..."

Dad smiled. "We can make that happen for you, honey."

"You're playing on the 12 and up team?" said Patrick, coming to stand next to her and smacking his jelly.

"Yup."

"Why is it 12 and up? That seems like a huge age range."

"Not enough people sign up for each age group to have its own team," Birdy paraphrased.

"I guess that's not surprising," said Patrick. "No one lives here."

"Why did we move to this godforsaken town anyway!" Chris wailed from behind them, grabbing their shoulders and shaking.

Patrick and Birdy both yelped in surprise, then all three of them collapsed into laughter. Dad closed his eyes and smiled helplessly, permitting himself a snort of mirth. The Cleary children coped with their strange circumstances by filtering them through a distinctly weird sense of humor. Their father, normally the picture of forbearance, could occasionally be made to smirk or even chuckle at these jokes. The kids worshipped these cracks in his armor, the signals he sent from his steadfast fortress that he, too, found their situation perplexing.

Birdy finished tying her cleats and met Dominic and Isaac at the head of a path in their woods. A mile on this path led them to a county park that butted up against the elementary and middle schools. Even on cloudy days, the place had the look of having been baked for decades in an unrelenting sun. There was a tired basketball court, a rusty playground, and two brown soccer fields. A smattering of ponytailed girls stood by one field, and a smattering of boys slouched by the other. The nets on the goals were limp and the lines were barely visible on the field, but Birdy's heart rose at the sight of it. Soccer had been a popular recess activity at every school she'd attended. She felt like she could never get enough.

"We'll walk you over to your field first," said Dominic.

"There's Mel!" said Isaac, waving to a girl whose freckles were visible even from this distance.

"Mel!" called Dominic as they approached. "This is Birdy."

"Hi! I've heard a lot about you!" she said with a smile. Mel's father had grown up with the Doppelski brothers and had enlisted in the Marines with Mr. Doppelski. Dominic and Isaac had known Mel their whole lives. She was whip-slender and six inches taller than

Birdy, with pale skin and straight black hair pulled into a slick pony-tail.

"Same here," said Birdy, "It's nice to finally meet you!"

"I'm so excited to have you on our team! Dominic and Isaac keep saying how fun it is to play with you."

"Well, I'll try to live up to the hype," said Birdy, warmed by Mel's instant friendliness. Mel laughed as a skinny girl with a tight blond ponytail appeared next to them.

"Hi Dominic!" said the skinny blond girl.

"Angela," he said lukewarmly. "Gotta go. Hope you ladies have fun," he said as he and Isaac took off for their field.

"I like your shirt," said Mel.

"Thanks!" said Birdy, glancing down at her Dunder-Mifflin tee.

"How do you like Divine Mercy?" said Mel.

"I like it," said Birdy hesitantly. "You're at St. Monica's, right?"

"Yeah," said Mel, in a similar tone. "I mean, so far."

"Did you go to these schools?" Birdy asked, pointing at the buildings behind them.

"No, I was at Conrad Primary, the K-8 school. It's over on the other side of downtown. My dad went there too, after St. Ann's closed."

A girl about Birdy's height walked up to them. "This is Kelly," Mel said.

"Hi," said, Kelly, smiling shyly. Two thick, honey-colored braids framed her face.

"Hi," said Birdy. She looked around for a coach, but she could only see girls around her age. The assembled players were character-ized by a collective lack of enthusiasm.

"Do you know who the coach is?" said Birdy.

Kelly started to answer, but then a tall girl jogged into the center of the circle. "Okay everyone," she called, "I'm Beth, and my dad is our coach but he can't make it tonight so I'm going to get practice started for us."

"Yes ma'am!" yelled Mel. Beth flashed a smile at her while Mel and Kelly fought back laughter.

"OKAY so I want you all to drop down and give me twenty!" roared Beth in her best drill sergeant voice. Birdy chuckled as she dropped down, making her way through the pushups. When she was done, most of the other girls had given up and were sprawled complaining on the grass.

"Great," Beth said over their moans. "Now let's get up and do three laps around the field!" In response, Angela the skinny blond girl walked to the sideline to sit and drink her water, after having run not a single step. Mel stared after her, apparently outraged.

Beth jogged up to Angela and cajoled her into joining the group, before jogging back to the touch line and yelling at everyone to get behind her. After the run, they got in a circle to stretch, and Beth made everyone say their school and grade. Despite the team's official age range, everyone was a freshman or sophomore. Beth, Mel, and Kelly, went to St. Monica's, the other Catholic high school in Conrad. So did Angela. The other six girls went to Conrad High, but everyone on the team had known each other since at least middle school.

St. Monica's was co-ed, but as Birdy learned in the warmup chit-chat, not many boys went there. St. Monica's didn't have any sports teams, so a lot of people opted for Conrad High. Unfortunately, Conrad High's teams were aggressively mediocre. Birdy inferred this was why the members of the Conrad Rec League appeared to be scraped from the bottom of the heart and talent barrel. Most were there under protest and threat of grounding.

At the end of practice, Dominic and Isaac came back to Birdy's field.

"Hi Dominic!" said Angela, pawing his arm. "How's school going this year?"

"Pretty good," he said. "Ready to go, Birdy?"

"Yeah, hold on," said Birdy, gathering her things. "Nice meeting you," she said to Angela.

"You too," said Angela. "Bye Dom," she said in a much perkier voice. She put out her arms for a hug, which Dominic gave her limply. Then Birdy, Dominic, and Isaac walked over to the path through the woods.

"Thanks again for walking with me, it's really nice of you."

"Of course, I wouldn't leave you here," said Dominic. "Girls shouldn't walk home alone in the dark."

"How'd your practice go?" Isaac said.

"It was... fine," said Birdy. "A few girls were really fun to play with. Mel seems awesome."

"Yeah, she's cool," Isaac agreed. He grinned. "And were some girls not so fun to play with?"

Birdy laughed. "Well, it seemed like a lot of them just didn't really want to be there."

"Like who?" Isaac prodded.

"Like... everyone except for Mel and Kelly and Beth. Do you know Kelly and Beth?"

"Yeah," said Isaac. "What did you think of Angela?" He glanced at Dominic as he said this, and so did Birdy. It seemed like he was friends with Angela, sort of, so she didn't want to be rude.

"She... didn't seem to be enjoying herself that much. Beth got her playing after a while though."

Dominic's face was impassive, but then he declared, "Angela's a slut."

Birdy was taken aback by his bald use of this epithet, but Isaac wasn't. "And how do you know that?"

"Trust me," said Dominic.

Birdy glanced at Isaac, whose expression was cynical. "Well, how was your practice?" she said, trying to smooth over whatever had just happened.

"It was fine," said Dominic. "Most of the guys who play with us want to be there, they're just not that good."

"Sorry," said Birdy.

"Your brothers are so lucky they go to a real school with real teams and more than like 10 people," he said, dropping his ball in front of him and dribbling it along.

"Yeah," Birdy sighed. "I wish I could go to Bosco."

"I don't think you can go there," said Dominic.

"Why?" she said with mock seriousness.

"Males and female shouldn't mix in that type of environment."

Birdy and Isaac exchanged a glance. "What, like high school?" said Birdy.

"Like a religious environment."

"Like... Divine Mercy?"

"No, like Divine Mercy is really small so we kind of have to mix everyone together. But it's better if you can have guys and girls at separate schools so you don't warp the male authority of the church."

Do you even know what warp means? "Where does it say *that* in the Catechism?" said Birdy.

"It's just one of those things." Dominic's face grew nastier.

"I've gone to Catholic school my whole life and I've *never* heard that before," said Birdy, getting annoyed.

"Well, a lot of Catholic schools aren't really Catholic. That's why my dad wanted to start Divine Mercy in the first place." Dominic's voice was now extremely condescending, which had the effect of kerosene on Birdy's irritation.

"But he let girls in."

"Well he doesn't want Sarah and Hannah and Rebecca to have to go to St. Monica's someday. So it's a co-ed school. But still it's better not to mix them."

"Show me where it says that in the Catechism."

Dominic dropped the snootiness. "Sorry, sorry, I didn't mean to upset the all-knowing Birdy," he said. He smiled and put an arm around her. "I mean, Divine Mercy's not *that* bad, I do like having *you* around."

Birdy's wrath simmered down. Isaac stared up at the brightening moon.

THE NEXT MORNING, BIRDY walked into Biology and sat beside Fred. So far she and Fred were uneasy with each other. Her first day correction appeared to have bothered him on a fundamental level. Now, every time she spoke, he felt the need to add supplementary comments.

"Here, I need you to look this over," said Fred, shoving a paper in front of her. It was interesting how he acted like he was smarter than her until he needed to hand something in. They had dissected a worm and were supposed to explain its circulatory system in the discussion section. Fred had insisted on doing the write-up and said she could edit it later. Birdy looked down at the paper.

...The blood now has a choice. It can choose to go to the left to circulate through the heart, or to the right to go through the lungs....

Birdy looked up from the page. "Well... it sounds like you understand the process. I think there is some grammar you could fix though."

"I'm pretty sure Mr. Murry just wants to know we understand."

I'm pretty sure you're getting Mr. Murry confused with your mom.

The CHOC families loved homeschooling because it could be anything they wanted it to be. They could focus on what they felt was important, rather than the contrived standards of the corrupt government or lackadaisical archdiocese. Consequently, Divine Mercy had a student population of uneven skill sets. Some families knew their math facts as well as they knew the Hail Mary. Other families could recite all the parts of speech in song form, though whether they could apply this knowledge to strengthening their compositions was a different story. Some families could point to every positive impact Christianity had ever had on societal advancement. Some families were Just Catholic and knew all the popes back to St. Peter, but didn't necessarily have any historical, geographical, or scientific context in which to anchor this information. All they needed to know was that the Church had been right, was still right, and would be right again, forever and ever.

For her part, Birdy had been raised in a home full of good books, and a family who liked reading them. Her thought patterns were obsessive and repetitive, which had its drawbacks but was certainly useful when it came to memorizing information. She had always thrived in school. Fred, for no discernible reason, had a reputation as an intellectual, and Birdy had recently disturbed it.

But Birdy had no room to care about Fred's social status. All Mom and Dad's moves and job changes had brought them to their mid-forties without a nest egg. Or even a nest. At random intervals, Mom issued shrill commands that they NOT MENTION they were renting their house to anyone, not even the Doppelskis. Their house had been for sale after years as a rental, but the bank was not impressed by the Clearys' credit score, and in a miracle of generosity, the seller offered to continue his career as a landlord and increased the rent by a mere hundred dollars per month. They were paying too much for a house that wasn't theirs and burning gas on commutes to low-paying jobs. If Birdy was going to go to college someday, she would need as much scholarship money as possible.

Consequently, she absolutely would not hand this lab report in for her own grade. "The rubric says the content needs to be communicated clearly and effectively. Blood doesn't have a choice. It's blood. It just goes."

"Fine. Fix it if you're so freaking smart." Fred slammed his pencil on the table and crossed his arms.

Freaking? Fred must really be irritated to be edging so close to actual curse words.

"I will." Birdy took out her red pen and attacked.

On Saturday, Birdy woke to voices outside. She peered through the blinds and saw Mom, Ms. Karen, and Mrs. Doppelski standing in the front yard, dressed to move. Birdy cracked open her window.

Birdy was an observer, a predisposition that had funneled her directly to her vice of eavesdropping. Since her toddler days, Birdy's brothers had deputized her to listen outside doorways because though she was quiet and looked innocent, she could repeat entire conversations verbatim. Even when she didn't set out to eavesdrop, opportune moments often seemed to fall in her lap. Or into her yard.

"It's just so big!" Ms. Karen was saying.

"I know, but I swear by it!" Mom said, hoisting her water jug like the holy grail. "My skin's amazing now, my head is so much clearer, my body hurts less, and yes I have to go to the bathroom every five minutes but that was true about the minute I first got pregnant anyway, so whatever!" Birdy wrinkled her nose at this, but the other two women found it hilarious.

"Okay, I need one," said Ms. Karen.

"Where do they sell those?" said Mrs. Doppelski. "Walmart?"

"I actually got this when I had that hospital stay," said Mom.

"Oh," said Mrs. Doppelski softly.

"So where's Arthur?" said Ms. Karen quickly.

"He went down to Bosco with Chris for soccer. He likes watching the games when he can, he used to always help coach the kids' teams when they were younger, but it just hurts his knees so bad now. When I first met him, though, I thought he *had* to be the coach of *something*." This was Mom laying the bait for a story.

"How did you two meet?" Mrs. Doppelski asked, eagerly snatching the dropped hint.

"Well, after Arthur couldn't stay in the Marines, he decided to try teaching, and he got hired at this school called St. Cecelia's. And I always loved music so much that I decided to be a music teacher, but I just—" Mom's back was to Birdy, so she mentally supplied the torment on Mom's face.

"Couldn't stand listening to 30 kids playing recorder all day?" guessed Ms. Karen.

"EXACTLY!" said Mom. "And the public school I was in—well, I don't have to tell you—"

"Oh my gosh, if they're anything like the ones in Conrad—"

"What happened?" said Mrs. Doppelski.

"Okay, so that's a whole other story, but anyway, after two years I said I was DONE. I never wanted to teach again. But I just love *being* in schools, you know? I love seeing kids learn, and all the fun crafts, and that school calendar is so convenient. So I was going to Mass at St. Cecelia's, and I saw in the bulletin that the school needed a secretary, so I walked right in on Monday and got the job!"

"Wow!" said Mrs. Doppelski.

"Yeah," said Mom. "So I'm there, first week of school, sitting at my desk, reading *Kristin Lavransdatter,* have you ever read that?"

"No," said both Doppelski ladies.

"Oh, it's so good, we have like three copies, I'll lend you some! But anyway, I'm sitting there reading, and this handsome man walks into the office. And he just had the kindest eyes but he looked *so* strong and I thought he must be the football coach. And then he looks at my book and goes, 'That's one of my favorites.' And I go, 'I think it's going to be one of mine, too!'"

Mom's version of this tale had many variations—sometimes the sun was shining through the window, sometimes it was raining outside, sometimes she had never seen Dad before in her life, sometimes she had already seen him in the halls and just knew he'd be her husband someday. Dad's version was economical and always the same: "Well, I saw a beautiful woman reading an excellent book, and I thought I'd better say something."

Mom tailored today's conclusion for her current audience: "And after all that, we just knew our family always needed to be in Catholic schools."

But that was a single neat chapter of the Cleary saga. Just as Dad liked to learn the history of their towns, lately Birdy had been trying to piece together the history of their family, trying to understand the sequence of events that had led them here to Conrad without Peter. Mom and Dad had such sweet beginnings, but tragedy caught up to them and cracked their fault lines wide open.

Only 68 Americans died in Vietnam in 1973, and Dad's dad was one of them. Dad and his brother grew up in Arizona, striving to impress their deceased father and their kind and unflappable mom. This mindset drove Dad all the way to Annapolis, where he discovered he liked seasons, and where he decided to settle after his accident.

Mom and her brother grew up with unkind and volatile parents who died together in a car accident when she was in college. Patrick theorized their accident was the reason Mom was so fragile and worried. Peter used to say her parents made her that way, before they died. Birdy thought it might also be related to Grandma Cleary, who her parents still couldn't mention without crying.

When Mom was pregnant with Peter, Grandma moved all the way from Flagstaff to the apartment building next door. They all planned for her to take care of Peter when Mom went back to work. But in her kind and unflappable way, she never told anyone about the pains she'd been having in her side. One day Mom walked over for an afternoon cup of tea and found her curled up on the floor. She called an ambulance, but by then it was too late. Grandma died of pancreatic cancer three months after she moved, one month before Peter's birth.

"You two are so cute," Mrs. Doppelski was saying.

"So how long were you at St. Cecelia's?" said Ms. Karen.

"Four years," said Mom. "We loved the Annapolis area, and then we were in Virginia for a few years, and then we went back to Maryland when Birdy started kindergarten, and I started working again, and when she finished first grade we decided that school wasn't a great fit anymore, so we moved."

At the end of Birdy's first grade year, Mom made a clerical error that ruined the report cards for the whole school. Mom's soul-crushing embarrassment over this incident was the impetus for the first move Birdy remembered being sad about. They moved again after second grade, and again after third, seeking schools with the proper combination of openings and employee tuition breaks. When Birdy was starting fifth grade and Peter was starting ninth, they landed at St. Francis, a K-12 Catholic school where Dad could teach history, Mom could work in the school office, and all the kids could attend for free. They made it three full school years before their most painful move of all, to Conrad.

"It's been a little tough sometimes," said Mom, "but it's all so worth it to me for my kids to have a good education."

"That's amazing that you've done all that," said Ms. Karen. "I've always lived here, and I always will, but sometimes I feel like there's more out there and I just don't know how to get it, you know? And I don't want my kids to feel that way."

"Oh, I know what you mean. At Bosco, they have this new science lab, it's gorgeous! I wouldn't know what to do with any of that stuff, but I'm so glad my boys get to learn how!"

"It's too bad we can't have something like *that* at Divine Mercy," said Ms. Karen.

"Well, we just have to remember we're raising saints, not scholars," said Mrs. Doppelski with her nervous giggle.

This quip was popular in the CHOC circle. Mom had been known to rage against it in private ("Haven't they HEARD of St. Thomas AQUInus?") but she didn't this time.

"It's so nice how much everyone cares about their faith here," said Mom. "Some of the schools we just had to leave because—"

"Tammy!" came a shout, and Mrs. Doppelski jumped.

"We need you back home," barked Mr. Doppelski, coming into view.

"Jude, we haven't even gotten started yet!" said Mom, stomping her foot a little.

"Well, I'm really sorry to interrupt, ladies," said Mr. Doppelski, smiling. "I know how much Tammy wants to lose the baby weight—" He took a pinch of her waist "—but the baby wants her." Mrs. Doppelski giggled.

"Oh my gosh, you're so rude, she's tiny!" said Mom, but she was giggling too.

Birdy shut her window and pulled her covers back over her head.

6

WHEN THE DOPPELSKIS DROPPED Birdy off on Wednesday, Mary was waiting under the maple tree in the backyard. "HI!" said Mary, squeezing Birdy. "This is so exciting!"

"I'm so glad you're here!" said Birdy, fishing out her keys. "Come on in!" Birdy showed Mary around while Mary told her about the youth retreat she had gone on the previous weekend.

"You have to come next time," said Mary, sprawling on Birdy's bed. "It's like going to Praise Night for two whole days in a row!"

"Wow," said Birdy. They heard the doorbell and Mary straightened.

"Do you think that's him?" said Mary.

"I think so," said Birdy, smiling. Mary flew down the stairs and opened the door.

"Dominic!" Mary shrieked.

"Mary!" he said, picking her up as he hugged her. Then he put her down and looked over her head at Birdy, who was still on the stairs. "Why do you always lock the door?"

Birdy dug her fingernail into the banister. "I mean, I'm here by myself..." She didn't want to explain Mom's egress-related hangups to Dominic.

"Doesn't your dad have a gun? He was a Marine, right? Almost?"

Excuse me? "I mean he has one, but he doesn't use it. I don't even know where it is."

Dominic cocked his head like Birdy was slow to understand the point. "Well, if you knew how to use that, you wouldn't be so nervous about robbers." Mary laughed and Dominic turned his attention to her. "How have *you* been?"

Birdy descended the stairs, feeling like flies were buzzing in her ears and limbs. She went to the kitchen table and started taking out her homework, but every time she sat down she realized she was missing something else she needed. She bounced in and out of her chair, somehow finding it impossible to remain seated while digging through her backpack. Dominic, meanwhile, managed to take out all of his supplies with one arm around Mary. He was in Peter's chair.

Mary leaned on Dominic to look at his proof. "What even is that?"

"Geometry." He sounded incredulous.

"Holy shoot, I could never do that. It looks so hard!" Birdy's buzzing nerves melted away at the look on Mary's face. Mary knew how to make all kinds of beautiful crafts, and she knew a lot about saints, but she always acted like other academic disciplines were a waste of time. Conrad County homeschooling parents had to present academic portfolios to the school board each semester to prove they were really teaching. Last spring, Mary had laughingly relayed to Birdy her family's rush to fabricate the minimum required documents. "It's so much better for you to just be free and not stuck in a building all day," she had said. But as she stared at Dominic's neat work page, she looked dismayed.

"You could totally do it," said Birdy loyally. "It's kind of like solving a puzzle."

Mary's eyes widened. "Are you in this class too?"

"Yeah," said Birdy.

"Oh, wow," said Mary. "What's it like being in *school?*" She said the word like it tasted bad.

Dominic leaned back on his chair legs. "It's nice having somewhere to go every day. I wish you were there, though."

"I know! I wish I could hang out with you guys all day," said Mary, pouting. Birdy said nothing. She hadn't minded her brief time homeschooling, during which she had entirely taught herself, but she was glad to be back in school. Not that she fit in very well there.

She continued her problem set and Mary and Dominic grew quiet. In a few glances, Birdy ascertained that they were exchanging notes in his notebook. Then Mary stood up.

"I need to go to the bathroom." Before Birdy could open her mouth, Dominic leapt to his feet too.

"I'll show you where it is," he said. This was unnecessary on multiple levels, and Birdy smirked at them both.

"Have fun in the bathroom," she said. Mary beamed at her and in a moment their footsteps had faded up the kitchen staircase. She figured they would be away for a few minutes, but she had completely finished her Geometry and was halfway through her Biology review page when the doorbell rang again. Mary pounded down the stairs an instant later, smoothing her hair.

"Joey's here!" she said, grabbing Birdy for a big hug. "Thanks so much, it was so good to see you, you're such an amazing friend,

I'll call you soon, I love you!" Birdy laughed, enjoying Mary's buoyant energy as she dashed down the hallway and out the door.

Still smiling, Birdy turned to find Dominic standing right behind her.

"Shit!" she yelled.

Dominic cracked up. "Language, Birdy," he said shaking his finger at her.

"Oh, shut up," she said, putting a hand on her pounding heart as she backed into the table. "You scared the crap out of me!"

He stepped closer, seeming to enjoy himself. "Why are you so nervous? Are you worried Mary will know you know cuss words?"

Birdy felt hot and drained her water glass. "How was the bathroom?" she asked pointedly.

Dominic smiled. "Oh, it was good." He started packing his backpack. "Your room was nice too." Birdy tensed. "I'd better head out too." He looked around. "When are your parents getting home?"

Birdy shrugged. "Like 6, maybe. Or 7."

"You're here by yourself so much."

Birdy shrugged again. "That's fine with me." It was. It was more peaceful than the alternative.

He looked at her intently, and Birdy became aware that they were very much alone. Then he enfolded her in a slow hug, which smelled an awful lot like Mary's shampoo. "Well thanks for having me over. See you tomorrow."

"Sure, anytime," said Birdy, shrugging again. *Stop shrugging!* "See you then."

As soon as he left, Birdy ran upstairs to her closet. She hoisted aside a cardboard box, opened the trunk beneath it, unzipped an old black backpack, and found her notebooks, undisturbed.

Birdy was a journaler, but she was sneaky about it. She never described her life in a narrative style. Instead, she wrote random scenes where the characters were dealing with some version of whatever was distressing her. Despite her layers of privacy measures, the idea of Dominic snooping around her room was unnerving, and, suddenly, easy to picture. She bristled at the memory of his comment about Dad. Then she thought of Mary's reaction to their Geometry homework and her heart wrenched again.

Mary was the third child in her family of eight, and the oldest girl. The Vespas' big secret was that two years previously, the oldest brother had impregnated his unauthorized girlfriend. This baby had only lived for a few weeks in utero before dying of natural causes, a relief to the Vespa family. After what happened with her brother, Mary's parents forbade her from dating, courting, or so much as linking pinkies with any male, anywhere.

When Birdy compared her home to these circumstances, it was easy to forget that she herself lived in an emotional minefield. It occurred to Birdy that for all she knew about Mary, Mary knew comparatively little about the Cleary family's dirt. This was fine, as Birdy had never offered it and Mary never asked. Birdy didn't even know if she could explain it, given the chance.

Even though Mary and Dominic were a year older than Birdy, sometimes Mary seemed younger than both of them. She used the term "playdate" to talk about hanging out, which Birdy still found jarring. She saw herself as the benevolent heroine in the world's plot, quirky, sweet, and vivacious. She preferred praise music and Disney music, disparaging anything you could find on the radio as too worldly.

Though Dominic had also been raised under the CHOC shelter, something about him felt more familiar to Birdy. He liked music that wasn't Christian, he liked movies that had cuss words, he liked contact sports and could play them well. He laughed in good humor, without stopping to calculate if the joke's subject matter was too secular. Being his friend had come completely naturally to Birdy, but she always pulled herself up short.

Back in April, Dominic had walked up to her, waving his digital camera. "Check this out, Birdy," he said, "I made something for my mom's birthday." She looked at the display and was amazed to see his own house, replicated in miniature as a birdhouse.

"Oh my gosh!" exclaimed Birdy. "You made that?"

"Yeah!" he smiled.

She leaned in and pushed the zoom button so she could see it better. "It looks just like your house! I love how intricately you painted it!" She looked up and saw an expression of pleased shock on Dominic's face.

"Thanks!" he said. "That's exactly what I like about it!" He seemed energized by her admiration and scrolled backwards so he could show her how he had designed, cut, and assembled each piece. He'd documented the entire project. Normally Dominic was busy constructing a joke or scheme of some sort, and this uncynical enthusiasm brought a sweet light to his face that opened something in her chest. She had thought his eyes were brown like hers, flat and unchanging like chocolate or mud. But now she noticed swirls of green and gold that came alive as he talked, dark eyelashes that swooped into an unbelievable curl, and crinkled edges that melted into a happy smile.

Birdy had been trying to pretend that moment away ever since. And now she lived in fear that if she made one false move, it would all come crashing down. Her parents uprooted their lives at the first sign of trouble, but it felt like the move to Conrad might stick. Mom was attached to Karen and Tammy, probably because they found her wise. Dad was less enamored of the neighbors, but liked his new job. Patrick and Chris were so close to graduating. Birdy already had dear friends who she didn't want to leave behind. And the thought of moving away from somewhere Peter had never even visited was unthinkable.

Mary's bubbly kindness more than made up for the times when Birdy worried Mary would disapprove of her full self, which she had never meant to hide. Birdy had not counted on getting along so well with Dominic, or the level to which their lives would become intertwined. But he had been Mary's dream first. Birdy was always ready to join in the fun, but Mary and Dominic both felt it was their job to make things fun. They deserved each other, and Birdy wanted to stay out of their way.

She wouldn't do anything about that sneaking want within her. She could make this sacrifice for her best friend.

THE NEXT TUESDAY AFTER school, Birdy was halfway through a proof when she heard the front door open. Birdy put down her pencil, heart pounding, and peeked out the window. Mom was home early. She was trying to shut her blinds when her bedroom door burst open.

They stared at each other, Birdy guilty, Mom furious.

"What are you doing?" Mom's voice was shaking.

"I, I, I," said Birdy.

"Are you trying to shut your blinds? Did you leave them open when I wasn't home?"

"I," said Birdy.

"ANSWER ME!" Mom yelled.

"I forgot! I'm sorry! I'm shutting them!"

"They're open all over the whole house!" Mom slammed her water jug onto the desk. "I have to be able to trust you! I can't believe you have been deliberately deceiving me! I'm astounded!"

"Mom, I just wanted some sunlight! There is nothing in this house that is going to be ruined by excess sunlight!"

"Don't yell at me! Don't you talk to me like that! It doesn't matter what you thought! I need to go to work and I need you to do your part! How DARE you!"

She screamed louder with every sentence, so breathless with betrayal it was as though she'd found Birdy dealing drugs. Birdy's heart knocked against her chest, forbidden thoughts pummeling her skull. *It's not fair, this is so fucking stupid, it feels like a tomb in here, I just wanted to breathe, you just want to control me, no wonder Peter hates you.* But she would never say those things. Mom was seething, shuddering, and Birdy knew the next act of this sick play. It was time to defuse the bomb.

She took a deep breath, easily found some tears, and exhaled remorse. "Mom, you're right, I'm so sorry. I was so thoughtless. I should have thought about what you wanted and not what I wanted. Sorry. It was selfish." Groveling and self-flagellation were critical components of defusing the bomb.

Mom relaxed a bit. "I just need you to listen to me, honey. If our electricity bills are too high or we need to replace the couches, we just won't have enough money left over for your tuition."

"I'm so sorry Mom." Birdy's insides were boiling. Her face was empty. She hugged her mother.

Later, Mom told the family the dentist's office would be closing two hours early all week while the equipment underwent maintenance. Birdy broke the news to Dominic on Wednesday. "My mom's going to be home this afternoon, sorry."

"Oh," he said. "Is Mary still coming?"

"Yeah."

"Well then I'll be there! Not that I wouldn't come anyway."

Birdy gave him a give-me-a-break look, and he protested. "No, really!"

They chose the living room for work that afternoon. Work consisted of Mary and Dominic snuggling and snickering on one couch while Birdy did her Geometry problem set on the other couch. When they heard a key in the front door, Dominic sprang from his seat, coming to stand in a position equidistant from Mary and Birdy. Mom entered, laden with her water jug, lunch box, backpack, purse, and two additional tote bags.

"Hi guys!" said Mom cheerily.

"Mrs. C!" said Dominic. "Let me take those for you!"

"Oh, thanks hon! I was really struggling to unlock the door and hold them at the same time." She looked over at Birdy as Dominic put her bags on the floor. "You don't need to lock up when you're here with friends, honey!"

"That's what I always say to her, Mrs. C!" said Dominic. Birdy felt an unfamiliar hatred for him surge within her.

"She's probably worried because she's always reading creepy books. She doesn't need to worry about anything with you around, Dominic!"

Mary contributed a peal of laughter, and then Mom started opening all the blinds. "Birdy, you're keeping it so dark in here! It's such a nice day outside!" Birdy's brain detonated, but she kept her face still.

"Yesterday you said to keep the blinds shut," Birdy said evenly.

"Oh, just sometimes," said Mom. "You must have misunderstood me."

Birdy pushed her pencil so hard into her paper that the tip broke. Neither Mom nor Mary noticed this, as they were now talking about some cute curtains Mary had seen at Wal-Mart. Dominic, however, observed the moment with the air of one discovering a trinket at his feet, finding it amusing, and pocketing it for future inspection.

7

THE OCTOBER PRAISE NIGHT was at the Vespas' house. Mary called Birdy the day before to talk about how exciting it was. "Oh and by the way," she said at the end of the call, "my mom doesn't know that I go over to hang out at your house every week. I told her I go to a prayer group with one of my other homeschool friends instead. But it's not really a lie because we do say grace before we eat!" It was a lie. They'd never said grace. Birdy didn't know how to explain she was hurt, so she agreed not to mention their weekly visits to Mrs. Vespa.

Birdy was still rattled by Mary's casual revelation when she arrived on Friday, but Mary ran to greet her and ushered her into the kitchen. A frail woman with fine blond curls and huge brown eyes floated over to them. She wore a long brown skirt, a tightly buttoned floral blouse, a scapular, and two Miraculous Medals. She took Birdy's hand in both of hers and didn't let go as she said, "Welcome to our home, I'm Grace Vespa. And what is your name, angel?"

Thunderstruck by this term of endearment, Birdy had to gather herself for a second before saying. "Birdy. I'm Birdy Cleary."

"And how did you hear about our praise night?"

Birdy had thought Mrs. Vespa would already know who she was. She stammered for an answer, but Mary jumped in.

"Mom, she goes to Divine Mercy. She knows the Doppelskis. We met at the barn dance a while ago."

Mrs. Vespa blinked her large eyes at Mary, then swiveled them back to Birdy.

"And do all of your siblings go to Divine Mercy? Or is your mother still homeschooling the younger ones, like Mrs. Doppelski does?"

"What? Well, no, nobody, I'm the youngest, my brothers go to Bosco."

"And how many brothers do you have, angel?"

"Three." She wasn't going to explain anything about Peter to Mrs. Vespa, who did some simple addition before changing topics. "Birdy! So unusual! Is it a nickname?"

"Yeah, it's short for Bernadette."

Mrs. Vespa was devastated. "Bernadette!" She pumped Birdy's sweating hand in her cool ones. "What a shame you go by Birdy instead! Bernadette is one of the great saints of our church!"

Birdy tried to respond with adequate piety. "Um, well, yes, she's good, she's, well, I'm not really, I just like Birdy more. It's more me." That last part made her sound like she was on some Nick at Nite show. *You are so stupid!*

Mrs. Vespa's eyes contorted with sorrow for Birdy's impoverished soul. "But don't you feel inspired by St. Bernadette's beautiful example?"

"I've just always gone by Birdy," said Birdy. Her left knee started to wobble.

"Mom, let her be! Not everyone has to be named after Mama Mary!" laughed Mary, disrupting the tension and leaving Birdy grateful. Helpfully, Mary's one year old sister ran up howling and yanked her mom's skirt. Mrs. Vespa scooped her up, then regarded her daughter's best friend with large, empty eyes. "I'll never be able to call you Birdy. Bernadette it is. So lovely to meet you, angel." She floated away.

Birdy couldn't understand how she could sometimes be confident and witty and fun, be basically secure and happy with herself inside, while also frequently feeling like there was a beast inside her, coiling her innards round and round its fist, disabling her lungs, throat, and vocal cords while her heart and stomach went nuts. During these times, she could at best stand motionless and silent, and at worst stutter and shake violently.

Mary never seemed to have this problem. She was the darling of CHOC. Birdy had gathered that one reason for both her confidence and her popularity was the way she so expertly herded her younger siblings. Large families with teenage daughters who could run the show were ensuring the future of Catholicism in America.

As a cradle Catholic, Birdy did not find large families shocking, but she had been surprised by how many there were in Conrad. The Harts had seven kids and were pretty normal, if you overlooked the way Polly carried a collection of saint cards around in a Pokémon binder. Mrs. Vespa, on the other hand, was evidently one of those who used family size to ascertain Real Catholic status. Four kids did not appear to be enough.

Mom had given birth to her sons in rapid succession, delivering each one in three consecutive Aprils via C-section. When it was Birdy's turn to be born, Mom had bled severely and needed an emergency hysterectomy. "I was so worried we wouldn't bond and you wouldn't nurse, but you did!" Birdy's pleasant disposition after the crisis of her birth was another miracle in Mom's book. And so Birdy had entered the world, requiring little maintenance in dire circumstances.

Mom was sometimes wistful about the impossibility of future siblings for the kids. Never more so than when she was socializing with moms of many. In every new Catholic community they joined, Mom worked in pieces of the emergency hysterectomy story early and often, so as to designate herself as someone who would have had more if she could. It always made Birdy feel sorry for Mom, but also annoyed. No one needed to know why their family wasn't bigger. God knew they weren't doing so hot as it was.

Dominic was the oldest by four years in his family. When he was two, Mrs. Doppelski had finally converted to Catholicism, and the couple had ditched birth control in all its forms forever and ever. Not to be outdone, Abe and Karen followed suit by the next Easter. They had managed to conceive Joseph during this interval, a minor victory for Abe, who normally did not win in his lifelong competition with his brother. But Tammy had upped the ante by giving birth to twins just a year after that. Cosmas and Damian were named for a set of twin brothers who, sometime in the 3rd century, had cultivated illustrious careers as both doctors and martyrs. The race had been on ever since their birth. The Dark Doppelskis' current lineup consisted of Dominic,15, Coz and Damian, 11, Frankie, 9, Steve, 8, Sarah, 5, Bobby, 3, Hannah, 2, and Rebecca, 4 months. The Light Doppelskis were one man short with Isaac, 14, Joseph, 12, Justin, 10, David, 9, Maria, 8, Theresa, 6, Gus, 4, Helen, 1.

"Come on," said Mary, linking arms with Birdy and dragging her outside. "We're going to play a humongous game of hide and seek. It's so fun when you have a million people! I'm so glad you're here!"

The humongous game of Hide and Seek was indeed fun with a million people, though the player with whom Mary would have most liked to hide was not in attendance. The Doppelski grandparents were in town for the evening, so while Birdy and Mary hid in a tree and laughed till their faces hurt, Dominic, Isaac, and all their siblings endured an awkward dinner at Conrad's once-fancy, now derelict Washington Inn.

Mrs. Doppelski shared her lamentations about her cold and absent in-laws with Mom during their Saturday morning walk. They had moved to Florida when Jude and Abe were still in the military, and now spent one week a year briefly visiting their five sons. They had managed to fit in three at dinner last night— a brother named Joshua had driven over from College Park—so they were ahead of schedule and already in Virgina visiting another brother named Larry. Jude and Abe always bickered before and after these visits, annoying everyone else in the family.

Mom felt she had the perfect book on the subject—*Story of a Soul* by St. Therese of Lisieux. As St. Therese died a 24-year-old nun, the book had nothing to do with frustrating in-laws, but it was Mom's go-to guide for enduring suffering. She promised to bring the book over on Sunday, but when they got home from Mass, the upstairs toilet was leaking through the ceiling. Mike, their landlord, righted things with Dad's help, but the stress of the situation rendered Mom immobile for the rest of the day. She tasked Birdy with bringing the book over instead. Birdy didn't argue. She had found an article in that morning's paper she thought Dominic would like, and she wanted to give it to him.

It was just after one when Birdy walked into the Doppelskis'. She heard Mrs. Doppelski's voice upstairs, telling the kids to see who could be the first one to pick up 50 toys. In the kitchen, the smell of fried bacon filled the air, and Birdy's stomach grumbled. Mr. Doppelski was tackling a mountain of dishes, Coz was drying beside him, and Dominic was putting away the remaining food.

"Want a piece?" Dominic said, holding out a piece of bacon.

"Sure!" she said, putting the book on the table and tucking in. Dominic smiled and went back to his task.

"Did your dad get a new car, Ms. Birdy?" said Mr. Doppelski over his shoulder. "I saw a nice pickup in your driveway before."

Distracted by her bacon, she replied, "Oh, that's the landlord's." As soon as she said it, she remembered that Mom didn't want her to mention they were renting. *Crap.* Mr. Doppelski nodded in satisfaction, and Birdy suspected that was exactly the answer he'd been after. *Crap!*

She looked anxiously at Mr. Doppelski's back, and then she noticed Coz had huge shiner on his eye.

"Oh my gosh, Coz! Are you okay?"

Coz's eyes darted to hers and his mouth opened. "Fell off his skateboard," said Mr. Doppelski. "Gotta learn to stick that landing, buddy!" Coz shut his mouth and nodded.

"How did you even do that?" said Birdy. "You must have landed right on your face!"

Normally Coz was eager to share a war story, but he wasn't forthcoming this time.

"He's a little embarrassed about it," said Dominic, shutting the fridge. "He totally wiped out." He glanced at Coz and then came to stand with Birdy. This reminded her of the other reason for her visit.

"Oh, Dominic, I found this article in the paper about electric cars, and it made me think of what you were telling me a few days ago about engines." Birdy reached into her pocket and pulled out the clipping from the *Conrad Sun*.

Dominic stared at her, looking baffled. "Wow, thanks!" he said.

Embarrassment crept into Birdy's sides. It had seemed like a normal thing to do for someone she cared about—her dad was always cutting out articles or making photocopies of book pages and sending them to people. But Dominic was looking at her like she was an alien. An alien he was pleased with, but still.

Mr. Doppelski zipped over and plucked the article away from her, dripping wet suds all over it. "Aw, she cut it out just for you, buddy! Isaac's gonna be jealous!"

Birdy now begged God to strike her dead. *Please. A heart attack, an aneurysm, poisoned bacon, anything.* She had thought this was a nice, normal, *platonic* thing to do for a friend. Her dad did it all the time!

Dominic laughed along with his dad, but then took the article back from him. He gave Birdy a soft smile, folded the clipping, and put it in his pocket.

"I'm excited to read it," he told her.

The next day at school, Dominic was especially attentive to Birdy. He hugged her more than she thought was necessary, complimented her on her headband that she wasn't sure about, told her she had beautiful eyes, and wrote her notes in class. He put his arm around her in Geometry and played with her hair. She was stiff at these advances, worrying that she'd misfired, that he'd misinterpreted, or maybe that he'd read her exactly right and was now inviting her into something illicit.

On Tuesday, Dominic barely spoke to Birdy at all. And on Wednesday, he treated her like normal and then initiated Makeout Phase with Mary while all three of them were standing in her bedroom. "Well, guess I'd better be going," Birdy said with false cheer. Mary gave a muffled farewell.

She tried to act like this light switch treatment didn't bother her, but the truth was that her thoughts had turned to a brutal self-interrogation.

Why did you cut out that article for him?

I just thought he would like it!

Why?

He's my friend!

Oh? Do you think about all your friends constantly? Or just him?

Shut up. *He and Mary are... something. End of story.*

But it kind of seems like he likes you sometimes.

That's exactly the problem.

That's why it's the end of the story.

ON THURSDAY, BIRDY SAT with Olivia, finishing her lunch. Dominic had spent the morning out of school dressing deer he had killed before dawn—a perk of being the son of a founding father. He walked in and surveyed the room, then went up to Margaret's table.

"Margaret!" he said.

She looked up at him and squealed "Dominic!"

"Wow, your hair looks stunning today," he said to her, eyes roving across her face.

Plink. A drop of blood disturbed the clear waters of Birdy's consciousness. She would revisit this moment ad nauseam for years to come, the moment it clicked that her entire concept of Dominic was wrong.

Margaret lit up at his compliment. "Thanks! My mom blow dried it for me."

Birdy couldn't fathom her own mother doing this for her, or herself wanting it to be done. Was that why Margaret's hair was all shiny?

"Well, it looks really smooth..."

Birdy threw away her trash and left the room, a pulse of confusion awakening in her gut. Dominic, as the son of Mr. Doppelski, was allowed to get away with a little bit of mischief. Mischief included late arrivals, pranks, and teasing, but it was also a euphemism for the way he acted around girls. The Divine Mercy moms often made laughing references to Dominic's flirtatiousness, which was supposedly neutralized by Mr. Doppelski's well-known rule against Dominic dating. The girls were all tasked with being modest so they could maintain their chastity, but no one batted an eye when Dominic gave their daughters prolonged hugs and complimented their beauty.

Birdy knew a girl who acted the way Dominic did would be burned at the stake, but that seemed like a problem with the adults and not the behavior itself. The other boys at Divine Mercy were terrified of girls, and she preferred Dominic's openness. Most of the time he seemed harmless, if confusing. But he had just recycled the compliment he used before kissing Mary for the first time. And that didn't seem so harmless.

Her last class that day was Latin, and as usual she sat next to Isaac. During their dialogue exercise he kept her laughing with a series of intentionally poor translations. Afterwards, she wandered down the hallway hungry, wondering what she could make for dinner tonight. She thought she was alone.

A heavy arm looped across her shoulders. "Those pants look good on you," said Dominic.

In trying to explain Dominic's behavior to herself, Birdy had often fallen back on the classic "He thinks of me like a sister." But she couldn't sell that one as a brotherly comment. "Oh... thanks," she said. He pulled her closer to him, but she noticed her shoe was untied. Not a dire situation for a boat shoe, but convenient in this moment. She bent down to fix it, then stood.

He put his arm around her again. "How was your day?"

She shook his arm off in a few quick steps and continued the conversation, all while a question echoed in her brain: *What. Was. That?*

They were just friends. He treated everyone like this, so everyone said. But she knew, knew, knew he would not have done that in front of Mary.

THAT EVENING, BIRDY FOUND only Dominic waiting to walk to soccer. "Isaac has to have his tutoring again tonight because his tutor's busy next Wednesday," he said as they set out.

"Oh, that stinks," said Birdy.

"Aw, you miss him?" Dominic said this reflexively, but there was no goofiness behind it. They walked along the path together, crunching leaves into a deafening silence. It had been a strange week, and the usual ease that existed between them was gone. The sun was already low in the sky. It would be dark before practice ended.

So few people showed up that the boys and girls joined forces for a scrimmage. The boys had a new player, a tall and lanky guy who most of the other kids seemed to already know. He wore a backwards cap, which he kept taking off and tapping on his hand, revealing smushed dirty blond hair. At first Birdy thought he was staring into space, but he was more serious than he appeared. He played offense to Mel's defense, and things turned cutthroat every time one of them got possession. Birdy also had a smackdown with a rat-faced guy named Sam, who always spoke to the girls in a singsong voice and touched their waists when they got close. After leaving him groaning on the ground, Birdy passed to Beth, who scored the only goal of the game.

After practice, Birdy knelt to take a long drink of water. Beth plopped down beside her and started changing from her cleats to her sneakers.

"Is that your bike?" Birdy asked, pointing to the red bicycle on the grass.

"Yeah," said Beth, making a tidy knot on her left shoe. "It's such a nice night!"

Birdy smiled. She thought it was on the chilly side, but Beth seemed like exactly the type of person who would chase an hour of soccer with a nippy bike ride and enjoy it. Beth slung on her backpack, shoved her pink helmet over her blond ponytail and got on her bike.

"Well, I would say good game tonight but—it wasn't the best." Birdy laughed as Beth went on. "But it was really fun to play with you! That one tackle was beautiful."

"Well, I was getting tired of him trying to touch me," said Birdy. "Thanks for being on the other side."

Once Beth had launched off into the darkness, Birdy looked around for Dominic. She found him standing on the sidelines with his hands on Angela's hips. Angela was giggling madly and rubbing his arms. *What the hell?* Dominic looked straight at Birdy and raised his eyebrows. Then he scooped Angela up and carried her to the other side of the field.

Birdy's armpits were cold with sweat, but the rest of her was hot with fury. Her heart galloped like she was still running sprints. She didn't want to walk through the dark forest alone without a flashlight, and she wasn't about to wait around for Dominic. So she headed for the silent street to take the long way.

Birdy's cleats scraped precariously on the blacktop, but the shoulder was too overgrown with prickly weeds to walk on. The road wasn't much lighter than the path through the woods. A car passed by her slowly, then turned around. Birdy retracted as it approached, but then she saw a familiar face.

"Hey Birdy, we can give you a ride," called Mel, who was leaning out her window with a friendly smile. "Right?" she said to the redheaded lady in the driver's seat.

"Of course!" said the lady, who must have been Mel's mom.

"Oh, wow, okay, thanks!" said Birdy. She opened the door to the back seat and was surprised to find the new boy folded into it. "Uhhh, sorry," she said, flinching backwards. "I'll just..." she said, preparing to walk around to the other door.

"Oh, I'll just..." he said, scooting over to the other side of the bench. "Okay" she said, wavering in indecision for a moment. She weighed whether her parents would be more displeased about her walking home in the dark or driving with an unknown guy. She figured it was okay if there was a mom in the car. She eased in and buckled up.

"I'm Mrs. Holloway, sweetie," said Mel's mom.

Mel turned around in her seat and gestured at the boy. "And this is Vince. He's my neighbor."

"Hi," said Birdy.

"Hey," said Vince. "Mel saw you walking and said we needed to pull over immediately."

"It's true," said Mrs. Holloway.

"Well between knowing you from soccer and everything Dominic and Isaac have said about you, I figured you weren't one of those murdering hitch hikers. Where are they anyway? Don't you usually walk with them?"

"Yeah, but Isaac couldn't come tonight and Dominic... got distracted."

"Oh yeah, I met the distraction. She is not your best player," said Vince.

"Our sports teams are challenged around here," sighed Mel. "So, Dominic talking to a skanky girl, big surprise."

Birdy laughed, feeling guilty but gleeful, and slightly surprised Mel would say this in front of her mom.

"Mel," said Mrs. Holloway, her correction somewhat negated by her snort of laughter.

"I would say I can't believe Dominic ditched you, except I totally can," said Vince. Birdy's stomach squirmed. "Do you know him too?"

"Yup," said Vince. "We were in the same class until he started homeschooling."

"No way!" said Birdy.

"Yup, and Dominic and I were like best buddies. He and I actually used to leave Mel out of everything. He would go over there to play and then I would show up and we'd hide from her for two hours. But eventually I realized she's cool. And Dom is... himself. So now we just see each other every once in a while. I only came tonight because football practice was cancelled."

Mel turned around in her seat again. "Tell her why."

Vince rolled his eyes. "My coach sprained his ankle. Stepping on his dog's toy. He stepped on it, tripped down the stairs, and sprained his ankle. And who did he call to bring him to the hospital? The defensive coach. But then the other offensive coach has some emergency with his tractor, and I don't know, I guess the assistants are busy sleeping or something. So that's it, practice cancelled, we're on our own to work out tonight."

"Wow," said Birdy, thinking of the complex chain of command that headed Chris's JV soccer team at Bosco. "I guess the sports teams really are challenged around here."

"Yeah, it's sad," said Mel, "You know like in movies where the small town doesn't have much, but at least everyone can rally around the football team or whatever? We don't even have that."

"Have you heard anything about when we're going to have a game?" said Birdy.

"Nope," said Mel, "Normally we would have had one by now, but no one knows anything about it."

Mrs. Holloway looked at Birdy in the rearview mirror. "CRL doesn't do anything to organize you kids other than take our money. It's impossible to get in touch with them. It's ridiculous."

"Is Beth's dad ever going to come to practice?" asked Birdy.

A scowl creased Mel's merry face. "I don't know. Beth swears he will. But he lets her down a lot."

They pulled up in front of Birdy's house. No one was even home.

"Thanks so much for the ride!" said Birdy. "I really appreciate it."

"Of course!" Mel cried. "We can't let anything happen to you. Without you we would be screwed. I know, because we didn't have you last year, and we were screwed. I don't know why anyone besides you, Beth and Kelly even plays. They don't even like it!"

"Nice job out there," said Vince.

Birdy smiled and went into her dark house.

8

DURING THE SCHOOL YEAR, the Catholic youths of Conrad gained another option for group worship. St. Paul's hosted its own Praise Night every third Friday of the month, except it was called Songs and Teens. Chris drove Birdy through Conrad's crumbly downtown for the October meeting.

"Are you excited?" he asked.

"I don't know," said Birdy, "it could be fun."

Chris made a cynical noise and stopped in front of St. Paul's. Floodlights illuminated its stained-glass doors.

"Do you know where you're supposed to go?" said Chris.

"Kind of," said Birdy, climbing out of the car. She spotted a sign for the parish hall and motioned a thumbs-up to Chris, who pulled away as she followed the path to a squat brick building. She entered a long room with a stage at one end and tables scattered throughout. To her surprise, the first familiar face she saw was Kelly's.

"Hi," said Kelly. Her voice was soft, but she looked as pleased as Birdy felt.

"Hi," said Birdy.

"I like your shoes."

"Thanks!" said Birdy, glancing down at her Converse knock-offs. "You look really nice." She did. Kelly wore a pink babydoll top and glittered with the type of accessories collection that always confounded Birdy. Earrings, necklace, a scarf, rings, bracelets. Her honey-colored hair, which Birdy had only ever seen in two thick French braids, framed her kind face in gentle curls. "I've never seen your hair down before, it's so pretty!"

"Oh, thanks!" said Kelly. "It's not like this is how it naturally looks down though, I used a curling iron."

"Oh," said Birdy, realizing this might be another piece of hair knowledge she was lacking.

"I think Mel and Beth will be here soon too," said Kelly.

"Oh, cool," said Birdy, "do you guys always come to this?"

Kelly shrugged one shoulder. "Every few months. It's a little... weird sometimes, but it's something to do together, you know?"

Birdy nodded. "That makes sense to me.

It got quiet. Birdy searched for something to say.

"Mel actually gave me a ride home last night," she offered.

"Yeah, she told us that!" Kelly became animated. "She actually lives behind me. Our yards connect."

"Oh, cool," said Birdy. "That must be fun."

"It is," smiled Kelly. "And then Beth lives a few miles away, but she rides her bike everywhere so she comes over to us all the time. Our houses are right next to the woods and we have a couple spots in them where we like to go hang out, it's pretty fun. You should come over sometime!"

"Absolutely you should," said Mel.

They turned around to see Mel's smiling, freckled face and Beth by her side.

"We need to show you the watering hole," said Beth, tossing her long blond hair behind her back. "It's not a real watering hole, it's actually just a clearing by the creek, but Mel named it that when she was little."

"I really liked the Lion King," Mel explained.

"Past tense?" said Kelly.

"Okay, I really like the Lion King."

"I used to love that movie too," said Birdy. "But I haven't seen it in forever because my old dog destroyed the tape."

"Oooh, my little sister destroyed The Little Mermaid!" said Mel.

"No real loss," said Beth.

Kelly gasped in indignation while the rest of them laughed.

"Some Saturday you should come over and we can all play soccer hang out," said Mel.

"That would be great," said Birdy, "Do you—"

"OH MY GOSH HI!" said Mary.

Everyone whirled around. Mary tackled Birdy in a hug and started talking a mile a minute. "Oh my gosh, I am so glad you're here! This praise night is nowhere near as good as the ones that CHOC does but it's fine. Oh my gosh, is *you know who* here yet?"

"Voldemort?" said Beth.

Birdy laughed, but Mary looked disapproving. "Um... *no.* I don't read those books. I'm talking about someone *else.*" She gave Birdy the look of one dropping a major hint, as if Birdy didn't already know who Mary was talking about.

Something about discussing Dominic as an object of intrigue in front of her soccer friends was off-putting. Back when their friendship had been confined to the neighborhood, Birdy had mistaken Dominic's friendliness for trustworthiness. Evidently, Mel had been under no such delusions, and Birdy was growing embarrassed that she was just now understanding this other side of him. It was uncomfortable for these two opposing views to collide in person, and now she wasn't sure how to answer Mary. Did Mary not want her to reveal who she was talking about?

"Oh look, Dominic and Isaac are here," said Mel.

Mary turned up her smile to 1000 watts as they approached.

"Hello girls, you're all looking lovely this evening," said Dominic, looking right at Mary.

"Hey Dominic," said Mel, unflustered.

"Do you all know each other, or do you just know Birdy?" said Isaac, pointing around.

"I saw you here last year, *sometimes,*" said Mary pointedly at the soccer crew.

"Yeah, didn't we all do that musical chairs game?" said Mel.

"Gather round folks," called a plump younger lady in a loose black sweater, jeans and clogs. "For those of you who don't know me I'm Carly, and I'm the youth minister here at St. Paul's. It's time for us all to get started, so let's have our friend Matt lead us in prayer."

Their friend Matt, a short and bearded fellow, did as he was invited and then pulled out his guitar. Matt was a better musician than Kyle, but he played all the same songs and made them spend a full seven minutes with their eyes closed in reflection. Crying rapturously did not appear to be a requirement at Songs at Teens, but Birdy could still hear Mary sniffling.

Afterwards, Carly announced it was time for Fellowship and Fun. Birdy turned to ask Beth what that involved, but Mary had other plans.

"Birdy and I need to go do something," she said, grabbing Birdy's arm and steering her forward. "Out on the *deck,*" she said in Dominic's direction. They were out the door in a moment, standing in crisp, clear air on a balcony that overlooked a walled garden.

"Ugh, I really like Praise Night more than Songs and Teens. There are just all these public schoolers here and you just know they don't really *care* as much," said Mary.

"Well, Mel and Beth and Kelly go to St. Monica's," said Birdy. "They're on my soccer team."

"Oh, St. Monica's is just as bad as public school," said Mary confidently. "It—" The fluorescent smile was back. Dominic had joined them.

"Mary, what's up gorgeous? That shirt looks so good on you," said Dominic, giving her a huge hug. Birdy's whole body felt hot.

Mary pulled away from the hug but left an arm around his waist. "I like yours too!" Then she giggled at her own wit.

"It's nice being out here alone with you on a night like this," said Dominic.

Mary continued giggling uncontrollably and glanced at Birdy, who took the hint.

"Bye," she whispered.

The fellowship hall felt hot and stuffy compared to the quiet night. Birdy went to the snack table and piled cookies and chips on a paper plate. They didn't taste good.

Mel materialized by her side. "So," she said. "This mystery man of your friend's."

"Voldemort," said Birdy around a mouthful of cookie.

"Yeah. Voldemort. It's Dominic, right?"

"Wow, how did you guess?" said Birdy. "You weren't fooled by that clever ruse?" She felt a little guilty, like she was talking about Mary behind her back, but her feelings were prickly at the moment.

Mel laughed. Then she softened. "You seemed pretty shaken up last night when we gave you a ride home. I thought it was just because he was being rude to you but--- it's because he's got something going on with your friend too, isn't it?"

Like Mary, Mel was more outgoing than Birdy could ever dream of being. But being in her company felt different. It was less like being swept up in a whirlwind and more like being seen.

"Yeah," she said. It was hard to talk.

Mel watched her. "I really meant it when I said you should come over some time. Can I have your phone number?"

"Sure," said Birdy, and she gave it.

"Do you want to come play Apples to Apples?" said Mel.

"I love that game!" said Birdy, and they went to a table to play. She didn't see Mary again until she left.

ON SUNDAY AT CHURCH, Dominic struck up a conversation with Birdy about electric cars, giving no sign of the weirdness that had followed her ill-fated journalistic offering. All that week, he was simply nice and friendly, refraining from complimenting or even touching her. Isaac came along with Dominic to the Wednesday study group since his tutor was busy. Isaac and Mary got into such a lively discussion about *Finding Nemo* that Dominic and Mary's personal time was heavily curtailed, but Dominic didn't act resentful.

On Thursday, Joseph finally wheedled his way into being allowed to tag along to soccer, and he bounded like a puppy all the way to the fields while Birdy, Isaac, and Dominic trailed. Birdy went straight over to Mel when they reached the field.

"So, you said you have a little sister?" she asked once they'd started drills.

"Two! They go to Conrad Primary." Mel passed the ball to Birdy. "But my mom is the guidance counselor at St. Monica's, so we can go there for free for high school."

"Oh, that's just like my brothers! My dad's a teacher at Bosco, so they can go there for free too."

"Oh, wow, Bosco is like super fancy right?"

"Yeah, we would never be able to afford it normally."

"I get that. My dad is a cop."

With that, Mel and Birdy had transmitted their poorish-kid bat signals, and the comfort of mutual understanding settled between them.

"I guess Vince's football practice wasn't canceled tonight?"

Mel's smile took on a width disproportionate to Birdy's question. "Nope, he's back to business."

After practice, the Doppelski boys came over to the girls' field. Angela slunk over to Dominic expectantly, but all he gave her was a one-armed hug and notification that she had grass on her nose. She drifted away downcast.

Mel quirked her eyebrows at Birdy. "Do you want a ride tonight?"

Birdy opened her mouth, unsure what to say, but Joseph whipped his head back and forth between them. "Birdy—wait—you're not going with Mel are you? I brought a flashlight for you!" He rummaged in his backpack. Wanting to solidify his place in the pack, Joseph had come prepared with four flashlights.

Birdy could not bring herself to ruin the hopeful look on Joseph's face. She took the flashlight and exchanged grins with Mel. "I guess I'm walking back tonight. Thanks though!" She waved to Beth and Kelly as Dominic and Isaac took up their flashlights too. They set off down the path, and the trip back home through the dark woods was spooky fun.

Birdy was almost ready to let the weirdness of the previous week slide. If Dominic had let things lie where they were, she might have. But he took his penance a step too far. At the end of the trail, Victoria Street's porch lights became visible. Birdy gave back her flashlight and turned right as Isaac and Joseph turned left.

Dominic looked between the two parties, then said "Come on Isaac, it's pitch black. You can't let Birdy walk all the way home alone in this!" He shook his head at her in apology for Isaac, and a finger of disquiet crawled up her spine.

The last week of October brought a bout of unrelenting rain that cancelled soccer, Halloween and the CHOC All-Saints Day party. The only noise to be heard on Victoria Street was that of pounding water. On Tuesday, Mary called to say the St. Paul's rectory basement had flooded and she was going to be helping clean it up tomorrow afternoon. On Wednesday, Birdy's bedroom ceiling started leaking and was remedied with a drip bucket. On Friday, she sprinted through the downpour from her house to the Dark Doppelski van. Isaac slumped against the window of the first bench, dozing. Dominic was in the front seat.

"Hi Birdy!" said Frankie, bouncing in place on the second bench. His newly adult teeth took up a lot of real estate in his mouth. "Look what happened!" He pointed to a brilliant black eye that wasn't there yesterday.

"I was doing a big flip on my skateboard and then I twisted in the air like this and then I almost landed but then this big squirrel came and ran in front of me and I didn't want to run over it so then I did *this* and then I fell right on my face right on the ground!"

But it's been pouring all week. The purple of the bruise lent a hauntingly beautiful depth to Frankie's brown eyes. He looked at her expectantly.

"You were skateboarding in the rain?" said Birdy.

Frankie's face fell and he looked at the driver's seat. Mr. Doppelski's right hand rested casually on the steering wheel, a round white scar shining in the dull light. He didn't look back at them as he said, "That's probably why you slipped, bud!"

Frankie nodded rapidly and went on to tell Birdy about how the squirrel had then run over his leg and almost jumped on his face. Birdy looked again at the ridges of Mr. Doppelski's knuckles, and then felt a magnetic pull to Dominic, who was watching her closely. She met his blithe, probing smile, and she knew.

Not a skateboard accident.

9

THE RAIN WAS STILL pouring late that afternoon when Jude Doppelski went back to school. He hunched his body against the door to keep his hands dry as he put the key in the lock. Then he stepped into the hallway and relocked the door as he shook raindrops from his hair and shoulders.

Divine Mercy still smelled like it did back when it was St. Ann's, like the same moldy sandwich was hiding somewhere. In fact, Jude had once taken all the sandwiches from all the lunch bags and hidden them around the school. Everyone complained about how hungry they were at lunchtime, but the better part started a few days later. Eddie Grouse's sandwich was the first to give the game away. Jude pulled his prank on a Friday in March. It was Lent, and Eddie had packed tuna salad. By Monday the whole place smelled like death. It didn't take Sister Josephine long to locate the offender under a radiator. After that, she was on the warpath, locating the rest of the sandwiches with unnerving speed. John Holloway had kept watch while Jude robbed the lunch bags and nearly confessed every time she found another sandwich. He hated disappointing Sister Josephine, who had a knockout smile despite her habit. But he managed to hold it together. John also hated getting in trouble.

Jude peeked in every classroom till he found what he was looking for. That afternoon, he had overheard Dom and Damien plotting how one of them could sneak into school during Mass that weekend, because Dom was pretty sure he left his geometry notebook there.

"Well, that's a problem," Jude had said from behind them. Dom and Damien flinched and gawked at Jude, looking guilty as hell.

"You don't want to leave all your homework for Sunday, do you bud? I can grab it for you, I need to head back over there later on today. Where'd ya leave it?"

Dominic spluttered out his answer. Jude stepped in close and gave him a little thump on the chest. "Relax, boy."

Dominic's notebook rested on a folding table in room 3. It was sitting right there in plain sight—he must have been distracted by some girl or another. All the more reason the kid did not need a girlfriend. Jude tucked the blue spiral under his arm and looked around. He was standing in his second-grade classroom. Second grade was when Jude figured out he should always sit to John's right during tests. John was left-handed and sat up really straight, so it was easy to see his paper. Some of the nuns were wise to him though, so he wasn't able to fully capitalize on this discovery until they all had to transfer to Conrad Primary in the middle of 6th grade.

To Jude, the world looked like a panel of buttons begging to be pushed, especially back then. Dom and some of his other kids were the same way. That was one reason Jude had gotten interested in homeschooling. Give the kids a chance to do something other than sit and write shit down, and they had more life skills than some adults before age 10. That seemed to help them when it was time to sit down to work, too. Now that he was back in school, Dom was doing just fine.

Jude wasn't always the best student, but he had a lot of friends. Meanwhile Abe was always getting stupid prizes. Not even the smart people prizes, more like good citizen prizes and shit. One time Abe won student of the month or maybe the St. Joachim Award or something. Anyway, he got the certificate in front of the whole school, and Dad got a frame for it and everything. Jude waited three days and then threw a baseball right at it and broke the frame, whoops. Dad gave Jude hell of course, but that time it was worth it.

Jude hunched again to navigate the narrow breezeway that led from the school into the church building. The altar stood in silence, a single cloth laying on top of it. A single *linen*, actually. Father Gerard used to be very strict on that point. Linens, chalice, vestments, alb, tabernacle, ambo, aspergillum. The specialized vocabulary of altar boys. At least back then. Dom, Coz, and Damien were all serving now, but Jude was the one who had to teach them that stuff. Father Bill didn't run a very tight ship.

But that was okay. Father Bill required other people to do his thinking for him, which was exactly the type of person Jude enjoyed having around. That was why Jude was here right now. Years ago, after Abe had elected himself as the least necessary usher of all time, the three of them were talking about how to manage the collection funds. Before Abe could say anything, Jude interjected.

"You know, we don't want to have just one person handling the collection—it's better to share that type of burden. How about Abe handles the basket and all during Mass, and I'll take care of gathering up all the money and putting it in the bank?"

Father Bill agreed, confused, and Abe plastered on the same smile he always used when he was trying to act like he liked Jude's ideas. Jude got himself an extra set of keys out of the arrangement, and now he came over once a week to pick up the money and deposit it. The problem recently was that Abe had started tasking his boys with putting the collection basket in a safe spot after Mass on Sundays. Whenever it was Isaac's week to handle the basket, he always put it somewhere weird. Jude wasn't sure if Isaac was being stupid or if he was fucking with him. He was pretty sure it was the latter, which is why he'd never said anything—he wouldn't give Isaac the satisfaction. But today he didn't mind spending the extra few minutes hunting the basket down. He had a bit of cabin fever. The stupid rain meant that every time he stopped by the house, it was crawling with his muddy kids.

The weather made him think of the fall when he was in fifth grade. For six days in a row, it rained so hard that the nuns made them do indoor recess, but that made the kids go crazy, even kids like Abe. Father Gerard walked into the lunchroom one day, took one look at the wild kids and the angry nuns, and announced it was time to go outside. Sister Josephine looked a little annoyed but mostly amused, he remembered that. Father Gerard took them out and they played kickball in the mud and got soaked but had a blast.

That was Father Gerard. He was strict on a lot of points, but he was still fun. Much smarter than Father Bill, and much nicer than Jude's actual father. He used to play football with them sometimes, which is how Jude learned to find his man and fire the ball down the line. His own dad was busy drinking or something while Father Gerard helped Jude learn to throw bombs.

Maybe he thought that would help Jude be less of a trouble-maker, but that didn't work too well. A few days after that kickball game, he and Abe were serving Mass, kneeling during the consecration. Abe's eyes were shut tight. A candle flickered in its holder right by Jude's elbow. Ultimately, he was a boy with a candle, and he just had to do it. It took two tries for the flame to catch Abe's alb on fire. Once it took off, people started running around like crazy looking for water. Abe had rolled around sobbing and leaving smoldering clumps of carpet all over the altar.

Yeah, Father Gerard liked Jude, but didn't like that prank so much. He'd made Jude stay behind after to clean up the mess, while Abe got to go home and cry about it. All that was probably why Abe didn't make his own sons be altar boys, though of course they'd never talked about it. Jude remembered how Abe had shrieked that day, and it was funny all over again. His laughter echoed back to him in the empty church.

If it happened nowadays, they could just ask Maggie Cleary and her absolutely enormous water jug to take care of things. God, that woman irritated him. Jude thought Arthur could be useful, but his wife was a piece of work. She never stopped talking and was a total scatterbrain, worked all the time but apparently not enough for the Clearys to afford to keep their house from looking like shit. And she was always getting Tammy distracted from the real world, throwing new books at her, dragging her on walks like a puppy, talking her ear off about whatever dumb show she was watching. All that was occasionally convenient, so he was letting in slide, for now. It helped that he could depend on Maggie to laugh when he was being funny.

Birdy was the opposite of her mom. Tammy and the kids adored her, but she was practically mute around Jude. Half the time when he spoke to her she did nothing but stare back at him with huge, worried brown eyes, looking exactly like a deer before he shot it.

Dom and Isaac had always gotten along annoyingly well, but over the last few months Birdy had driven a wedge between them. It was funny to watch how Dom was always getting Isaac's goat over her, but it was even funnier to watch her with Dominic. She would laugh and smile and hang on his every word, but as soon as he pulled his flirty crap she either gave him the same doomed-deer look or acted like it hadn't happened at all. Still, Jude was pretty sure Dom would land her in the end. He stood a better chance than Isaac, at least. That was obvious.

Jude now stood in the doorway to the sacristy. He stared into the blackness for a moment. Then he flicked a finger up to the light switch. The sacristy looked mostly the same as it did back then. A single bulb shed dusty yellow light on the room. Brown cabinets, drop ceiling, cold linoleum floor, tall cabinet in the corner. The collection basket sat in front of a cabinet where there used to be a chair. Jude clenched his fist and immediately winced. His hand was still sore from yesterday. He flexed it as he strode forward to the basket, crouched down, and sorted the bills into a neat stack.

He shook the basket and peered inside. No coins today. He plucked a ten-dollar bill from the top of the stack and shoved the rest in his pocket. He turned off the light and strode back across the altar and down the center aisle of the darkening church, fluttering the bill in his fingers. Then he stopped, folded it longways, and tapped the sharp seam against his chin. Jude had an idea. He smiled as it blossomed in his brain, driving out the chill in the air and the gloom in the sky and thoughts of rainy Sundays long ago.

Jude put the bill in his wallet and stepped out the front doors of St. Ann's church into the downpour. He locked the door behind him, of course. Wouldn't want anyone to rob the place.

Winter 2008

1

BIRDY MOVED THE WATER bucket full of ceiling drips and opened her window. No one outside noticed the obnoxious screech. Cold air wafted through the ripped screen and Birdy wrapped herself in an American flag quilt, one product of Mom's brief but intense quilting phase years earlier. With blanketed hands, she moved her desk chair beside the open window.

Birdy had been thrilled when winter break began. She was tired of waking up in the dark, of homework, and of other people. But as soon as the stresses of school receded, the stresses of home stepped up to the plate. Peter hadn't come home for Thanksgiving because he was working, so all of Mom's holiday happiness hung on him coming for Christmas. She had fretfully arranged her Santa collection, set out her twelve nativity scenes, and handmade an Advent wreath while blasting and singing along to Harry Connick Jr.'s holiday album. Then, on December 23, the email had arrived.

From: icanseeclearynow@aol.com
To:bluebirdy@aol.com,patchythepirate32@aol.com,
ccleary292@aol.com
Hey guys,
I'm going to call Mom and Dad later but just as a warning, I'm not coming home for Christmas. I can get paid overtime to work the next three days and I need the money. I'm really sorry, I'll miss you guys.
   Love, Peter

Patrick had called Chris and Birdy into the oubliette to show them, and they had a whispered conference.

"Mom's going to be so upset," said Birdy.

"I don't get it," said Chris, his face blotchy red. "He could just come home some other day. Doesn't he ever get a day off?"

Patrick sighed. "I don't know." He elected to take them out for some last minute Christmas shopping in hopes of avoiding the moment of the call. They had returned home to the smell of singed cookies and the sound of Mom's sobs. Birdy comforted Mom while Chris dove to rescue the Pillsburies. Patrick refilled Mom's water jug while Dad scrounged up snacks for a Christmas movie night. There was nothing like a holiday disappointment to help them all bury their feelings.

At Christmas Eve Mass, Mr. Abe strode up to Dad, looking purposeful from his pocket square to his wingtip shoes. Throughout the fall, the Doppelski brothers had repeatedly insisted to Dad that they needed to have a beer, shoot the shit, have some man time. Dad was unenthusiastic at this prospect, to Mom's dismay. But this time, perhaps to buoy Mom's feelings, he smiled as Abe approached. "I'm glad to see you," he said. "Why don't we have that beer next Saturday?"

 On Christmas morning, each kid got a Dutch oven, although none of them knew what that was at first.

"It's a... pot?" said Patrick.

"Oh wow, Mom gave us pot for Christmas, thanks Mom, my friends at school love pot," said Chris, barely keeping the scorn from his voice.

"It's a nice color," said Birdy. Hers was white, Patrick's was blue, Chris's was red.

"You guys, these are SO useful. You'll love having them when you're older. You can cook up a big pot of soup and feed your whole family for days," said Mom.

"Wow, what a novel concept," said Chris.

"Don't you like them?" said Mom tearfully.

"I love mine! Mom, open your present," said Birdy, diving under the tree to extract her gift for Mom.

"Oh, I told you not to get me anything," said Mom as she eagerly unwrapped the Santa paper. "Oooo!" She put on her new fuzzy pink slippers and sat admiring her feet.

"Uh, kids, there's also some other stuff..." said Dad, gesturing at a few more presents. Birdy suspected he had no idea what was in them. Normally he handled the stockings, which explained everyone's new pens and candy. The kids each unwrapped a navy blue hoodie. Birdy's was a men's medium, but Mom assured her she would grow into it. They had also each gotten a planner, so they could start learning to keep track of their own schedules.

"I know it's not too much this year, kids, money is tight. But those Dutch ovens will last you forever," said Mom.

"Yeah, I'll hardly put any wear and tear on mine," said Chris.

Patrick put his on his head. "Plus it doubles as a hat."

"Ewww, take that off!" said Mom.

Miraculously, they made it through Christmas morning with no fights, and enjoyed a relatively tasty pot roast for dinner. Chris took the opportunity to continue with his pot-related humor, making Mom giggle and Dad frown. But as soon as their parents retired for the night, Chris dropped the jokes and launched into a rant about how stupid their presents were, how it was like this every year and how Peter had the right idea of not coming home. Birdy couldn't argue with any of it, but it was still depressing.

The next day passed in a haze of eating candy from their stockings and lying around watching Christmas movies. Then Chris and Patrick started working again, and Birdy was quite bored.

So it was that on the Saturday before school started again, Birdy was seeking entertainment. Dad, Mr. Doppelski, and Mr. Abe were outside her window, standing around the portable fire pit Mr. Doppelski had dragged over. Mr. Abe had brought the beer cooler. The brothers had incorrectly assumed that Dad would provide the lawn chairs.

Birdy alerted Chris and Patrick that the beer around the fire was happening, and they immediately tasked her with espionage.

Chris: birdy. You HAVE to tell us what they discuss. Mr doppelski will probably be like "hey wanna hear about how stupid my wife is" and dad will be like "Jude, I think that is morally wrong"
Patrick: 10 bucks says dad asks abe what book hes read lately and abes never read one in his life

Dad was not much of a beer drinker, or much of an anything drinker, so by the time Abe and Jude were on their third bottles, he was still destroying the label on his first. The conversation began with Abe bragging about the great deal he got on his new truck, and then Mr. Doppelski interrupted with his predictions for the remainder of the Redskins' season. Abe tried to assert his dominance by smack talking Mr. Doppelski's tenure as a quarterback for the Conrad Minutemen.

"He had all these complicated idea for the plays he wanted them to run but they never made any sense. Never made the playoffs under him. Now, *my* senior year, we made it to states," said Abe.

"Yeah, and you missed the tackle with ten seconds on the clock," said Jude. "We're up 24-21, Keith Murphy from Severna Park is pounding down the field, and he's not even a fast guy, no one's there but Abe, and it should be a piece of cake, but as usual, Abe completely whiffs—" he mimed stumbling and flailing his arms— "and they pull ahead and win."

Dad steered the conversation into more neutral territory by offering some high school football memories of his own—he'd had both a win and a loss at states—and this led the Doppelski brothers back into peace and discussion of the Redskins.

For the eavesdropper, it was nothing too juicy. Dad was interested in but not passionate about the NFL, so he didn't say much. Bored of hearing how Sean Taylor's death was affecting the season, she opened *To Kill a Mockingbird* and tried to find where she had left off.

"Mike Tucker owns this house, right?" demanded Mr. Abe's carrying voice.

Birdy looked up.

"Can't believe you're still renting, man! You're even older than me!" Abe gave Dad a friendly punch on the shoulder. Dad clenched his fist.

Mr. Doppelski tuned in. "You happy with how he handles things around here? Looks like it could use some better upkeep."

Their eyes all turned to the unkempt lawn, the destroyed front door screen, the drooping gutters.

Dad was no fool, and had their number now. He cleared his throat. "Mike sends repair people quick enough when we call him."

"Don't you hate that though? Man buys a house just for profit, becomes a landlord, and doesn't even want to get his elbows greasy with taking care of the house himself." Abe's tone implied that un-greased elbows were everything wrong with the world.

Dad shrugged. "People have different strengths."

"You ever think about how it would be to have us taking care of this place instead?" said Mr. Abe, as though this had just occurred to him. "We could come over real quick anytime you had a prob-lem."

Dad shifted in his shoes. "But Mike Tucker already sends peo-ple when we have a problem."

Jude pointed an explanatory finger away from his beer bottle and adopted his Sunday morning clip. "Well, see, Mike's always been a little funny about this house. He lived here when his kids were young, they're a bit younger than us. All the houses on this street were slapped together in the 70s and without good maintenance they fall right apart. Mike's been renting it out for years, and you know renters don't take good care of their property. So when the last peo-ple moved out he swore he would finally sell it, but it seems like he chickened out again when you came along. He might feel better let-ting it go to the right hands though. So there's a few things we could do. If you put in a good word, we can work out a contract with Mike so DBC gets any work that needs to be done here. Or we see if he's interested in selling to us, and DBC becomes the owner."

Yikes. As Mom was fond of telling her, Birdy was no expert at home management, but even she knew either arrangement would be unbearably awkward.

"Oh, there's no need for all that. Wouldn't want to call you away from home when you're home."

"Oh, it would be no problem, I'd be happy to trade fixing the shit my wife broke to fixing the shit your wife broke!" Mr. Doppelski cackled and Abe joined in. Dad stood tall and stared them down, unsmiling. Their laughter squeaked to a halt.

"My wife doesn't break things." *Well, not on a regular basis,* thought the listening spy, but she appreciated her father's gallantry. "Thanks for your interest, but we're doing just fine here."

The Doppelski brothers' cunning plan had slipped through their fingers and hit the brick wall of Dad. They stared back at him, lost for words.

"So," said Dad, sipping his beer, "Read any good books recently?"

Patrick: You owe me $10

2

AFTER A WEEK BACK at school, Birdy was ready for summer. Their first English assignment was a descriptive essay detailing how God had spoken to them at Christmas Mass that year. In History, they started a four-week unit about the scant role of Catholicism in the American Revolution. In Biology, they started the reproduction unit, prompting Fred to say in a loud whisper "I don't know that this is appropriate." And on Friday, Dominic told Olivia her new haircut was gorgeous and carried her from the locker room to the lunchroom.

On their way to the parking lot that afternoon, Dominic poked Birdy in the back and said, "You get shotgun, Birdy, we're all sick of Abe talking about his truck."

She turned around to object and found Isaac smiling helplessly and Joseph wearing the grin of a madman, thrilled to be in on the conspiracy for once. Dominic patted her on the head before shoving her slightly backwards and dashing for the back door of the F-450, his cousins on his heels. Birdy sighed and climbed into the towering front seat. The engine was loud, but it had nothing on Abe.

"What do you think?" he asked her, gesturing around the cab.

"Uh, it's nice."

"It's a lot of truck, but I like it," he said modestly. She nodded. He raked a hand through his short hair and rested a flannelled elbow on the console.

"I thought we might get to meet your biggest brother this Christmas."

"He had to work," said Birdy, looking out the window.

"Where's he working?"

"A store." Birdy didn't know which of Peter's jobs had kept him away from them, and her shame over this fact soured her voice.

Abe was annoyed. "You know, you could be a little politer. Our family is bringing you back and forth to school every stinking day."

"Sorry!" she panted, sick with embarrassment. "I just forgot which store."

Abe settled back, satisfied with her remorse. "Now if you want a story about how keeping a good, friendly attitude will really pay off..." He launched into an endless tale about how one of his old buddies who worked at a Ford dealership called him first when he slashed the price on this truck. Birdy was obliged to listen attentively while the boys snickered in the backseat.

Abe's disgruntlement turned out to be the first beat of a new rhythm. On Wednesday morning, Birdy got in the van to find Dominic in the driver's seat and his mom beside him.

"Did you get your learner's permit?" said Birdy.

"Obviously," said Dominic, drumming his fingers on the gear-shift.

Sarah scowled at Birdy as she buckled her seatbelt and said, "You look really ugly today."

"Awww, that's not very nice," said Birdy.

Dominic rolled his eyes. "Geez, Birdy, give her a break."

On Thursday afternoon, Hannah used an Etch-a-Sketch to smack blood from Gus's forehead, then screeched to wake the dead when Birdy wrenched it away from her. Mr. Doppelski merely observed this incident and passed back a Band-aid, but the next morning, Steve tapped her on the shoulder as soon as she sat down.

"My dad says you're not very helpful." Mrs. Doppelski giggled uncomfortably from the passenger's seat.

The little Doppelskis were always boisterous, but they had apparently resolved to go insane in the new year, and somehow it was Birdy's duty to quell the chaos in the backseat. She did her best, but it was never right. Fourteen years as the peaceful baby sister had prepared her to soothe children through play and cuddles, but it had in no way prepared her to discipline them.

The very involved dads seemed exasperated not with the behavior of their kids, but with Birdy's inability to control it. About half the time she got in the car, she felt distinctly unwelcome. Birdy took to cycling through the possible reasons why things had changed. She thought about it so much it wore grooves in her brain.

Maybe she had outlived her usefulness now that Dad had rejected the offer to let DBC take on their house. Or maybe the difficulty of running the school on top of the business was getting to Mr. Doppelski and spreading to the rest of them. Birdy knew how stress could spread its mantle across a household, and she knew Mr. Doppelski was nowhere near as laid-back as he liked to appear.

Or maybe Dominic was the source of the rancor. Continuing to facilitate his relationship with Mary while watching him play the rest of the girls in school like pathetic string instruments made her feel sick. Perhaps sensing he'd lost her allegiance, he'd doubled down on his teasing about Isaac, but she could no longer bring herself to offer Mary as a rebuttal. Where she used to joke along, she was now silent, and if this happened when Mr. Doppelski was in the car, she could always feel him scrutinizing her reaction and giving it a failing grade. Dominic was otherwise rude to her more days than not, but whenever he acted normal, she rushed to play along, trying to reenact their old friendship.

Birdy had the distinct feeling she had been under consideration by the adults as a valuable entity—a business vector, a babysitter, a means of pitting their sons against each other—and, having been found wanting, was now being discarded. She was fine with being phased out of the position for which she had never asked to be considered. The problem was, she still needed a ride home.

Late in January, Dominic pulled the van into her driveway. In her desperation not to step on anyone's toes, she had played peekaboo with Rebecca the whole car ride, ignoring the war raging between Gus and David behind her but at least keeping the baby happy. Unfortunately, she didn't notice Bobby opening her backpack and scribbling on her history notes.

"Oh, I need that buddy," she said, peeling his sticky fingers off her notebook.

"'Tupid bitch," he said in his sweet voice.

She ground out a smile as she stuffed her notebook in her bag, trying to appear unruffled by both the loss of an evening's work and having been cursed at by a child.

Mr. Doppelski turned around in his seat to watch the exchange between Bobby and Birdy.

"You've got to watch those boys, they just get ideas and they can't help themselves," he drawled.

Birdy looked at Mr. Doppelski. His eyes were so much like Dominic's, especially when they held her in that stare of mean amusement, smiling on the edges but dead in the pupils. Today they gave her those same painful butterflies. "Maybe they could help it if they tried," she said.

She succeeded in zipping her bag and stood up into a crouch. Her left knee wobbled.

"Wow, Dad," said Dominic, "Did you hear that sass?"

Birdy couldn't tell if Dominic was on her side or not. His expression matched his father's.

"Are you trying to tell me how to raise my kids?" Mr. Doppelski dropped all pretense of goofiness and his voice turned silky with anger.

"Nope," said Birdy, in retreat now. "Thank you very much for the ride."

She pivoted for the van's double doors, opening just one of them in a frazzled attempt to take up minimal time and space while exiting. The metal latch jutting from the closed door gouged her in the ribs as she hopped out, but she didn't make a sound. As soon as she freed her backpack from the too-small opening, she slammed the door shut and speedwalked into her cold, dark house.

The front staircase rose into the gloom. She dropped her backpack in front of it, headed for the couch, and drove her face into the cushions. For so long, the wild and free Doppelskis were a fun retreat from her family's stifling depression, but in this moment, she preferred the safe, empty silence of her own home.

Shortly thereafter, a nasty wave of influenza swept through Conrad. Five Divine Mercy families caught it, which opened a huge void in the student population. The *Conrad Sun* published frantic articles about "the ghostly halls of St. Monica's and the gloomy walls of Conrad High, which flashed one back to that terrible time when so many families moved out of town."

Mr. Doppelski was scoffing at the sensation when his fever struck. The rest of the clan followed in short order. Birdy had a week of respite from what was turning into the most uncomfortable carpool in history while they malingered. Mom took some of her scarce PTO and went on a hand sanitizing rampage, leaping to squirt alcohol gel on anyone who so much as sniffled.

This was how Birdy found herself by Mary's side at a sparsely populated Praise Night, not a single Doppelski in sight. Birdy realized with a pang that this was the first time they'd been together without Dominic since October. But that didn't stop Mary from making him the exclusive topic of conversation.

"I just can't wait till we're a little older," she said with a faraway smile. "It's kind of fun to have this secret romance going on, but it'll be so nice when we can walk down the street holding hands too. I can just imagine us with all our kids in a big line behind us."

You have to tell her. You have to say something.

"It's so sad to be at Praise Night without him! I love how he's just such a good guy. Most boys wouldn't spend their free time praising God, you know? And all those public schoolers you see at Songs and Teens, they're just there for the wrong reasons. You just know they don't care about chastity and being a gentleman and respecting God's plan for how families should be, like he does."

Say it. She's your friend. She deserves to know.

"What's wrong?" Mary asked. She had finally looked at Birdy and noticed the expression on her face.

"Mary... he... he's not always as good as he seems, I don't think."

"Who?" said Mary, like Birdy was crazy.

"Dominic. He... he's really kind of... touchy feely a lot with girls at school and... and soccer sometimes." Mary continued to stare. "I mean like, he always picks girls up and says they look beautiful and plays with their hair and stuff."

"Like who?"

"Like... like Margaret, and Olivia, and Polly, and.... and... and it seems weird and I just... thought you might want to know." Her voice dwindled away.

For a moment, Mary looked outraged. Then she smiled. "Well, it's kind of a secret that we're together, so he has to act like himself, right? He's always been such a big flirt." Even as she said this, her face slipped repeatedly from composure to anger. It was like watching someone trying to prevent a wall of Jello from collapsing.

3

BY THE TIME SONGS and Teens rolled around, the health of the masses was restored, and Dominic and Mary's affair with it. Birdy wore a long-sleeve black t-shirt with jeans to the gathering. Mary wore a True Love Waits t-shirt and a long white skirt. They stood together until Dominic snuck up behind Mary and put his hands over her eyes.

"Guess who!"

Birdy slipped away, leaving Mary in coy speculation. Mel, Beth, and Kelly were waiting for her by the door.

"Birdy! I'm so glad you're here! We were just talking—can we do the sleep over tomorrow night?" Mel asked, bouncing on her tip-toes.

"Wow!" said Birdy. "Yes! Well, maybe, I don't know, I'm pretty sure it'll work this time though!"

"Please! We have to make this happen! I checked, there's no flu or snowstorms to ruin our plans this time."

"Our lives are emptier without you," said Beth, pretending to break down in tears.

"Can I come?" said Isaac, who had wandered over.

"Ew," said Mel, shoving him backwards via his forehead. He laughed and wandered away again.

When Birdy got home, she found Mom.

"Mom, can I go to a sleepover tomorrow night?"

Mom thought. "Probably! With Mary?"

"No, Mel."

"Mel who?"

"Mel Holloway, she was on my soccer team."

"Why aren't you having a sleepover with Mary?"

This question felt a bit like being bludgeoned with a blunt object, but Birdy glossed over it. "Well, Mel invited me on a sleepover, Mary didn't."

Mom thought again. "Where does she go to school?"

"St. Monica's."

"How did she even get in touch with you?" Mom's shock implied St. Monica's was a remote planet.

"She goes to Songs and Teens at St. Paul's. Dominic and Isaac know her too, her dad is like best friends with Mr. Doppelski. They were in the Marines together."

These were the right points to make. Mom now felt the sleepover would be sufficiently wholesome, but she had one more worry.

"What about church?"

"I can go with Mel's family in the morning. They go to 9 o clock Mass at St. Paul's."

Mel's neighborhood was ten minutes away by car, though neighborhood was a generous term; it was more like some houses that happened to be near each other. When Dad pulled up, a police cruiser was in the driveway.

"What's going on here?" said Dad, getting out of the truck. Birdy started to unbuckle, but he pointed his finger and commanded "Stay there."

"Dad—" said Birdy, but he was already halfway up the stone walkway. He rapped on the front door and stood with his arms crossed. Mrs. Holloway answered the door and they started talking, Mrs. Holloway gesturing enthusiastically and Dad's posture relaxing by degrees. He turned to the truck and waved Birdy over, smiling now.

"You didn't tell me Mel's dad was a police officer!" said Dad.

"Oh," said Birdy, who hadn't realized this was critical information.

"He's still sleeping after his shift but he'll probably be waking up soon!" said Mrs. Holloway. Red curls danced from her high bun.

Mel appeared beside her. "Birdy! Come on in!"

Dad departed, concerns assuaged, and Mel yanked Birdy inside for a tour of the house. The downstairs had a sunny kitchen and a comfy living room. The basement was unfinished and creepy but had ancient pool table.

Mel's sister Bailey was busy chalking a cue stick. "I'm working on my game," she explained dispassionately.

When they got upstairs they had to tiptoe. "My dad's sleeping in there, he worked last night," whispered Mel, pointing to a room at the end of the narrow hall.

"This is my room!" said Mel's other little sister, who was tailing them.

"Shhh, Jessie! Yeah, that's Jessie's room, and that's Bailey's room, and there's the bathroom, and here's my room." She shut the door behind them, to Jessie's vocal outrage in the hall. Mel stuck her head out the door. "Jessie, quiet! You'll wake Dad!" She popped back inside her room. "Okay, we can talk normal now."

Mel's room had pink walls, ten posters, and an overflowing dresser. Her bed was beside the window, and she bounced down on the neon green comforter. "Look, you can see Kelly and Vince's houses from here." Mel's wide brown lawn melted into another wide brown lawn, which ended at the stone patio of a huge white house.

"That's Kelly's," said Mel, tapping the house on the window, "and Vince's is that way." She tapped a plume of chimney smoke rising from the bare tree tops. "Oh look, here she comes!" Kelly was bundled in a parka, scarf, and hat, and was trudging across the back-yards.

They went out to greet her. "Is Beth here yet?" said Kelly.

"Of course not," said Mel. She looked at Birdy to explain.

"Beth insists on riding her bike everywhere. *Everywhere!* Even though she lives three miles away, and it's super hilly, and there are no sidewalks, and there's no shoulder, and it's freezing. So she'll be here in a bit, but she's normally a little late."

"Is that her?" said Birdy, pointing behind them. Someone was coasting down the hill on a red bike, blond hair streaming from her helmet in the wind. She veered into the yard and barely slowed down as she approached, skidding to a stop just in front of them. Beth took off her helmet and shook her head upside down.

"Hey guys," she called, raking her hands through her hair.

"Beth! You got here just after Kelly! You're so punctual today!"

Beth flipped her head up and laughed. "I left extra early, I didn't want to miss Birdy's first time at Mel's house."

"I'm honored," laughed Birdy.

"Aren't you freezing?" Kelly asked Beth from inside her layers.

"No, Kelly, I had my blood pumping, which works even better than four coats for staying warm! How's your presentation coming?"

"Oh my gosh, Will is the worst partner in the world," moaned Kelly.

"I think Ryan might be worse," said Mel. She addressed Birdy again. "We each have to do a presentation for Biology about the growth cycle of a certain plant. It's twenty percent of our grade so it's a big deal, and it's supposed to be really detailed and professional.

"The work part is fine," said Kelly. "It's the people that suck."

"At least Will is cute," said Beth. "I have Angela."

"Prune?" said Birdy.

"Yup," said Beth, "And she's just as good at Bio as she is at soccer, let me tell you."

"Oh no," laughed Birdy.

"Oh yes. It's actually a pretty interesting topic, so I don't even mind doing all the work, but I'm so sick of her whining about it. Plus, she always tries to get me to talk bad about them!" she exclaimed, gesturing to Mel and Kelly.

"Like you could ever say anything bad about me," said Mel, tossing her hair.

"But really though!" said Beth, as Kelly nodded her agreement.

Birdy shivered in the cold air as she smiled around at her friends. No one was trying to convince her that Harry Potter was evil, or that the rosary was just as fun as soccer. No one was wearing a Modest Is Hottest t-shirt while trying to orchestrate a makeout session behind a shed. It was the first time she'd felt relaxed in weeks.

The front door opened, and a man wearing pajama pants and a sweatshirt walked out. He seemed surprised by the group of girls standing in the yard and hesitated before walking over.

Mel and her mom and sisters were all so vivacious that Birdy expected her dad to be similar, but he was not. Officer Holloway was haggard, clutching a coffee cup. His hair was as dark as Mel's, but he kept it very short like Birdy's dad did. His stride as he approached them was as stiff as his smile.

"Hi, Melly," he rasped. He cleared his throat. "Sorry, just waking up." He squinted like the overcast day was too bright for him, his pale blue eyes hiding in the slits of his eyelids.

"Dad, this is Birdy Cleary, she's our friend from soccer and she goes to Divine Mercy, she lives on the same street as the Doppelskis."

"Oh," said Officer Holloway. "Jude got you in his school huh?"

"Yeah," said Birdy, not sure what his tone implied.

He nodded. "Well, I've known Jude Doppelski since I was younger than you all." His eye slits found Beth. "You biked here, Beth?"

"Yup!" said Beth with pride.

Officer Holloway shook his head. "Please be careful, hon."

"I am careful! I only had to dodge like two eighteen wheelers and three serial killers."

In response to her teasing, his whole body sagged. He looked to Kelly. "Mom and Dad doing okay?"

"They're good," said Kelly softly. Her eyes were pools of sadness as she looked back at Officer Holloway.

"Good," he nodded, before she had finished speaking. "Well, I just got a call, I need to head back into the station for a minute, skipped a line on some paperwork."

Mel looked stricken, but then her face hardened. "'Kay."

"Glad to meet you, Birdy," said Officer Holloway as he turned back to the house. He shut the door behind him gently, and then everyone looked at Mel.

"So, yeah," said Mel, sounding gloomy. "That's my dad."

MRS. HOLLOWAY MADE THE girls steaming mugs of hot chocolate, which they brought up to Mel's room along with a package of Oreos.

"Sorry about my dad," said Mel. "He always acts like it's a pain to be around us. Like not just us like my friends, like my whole family. It sucks." She deconstructed three Oreos as she talked. "When I was little, I thought he was this superhero. He went to work in his uniform, and he looked so handsome and strong and he had his cool car and everything. Anytime he missed a soccer game or a party or whatever it was because he was stopping bad guys, so even if I was disappointed, I could put that aside." She stabbed at a tower of creme filling. "But at some point, he started hating his life. He started working night shift more after Jessie was born because it pays better, but it just sucked the life out of him. My mom says he's just exhausted and stressed and it's not his fault, he's making a sacrifice for all of us. But he doesn't even seem to want to be around us when he's home. I mean God, I get super tired too sometimes!" She swept the creme tower angrily into her mouth.

"I'm sorry, Mel," said Birdy. "I didn't feel like he was rude to me or anything though, don't worry."

"That's nice of you," said Mel, smacking her creme, "But he can really be a jerk. He's not mean, exactly, but it's more like he just acts like we don't exist half the time." She gestured at Beth and Kelly. "They remember when he was nice." Kelly nodded reluctantly.

"But you're not the only one with a weird family," said Beth. "My parents hate each other. And they're not crazy about me either." Mel tipped her head in acknowledgment.

"That sucks," said Birdy.

"Yeah," said Beth. "Is your family weird?"

Birdy laughed in surprise. "Yeah, actually."

"What's weird about them?" said Mel.

Birdy thought for a minute. Mom always implored her not to tell anyone about their family's problems, and she never did. Mom was terrified someone would think badly of her, but Birdy simply felt it was all too hard to explain. But Christmas still smarted, and her heart ached at the sight of the kind and happy Mel brought so low. She didn't want her to feel alone.

"How much do you want to know?" asked Birdy.

"Anything you want to tell us," said Kelly.

"Well, what you were saying about your dad's job reminded me of it a little, Mel. Except it's kind of the opposite. My parents are super committed to Catholic schools, but we can't really afford them. So they always find one at least one of them can work at so we can have discounts or scholarships, but the problem is my mom is really good at getting new jobs but not at keeping them. It's not even like she gets fired. It's like one thing will go wrong and she gets embarrassed, like just humiliated, and then she's so ashamed that she needs a whole new job and we have to move away."

Mom and Dad always announced their relocations with an aura of mission and nobility, saying Catholic education was paramount and they needed to go where they could best make that happen. This gave all four kids permanently installed savior complexes by age five, though Chris's was directed more at athletics than at family life. But everyone could see the real impetus for the moves, and the injustice simmered in their veins.

"It's just so frustrating. And even in between the times we're moving, things are still weird."

"Like how?" asked Beth.

Birdy took a deep breath. "Like... so, you know I like to read. Well, I also really like to write. And so does my oldest brother, Peter. But I'm not always that good at saying the right thing out loud. And he... is."

True to his name, Peter had always been a rock for his siblings, putting on a good attitude when things went wrong. If there was nothing positive to focus on, he could at least muster a black-humored joke. But as he moved through high school, all his endless patience crammed into a fast-moving hourglass. He started fighting with their parents, saying things the siblings had previously said only to each other.

Birdy wasn't always a sneaky journaler. Inspired by the *Dear America* series, she had spent her elementary school years meticulously documenting her days, though nothing as exciting as the Civil War ever happened to her. As Peter's unrest grew, writing became her lifeline. Patrick was contemplative about the conflicts and Chris all but popped popcorn to watch them, but Birdy found them crushing. She thought no one would understand how she felt, so she wrote.

One Saturday towards the end of 7th grade, Birdy returned from her friend's house to find Mom standing in her bedroom, seething.

"I found it," said Mom.

"Found what?" said Birdy.

"This." She brandished Birdy's brown pleather notebook, which was filled with choice words about Mom. Mom made Birdy rip the diary to shreds page by page, and when she was done, she designated her as the only person in the house who would wash dishes for the next two months.

Birdy drew designs in Mel's carpet with her finger as she talked. She felt her face moving in weird shapes as she wondered how they would receive her tale—would they think this was just a funny crazy family story, or did it sound as horrific as it had felt? She dared herself to glance up at her friends' faces and found shock on Kelly's, concentration on Mel's, and recognition on Beth's. All three were listening, no one was laughing. She choked up for just a moment, then cleared her throat. "But that's not even what the weird part is."

Peter was a junior at the time of the journal incident. That school year was a war zone, but things went nuclear in the summer. Mom and Dad called them for a family meeting, always a bad sign. They had decided St. Francis was not serving their family anymore, and Dad was looking for a new job at a school that would serve them better.

Patrick, Chris, and Birdy looked to Peter. Peter's brown eyes glittered with tears, his unfairly lush eyelashes reaching towards Dad.

"But it's my senior year," he said. His elbows were on his knees, his hands clasped between them in a posture of unconscious prayer. He had a sweet girlfriend, he was the president of the chess club, and he had been planning his senior prank since he was a freshman.

"This is just one year in the whole rest of your life, Peter," said Mom. "Besides, you're halfway out of there anyway. You already quit the paper."

As long as Birdy lived, the memory of the look on Peter's face would destroy her. *He hates them,* she'd thought, *he hates them.* He got up and left the room without a word, but that wasn't the end of it. Not at all.

They started the new school year like normal, but Dad continued to scout out a new job. He and Mom started pushing Peter to apply to college, but Peter pointed out he had no money to go. Mom kept saying he could take out a loan until Peter, who was acing calculus, presented them with a chart illustrating just how long it would take him to repay a loan at today's interest rates. Mom and Dad did not appreciate the concreteness of his argument and tried to steer things back to more emotional territory. Mom said he was such a good student he would probably get a scholarship, anyway. Peter responded by failing every class. Dad proposed he join the Marines and Peter said he couldn't see how that would lead to a fulfilling life, wounding Dad to his core. They thought it was all noise, and Dad accepted the spot at Bosco. Miraculously, they said, the history teacher had just quit, and his three sons had left open spots. But Peter didn't fold. Instead, he dropped out of high school, got a few jobs, and moved to his friend's basement futon. The Clearys fled town in pain, and Peter didn't come.

Birdy leaned back against Mel's bed and looked up from her carpet drawings.

"So basically, my parents are really strange and can't stay in one place, and my brother is over it. And he has a point, but they're really sad about it. And now he doesn't even talk to my other brothers and me that much—" she paused to let another lump recede from her throat "—so things are even weirder than usual right now. Except my mom thinks that everything we've been through so far has led us here to Conrad. My dad really likes his job, and it's a good school for my brothers. The whole thing with Peter really freaked them out, so I'm hoping they'll want to stay till we finish high school. And we moved down the street from the Doppelskis, who my mom thinks are so amazing. So, that's good, I guess. I don't know."

"Well, I'm really glad you moved here!" said Mel.

"I actually am too," said Birdy. She looked at Kelly, who was silently absorbing the conversation. "How about you, Kelly, is your family weird?"

"Well, they're a little OCD," ventured Kelly.

"Oh my God, her family is the nicest freaking family in the universe!" yelled Beth. "Just you wait until you meet them, it's unreal!"

4

THANKS TO THE SLEEPOVER, Birdy was invigorated instead of anxious when she climbed into the Light Doppelski van on Monday morning. Mr. Abe was at the wheel and Isaac had claimed the front seat, so she sat beside Dominic in the first row.

"Why weren't you at church yesterday?" said Dominic.

"I went to church with Mel. I slept over at her house on Saturday night."

"Oh! Well, Isaac missed you," he said, nudging her knee with his.

"I actually didn't realize you were gone," said Isaac.

"Ha!" Mr. Abe interjected. "Don't tell me that. Both of you were looking around like lost puppies the whole time."

Birdy sighed, wondering yet again how to get out of this conversation, but Abe had no trouble filling her silence.

"They wanted to see you all dressed up for Sunday. It's hard for boys to focus when there's a young lady around. This time you weren't even there! I don't know how Isaac's still doing so good in school!"

Dominic didn't appreciate his uncle appropriating his comedy routine, so he took a new tack. "If he went to Bosco it'd be a whole different story."

His tone was deliberate, designed to make them react, but nobody did; Birdy was puzzled, Isaac was blank, and Mr. Abe was distracted because "Low" by Flo Rida came on the radio.

"Oh, God I'm so sick of this crap," he grumbled. "Low," a ballad to the movements of a woman's generous rear end, as sung from the perspective of a gentleman's club patron, was inescapable on the pop stations that winter. "This is just disgusting. And you wonder why their families are so messed up. They go spend all their money in a place like this, and then they're broke and need the government to bail their ass out. And now one of them is trying to be President? We're all gonna be broke next! I don't know why you put this crap on my radio." This last was directed to Isaac, who shrugged, impenitent. Mr. Abe stabbed his presets until he landed on a country station.

"Now that's better," he said, as "Honkytonk Badonkadonk" by Trace Adkins filled their soundwaves. "Honkytonk Badonkadonk" was another ode to a large derriere in a drinking establishment, but as its singer was white, it was more wholesome in Mr. Abe's book.

BY NOW, PATRICK AND Chris were immersed in life at Bosco. They had constant practices, club meetings, and work shifts, and spent many evenings and weekends at the houses of friends who lived near school. Birdy didn't blame them for being gone so much, but she was starting to feel like an only child.

One rare Friday evening, everyone was around the table for dinner eating burned rice and dry chicken.

"It's so nice to have everyone together," said Mom. Peter's empty chair begged to differ.

"How was everyone's day?" Dad asked.

No one answered at first.

Chris fiddled with his food and glanced up. "I was wondering if I could get some new uniform pants? Mine are getting too small."

"Well, maybe you can have some of Dad's pants. He has some black pants he never wears."

"But I need navy pants. And I'm taller than Dad."

Mom looked skeptical. "Are they really going to notice the difference between black and navy?"

"Yes! They're two different colors!"

"No one can even tell the difference."

"Just because you can't doesn't mean no one else can! And didn't you hear me say I'm taller than Dad?" Chris clutched his fork.

"No you're not! Not yet," said Mom, crossing her arms.

Chris shot to his feet. "Look," he said, ready to walk over to where Dad sat, but Dad put out a calming hand. "Son, you can get the pants you need."

Chris relaxed, but now Mom was angry. "No one ever cares what I think! Why even ask me if you're just going to ignore everything I say?"

Birdy stared at her plate, not hungry in the slightest.

"Maggie," said Dad in soothing tones, "I still have all kinds of gift cards my students gave me for Christmas. There's plenty to get Chris a few new pairs of pants."

Mom sat back. "You're lucky to have such a generous father," she said to Chris.

Chris nodded once. For a moment everything seemed stable. Then he got up and threw his food away. "I can't eat this shit."

During the ensuing screaming match, Birdy concentrated on washing down each gristly bite of chicken with gulps of water. The fight ended with Mom assigning Chris cleanup duty, which would supposedly teach him gratitude. She announced she was going to shower, and Dad retreated to the living room. Chris half-assed the cleaning job while Birdy and Patrick picked up his slack. When they were done, Patrick propped the broom in its corner and looked at his siblings. "Want to go see a movie?"

They drove to Woods Crossing Shops in silence. Then Patrick deadpanned, "You know, they say family dinners are the key to a stable home life." Chris and Birdy half-laughed, half-cried at this as they pulled into the parking lot. The movie was stupid, but it lightened their spirits. Afterwards, Patrick bought them all milkshakes, which they sipped at outdoor stone tables. It was too cold for milkshakes, but none of them were ready to go home.

Chris nudged Birdy's foot with his shoe. "I'm sorry for what I said about the dinner, Birdy. I forgot you were the one who made it."

"It's okay," she said, "It was gross."

"Still."

"How's everything been with you, Bird?" asked Patrick.

"It's okay," said Birdy. She was not in the mood to listen to Chris gloat over having judged Dominic so accurately. "School sucks. How was your week?"

Patrick sipped his milkshake. "It was okay. All my friends went on a ski trip this weekend without me."

"Oh no, they didn't invite you?" Birdy cried, indignant.

"No, I just couldn't afford it. And I'm pretty sure the girl I want to ask to prom is going, and I'm pretty sure Longwood is going to try to get with her, and I'm pretty sure she likes him more than me. So that sucks." Bryce Longwood was an unfortunate member of Patrick's social circle who drove a BMW and told boring stories of summering on Nantucket.

"Aw, Patrick, you shouldn't have bought us these milkshakes then!" said Birdy.

Chris said "Well, of course you can't compete with *Longwood*."

Patrick flipped Chris off and shrugged at Birdy. "That milkshake costs like one percent of renting one ski for a day."

Chris smiled. "Well, I'm home tonight because I don't get paid until tomorrow and I'm broke." He sucked the dregs of his milkshake loudly. "Probably because I keep buying Five Guys for lunch."

"Well, I didn't have any plans, so I'm glad you guys are home," said Birdy. "This is a lot more fun than Praise Night."

Chris put his arm around Birdy. "We can have our own Praise Night if you want."

"No."

Chris started singing his own version of a classic. "Our God, is a pretty cool guy, he gave—"

"—us air and stuff to breathe, so we would not die—" Patrick joined in.

"Shut up," Birdy said.

"OUR GOD IS A PRETTY COOL GUY!" they finished to-gether. Birdy put her head down on the table as Chris continued improvising every verse with hand motions so reverent they would have made Kyle Amon weep.

Spring 2008

1

BIRDY WAS DIGGING THROUGH her dresser for a sweatshirt when Dominic appeared in her doorway.

"Want to come down and wait for Mary?" His eager posture beckoned her to get moving. Birdy was annoyed with him for directing her around her own house, but she was about to go down anyway.

"Yeah, I'm coming," she said, pulling on a black hoodie. Dominic headed for the back stairway and Birdy followed. At the top of the stairs was a door that the Clearys always left open. He shut it and looked at her.

"Okay, time to open the door," said Birdy, but his hand was still on the knob. He smirked, daring her to wrestle his hand away, but she turned for the front staircase. "See you down there," she called. She heard him open the door and pound down the stairs. He met her in the front hall, looking triumphant.

"I win," he said.

"Congratulations." She spread out her homework on the kitchen table while he peeked through the living room window. Then he came in the kitchen.

"We have that same door at our house."

"Our houses have all the same doors."

"Yeah, but ours locks."

"I know, so Rebecca won't fall down that way, right?"

"Yeah, but your lock doesn't work."

Well, everything in my house is broken, genius, thought Birdy, but she only shrugged.

Dominic went on. "It's funny how you're so weird about locking everything up, but then that lock doesn't even work."

Birdy looked at him. "Well, why would we need to lock that door anyway? There aren't any babies in this house."

Dominic smiled at her just as Mary pounded on the front door. He let her inside and Birdy heard them commence their greeting ritual in the hallway. Then Mary arrived in the kitchen in her usual flurry of hugs and chatter. Today it felt tiring, but Birdy didn't have to endure it for long.

"Come on Mary," Dominic said. "I want to show you something upstairs." He took her hand and led her up the kitchen steps. He shut the door behind them.

This order of events was now typical—Dominic being unsettling when he was alone with Birdy and then whisking Mary away as soon as she arrived. Birdy despised the whole situation, but she didn't know how to stop it without them getting mad at her. She lived for disruptions to Joey Vespa's schedule that freed her from having to host their rendezvous. Mary always called Birdy the day after their "dates" to debrief. It was a lot of Dominic telling Mary how amazing she was, peppered with kissing that was romantic, filled her with butterflies, made her feel like she was on top of the world, and was like a dream come true.

These conversations were sandpaper to Birdy's internal organs. Dominic was obviously not to be trusted, but she'd said her piece already and Mary was apparently going to ignore it. Besides, based on Mary's reports, the sweet things he said to her were more specific and personal than the things he said to other girls. So maybe that meant something. But Birdy didn't think so anymore.

On Tuesday afternoon, Birdy and the Doppelskis waited outside school. Everyone else had left 45 minutes ago. The sky was a brilliant blue, but a cold wind pounded them. Birdy put on her hood and shoved her hands deep in her pockets. She had worn her light jacket, desperate for it to be sufficient.

Mr. Doppelski screeched up in the Escort. As the kids walked over, he climbed out and hurled the keys at Dominic. Dominic tripped and fumbled the catch, looking uncharacteristically klutzy. The part of Birdy that was now constantly pissed at him laughed at this, but she also felt sorry for him. He righted himself and got in the car. Mr. Doppelski settled into the passenger's side, reached across the console, and used the keychain bottle opener to crack his beer.

From his mean and loquacious manner, Birdy thought it might not have been his first of the afternoon. Mr. Doppelski dug into Dominic, asking him how his math test had gone, asking him why he hadn't emptied the dishwasher that morning, asking him if he was going to be ready to hunt turkeys in the morning or if he was going to sleep in like a lazy bitch again. Dominic answered with as few words as possible, radiating a tension so raw it felt indecent to witness. Birdy burrowed her body into the door while Isaac and Joseph sat motionless by her side.

Mom's car was in the driveway when they got home. Dominic whirled around in his seat. "What the hell, Birdy? Your mom's home, why didn't she just get you from school?"

Birdy tried not to show how much this hurt her feelings.

"I don't know. I didn't know she was going to be home." She hated the defensive whine that made its way into the last word.

"Does she make dinner on nights when she gets home early? Or do you still have to do it?"

"I don't know. She might not if she's tired."

Mr. Doppelski hooted. "Your dad better tell her to earn her keep!"

Birdy was furious on behalf of both of her parents. "Well, she is. She's *working.* And she's tired when she gets home."

Mr. Doppelski was nothing but amused by her anger as he gestured at her with his beer bottle. "Oooh, she's a feisty one! Some man's gonna have to whip you into shape!"

The whole car ride had been uncomfortable new territory, but now it felt downright dangerous. All she wanted was a way out.

She arranged her face into a smile. "Heh."

Mr. Doppelski turned to Dominic. "Who's it gonna be? You?" Dominic turned away.

"We know it's not gonna be Isaac!" Mr. Doppelski cackled. Isaac stared back at his uncle, all his usual merriment absent. Joseph shrunk beside Birdy, clearly hoping to avoid being targeted too. Mr. Doppelski noticed. "Oh, don't worry, buddy, you don't have to handle this one, she's a little too much for the likes of you right now!"

What was that supposed to mean? Joseph inched away from her towards Isaac. Birdy's heart was pounding and her hands were slippery as she pulled up the lock on the door. Feeling the need to fix things somehow, she said, "Thank you for the ride," and rushed out of the car. She slammed the door behind her and tried to flee, but jerked to a halt. Her backpack strap was stuck in the car door. Mr. Doppelski's mocking laughter rang in her ears once more as she freed herself, and then she bolted for the house.

Mom was on the couch, entranced. Simon Cowell was on the TV sneering at someone who had been foolish enough to sing badly in front of a large crowd.

"Hi honey! I came home sick. I don't feel good at all."

Birdy watched her mom, who looked fine. "It's okay Mom. Sorry you're feeling bad. Do you need anything?"

"I'm just catching the latest! I'm not hungry. Just get yourself some food when you get a chance...oh, could you give me a blanket?" Birdy took a blanket from the other couch and draped it over Mom's shoulders.

After Birdy made dinner, Mom declared herself fine and ready to go to work the next day. Birdy stayed up almost the whole night making flashcards for her upcoming Biology test and "editing" the latest lab report. The computer randomly shut off twice while she was working, and on the second time she had to rewrite an entire unsaved page. When she tried to print the report, there was a paper jam. She finally fell into bed around 3. In the morning, she overslept and was almost late making it into the Light Doppelski van.

Isaac and Mr. Abe took in her disheveled appearance with twin glances of bemusement. Her hair hung in greasy tangles and her pants bore stains from yesterday's lunch. Dominic was coming straight from hunting to school, and no one else in the van dared speak to her. When they got to Divine Mercy, Birdy found a free cubby and pulled her bio stuff out of her backpack.

"It's Birdy!"

Dominic was behind her, apparently happy to see her today.

"So can I come over later?"

"Yeah, yeah. That's fine," said Birdy. She wanted nothing more than to take a nap under her purple comforter. But it was Wednesday.

"Sweet! Hey, you okay? You look exhausted."

"Yeah, I'm fine. I am exhausted" she said.

"Were you up late IMing Isaac?"

"Shut up," she groaned, punching him lightly on the arm.

"Because he was up really late last night on the computer, and I'm pretty sure he would only do that for someone he really, *really,* cared about."

As she attempted to glare at this annoyance, a giant yawn overtook her, and she indulged in it a bit theatrically, squeezing her eyes shut and stretching her arms over her head. When she resurfaced, Dominic's eyes were locked on her chest.

Shit. She crossed her arms fast. Dominic brought his eyes to her face, unashamed. A sneaky smile played on his lips.

"Your hair looks different today" he said. He reached out as if to touch it, and Birdy slapped his hand away.

"Stop! I don't know why you always have to act like that!" she snapped.

"Act like what? I just wanted to feel your hair. It looked pretty."

It didn't, and they both knew it. She met his icy stare, wanting to challenge him but unable to speak.

"Chill, girl," he murmured. He hugged her and then walked away.

The rest of the day was awkward, made worse by her continuously twitching eyelids. Birdy made sure she got to Geometry with

Polly so she wouldn't have to sit next to Dominic. She handed in the lab report to Mr. Murry, who glanced over it.

"This looks like really good work, Birdy," he said, licking his fingers to turn the pages.

"Thank you, sir," said Fred from beside her.

Mr. Murry regarded him as he might a puzzling microorganism. "I was talking to Birdy."

When Birdy got home, she found Mary sitting under the maple tree, which had the very beginnings of green buds. They went up to her room, leaving the front door unlocked for Dominic.

"Your hair looks so good!" Birdy told Mary. "It's even curlier than usual!"

"Oh my gosh, thanks! Do you think he's gonna like it?"

"Yeah, I'm sure—what did you do to it?"

"Okay, I have to bring it next time, you mix a little bit of gel with a whole bunch of this cream and then you—" Birdy never learned Mary's hair secrets because Dominic appeared in her doorway, freshly changed out of his uniform.

"Hi," Mary sighed, devotion spewing from her pores. Birdy's stomach clenched at the sight of him, and she turned away to gather what she needed to do homework downstairs. It was a struggle—her mind was pure mush. When she turned back, they were already sitting on her bed.

"So, Birdy, is your mom going to come home early today?" Dominic asked, not looking at her.

"No, definitely not today. She has a doctor's appointment after work and then she wants to stop in at some craft store on the way back."

Dominic nodded his approval. Birdy left to work in the kitchen, but halfway down the stairs she realized she'd forgotten her flashcards.

The carpets were thick, muffling her footsteps as she went back to her room. The doors, on the other hand, were made of what was essentially thick cardboard. It was easy to hear what they were saying inside.

"She's a little intense, huh?" said Dominic.

"Oh, she's such a little nerd. She's so cute."

"She takes things so seriously. She got all mad when I touched her hair, like I was going to mess it up or something. It's not like it looked good in the first place. And Fred said she's so annoying about their lab reports, she always rewrites everything he does."

"She's such a nerd. She's like a mom or something. She's so cute."

"You know who's really cute..."

Mary giggled and then all Birdy could hear was the creak of her own bedsprings. She waited, face on fire, then opened the door, averting her eyes as they rearranged themselves.

"Forgot my flashcards," she said to the floor. She went to her bedside table to get them. Then, she couldn't help it. She looked up.

Dominic wore that dead-eyed smirk from earlier, but it was Mary she wanted to see. Mary had a huge smile on her face and worry in her eyes. She was clearly wondering if Birdy had heard what they said.

"See ya in a bit," Birdy croaked. In her head, she yelled at them to get the hell out of her room. In real life, she went back downstairs. In her head, Mary dumped Dominic and then followed Birdy, crying and apologizing. In real life, Birdy sat alone at the kitchen table. In her head, she aced the Bio test, got a full ride to Harvard, made world-changing discoveries, won a Nobel Prize, and basked in the perks of being an intense little nerd. In real life, she couldn't read her flashcards because she was blinded by tears.

She didn't let them fall. Declining to be hurt was her specialty. She put her head down on her arms to talk herself down.

I'm sure she didn't mean it, she told herself. *She's just going through a lot.*

So are you, herself whispered back.

I'm fine, she argued. *I can handle more than she can.*

If Birdy had really handled it, if she had marched back upstairs and kicked them out, she might have traded a splash of pain for the deluge that would come in the next weeks. Instead, she kept her eyes shut in the dark safety of her arms, and fell asleep.

She jerked awake to footsteps pounding down the stairs.

"Hey, Birdy!" Dominic said with too much pep as she sat up, dazed. He was holding her bedsheets. "Can I use your washing machine?"

Despite her hurt feelings, she felt her mouth pulling into a smile at the sight of his apologetic face. "Um... why? What did you do to my room?"

"Well, you see, Mary here was telling me a hilarious story about the time she broke her foot kicking a bowling ball, and I was laughing so hard I spilled my Gatorade all over your bed, so I decided to just bring them down here for you and put them in the wash." Smile.

Mary laughed loudly. "It was soooo funny! I almost peed my pants I was laughing so hard."

Birdy stood up, wondering if the rest of the day had possibly been a bad dream.

"Well, thanks, I guess? You can bring them over here." She went to the kitchen closet and shoved the folding door aside, keeping a hand near the top to keep it from falling off its track. He opened the washer and looked at the pile of wrinkled, damp clothes inside.

Dominic looked at her and shook his head. "Birdy, come on, this should have been moved as soon as you got home! At our house, someone is basically always moving a load of laundry."

He said it with a smile, but her blood boiled. Dominic always acted like she shouldn't have to do chores but then criticized her for the way she had or hadn't done them. He was so comfortable with disparaging her family's way of doing things, and even if he was sometimes right, she hated that about him.

But maybe he felt bad for being rude earlier and was trying to tease his way back into her good graces. She decided to throw him a bone. When he turned around to load the washing machine, she could see the seams and tag of his white T-shirt.

"Well, you messed up my sheets *and* your shirt's on inside out, so maybe I'm not the only incompetent one here."

She was trying to joke, but Dominic and Mary both flinched so obviously that Birdy knew she had somehow messed up. Her palms sweated. Maybe it wasn't okay to tease Dominic when Mary was around. But she was trying to treat him like one of her brothers, trying to distance herself from what she had heard him say and the unpleasant truth of her feelings. Was she going to do everything wrong today?

Dominic recovered first, with an easy chuckle. "I just have better things to do than fuss over my clothes, because I'm not a fag. Now, when you wash sheets," he said in a tone of voice like he was explaining this to his Sarah, "you put the water on hot"—he took a minute to find the hot setting, while Birdy and Mary laughed —"you put the water on hot, and then you put the water on deep, and then you put in your laundry detergent—oooo, you're fancy, you use Tide, wow—and then"—he slammed the lid shut— "You turn it on."

"Well, thank you for that explanation, I'm so grateful," said Birdy. "And now if you will excuse me, I need to make some spaghetti, because believe it or not I actually know how to do that."

Dominic chuckled and Mary scurried into the living room to peer out the window. "Oh, Joey's here!" She hugged Birdy, who then busied herself with locating the spaghetti while Dominic and Mary said goodbye.

Mary rushed out the door, and Dominic waited with Birdy for a minute. "Aaaaand the coast is clear!" he said as the Saturn choked away. "Are you inviting me for spaghetti?"

"Do you want spaghetti? It's going to be very plain, I'm sure you'll love it."

He laughed. "No, no, I'd love to stay with you but I should get going. And I'm sorry."

Birdy's heart rose. "For what?"

"For spilling on your sheets? Remember that whole thing from a few minutes ago? Aren't you supposed to be all smart?"

She forced a smile. "Sure, no problem. Thanks for washing them, you didn't have to do that." *How am I the one thanking you right now?*

"Just remember to put them in the dryer," he ventured.

A wall rose between them. There was an awkward pause.

"Well... see ya," she said.

As she turned away, he grabbed her for a hug, held on for a second too long, and left.

2

EASTER CAME AND WENT in a flurry of incense, chocolate, and grandiose Mass readings by Mr. Doppelski. To Birdy's relief, everyone's holiday activities impeded the next two Wednesday gatherings, so Birdy didn't see Mary until the April Praise Night, which the Vespas were hosting once again. Mrs. Vespa stopped Birdy on her way down to the basement.

"So lovely to see you again, Bernadette," she said, touching Birdy's shoulders. Mrs. Vespa was the only adult Birdy knew who was shorter than her.

"Hi Mrs. Vespa," said Birdy.

"Mary mentioned how you've been needing extra support at the prayer group."

Oh, did she?

"We all go through these times of struggle. But remember, the Lord is just testing you. I'll be praying for you, angel."

"Thanks," said Birdy. *I need it.*

Kyle must have had an axe to grind that evening, for the music was especially keening and the meditation was especially pointed. "Boys, close your eyes, and open your hearts. Commit yourselves to purity in heart and soul. Guard yourselves from temptation. Girls, guard your Christian brothers, guard their hearts by guarding their eyes, and strive not to lead them astray. Think of God's own mother, the Virgin Mary. She didn't wear tube tops or short shorts. She was beautiful like a flower, and natural like one, too. Strive to be a beautiful flower like her. Look to her example in all you do. Don't be a weed that chokes your brothers." Mary smiled blissfully while Dominic nodded in agreement. Isaac rubbed his nose.

Afterwards, Birdy used the bathroom and spent a few minutes stalling before she had to face the world again. Isaac was outside the door when she opened it.

"You were in there for a while."

"Stalker."

"I'm just saying, everyone's going to think you were pooping."

"I was looking at the shrine to Jesus that's above the toilet." This sounded like a joke, but it was true.

"Were you praying the rosary or something? You took forever!"

"Why are you standing around outside the bathroom anyway?"

"Because I need to pee!"

"Well then why don't you go do that instead of interrogating me!"

Dominic's mocking voice sliced through their laughter. "Awww, look at them."

Birdy flinched. It was a typical comment from Dominic, but he had a mean glint in his eye and his arm slung around Mary like a prize and these things flipped a switch of blind rage inside her. She was trying to think of a response that wouldn't make Isaac feel bad, but then Mary spoke.

"I'm so happy for her that she's finally talking to a boy! I'm so proud!" She looked up at Dominic for approval, and he did approve. Their shoulders turned toward each other in laughter as Birdy's heart ripped to shreds. She glanced over at Isaac, who was looking between the other three and calculating the situation. He put on a performatively sheepish grin.

"I'd be lucky if Birdy would talk to me, but she's always too busy trying to escape from Fred." Birdy flooded with gratitude at this small kindness. Dominic laughed in spite of himself and looked at something to Birdy's left.

"Speaking of which..."

Fred rushed up to them with Josh close behind. "Birdy! I just asked everyone else what they got on their lab report."

Rude, Birdy thought, but he went on.

"We got the highest grade in the class! By a lot! Like Isaac and Josh got the next highest grade and all they got was a B-plus!" He held his hand out for a moist high five.

"Wanna come play volleyball?" Normally this would be a no, but this time Birdy took the escape hatch. Volleyball did not include enough body slamming for her current mood, but the movement helped her wrench her spiraling thoughts back into her body. Isaac also joined, presumably after using the bathroom, and so did Mary and Dominic eventually.

When Dad arrived, Mary gave Birdy a huge hug. "I'm so glad we're best friends," she said, once again wearing that eager smile as if she hoped Birdy would forget what she'd said earlier. Birdy couldn't answer.

In the car, she told Dad she had a headache. When they got home, she brushed her teeth on the way down the hallway, put on sweatpants, and dove straight under her covers. The hurt of the night still pulsed through her body. She rolled on her back and stared up at the glowing stars some other kid had left behind. *Enough is enough.* She wasn't going to let them use her anymore. They could figure out how to see each other without treating her like dirt along the way.

They'll be so mad at me. Mary's feelings will be hurt. She'll think I'm being a bad friend. But I don't care. That last part was a lie. She did care, she cared ruinously, but she knew her decision was right. But it was also anticlimactic because she didn't hear from Mary for three weeks.

The deal was that Mary was always the one to call Birdy and never vice versa. At first Birdy had thought nothing of this; Mary was way more eager to place calls than she was. Eventually she had realized Mary had to be the one to call because she was sneaking around her mom. After a week had passed since Praise Night with no word from Mary, Birdy grew uneasy. Spring soccer started and Birdy lived for the weekly relief of sprinting and kicking and Mel, Beth, and Kelly. They all went to Songs and Teens together, but Mary wasn't there. Dominic kept things cordial enough between them so that on

Wednesdays he could stand close and murmur "Is she coming over today?" and she could say "Not this week." On the third Wednesday, he looked down at her, suspicious. As usual, she only shrugged.

That Sunday, she finally got a call.

"Hey Birdy!" said Mary on the other end.

"Mary! How have you—"

"Oh, great, hey can I come by today? At like three?"

"Yeah sure, I—"

"Oh, yay, I've missed you! See you then!" She hung up.

That was weird. Birdy looked down at the receiver in her hand. *But she did say she'd missed me.*

The day was quiet and hot, the trees and sky in stagnant postures more typical of late summer. Birdy curled up on the couch and tried to read, but kept peeking out the curtain. At 3:08, she heard a car door slam. She leapt from the couch and went to greet her friend.

Joey's Saturn wasn't outside. Instead, a green Dodge 15-seater idled on Victoria Street, with Grace Vespa at the wheel. Mary stood in the driveway, sweating.

"Hey, Mary!"

Mary stared at Birdy, afraid.

"What's wrong?"

Mary took a deep breath.

"Once, there was a girl. She was a princess. And there was a boy she loved, a knight from a forbidden kingdom. And she had a lady in waiting who she *thought* was the best friend in the world. And the girl and the boy loved each other so much and they just needed to be together, and the friend helped them, for a little while. And then it all went wrong. The friend started getting jealous, she didn't understand why they didn't want her around. She was acting like it was a bad idea for them to be together, and that hurt so much. But it didn't stop them from being in love. But the girl's family didn't understand either. No one did. And when the king and queen found out about the knight, they decided to send the princess away."

Birdy stood speechless, trying to decipher the fable to which she had just been subjected.

"I'm moving. To New Hampshire."

Birdy stepped forward, but Mary stepped back.

"Dominic and I, we... we did it, we... had...*it.*"

Oh. My bed.

"I thought I was pregnant. It turned out I wasn't." She sounded wistful. "But I took one of my mom's tests. She always has a whole box so I thought she wouldn't realize, but she noticed it was gone, and she found it in the downstairs trash. I told her that you took it at Praise Night, that you had a boyfriend at school. And then my parents went through my stuff and found this bracelet Dom made for me. They decided they wouldn't say anything to your parents or Dominic's parents about it. People look up to my parents, you know, and the Doppelskis. It might cause a scandal if people found out, it could really hurt their faith. But they... they don't want me around you anymore."

"Me?"

"They think you were a bad influence on me. My mom found out I had been going to your house with Dominic all this time and it wasn't a real prayer group. And Mom said this is the sign they've been needing to send me to live with my aunt and uncle for a while. They're homeschoolers too, they'll help me there. I'm not really meant for college anyway but I can get my hairdressing license and work on my singing and do some acting classes."

Mary stepped back to deliver her final blow.

"And when I'm gone... I don't really want to—to talk to you when I'm gone. I know you like him. Dom. He told me you always flirt with him."

"Wh-what? Mary, I, he, we didn't, he was the one who—"

"I don't want to hear it" Mary said, and though Birdy felt like her soul was no longer attached to her body, she did notice that Mary had just delivered a perfect imitation of that black-and-white movie scene she so loved. "I called him yesterday to tell him what happened. My mom didn't even notice I was using the phone. I just told him what happened, and didn't even give him a chance to argue."

She wore a proud smile. "It'll all work out for the best for me. This is just what I need to grow myself into the person I'm meant to be."

Mary squared her shoulders. "See you when I see you, Birdy." She turned on her heel, then turned back. "Tell Dominic I said bye." She strutted off to the van, leaving Birdy rooted in place like a dead tree.

Grace smiled sweetly at Birdy and waved as they drove away. Birdy went inside and found Mom, who had been peeking out the window.

"Why was Mary here?" said Mom.

"She—came to say—she's moving," Birdy choked. She kept a hard internal thumb down on her hysteria, but this left her with a flat affect so unsettling that Mom insisted on staying home from work the next day to bring her to school. They were late getting out the door. The eerie stillness of Sunday had given way to a sweet breeze, and all the trees waved their new buds to greet the morning.

Birdy walked past study hall, and there was Dominic, hunched over with Margaret, laughing. He pulled a lock of her thick hair that bounced from behind her headband, and she giggled as he drew something on the notebook in front of them. He tickled her sides, then turned around. That was when he saw Birdy.

She had spent the year practicing stoicism, embracing the challenge of willing her feelings away. She had kept her face straight and her thoughts in check. She had believed that was the right thing to do. Today, she nailed Dominic to the wall with her eyes. He glanced behind him at Margaret, who was now giggling with Polly. Birdy turned away.

She walked in a trance to her cubby, grateful that the room was empty. She was sure her face resembled an Egyptian sarcophagus, solemn eyes and frozen features. *What the fuck was I doing all this year?*

The door shut behind her. She inhaled the scent of dog, laundry, and Axe. She knew it was him before she turned around.

For once, Dominic's face betrayed an emotion other than good humor or nonchalance. He looked scared.

"Birdy... I didn't mean for it all to happen like that. With Mary. I didn't know it would happen like that. I'm sorry for everything I've done, but just, please, please don't tell my parents."

Summer 2008

1

WALKING TO THE TRUCK was like walking through a swamp. Clumps of days-old mowed grass splotched over the lawn as Birdy picked her way through the yard. Birdy climbed in the truck and rolled down the window, breathing the smell of hot gasoline. Dad got in the truck and smiled at her.

"Ready, Sweetie?" The cab shuddered to life, vibrating the wooden rosary hanging from the rearview mirror.

Birdy had been silent and distracted for weeks. Mary's departure was an acceptable explanation of Birdy's malaise at first—they were such good friends, and Birdy had looked devastated when their conversation was over. So odd of her parents to just ship her off north like that, but then, Mom had always known Grace was odd. Plus, Birdy was about to start her period, and then she was on her period, and then, well sometime ovulating can make you moody too. Mom always found Birdy's menstrual cycle to be a convenient explanation when she did not meet expectations.

After three weeks had passed with Birdy's face made of stone and her brothers eliciting only distracted chuckles from her, the Clearys grew more concerned. Mom tried to warm her up with a girls' day, which backfired when they both got haircuts they hated. When she had rebuffed Mom's 100th demand to know what *else* was wrong, it was Dad's turn. And Dad's best medicine was breakfast food.

In the time of Birdy's hiatus from the world, the weather had shifted to unbearably hot. Humid wind whipped her face as they drove twenty minutes to the type of hole in the wall place Dad loved.

The air inside the restaurant smelled fried. Dad ordered a black coffee for himself and a hot chocolate for her. Hot chocolate was the last thing she felt like drinking on this suffocating morning, but she smiled and said thank you before leaving for the single occupant bathroom.

Birdy stared at herself in the mirror above the sink. Her hairline frizzed and strands of her newly shortened ponytail reached around her neck to strangle her. Zits dotted her forehead. Sweat stained the armpits of her shirt.

She was fifteen years old. She had never felt more stupid in her life.

Mary was gone. Everyone from CHOC knew she had gone to live with her aunt and uncle, who were expecting a baby under difficult medical circumstances. "How very like Mother Mary herself, going off to help a pregnant relative in need!" That was how Grace had put it when she emailed the CHOC listserv.

Dominic had cruised through the last weeks of school as though he had no cares in the world. He drove the van to school in the morning, charmed Margaret, Polly, and Olivia all day, and did skateboard tricks along Victoria Street in the evening. Birdy spoke to him as little as possible.

Isaac clearly sensed something was up and had taken to making nonstop conversation or proposing various activities whenever Birdy and Dominic were around each other. Birdy found this both annoying and sweet. If any of the Doppelski parents had noticed the change in her demeanor, they hadn't mentioned anything. When Mr. Abe dropped her off on the last day of school, she thanked him profusely for the year of rides, slammed the door, and said *Good riddance* in her head.

The trainwreck of her freshman year played on a constant loop in her mind, hurting her stomach and making her cheeks flush. In the bathroom, her face was hot. Trying to cool off, she splashed water on her face. Then she went back to breakfast.

In typical fashion, Dad had chosen a table at the back of the restaurant, his seat facing the wall, so he could survey the room for possible threats. He didn't see Birdy coming. The pretty waitress, who wasn't young but wasn't as old as Dad, approached.

"Ready for your eggs, hon?"

"Yes, ma'am."

"What do ya think?"

"They look delicious, thank you ma'am."

"I bet you'll eat them right up! Big strong guy like you! What are you, football player?"

"Former football player, current History teacher and dad of four."

"Ah, family man! Love it! Y'all got any fun plans today? It is so dang HOT out there all the sudden!" She fanned herself with her notepad.

"Well, I'm spending some time with my daughter today, and tonight I'll be watching a movie with my beautiful wife."

"Well, I hope you two have a good night, hon! I'll be back with your other plate in just a minute!" The waitress pranced off, and Birdy returned to her seat.

Dad already had his book out and was squinting at the pages. He'd forgotten his reading glasses. Birdy took out her own book, but she didn't read it. Instead, she looked at him.

He was a handsome man, it was true. His shoulders were still broad, his haircut neat. The strong brows and square jaw that overpowered Birdy's face were striking on him. It was far from the first time a random lady had paid him a compliment. But he always responded just like that—polite, detached, and mentioning his kids and his wife.

He didn't entertain himself by intimidating his children and their friends. He spent what little free time he had seeking truth and beauty in his books. He was kind to Mom and didn't laugh at her when she got upset, even when Birdy thought she deserved it. Birdy couldn't remember a day in her life when he hadn't asked her what she was reading and what the best part of her day had been. He wanted to protect her, but it wasn't that he thought she was weak. He just loved her.

Birdy's eyes filled with tears as she watched her father. Then she opened her book and waited for her breakfast.

2

AT THE END OF JUNE, Mel invited Birdy for another sleepover. When Chris dropped her off, Officer Holloway's car was not in the driveway. Mel ushered Birdy inside to show off the new TV in her room.

Kelly and Beth arrived while they were upstairs, and they went outside to play soccer. Then they sat around talking in the grass. Mel's little sisters kept coming out to visit, and Mel kept charging them with errands. In this way the girls acquired bug spray, towels to rest on, and a heaping pile of snacks and drinks.

Later they had pizza, took showers, and watched *Mean Girls* in Mel's room. "Other than the happy ending and the freedom to wear our own outfits, this is just like St. Monica's," Mel said as the credits rolled. Then she picked up the remote. Instead of turning the TV off, she started the movie over again and then crept out to the hallway. After a minute she returned and gave a thumbs up. "Coast is clear." She beamed a conspiratorial smile at Beth and Kelly, then over to Birdy.

"So... want to meet the admiral?"

From her closet, Mel produced a big plastic bottle of brown liquid. Its label said Admiral Nelson, and it featured a jaunty looking sailor on a big wooden ship.

Birdy's heart sped up as she thought about it. Her parents were fond of invoking the standard reminder not to jump off a cliff just because her friends were doing it. Consequently, an imaginary cliff carried out an active existence in Birdy's mind, standing erect in moments of moral quandary. Tonight, it loomed large.

Birdy was the queen of the unobtrusive rebellion. One false move around her house thrust everyone into misery, so her default mode was to steady the boat. But she needed to prove to herself that she lived this way because she loved her family, and not because she was weak. So she opened her secret windows, wore her plain shoes with bright interiors, and kept the peace.

And look where all that had gotten her. Her secret keeping and her silent battles, they were no match for the chaos other people could cook up. Couldn't she do something real for once?

Birdy sat up straight. "Yeah, I'll do it."

"Yes!" said Mel, laughing as she opened the lid. "Where'd I put the shot glass?" Kelly went over to the dresser and fished out a pink shot glass. "Here you go!"

Mel filled it up and presented it to Birdy with much fanfare.

"It's kinda gross but—"

Birdy tossed it back. It felt cold going down and made her nose scream, but a welcome warmth immediately radiated out from her chest and down through her limbs, lifting, lightening them.

She looked around. "Not bad," she giggled,

"Oh my God Birdy! We were all about to puke when we did it! You would just do it, no problem," laughed Kelly.

She took one more shot, which left her head swimming and her body feeling airy. Mel and Kelly took two each, Beth took four, and then Mel declared it was time to go for a walk. They crept loudly down the stairs and out the door. Mel led them to the woods as Birdy stared up at the sky. She could see a lot more stars here than at home. Then she stumbled on her own feet and tripped back down to planet earth. Beth almost cried with laughter as she helped Birdy stand. The girls found a spot at the edge of the tree line and plopped down into a sprawling diamond. Yellow pinpricks of light flashed a joyful Morse code in front of them like an extension of the stars above.

"Ohhh," said Birdy, "Look at all the lightning bugs! They're so pretty! Did you know fireflies can light up even when they're eggs?"

"Wow, Birdy," said Beth, "You know so much about bugs for a drunk person!"

"I'm not drunk!" protested Birdy.

"Oh yeah? If you're not drunk, then why haven't you noticed there's firefly on your forehead?" laughed Mel.

Birdy yelped and smacked herself in the head, crunching something beneath her palm.

"Oh no, I killed it!" Birdy shrieked.

"It never got to have glowing babies!" said Kelly. They laughed about this so ridiculously and for so long that when they were finally finished, Birdy conceded that yes, perhaps she was drunk.

"Hey, I keep meaning to ask you, are you doing soccer this fall again?" said Mel.

"Um, I don't know, I want to but honestly I think probably we can't afford it very much." There had been a lot of urgent murmurs about gas money lately.

"Same!" said Beth, for which Birdy was grateful.

"Me too," said Mel.

"But maybe we can just still meet up and play at the same time anyway," said Beth. "I mean they are not gonna come kick us off those fields, they don't even mow them or anything."

"They need us to keep the grass trampled," said Kelly.

"Maybe Vince would come sometimes if he wasn't busy. And I bet Isaac and Dominic would meet up and do it too," said Mel. "Have you seen much of them lately?"

Fly casual. "Well, I see them around the neighborhood. But school's over and we're not carpooling now."

"Is Dominic still hooking up with your one friend?"

"N-no. She... she moved."

A lone cricket chirped in response.

"So did you see—" Birdy began, but Mel interrupted.

"Wait. She moved? Where?"

"New Hampshire." Her voice cracked.

"I swear I saw her family last week," Mel said sharply. "Her mom's that bug-eyed lady, right?"

Birdy nodded. "Just Mary went."

"Why?"

Birdy had no idea how to answer that. Kelly looked straight at her.

"Are you okay?"

Birdy nodded. Then, before she could stop herself, her eyes filled with tears and the story poured out. She was amazed at how easily it flowed from her, this thing that had felt so humiliating that she couldn't even write about it in her journal. When she'd considered telling Chris and Patrick, the words had seemed to stick in her throat before she'd ever opened her mouth. *I guess I really am drunk.*

She told them all the times Dominic flirted with her, she told them all the times she'd rejected him, she told them how Mary had thrown it all back in her face. She told them how they'd ruined her bed and it was hard to even sleep there now. She told them how stupid she felt for helping orchestrate the idiotic arrangement that had only led to the loss of her best friend. But despite her altered state, she said nothing of the one secret at the core of her sorrow. *I didn't want to like him, but I did, I did, I did.* That was a raw nerve ending, to be avoided at all costs. In omitting that piece from the telling, she almost made it disappear.

The girls sat in awed silence when Birdy's tale was complete.

"Well, that is about the most fucked up thing I've ever heard," said Beth, at which Birdy chuckled.

"So, have things been weird with you and Dominic then? He's such a rat!" said Mel.

"Yeah, it's been weird, but we act like it's not weird, but it feels weird to me at least. It's very like formal now. You know? He asked me not to tell his parents and... well, I'm not going to. I don't want to protect him, exactly, but it's the same reason I never said anything in the first place, plus now his dad seems really... sorry, Mel, I know your dads are friends..."

"Oh, do not apologize," Mel said. "Mr. Doppelski is SUCH a creepy weirdo."

This sent them all into desperate giggles, during which Kelly had to drag herself to the woods so as not to pee her pants. When they were done laughing at Kelly for peeing in the woods, Birdy hiccupped and kept blabbing.

"Yeah Mr. Doppelski, he's like... really weird about women, and he talks shit about my mom to me, and one of the little boys called me a bitch one time and I just don't think that came from nowhere and he's just kind of a dick to his wife and kids but then he acts soooo holy at church. Like he does the readings so solemnly and everything and is Mr. Church Man. I think he would flip shit on Dominic. Like in a bad way. Like *bad.*" *And then Dominic would hate me.*

"That's so true about Mr. Doppelski being Mr. Church Man. But he really is such a dick! My mom can't stand him," said Mel. "I hate that about church. It's so full of nasty people."

"And they're such hypocrites!" said Kelly, outraged. "Like they're telling everyone what to do with their bodies all the time and meanwhile there's all this child abuse been going on forever. Like what the fuck!" The alcohol had loosened the expletives on Kelly's normally mild tongue.

"I'm not going to any church stuff at all anymore," Beth declared.

"Wow," said Birdy.

"Well, I found out, I can't go to St. Monica's anymore—"

"Oh nooo!" said Birdy.

"—because my parents ran out of money—," said Beth.

"Mine too!" Birdy interjected.

"—and I don't care anyway because it's all bullshit. I don't believe in that stuff anymore. So I'm not going to church stuff anymore, I have other shit to take care of you know?"

"I want to stop going too," said Mel. "My mom feels like we need to so my dad won't die at work though."

"My parents think they owe it to God because I was their miracle child," sighed Kelly.

Birdy felt that distinct and lonely feeling that everyone had changed their minds together, without her. She ripped grass from the earth and tried to articulate her response.

"Well, I mean, the church can be pretty fucked up and everything, not denying that at all, it can be so fucked up and everything, but I still think God is real and so I still feel like I should go to church because why not give like an hour of my time each week when I really do believe in God you know? Like the church says it's the, like the source or something, for truth in the world, like you'll find all truth through it."

No one said anything, but her inner chatterbox was free, so she added on. "And my parents would be sad and everything. Like you guys don't know my dad, but oh my gosh, he'd be so sad, it'd be so sad. He's so sad about Peter, I can't make it all even worse."

"Maybe you shouldn't live your life by what your parents want," said Beth.

"I feel like I can only live my life by what they want. They control everything I do." Birdy flopped backwards, staring at the stars.

It was quiet. "My parents never even know where I am" Beth said with a laugh. Then all at once she was sobbing. Her extra shots had landed.

"She always does this" Mel murmured to Birdy as Kelly enveloped Beth in a hug. They scooched in closer until all four girls were in a huddle. Beth continued crying and explained how her dad used to always coach her soccer team but had bailed for the last three seasons, and how her mom went shopping every day after work and always came home late with bags of food and clothes for only herself and didn't care what was going on with Beth. She got so lonely and wished she had a sibling, but her parents had told her many times that as soon as Beth was born they realized even one kid wasn't worth all the work involved.

Beth paused for air and looked at Birdy. "Birdy, you're like an amazing listener for a drunk person."

"Yeah, I'm sooo glad we're friends, Birdy. Soccer has been so much better with you around and it's just so nice to know that we aren't the only three girls in the world who aren't going to stab each other in the back as soon as we can," said Kelly

"Yeah, and like even though we might not agree about church and stuff, whatever! You're a good person, that's what matters!" Mel.

"Yeah, we're all good people," cried Birdy. "I don't care if you don't like church, I just love that you aren't pretending like you're all holy in church and then being total bitches outside of church."

"I love you guys!" said Kelly, her voice swelling with emotion. "You're all so fun and smart and beautiful!"

"And we're good at soccer!" snuffled Beth, which made everyone laugh again.

Moments later, Beth fell asleep, so they woke her and crept noisily back in the house. Kelly instructed them all to drink two glasses of water before they went to sleep to stave off hangovers the next day. Birdy followed this advice, settled into her nest of blankets on the floor, and then spiraled down to sleep.

3

MOM PACED AROUND THE HOUSE, alternately gulping water and stopping in the bathroom. Dad stood on Victoria Street, ready to flag down any arriving vehicles. Patrick, Birdy, and Chris lounged uncomfortably on the couches, arguing over whose feet were in whose space. After eighteen months of neglect, the spare bedroom upstairs was sparkling clean. The shades were open, the floors were vacuumed, and a squat, heavy cylinder of Christmas wrapping paper was on the kitchen table. For one night, Peter was coming home.

Like Peter, Patrick had no money to go to college, but unlike Peter, he had decided that was no hill to die on. He was accepted at a college in upstate New York and would be attending with the help of a small scholarship and a lot of loans. Though Peter had so far missed Thanksgiving, Christmas, Easter, and everyone's birthdays, he had called a week ago to say he wanted to spend time with the family before Patrick went away, and the Clearys leapt to attention.

Birdy looked out at Dad pacing the road and was momentarily floored by how much had happened to her since she'd last seen Peter. She had not grown any taller, but didn't feel the same inside at all.

Chris kept saying Mom was going to miss Peter's arrival while she was in the bathroom, but it was Birdy who missed the critical moment. The front door opened just as she was flushing. She rushed down the hall and took in the view from the top of the stairs.

Mom had Peter around the waist, saying, "Oh honey, I'm SO happy you finally came!" She drew back and said, with less enthusiasm, "And you have a beard."

"And what the—what is on your head?" said Patrick.

"He has a *bun*," said Chris in disbelief.

"What, you can't afford a haircut?" said Patrick.

"I'm a trendsetter," said Peter, and the giddiness in his voice awakened in Birdy a piece of long-dormant joy.

"Don't you love that, Dad?" Chris snorted.

"Ahh, it's fine," said Dad, his smile sparkling.

"Well, he does kind of look like a Viking now," said Birdy.

"Birdy!" Peter cried. He broke away from Mom and she rushed down the last few steps into his arms. They'd said goodbye in their old gravel driveway on a cold, gray morning, encumbered by bulky, oppressive winter coats. Now summer streamed through the still-open door, and he wore his threadbare Boba Fett shirt that had a different laundry smell but underneath it was still Peter, and the smell of him was blanket forts, stupid fights, Christmas movies, squirt gun battles, elaborate stories, and his same old soap.

She looked up. "Hi."

"Hi." He grinned, the hair and beard strange, the rest of him so familiar and beloved, ached for and missed, in the flesh and happy to see her.

"You *finally* came, this is such a treat!" Mom said as they ushered him through the house.

"Peter, I've been waiting all week to tell you—"

"Come on in, son, we're making steak—"

"Pete, can we show you the—"

"Wait did I tell you about the—"

"The kids will have to take you to—"

"What was with that sign on the way into town, is it—"

"'Not Your Ordinary Place?' I know, it's so stupid, but they don't realize how true it is, Conrad is—"

They dragged Peter through a tour of the house, bombarding him with stories, relishing his reactions to everything. They laughed like they did in their best times until they got to the kitchen table and found his unopened Christmas gifts in their condemning wrapping paper. Everyone stared for a minute until Mom said, "Open them!"

Peter unwrapped his sweatshirt (navy blue, too small), his planner (five months of remaining usefulness) and his Dutch oven (forest green).

"Thanks Mom," he said, "I love pot!"

"I already made that joke, yours isn't funny," Chris said loudly.

Peter snickered. Then he saw the intensity of Mom's gaze, waiting for his true opinion of the presents. "Really, Mom, thanks, it's great."

"Well, you're on your own now, you don't have us to cook for you anymore, so—" the kitchen timer beeped and both parents rushed over to the oven. Dad removed a baking sheet full of steaks and Peter cocked his head in confusion. One of his three jobs was as a waiter in a steakhouse. In honor of this, Mom had decided they should have steak for dinner, but as they did not own a grill, the oven was the solution. Now she urged Dad to cut the steaks open to make sure there was no pink.

"There isn't," said Dad.

"Well, let's cook them a little bit longer just in case."

"Do they need more seasoning?"

"Let me just put on a little more salt," said Mom, dumping a shower on each one.

Peter looked back at his siblings to mouth "What the fuuuuck," and then all four of them turned away from each other to laugh.

After the steaks had finished curing, they settled around the table, Peter automatically taking his old seat beside Dad. The first bite of steak was a shock, and the family proceeded to gulp water throughout the meal.

"What do you think of the neighborhood?" asked Mom.

"Seems nice," said Peter. "How do you like the neighbors?"

"Oh, we love them!" said Mom. No one else affirmed. "But they're away visiting their family right now, I wish you were staying longer so you could meet them."

"All your neighbors are visiting their family?" He was trying to tease, but he had not been around enough to know how territorial Mom was about the Doppelskis.

"Why are you saying it like that?" she said, sounding injured.

"Saying what like what?" said Peter, clueless to his error.

"Most of the neighbors are old people who never come out, but the dads of two of the families in the neighborhood are brothers, they're the ones who helped start my school, and they have a bunch of kids, and all of them are gone right now visiting another brother," Birdy clarified. It was depressing to summarize the Doppelskis in this perfunctory way. She pushed away the thought of Dominic grinning at her from Peter's chair.

"Ohhh," said Peter. Mom sighed, weary. A wisp of unrest entered the room on the wings of this stupid almost-fight. Tense silence festered as they all struggled with their brittle, salty steak.

Dad tried again. "Read anything good, Peter?"

"Yeah, I just finished reading *The Audacity of Hope,* which was really interesting," said Peter. Birdy did not understand the cause for the forced casualness in his voice, but Dad stopped chewing, and Patrick raised his eyebrows as though Peter had said something bold.

"And I've also been rereading Narnia just for something comfortable and familiar"—this seemed to both relax and confuse Dad—"because I was studying for my GED," he finished with even more forceful casualness.

Mom perked up. "Oh, Peter! When are you taking it?"

"I already did," said Peter. "Last week."

"You didn't tell us? Honey, we could have been praying for you!"

"Aw, don't you always pray for me, Mom?" Peter tried a disarming smile, which half worked.

"Yes," Mom began impatiently.

"Well, thanks! I passed."

"Are you thinking about college?"

"Not right now."

"But Peter, your SAT score was—"

"Wait, did I ever tell you about the gross guy in front of me during the SAT?" said Patrick.

"Oh, you have to tell him," said Birdy with much more enthusiasm than she normally brought to the table. Patrick explained, in even greater detail than in previous tellings, how the boy in front of him had picked an army of boogers from his nose during the test, steadily constructing a massive snot ball on the edge of his desk. Chris had his own bland tales to embellish about his own SAT, and the ensuing stories carried them through the rest of the meal.

When they finished eating, Peter rallied the siblings to clean the kitchen. They spent the afternoon catching up, which required several additional conversation redirections. For dinner, Peter and Patrick went out to pick up pizzas, a rare expense, but Mom wouldn't let Birdy and Chris go. Chris and Mom argued about this the whole time the older boys were gone, so they returned with happy faces to find a black cloud had settled over the house. After dinner, Mom told Dad, Chris, Birdy, and Patrick to clean up and dragged Peter upstairs to talk. Chris pantomimed instructions for Birdy to take out the trash and then creep up the front staircase and eavesdrop. She moved swiftly and arrived outside Peter's bedroom door to hear their muffled voices.

"—and it's all here for you, and there's plenty of work here you could find, I'm sure our neighbors would even give you a job, and we would just love to have you back."

"Mom—"

"You're always welcome, honey, we miss you so much."

"Mom—"

"And there's a great community college here, it's one of the things that brings people to the area, we know lots of people whose kids have loved it, you could—"

"Mom—that's really nice. I appreciate it. But I just put down a deposit on an apartment with a friend."

Birdy could practically hear Mom's shoulders sag. "Oh," she said, sounding broken. Next she sounded nasty. "What *friend?*"

Birdy crept back down the stairs. She didn't want to hear any more.

They watched *Groundhog Day* and laughed dutifully at their favorite jokes. After Mom and Dad went to bed, Chris kept trying to trash talk them, but Peter wouldn't bite, and they both grew surly. Birdy went to bed to escape the awkwardness and stayed awake for a long time.

In the morning, she found Peter and Dad downstairs eating frosted mini-wheats. Chris followed soon after, shockingly early for a summer morning, and plunked down beside Peter. Patrick and Mom were next and then they were all around the breakfast table together. The mood of the room was the evil twin of the days just before they moved to Conrad.

Peter rose, rinsed his bowl, and put it in the dishwasher. "Well," he said.

Mom instantly teared up. "You're sure you can't stay a little longer?"

"I'm working tonight," Peter said placatingly. "Thanks for having me."

"Did you like the steak? You didn't say."

"It was delicious," he said woodenly, the joy he'd brought home yesterday gone from his eyes. "Thanks."

After Peter left, the family retreated to separate corners to lick their wounds. Chris and Patrick left after lunch to hang out with friends. Mom and Dad soothed themselves with their annual viewing of *Gettysburg,* which Birdy had no desire to join. She pulled the family's decrepit copy of *The Lion, The Witch, and the Wardrobe* from a shelf and brought one of Mom's quilts—rainbow—out to the backyard. She spread it beneath the maple tree and started reading. Edmund was just tasting his Turkish delight when her phone buzzed. She flipped it open to find a text from Peter.

Peter: I was thinking on my drive home of how we used to pretend to be Peter and Lucy from Narnia and the one time when we got stuck in the closet and Patrick and Chris had to unscrew the door from its hinges lol

Birdy snorted at the memory. She had been thinking about it too. Peter had babysat them the time Dad took Mom to the hospital for heat stroke. At ten and nine, Patrick and Chris were not well equipped for the job, but they had managed under Peter's panicked instructions, and then they all worked together to put the door back on. It was egregiously misaligned and never shut again, but their parents had seemed to simply accept this without wondering what happened. She wrote back.

Birdy: Hahaha and I started crying cuz Chris said "Damn this damn screwdriver"
Peter: Lolol yes
Peter: I'm sorry things got kinda weird when I was home. I got to hear a lot about Patrick and Chris but not too much about you. How's life?

Oh, Peter. She couldn't answer truthfully, but she loved him for asking.

4

AS THE SUMMER MARCHED ON, Conrad accumulated a thick layer of bumper stickers, lawn signs, and billboards for John McCain, with a sprinkling for Ron Paul. Mr. Doppelski declared he'd take either one since they were both real Americans, unlike the opposition.

"His middle name is *Hussein!*" said Mom. "Like *Saddam Hussein!* Do people not notice that at all?"

Politics were simple in the CHOC-Divine Mercy domain. Babies were good and abortion was bad, which made anyone who supported abortion bad. Obama supported abortion, so he was bad, and political analysts near and far were happy to explain his additional flaws. Rush Limbaugh found it suspicious that his father was a Kenyan, and traitorous that he was running on a platform of change, as America was flawless. A letter to the *Conrad Sun* by one Abe Doppelski pointed out that the candidate who had never been a POW could not possibly care about the military. Mrs. Amon circulated an email to CHOC outlining all the qualities Obama shared with the foretold Antichrist.

In August, Chris bought the Spirit from Patrick, and Patrick put the money toward a sturdier CR-V. Constant moving had made Chris a packrat and Patrick the opposite, but even though Patrick easily fit all his worldly possessions into his new vehicle, Mom and Dad still escorted him to school. Chris and Birdy were excited for their two days of liberation, but first they had to say goodbye.

"Love you," said Birdy, her bare feet roasting on the driveway.

"Write now, ya hear?" said Chris, attempting to conceal his sadness with a falsetto prairie-lady voice.

"I will write, and text, and like all your Facebook posts so you look popular," Patrick said. They laughed and he smiled back at them. "I know I'm far away, but I'm here anytime you need me."

Birdy and Chris exercised their freedom by getting Chipotle twice, buying name brand snacks from Food Lion, and eating all of it in front of Chris's DVD collections of *The Office* and *Smallville.* The day Mom and Dad were to return, Birdy went for a run and saw Mr. Doppelski's Escort gliding down the road toward her. Already sluggish from the burrito she'd just devoured, Birdy did not want to chance an interaction, so she kept her eyes dead ahead. As the car passed, she saw in her peripheral vision that it wasn't Mr. Doppelski driving. It was Dominic, alone. He must have gotten his license. Birdy ran faster, growing nauseous as she considered what this might mean for the impending carpool.

But days before Birdy's sophomore year began, Mom had an announcement.

"I quit my job," she told them at breakfast, and Birdy felt the same horror she saw on Chris's face. But Mom was only half finished. "Karen said they needed a new secretary at St. Ann's, so I talked to Father Bill and he hired me!"

Their heart rates settled as Mom chatted about her new duties. She would be pushing the paperwork for its 2.5 collective weddings and baptisms per year, answering phonecalls and emails, saving gas money, and not getting yelled at for people's insurance woes. "And my hours match up with school hours," she said to Birdy with a fakely offhand laugh that made Chris grimace, "so now I can bring you there!"

"Cool," Birdy said, now suspecting Mom's job change had motives besides convenience. It would be hard for someone with her love of drama not to have inferred a connection between Mary's departure, Dominic's absence, and Birdy's melancholy. Mom's abnormally alert gut typically read situations upside down and backwards, but occasionally it got the book right side up. Whether she was trying to protect Birdy or simply trying to protect her walks with the Doppelski ladies, Mom had managed to kill the carpool.

Birdy was sick of the carpool and of the constant feeling that she was not meeting expectations she was neither willing nor able to meet. She was relieved Mom had managed to change jobs without making them all move. But her heart wrenched at the thought of no longer having a designated place in Dominic's life. Now they would have to seek each other out, and she didn't know if they would. Before everything had slipped down to hell, she had felt like she belonged somewhere, and now that feeling was off limits.

Fall 2008

1

"COURTSHIP IS THE FAITHFUL teen's answer to navigating romance in this secular world," intoned Father Bill, who had not been on a date since before World War II. "With courtship, teens can commit to a faithful, pure relationship, free from the pressures of sexual immorality, new wave feminism, and contraception. Courtship ensures that teens are properly supervised, that their parents know the young people they are seeing romantically, and that they can avoid the near occasion of sin by spending time together in wholesome settings."

The faithful teens being addressed sat listening in varying degrees of rapture. The desks in Room 3 were arranged in a straggling horseshoe. Birdy had taken the seat closest to the door. Isaac was sketching a mountain in his notebook. Margaret sat open mouthed and joyous. Fred nodded indulgently at each sentence, as though he had written the speech himself and found the priest's delivery of it acceptable. Dominic watched, polite.

It was the first day of school. The morning was hot and sticky, and Birdy had woken with agonizing cramps. She wished to be going anywhere else but school as she swallowed a heavy dose of Naproxen and put on her uniform, which was tighter now. She had loaded her things and Mom's things into the van, waited irritably for Mom to come outside, and exited the vehicle as soon as possible once they arrived at St. Ann's. Her first stop was a mandatory lecture for all high schoolers about the blessed world of courtship.

Courtship, according to Father Bill, was when teenagers oriented their dating lives towards marriage, and only saw people their parents had formally approved. This family-centric arrangement was supposed to help cultivate the respect necessary for a successful marriage, while conveniently erasing their sexual urges.

Birdy sat, sweating from pain, and eyed the newcomers for indicators of what they thought of the talk. The tall blond girl on the opposite end of the horseshoe smiled sweetly at Father Bill. A smaller blond beside her faced the priest with a neutral expression, tapping her pencil nonstop on the edge of her notebook. A skinny redheaded guy looked like he had cramps as bad as Birdy's.

"Faithful teens today are challenged to uphold their purity in a world that tells them to go and have intercourse with the first person who comes along. This damages teens, but there is a way out. Even for teens who have committed sins of impurity, courtship is one means of remaining pure and faithful while still enjoying a rich and fulfilling teen life."

Dominic had chosen the seat next to Birdy, and she was on fire. For months, their conversations had been brief, polite, and buffered by the presence of many other people.

Without taking his eyes from the priest, Dominic reached over and wrote in the margin of her notebook "Teen."

She immediately had to stifle a laugh. It was all the funnier because she was pleased he knew she would be annoyed by the repetition of the word "teen." He hadn't made such a specifically friendly gesture in months.

Fred's hand shot up. "Father, what are your recommendations for remaining chaste in this crazy, messed up world?"

Birdy took a deep breath. It wasn't that she doubted it was difficult to be chaste when one had any opportunities to the contrary—that much was obvious. What bothered her was Fred, who seemed to be both trying to suck up to the priest and make it clear he would never struggle with such a thing himself. She doodled a cartoon rolling its eyes. Dominic drew a smiley face underneath.

Father Bill had not planned to engage with his audience. Instead, he cleared his throat. "Well, let me introduce our guest, here," he said. "This is Mr. Mike Faducci." He handed the floor over to a middle aged, potbellied man who was effervescent with friendliness. He wore a polo shirt with a Redskins logo embroidered on the lapel. His shoulders were just broad enough that one could construe he had, at one time, played football more than he watched it.

"What's your name, young man?" he asked Fred.

"Fred Michaelson."

"Fred, great to meet you. And let me tell you, Fred, that's a tough question you've asked there. I wondered it myself for a good long time." He leaned forward affably. "Now, when I was born back in 1959..."

This lecture on courtship was provoked by rumors of a teen pregnancy at St. Monica's. That the pregnant teen had no apparent identity did not matter. It merely electrified what the Divine Mercy parents had tried to ignore for the last 14-16 years—their children were going to notice the (hopefully) opposite sex someday, just as they themselves once had.

The reaction was swift. To get in front of any unchaste behavior, they decided to crack down at the beginning of the school year. As luck had it, the patriarch of one of this year's new families was a moderately successful Catholic author who had written a great deal on chastity and many other subjects. *Farewell to Secular Sexuality: One Man's Journey to a Life of Faith and Fatherhood* was required reading for the faithful teens this year, and its author stood before them now. His daughter was the beautiful blond sitting across from Birdy.

The door opened and Mrs. Amon hissed into the room, "Sorry to interrupt, but it's time for next period." Mr. Faducci had just made it to the high school portion of his autobiography, when things would presumably have gotten interesting, but the time was up. Thus dismissed, the faithful teens rose with varying degrees of relief.

Fred went to the front of the room, seemingly determined to continue the conversation with Mr. Faducci, but Dominic cut in front of him, hand outstretched.

"Hello sir, I'm Dominic Doppelski."

Mr. Faducci was floored by the masculine assertiveness of Dominic's handshake.

"Dominic Doppelski! Nice to meet you, young man, and let me tell you, a handshake like that will get you far in life!"

"Thank you, sir! I noticed your polo shirt; I got to go to watch a day of training camp this summer..."

Birdy left, not wanting to listen to Dominic's schmoozing or Fred's ass kissing. Isaac quickly caught up to her.

"Well, that was riveting," said Isaac.

All the feelings Birdy had been suppressing for the past half hour came spilling out as laughter. "I'm just mad we never got to find out how to fight temptation in this crazy messed up world."

Fred stalked past them, evidently feeling it was more important to arrive to Latin on time than to learn how to fight temptation. His shoulders were so erect that Birdy was sure he had heard her comment.

"Whoops," said Birdy, shamefaced.

"Well, don't worry, I'm sure Dom will find out for us," Isaac said, glancing back down the hall with a smirk.

Birdy tried not to snort. "Yeah. Well, it's annoying, because I actually agree that you should treat the people you date with respect and honesty. It's just... something about that talk was so..." She didn't know how to say what she thought about it, but she didn't have to, because they made it to Latin, where Fred sat brooding. The girl who kept tapping her pencil during the courtship lecture walked in, looking guarded. Isaac waved to her and gestured to the empty chair beside him. She smiled shyly and sat down.

"Gabby, right?" he said. "Gabby Heron?"

"Yeah," said Gabby, whose voice was stronger than Birdy had expected from her timid appearance.

"Have you met Birdy?" Isaac leaned back so Birdy was visible. "Hey," said Birdy.

"Birdy?"

"Yeah, but I like to call her Big Bird," said Isaac.

Birdy rolled her eyes. "It's short for Bernadette, but please don't call me that *or* Big Bird," she said with a smile. Gabby smiled back.

"Okay, got it. Did you go here last year?"

"Yeah," said Birdy. "How are you liking it so far?"

"Well, so far I got to hear my uncle talk about courtship so... just a regular day in the life I guess."

Birdy laughed appreciatively at this as Mrs. Fischer, their Latin teacher, clomped into the room. "*In nomine patris, et filii, et spiritus sancti, amen...*"

By lunchtime, Birdy's cramps had settled to a dull roar, and her appetite had returned. She went to get her lunch bag from the locker room and found Dominic standing in front of her cubby, chatting merrily with the tall blond girl from the assembly that morning.

"Birdy!" said Dominic, more happily than he had in months. "Have you met Rachel?"

"Not yet," said Birdy, smiling.

Before she could say more, Dominic clapped a hand on her shoulder in a chummy fashion and said "Rachel, meet my friend Birdy, Birdy, meet my friend Rachel. Birdy lives down the street from me and Isaac."

Rachel smiled. Her skin was flawless. "It's so nice to meet you!"

"So nice to meet you too!" said Birdy. "I met Gabby earlier. Are you two bonding over living next door to your cousins?"

Rachel laughed surprisingly hard at this weak offering, and Dominic matched her output.

"I actually was just telling Rachel she needs to come to the back-to-school party on Friday. It was so fun last year, right?"

Birdy stared at Dominic's wide grin. "Yeah. So fun last year. Well, I was gonna get my lunch, if I could get past you...." She plucked it off the shelf. "See you later."

Birdy carried her lunch bag down the hall, feeling glum. Rachel was clearly Dominic's latest target. And what was Birdy? A convenient means by which Dominic could demonstrate that he had other friends who were females. This could stir jealousy in Rachel, making

Dominic look more interesting. It was a brilliant strategy, really. Maybe even an improvement over how he'd treated her around Mary. She just wished he had sat with her during the lecture because he cared about her and not because he wanted Rachel to like him.

2

THE QUEST TO IMPROVE Divine Mercy continued. During their summer walks, Ms. Karen had convinced Mom to join not only the parish staff, but also the school board. Now the two of them would join Mr. Doppelski, Mrs. Hart, Mrs. Strabinski, and Mrs. Amon on the first Wednesday of each month to discuss plans for the school's future, while Birdy and the other children of the board members fended for themselves on the grounds of St. Ann's. On a hot afternoon during the second week of school, Dominic stood waiting outside for Mr. Doppelski to arrive with a van full of kids for Dominic to take to the park during the meeting. Isaac had somehow escaped sharing this duty and had convinced Josh to join him in a very intense looking workout in the graveyard. Birdy didn't want to look through the American Girl catalogue with Margaret, Polly, and Olivia, so told them she was going to do homework.

Room 4 had an inconspicuous alcove with a single desk. Last year Birdy had told Dominic fondly that her third grade teacher had turned a similar space into a reading spot, and Dominic told her his dad said it used to be a timeout spot. Thereafter, they had referred to it as the desk of shame. She headed for it now, hoping no one would see her from the hallway and bother her. The lights were still on in the room.

The desk of shame was dusty. Birdy itched her nose and took out her chemistry. She was balancing her second equation when Mr. Doppelski's voice came from the hallway.

"Come on in here, ladies, let's get started."

Birdy opened her mouth to tell him she was in the room but tarried for a moment too long. The door shut, the chairs scraped, and the voices began their chatter.

Mr. Doppelski pulled a chair to the side of one of the folding tables. The angle of the desk of shame was such that Birdy could see his back, but she couldn't see anyone else and they couldn't see her. She didn't want to seem like a weirdo for hiding back here, so she figured she would just wait until the meeting was over.

"Well, I'll get us started. May the peace of Christ be with you all," said Mr. Doppelski, tilting back in his chair.

"And also with you," came Mrs. Amon's voice, "And I just wanted to say, some of us have been talking—"

"Hold on, hold on," said Mr. Doppelski. "We all read the emails, we know what's on your mind."

"Well, yes," said Mrs. Amon. "Some of us have the idea that Divine Mercy should seek to become affiliated with a parish and be under the wing of the archdiocese. And *some* of us want to stay independent because *we* aren't willing to gamble our children's education."

"It's not about *gambling* our children's education," said Ms. Karen's voice, "It's about having the resources to give them an education in the first place. I grew up in the Conrad schools, I know better than any of you what they don't have. I'm not about to send them where they can't say their grace before meals"—Birdy questioned how much Isaac would pine for this opportunity, if lost—"or where they're exposed to awful things all day, but that stuff is only part of what's wrong with the schools here. They're also missing a lot of basic resources, I'm talking things like enough books and desks, and the teachers are totally overwhelmed, and I don't want to see us go down that road."

"Becoming an archdiocese school would be just as bad," said Mrs. Amon.

"No, it wouldn't!" said Ms. Karen. "Joining the archdiocese could give us another source of funding—the county funding, it's *pathetic*—and with more funding, we could have more resources. We can't go on with no APs and half a science teacher forever. Maggie's kids have been to lots of Catholic schools all over the place, and in talking to her I've realized a lot of what's been missing from our school." Birdy's nose itched even more.

"Oh, Maggie's giving you some great ideas, huh?" said Mr. Doppelski.

Birdy didn't know how Mom could have raised Chris and not caught the mockery in Mr. Doppelski's voice, but she responded with gusto. "Oh, I just love this school, and I have so many ideas for ways we could make it better!"

"I'm glad we're all full of enthusiasm," said Mr. Doppelski. "Karen, you're saying joining the archdiocese would get us more funding, but did you actually compile any data on this? We could sure use more money, but we're going to need some kind of report to really make a decision one way or another. Has anyone done that? Crunched any numbers? Written anything down?"

There was silence in the room; Birdy imagined they were glancing around in embarrassment.

"I don't need the numbers to tell me what I think," said Mrs. Amon after a minute.

"Well, I did crunch some of the numbers," said Ms. Karen. "But I didn't write anything down. I'll put it together in a report for next time."

"Great," said Mr. Doppelski.

Mrs. Hart's reedy voice sounded. "I also took some notes, and Karen's right about us getting some more funding. But I also asked Father Tom at St. Paul's what he would think about reopening the school there using our group, and he said he wasn't sure about taking on a new financial risk right now."

"That's your sign right there," said Mrs. Amon triumphantly. "Father Tom runs that parish like a business, when his top priority should be our *souls*."

"Well, we don't exactly need him," said Mr. Doppelski. "We're already well set up right here."

Ms. Karen started, "I don't know about well set-up, not if we want to grow—"

"What's the goal of growth, though? Do we want to get bigger, or stronger?" interrupted Mrs. Strabinski.

"Well, who says we can't have both, Carly?" said Mr. Doppelski in a deeper than usual voice. *Gross,* thought Birdy, itching her nose vigorously.

"Besides, if we become a diocesan school, then they might make it so every teacher needs a college degree," said Mrs. Amon.

"Well, that's a good thing, isn't it?" said Mom.

"It might take some of the teachers out of the running," said Mrs. Amon tersely.

"Ohhhh," said Mom, catching on a moment too late.

"And if that were the case," said Mrs. Strabinski, "Then we would need to pay those teachers full salaries, and not just the stipends we're paying them now. And to cover the salaries, we would need to dramatically increase tuition, and that would edge out most of the students we already have."

"Not to mention we would have to adopt the archdiocese curriculum," said Mrs. Amon.

"It is a bit too rigorous," said Mrs. Strabinski.

"Rigorous? I'm not worried about *rigorous.* It's not nearly rigorous enough when it comes to the faith. I've looked through their high school religion texts. All these softball topics that have nothing to do with what our children really need to know." Mrs. Amon said this last part with ominous significance.

"But—" said Ms. Karen.

"Just think, if we were to open to—say the families that send their kids to *St. Monica's*"—this as though St. Monica's was a rotten cheese factory— "We would be forcing ourselves and our kids to associate with all those cafeteria Catholics. And that would just fly in the face of why we all started homeschooling in the first place."

"Well, you know, I've found out not everyone from St. Monica's is that bad," said Mom, unaware her friendly explanation would fall on hardened hearts. "Birdy has some really lovely friends who go there, their families might want—"

"All right, ladies, ladies, calm down please," said Mr. Doppelski. "We're getting a bit heated in here, don't ya think?" He continued to tip back in his chair. *Fall,* Birdy urged him, but of course he didn't. "Now there are some good points going around, but we can kick the can on that question a bit. The fact is, we need to figure out how we're gonna make more money *this* year." He leaned forward and Birdy heard his finger tap on the table. "Because *this* year, we got a few more families, that's great, but now St. Ann's is tightening its belt along with everyone else, so it makes no real difference in our margin. And we aren't gonna go shopping around for some other building either, because we aren't going to find something cheaper anywhere else. So we need a way to pull from the community to get attention on our school, and attract some more families." Birdy's nose started itching uncontrollably.

"Jude," said Ms. Karen, sounding exasperated, "That's what we were saying. If we become affiliated with a parish, we'll be a much greater part of the community, we'll have more resources to reach out to the community, and we'll bring in a *lot* more families." Birdy was getting the idea that Ms. Karen liked saying *resources.*

"Now, Karen, I agree," said Mr. Doppelski, reaching out a quieting hand. "But we just heard St. Paul's probably isn't on board, so that leaves St. Ann's. And right now, St. Ann's only has about six families with kids, and half of them already go to Divine Mercy. So maybe you better talk to your husband, Mr. Friendly, see what he's gonna do as our usher and outreach guy, to fix that." He tipped back in his chair again and crossed his arms over his chest. "Better yet, tell him to figure out how to bring more money in for DBC. Because to make money for the school, we're gonna have to spend some money, and that's gonna have to come out of our pockets."

Silence from Ms. Karen for a beat. Then she said, "I'll have to do that," in a tone of resolve.

"Now like I said, we need to talk about the way to make some money *this* year. And I've got a great idea, kids are gonna love it. We're gonna—"

Unfortunately, the dust triumphed at this moment and Birdy succumbed to a monstrous sneeze. There was a collective yelp and Mr. Doppelski toppled out of his chair. Mom said *"Birdy?"* and Mr.

Doppelski whipped his head around, stumbling backwards till he found her.

"Ms. Birdy! What are you doing in here?" He smiled for the benefit of his flock, but she could see in his eyes that he was mad. *Good.*

"Homework," she sniffed, getting out of her seat. "Sorry. I was already in here and I didn't want to interrupt." This felt like a rather lame explanation when she said it out loud. Mom looked amused, if puzzled, but Mrs. Amon wasn't smiling.

Mr. Doppelski pointed at the door. "Get out of here and don't repeat any of what you just heard." Birdy gathered up her books and put on her backpack. He jabbed a thumb in her direction and addressed the class. "That was the spot they used to sit us when we were bad," he said to general giggles. "Better keep your girl in line, Maggie!"

"Oh, you would never get in trouble, would you Jude," Mrs. Amon simpered.

"Oh, I got in trouble like you wouldn't believe, Roberta," Jude said from under his eyelashes, looking every inch the bashful hangdog. "I wasn't like your Honest Abe," he said to Karen, who smiled absently and chewed a thumbnail.

Revolted, Birdy shut the door on the continued giggles and found Isaac and Josh sitting in the hallway. Josh looked like he would never rise again.

"Why were you in there?" Isaac demanded.

"I was in there doing homework and they just started having the meeting," she shrugged.

"Oh," said Isaac. "Did you hear anything interesting?"

"Kinda," said Birdy. The boys were a bit pungent "How was your workout?"

"You tell me," said Isaac, flexing.

"I'm so sorry I asked," said Birdy. Josh looked like his embarrassment would kill him if his exhaustion didn't.

3

IN THE DAYS AFTER the meeting, Mom shone with new confidence. Her walks with Karen and Tammy doubled in pace as they discussed all there was to say about Divine Mercy and St. Ann's. The economy was bad, and literally anything that went wrong could be blamed on it, but Mom's new job was just her style, and the Clearys were saving hundreds of dollars per month on gas now that she wasn't commuting to Pennsylvania. Furthermore, she was convinced that given the housing crash, it was a miracle they'd never bought the house they lived in.

"We aren't underwater on our loan, because we don't have a loan!" Mom gushed to Dad one evening over dinner. Dad nodded carefully and took a huge bite of chicken.

Dominic had been promoted to the position of primary family chauffeur, which he loved. After school, he always made a big show of rounding up his passengers, which included Coz and Damien this year, or herding the little ones if a Doppelski adult had passed them off to him. Rachel gobbled up these displays of upstanding young manhood, smiling like an angel as Dominic twirled his keys on one finger and hoisted a preschooler on his hip. Birdy felt ancient in her jadedness at these proceedings. Nevertheless, she and Dominic were rapidly rekindling their friendship now that school was back in session.

Kelly was the only one of the girls who was officially signed up for fall soccer, but as the Conrad Rec League had no presence whatsoever at the fields, Birdy, Mel and Beth still went along to play every Tuesday. By now they were used to governing themselves at practice, and they soon fell into their usual routine of half-hearted drills and full throttle scrimmages. The Conrad High football coaches continued to be mired in personal struggles, so Vince joined their practices every few weeks, which always increased Mel's intensity.

At first, Birdy walked over to the soccer fields by herself, but Dominic, Isaac, and Joseph caught up with her the second week. Coz and Damien joined them the week after that, Joseph apparently having blazed the trail for younger siblings. These walks were fun and felt almost the same as before, but Mel's mom always drove her home.

Dominic's hasty, ass-covering apology in the locker room felt pathetically insufficient for all his transgressions. Birdy sometimes imagined he would come to her again in true sorrow and make things right between them, but she knew that was only a fantasy. Nevertheless, it was a lot more fun to talk to him and Isaac than it was to listen to Fred expound on the benefits of courting, hear Olivia daydream about her future nursery, or compare favorite saints with Margaret and Polly. And it was easier to be Dominic's friend when she wasn't sneaking around on his behalf.

Under these new circumstances, she managed to put her feelings for Dominic away. They lived on a shelf in her mind, in a box taped shut tight, guarded by her certainty that she could never date him. She didn't trust him, and that was that.

Until one Tuesday when she was unstoppable. She scored two goals, intercepted every pass in her area and knocked Isaac flat on his back. Afterwards, Dominic slung an arm around her.

"Birdy, you're a monster out there. You're always right where you need to be, and you zip around all these guys. They're falling over before they even know what happened. You amaze me!" And he smiled down at her.

Down fell the box, its contents flooding Birdy's veins. The secret she had been keeping from herself was out. And that was that.

That night, Birdy signed onto Facebook and was surprised to have a friend request from Ms. Karen. *Am I supposed to accept my friend's mom?* Curiosity made the decision for her. Karen Doppelski had always been a digital camera enthusiast, but she had also recently acquired a pink Razr flip phone that could upload pictures to the internet. Her albums were a mixture of well-lit flowers from her front yard and blurry pictures of her younger kids.

One afternoon, she posted a missive in her status: "Dear friends, you are invited to view my new project the Lord has placed in my heart: My Own Blog!"

Birdy followed a link to *Hallowed Home: A Blog about Home-schooling, Faith, and Family.* According to the About page, Ms. Karen was "trying her hand at cultivating a faithful family and a happy home." The Light Doppelskis' home had two distinct looks. One stemmed from Abe's attempts to one-up whatever had just happened at the house next door. The other stemmed from Ms. Karen's attempts to beautify small corners of the house with plants and cute bins from Wal-Mart. The kids normally ruined these vignettes within days, but the blog gave the impression that the entire *Hallowed Home* was stylish and neat.

Chris appeared over Birdy's shoulder. "Click on that," he said, pointing to a pixely "Homeschool FAQ" graphic.

"Who do you think is frequently asking the questions?" said Birdy.

"I've got a lot of questions," said Chris. He read aloud in imitation of Ms. Karen's loud, cheery voice:

"Q: Where do your kids do school?

A: Our kids do school anywhere that's comfortable! Even in they're pajamas!"

This seemed to defy the homepage picture of all the kids dressed in blues and whites, working diligently around the long, sunlit table. Ms. Karen had also authored a long post about the origins of Divine Mercy and her conviction to "responsably" help it grow. Every time Birdy clicked a new page a box popped up on the screen begging her to subscribe.

"Well? Are you going to?" said Chris after the fifth plea.

"No," said Birdy. "I don't want her to know I'm stalking her."

As the fall wore on, Mom took to regaling Dad, Chris, and Birdy with the latest Divine Mercy scoop over dinner. According to Mom's sources—she wouldn't say who—Mr. Doppelski had muscled his accounting slash treasurer slash president position into giving himself the last word on all financial planning decisions. This was breeding some awkwardness between Ms. Karen, who was annoyed, and Mrs. Doppelski, who supported her husband in all things. Mom was of the opinion that, while it was a bit annoying, Mr. Doppelski's forcefulness was valuable. Their money situation was tenuous, and he had concrete plans to stabilize it.

Mr. Doppelski couldn't make it to the October board meeting because he was closing on a new property, so the other board members decided to make it an open forum for all the Divine Mercy parents. Birdy played MASH with Gabby and Rachel during the meeting. After Rachel had ended up with Dominic as her future husband for the second time, Birdy left to use the restroom. On her way back outside, she paused beside Room 4. The door was propped open, as about half the attendees of the meeting were plagued by ever more frequent hot flashes.

"We founded this school to train our children in our faith! Do you *know* what goes on at St. Monica's?" Birdy knew a great deal of what went on at St. Monica's and was curious if Mrs. Amon's knowledge was accurate.

"I heard there were children *smoking* in the bathroom."

"I heard they were doing *more* in the bathroom." A pause for gasping. Unfortunately, both claims were accurate.

"They hired my husband to give a talk like he did for our kids, and no one signed up! Not ONE kid." That had to be Mrs. Faducci's voice.

"Well, that's the problem, they didn't make it mandatory."

"I doubt that would have helped."

"Why are you always eavesdropping?" said Isaac. Birdy jumped and turned around. Isaac stood grinning with Gabby and Michael, the skinny redheaded guy who had looked nauseous during the courtship talk.

"I wanted to hear Mrs. Amon talk shit about St. Monica's," said Birdy. This joke was a risk; she knew Isaac and Gabby would appreciate it, but she wasn't sure about Michael. He chuckled along with the other two and said, "My mom was really excited to go to this meeting today."

"I think it's like the social event of the month for some of these people," said Isaac.

Michael laughed even harder at that joke. The boys were stinky once again, but Michael seemed to have taken the workout better than Josh had.

"Did Josh not want to work out with you this time?" said Birdy.

"No, he said he had to work on our chemistry report. Which I *know* is a lie, since he always leaves everything for me to do."

They went back outside to find Dominic had returned with his van of siblings and cousins. They were in the cemetery, playing a literal interpretation of ghosts in the graveyard. Dominic was adhering to his habit of using this game as an opportunity for romance, and they found him and Rachel holding hands behind a particularly large headstone. Rachel turned red as a cherry, but Dominic smiled around at them as he casually released her hand.

"Hey guys," he said. "Wanna play?"

Birdy started having lunch with Isaac, Gabby, and Michael every day, with Dominic and Rachel sometimes joining them. Knowing and loving Beth, Birdy could not allow herself to resent Rachel purely for being tall, blond, and beautiful, but she kept having the strange urge to send a letter to Mary in New Hampshire saying *Don't worry—you're so much cooler than her.* Mary was warm and goofy and had likes and dislikes. Rachel was unquenchable, one-dimensional sweetness, without an ounce of unkindness in her body, not even the secret type like Birdy's. Sarcasm slid right off her, and she smiled nonstop. Eating lunch with her was like eating with someone's venerable grandmother.

Birdy worried Rachel wouldn't be able to take what Dominic might end up dishing out, but she tried to think maybe she was good for Dominic. Maybe the only thing missing on his journey to redemption was a saccharine girl. *Yes, maybe he'll finally be changed by a tall, blond, beautiful girl with no personality. Wouldn't that be great,* she thought, stabbing cold noodles with her fork while Rachel laughed gently at Dominic's wit.

The board members had decided Divine Mercy needed to both prepare the kids for college and have more clubs, so Birdy and her friends were forced to join the SAT prep club, facilitated by Mrs.

Strabinski. On Thursday afternoons, they spent an hour reviewing vocabulary, math concepts, and test taking strategies. During the first class, Dominic took the unprompted opportunity to explain to Rachel what a hypotenuse was.

"I know," smiled Rachel, totally unoffended.

On the first Tuesday in November, Barack Obama was elected. Mrs. Amon was too distraught to teach the next day, instead leading them through sob-wracked rosaries in both Religion and English class. Ms. Karen thought they should all get together and deepen their resolve for their school's mission, so the board meeting was canceled in favor of a school-wide prayer service. Even Mrs. Doppelski came, bringing all the kids with her.

After the prayer service, the parents stayed behind for a passionate discussion about how to protect their children from the evils to which they would soon all be subjected. The children in question awaited their imminent corruption in the parking lot. Isaac got Dominic to move the van over near the grass so he could attempt to back-flip off the hood, a move he had seen in the movie *Step Up*.

"Has anyone seen that?" said Isaac.

"No!" said Fred, looking harassed.

Margaret sighed. "I really, really want to. My mom said I could watch it after she edited it on the laptop.

Feeling the urge to annoy Margaret, Birdy said, "The movie was okay, but Channing Tatum is really cute." She saw Dominic raise his eyebrows at her, but she focused on Gabby, who giggled in agreement.

"Oh yeah, that guy is so ripped. That one scene where he lifted that girl over his head, I was shocked. He's so strong," said Isaac.

Birdy started to respond, but Dominic interrupted.

"Wow, keep it in your pants, Isaac. It's Adam and Eve, not Adam and Steve."

Everyone went silent at the sudden viciousness in his voice. Then the laughter began. It started with stifled giggles, then exploded to a roar. They were giddy at understanding the forbidden, edgy punchline, and they could indicate they were both savvy and holy if they just laughed hard enough.

Isaac laughed harder than anyone else. Birdy laughed too. But Dominic's casual nastiness writhed in her gut, a dreadful thing that just kept growing.

Winter 2009

1

From: icanseecleary@aol.com
Hey Bird Flu,
Merry Christmas! I missed you guys today. I'm trying to figure out my work situation so I can work somewhere that's actually closed on Christmas...Now I'm watching Home Alone and it's lame without you guys. How was everything? Anything I should know before I come home?

From: bluebirdy@aol.com
Hi Pee Tea,
We missed you too! I'm glad you'll be here, even if it's a few days after Christmas. Everything was okay today. Don't bring up the March for Life, Mom is very enthusiastic about it and will not accept anything less than matching enthusiasm when speaking of it. Patrick likes some girl named Kara and he told her she had nice hand towels and he is very embarrassed about that so you should definitely compliment him on his hand towels when you're here. We also got weird presents but I'm not going to tell you what they are. You get to find out for yourself just like the rest of us. We're going to watch Home Alone too but we'll save Christmas Story for when you're here. Merry Christmas ya filthy animal.

IN JANUARY OF EACH year, the Catholic youths of the DC and Baltimore metro areas were shipped en masse to their nation's capital to exercise their first amendment rights in a huge pro-life protest called the March for Life. By observing this ritual, they would learn that being virtuous, good citizens was nothing if not fun. In response to Obama's impending inauguration, the Divine Mercy parents threw together plans for their own DC odyssey. Over Christmas dinner, Mom had enthusiastically informed Patrick of the plans.

"I'm so excited—we're going to end abortion!" She pumped her fist in anticipation.

"Well, if Roe v. Wade were overturned, it would only end the right to abortion on a federal level," said Patrick. "Abortion wouldn't disappear overnight."

"Why are you being so negative about it?" Mom snapped.

"I'm just saying," said Patrick.

"Don't you *want* to end abortion?"

"I'm just saying, Roe v. Wade is—"

"Are you coming down for it?" Mom interrupted.

"Uh, no," said Patrick. "It'll be like two weeks after I go back and I need to work on my RA application for next year."

"Well it sounds like that school is doing wonders for your spirituality," Mom snarked.

"Well, I do feel like I've taken a vow of poverty," said Patrick.

Birdy was suddenly afflicted with a coughing fit, while Mom balled up her napkin, cast it down upon her plate, and stomped upstairs.

Mr. Doppelski charged the kids $40 a head to cover the cost of gas, Metro fare, and lunch. Almost every Divine Mercy family was on a tight budget, but for this cause, and for Mr. Doppelski, they willingly coughed up the cash. Mom and Dad both looked a little startled at the amount, but Dad disappeared into his room for a while and returned with some wrinkled bills.

The day of the March had a predicted high of 25 degrees. After watching the weather report, Mom remembered an urgent task she needed to do at work that day and called Tammy with her regrets. Dad and Chris dropped Birdy off in the St. Ann's parking lot before the sun had risen. They would be taking their own DC trip with Bosco. The two Doppelski vans and Mrs. Amon's car were already there, and their riders milled about the parking lot in the glow of Mr. Doppelski's headlights.

"Bye honey," said Dad, waving to the bystanders. "Did you bring gloves?"

"Yeah," said Birdy.

"Okay," he said, "Be safe out there." Birdy stepped out of the truck and into a nasty chill.

"Can't board if you don't pay!" said Mr. Doppelski, in a would-be fun voice, except Birdy knew he was serious. She handed him the folded bills from her pocket, and Mr. Doppelski straightened them and stuck them in an envelope. Birdy lowered her face into her coat collar. Slowly, most of the student body of Divine Mercy arrived, and Mr. Doppelski extracted their cash from them in the same breezily threatening manner each time.

"You hang onto this for me for the day, son," Mr. Doppelski eventually said to Dominic, holding out the now-bulging envelope. Birdy had noticed that when other adults were around, Mr. Doppelski liked making a show of entrusting his kids with mature duties. He also called them "son" and puffed out his chest a lot. Dominic put the envelope in his pocket.

Mr. Abe waved the kids around him for the first of the many prayer circles the day would hold. Mr. Abe squeezed his eyes shut and bent his head, his breath billowing around them as he spoke.

"Heavenly Father, you gave us this work to do today, and we're so grateful, Lord, we want to go out there and save these babies. Help us travel safe, keep us safe in the city from thugs and from people who don't like our mission, help us stand against these evil politicians and do what you've asked us to do."

*God...*Birdy started in her mind, but she didn't want to tack her prayer on the heels of Mr. Abe's slimy petitions. *Never mind. I don't know what I'm even asking you for.*

She ended up in the Light Doppelski's van with Isaac, Michael, Joseph, Gabby, several younger Doppelskis, Josh, and Fred. They drove 45 minutes to the Shady Grove Metro station. Mr. Doppelski,

Mr. Abe, and Mrs. Amon herded the kids onto the already packed train, and they lurched away.

Once his father was distracted by the task of navigating the Metro system, Dominic directed his attention to Rachel. They had both brought their digital cameras and kept posing for pictures that required them to smush their faces together. Birdy clutched the greasy pole and tried to distract Gabby, who was wigging out. Birdy had been on the Metro during several past summers when the Clearys toured the monuments and memorials, but Gabby was nauseous from the train's movement and worried by the other occupants of the train, who looked less and less like Conrad-area homeschoolers the further south they went.

They missed their transfer point and spent an extra hour correcting course. When they made it to their final train, Mrs. Amon dove for one of the peeling orange seats.

"Need to catch my breath," she gasped.

When they reached their stop, Mr. Abe urged them to get going and counted all of them, but missed Polly, who was absorbed with the map. She noticed they were leaving just in time and dove through the closing doors with shocking athleticism. After she had finally calmed down, the crew of heroes marched through the Metro station and climbed a broken escalator out into the winter sunlight.

Mr. Doppelski directed them to a low stone wall in front of a tall office building. "We better have lunch before we get going," he said, taking off his backpack. Birdy had assumed they would find a McDonald's or something, but lunch turned out to be apples and granola bars that Mr. Doppelski had been carrying the whole time. Birdy was last in the food line and ended up standing right beside Mrs. Amon.

"You know, I'm so thankful we have you to lead us all out here," said Mrs. Amon, touching Mr. Doppelski's arm like it might be hot.

"Of course!" said Mr. Doppelski. "We've got to give these kids a good example. They're exercising their right to protest, they're standing up to the government, and they're learning some valuable lessons. These feminazis want to keep abortion around to just bail them out of their mistakes, but life just don't work like that. If they're not ready to be mommies, then they shouldn't do what turns you into mommies, right? That's something all these young ladies should learn before they get much older." He pointed his head at Birdy. Mr. Abe looked at her too and punctuated his brother's statement with a hard nod. Mrs. Amon gushed her agreement. Birdy looked down at her bruised apple, feeling queasy.

After their "meal," they headed for Constitution Avenue. The rally they were supposed to attend was already over, so they joined a thick stream of marchers, bundled up for their walk to the Supreme Court and pumping signs. Michael leaned close to Isaac and pointed to the signs.

"How'd we get out of carrying those?" he muttered. Isaac grinned back at him.

"Oh look, kids, we've got some counterprotesters," said Mr. Abe, sounding triumphantly grim.

A tall woman in a blue parka stood on a wall and chanted through a megaphone, "KEEP YOUR LAWS OFF MY BODY!" A shorter woman on the ground waved a sign that read "THE GOP does NOT care about BORN children!!" A third person, whose features were indistinguishable beneath their many layers, waved a sign with an entire paragraph of arguments: "Dear Anti Choice Protesters: Abortion Gives Women The Right To Bodily Autonomy. Why Do You Want To Force Women To Carry Unwanted Pregnancies But You Dont Want To Fix Education Improve Welfare Or Provide National Healthcare? I Think The Answer Is That You Dont Actually Care About Women or Children!!!!!"

"Communists!" Margaret squeaked boldly in their direction.

"What's the gop?" wondered Polly.

Birdy slowed down to reread the sign. Grammatical oddities aside, it unlocked a secret door in her mind. She'd never questioned banning abortion because it had always been about saving the babies, and babies were delightful. But she'd seen Mrs. Doppelski floored by nausea, sciatica, and something called round ligaments. She'd heard Mom's birth horror stories and lived the chaos of a struggling family. When anyone mentioned women in the context of abortion, it was to designate them as either heroic pro-lifers or selfish pro-choicers. No talk of their suffering, other than how redemptive it was. No talk of helping them take care of the babies, once born. No talk of boys avoiding doing what turned them into daddies.

If anyone else's worldview was being disturbed, they didn't show it. In front of her, Dominic was tickling Rachel's side while she giggled uncontrollably. Then he pulled his cell phone out of his pocket, and the envelope of cash fell to the ground. He didn't notice because he was using his cell phone to snap a picture of himself and Rachel. They marched on, unaware. Birdy picked up the envelope, then dashed forward.

"Dominic, you—"

"Not now, Birdy," he said, not sparing her a glance.

"But you—"

"Shhhhh, I'm showing Rachel around DC," he said, snaking his arm around Rachel's shoulders and steering them away from Birdy. Rachel looked back through the space between them and giggled at Birdy, like, *Oh, him, he's so funny, right?*

Birdy kept her face still and slowed down, letting Margaret, Polly and Josh fill the space between herself and Dominic and Rachel. *Do not cry,* she commanded herself. Mr. Doppelski was busy expounding about something or other to Mrs. Amon, so she didn't want to hand the envelope to him. She shoved it into the pocket of her innermost hoodie and zipped her coat over top.

They trudged along DC's wide streets, splendid buildings above their heads, trash beneath their feet. In the distance, she spotted Nancy Vespa and her brood, but no one else noticed. She balled her hands inside her thin gloves as they finished their walk and unceremoniously pivoted to the nearest Metro station. *Was that it?* Margaret, Polly, Rachel and Gabby were all talking about how amazing it had been, but Birdy didn't join. At the end of this cold and miserable day, all she felt was doubt.

On the way home, Mr. Abe treated them to a lecture about how it was more important than ever that they go to these protests because a socialist was in the White House now. He wasn't even a real American, he was born in Kenya, and we weren't going to let him bring this country down. As he talked, he downed three granola bars he had apparently pilfered from his brother. They passed numerous exit signs advertising Taco Bell, McDonalds, and Burger King, but they never stopped. Birdy's stomach gurgled in its neglect. She leaned her forehead on the cool window to stave off her incoming headache.

They made it back to the St. Ann's parking lot, where several parents were already waiting. Mr. Abe looked over his shoulder at Birdy.

"We giving you a ride home, little lady?"

Birdy shook her head. "My mom's coming."

"All right," said Abe as she climbed out of the van. "It sure looks cold out there."

Mrs. Amon and Margaret drove away, and Mr. Abe left with his kids and some of Dominic's siblings. Then Mr. Michaelson came to get Fred, leaving Birdy alone with Dominic and Mr. Doppelski. Trying to be unobtrusive, she hunched against their van, warming her nose inside her coat. Dominic and Mr. Doppelski stood in the pool of the streetlight's illumination. Mr. Doppelski finished waving to Mr. Michaelson, then turned upon his son.

"Dom, where's that envelope?"

Dominic reached for his pocket, then stared at his dad. "...envelope?"

Birdy smiled inside. *Not so cool now, are you?*

No, he wasn't. The snide and confident Dominic from earlier was gone. In his place stood a boy in pure panic, stuttering, scared, stuck.

"Yes. Envelope."

Dominic kept his eyes on his dad as he touched all his pockets, gently, as if to do so without being noticed.

"I... don't... have it."

Birdy stopped smiling inside.

"Do you mean to tell me," said Mr. Doppelski in a deadly voice, "that the money I told you to hang onto, that I trusted you with, is somewhere back in DC? Some black crackhead probably stole it out of your pocket on the Metro, and you let him because you were too busy following your goddamn dick around."

Oh no.

He took a quick step at his son and grabbed the front of his coat.

No.

"Hey, Mr. Doppelski, wait," said Birdy.

Two sets of dark eyes snapped toward her. Birdy walked forward and dug under her many layers, her cold fingers closing around the fat envelope. Instinct told her to play dumb. Pitching her voice a smidge higher, she said, "I found this earlier, but I didn't know what it was. Is this what you needed?"

Gratitude and understanding flooded Dominic's face as he beheld Birdy's outstretched hand. Birdy widened her eyes up at Mr. Doppelski, channeling innocence, momentarily grateful for her cute-but-not-hot face. Mr. Doppelski snatched the envelope from her. He thumbed through its contents, then let out a bark of laughter just as Mom pulled into the parking lot.

"Well, you're just full of surprises Miss Birdy! Come on, boy. We need to take this to the bank."

He bounced back to the van, mood sunny. Dominic followed him, but he walked backward for a second. "Thank you" he mouthed, hands over his heart.

On Friday, Dominic made a point of flagging Birdy down to sit with him and Rachel at lunch. On Wednesday, he sheltered her history project with his jacket as she carried it inside through the rain. Now it was Thursday, and Dominic and Birdy were waiting in the classroom before SAT prep class began. Rain was still pounding on the classroom's single window, but their seat was next to the radiator and the room felt cozy. Mrs. Strabinski was late, and so was everyone else, so they were alone at the table. Dominic was going over the vocabulary words he was supposed to have learned already.

He took her notebook. "What does integrity mean? Like could I say that statue has integrity?"

Birdy marshalled her best manners. "Um, not really, like maybe as part of an involved metaphor or something, but integrity is more like when a person does the right thing. When no one is watching."

Their eyes met awkwardly, and then Birdy looked back at her textbook. Dominic kept looking through her notebook.

"Wow, you take such good notes. Can you just take the SAT for me?"

"Nope. Because I have integrity." She made a smug face.

"Touche," he laughed. "Okay, well here's a note for you."

He found a blank page and wrote something in one corner as butterflies mounted in Birdy's stomach. He slid the notebook over to her.

Birdy- Your a better friend then I deserve! Thanks for everything girl.

He smiled at her then with such open tenderness that the oceans of resentment in her heart evaporated. All she felt for him was love. She smiled back, then looked away so she wouldn't cry.

That evening, Birdy sat curled on the other end of the couch from Mom, who was enthralled with the latest episode of American Idol. During the ad break, she switched to the news. Tonight's story featured a huge gay marriage protest taking place in Florida.

"I can't believe they didn't cover the March for Life at all, but they cover this!" said Mom, turning up the volume. The camera panned over a crowd of men who were wearing shorts and tank tops that Birdy would surely not be permitted to wear.

"It's ridiculous, these people have no willpower," Mom said, gathering another handful of popcorn. "It's so sick to like someone who has all the same... *equipment* as you do! They're just so self-absorbed. And now it's just the popular thing to do! They just act that way to seem glamorous!"

It was a conversational hike Mom was fond of taking, and Birdy already knew every step. Today, she could only think of how her stomach had felt when Dominic had written in her notebook.

She'd tried and tried to turn her feelings off. She had no future with Dominic. She could never date him, would never marry him. She wouldn't want to raise his children, couldn't share her life and her dreams with him. She would give anything to stop wanting him. And what she wanted most in the world was for him to want her back.

No one could choose who they loved. No one would ever choose to feel this way. This wasn't glamorous. It was misery.

"Well? You're not saying anything!"

Birdy glanced at her mom and then back at the TV.

"You're so unreadable lately!"

Birdy headed for the kitchen stairs. "I have cramps," she called back over her shoulder.

2

OFFICER JOHN HOLLOWAY WAS a miserable man. He waited at the bar, thumbing the condensation on his beer bottle. He should have just gone home, seen the girls, gone to bed at the same time as Lily. But he was afraid to be home.

Before Mel was born, John thought he knew what tired was. When he was new to the Conrad Police Department, he'd always worked nights. He and Lily found joy in the hours they scraped together on his days off, and his constant sleepiness was more of a joke than a burden, more of an excuse for him to yawn dramatically and tell Lily he needed her to put him to bed. He started working days right before Mel was born, thinking he'd gamed the system because he could get along just fine on little sleep. That first night in the hospital, he'd paced the dim room with Mel, his eyelids locking shut each time he blinked, scared to sit down because he was worried he would fall asleep and drop her. He didn't mention this to Lily, who had just spent thirty-four hours in labor.

When they got home, he realized there were to be no more luxurious, sunlit naps under their white quilt. Mel had been vocal and energetic from day one, and she refused to fall for his singing and rocking bullshit—she merely appraised him with her bright little eyes, making it plain she would not be sleeping anytime soon. As the weeks of life with a newborn went on, his brain felt progressively more like a sieve. Simple words eluded him. He would think of something he needed to do, and then instantly forget what it was, feeling the phantom of the task poking at his brain but unable to grasp it.

But Mel, and then Bailey and Jessie, had eventually slept, and the holes in his brain closed, mostly. They'd had a happy few years back then. But three little girls cost money, so when Mel was eight, he went back to nights. The money was better, and he was around during the day with the girls sometimes. It had seemed like a great idea. That time, he really thought he knew what tired was.

Two months into his new shift, Officer Mark Farrow shot a guy named Will Straw. Will was twenty, not the most prudent of ages, and he had a gun and fifty-nine stolen dollars. John ordered him to drop the weapon and put his hands up. Will was drunk, so he put his hands up without dropping the weapon. Farrow shot him without another warning. John stepped up to confirm death, and that was when he noticed the gun was a toy.

John's boss opted to keep that detail internal. "Farrow did what he had to do," he told John. "Straw was violent, he was holding the weapon in a threatening manner. Farrow was protecting all of you." John had remained silent. He could see himself in Farrow's shoes, could see how it would be to charge into battle exhausted and enraged and find a man with a gun who might kill you, and just pull the trigger because there was no such thing as talking things out when you were that tired and your one goal was to stop the threat. But whenever he thought of Will's poor, dumb, dead, face, he thought of Sister Josephine.

Sister Josephine, when he was in fourth grade and spring was in the air, saying she had one more thing to tell them before she released them to Easter break.

"I know you've heard this story before, but listen close, because it's really the secret to everything." On John's left, Agnes Wilcox's hair ribbons quivered to attention. She loved secrets.

"When Jesus was dying, there were two thieves up there with him. One of them made fun of Jesus, but the other one recognized what Jesus was. He asked Jesus for one more chance, and Jesus gave it to him. And that's the secret. No matter who you are, no matter what you've done, Jesus will love you till the last moment of your life."

Agnes Wilcox looked crestfallen. She'd heard this one already.

Sister Josephine smiled at her. "That's a big deal, Agnes! Love isn't just something we talk about. It's a real force. It's powerful, stronger than Superman. You know how I know?"

"How?" Agnes gasped, rallying.

"My little sister had a baby last year, and I finally got to meet him over Christmas," said Sister Josephine. "When I see them look at each other, I see love flowing as big and strong as the Hickory River." She flung her arms out wide. "Baby Charlie does terribly rude things. He threw his sweet potatoes on her new pants! But she keeps pouring her love into him, and it shines right back out. He crawls around like the proudest kid in the world, because he's wrapped in her love everywhere he goes."

"And our parents' love is like God's love," said Agnes reverently. On John's left, Jude snorted, but Sister Josephine didn't miss a trick. She looked at Jude for a moment before answering.

"Parents are people, and people don't always get things right. So even if your parents aren't as nice as my sister—" she ignored Agnes's indignation "—God's love will fill you up and make you strong, if you go to him. But he wants us to love each other the way he loves us, so we have to share. The trick is to remember that everyone was once a baby like my nephew. We can expect them to take up more responsibility as they grow," she tossed to Jude, anticipating that he would ask if he could throw his sweet potatoes at her, "But we're all precious to God, so we should all be precious to each other, too."

It was embarrassing how often John flashed back to elementary religion class, but Sister Josephine's passionate insistence on the value of every single soul was the thing that put him in the church pew on at least some Sundays. Though it was also the thing that kept him away on the other Sundays. He preferred not to think about how he would square things with God if he ever shot someone. He preferred not to explain to God that one of his cherished, precious lives was worth only fifty-nine dollars.

So now John knew about tired, and he knew about disappointment, too, if disappointment was the word for churning with bitterness at your failures. John didn't want the blood of a young fool on his hands, so now he exerted all his efforts to keeping his rage under control. Everyone at work gulped pots of black coffee as a matter of course, but for John it was the key to basic functioning, and an insufficient one at that. The coffee took the edge off his sleepiness, but it also removed the soft lining from his anger. It was always waiting right there on the surface, ready to drown anything that touched it.

It screamed inside him even when he went home. He could only sleep so well during the day in an old, thin house occupied by his four lively ladies. He didn't want to lose his shit at them, so he didn't talk to them very much. John sipped his beer and thought about Lily back in their crusty first apartment, laughing her outrageous laugh and melting into his arms. Now his arms rested on the sticky black bar top, taunting him in their emptiness. Mel used to look at him like he was her hero, and that used to carry him through the long hours at work. Mel didn't look at him like that anymore. Bailey and Jessie never had.

He hated his job, hated busting up petty criminals, hated the criminals for being so petty. He could feel his girls slipping away, and there he was dedicating all his time to something he didn't believe in anymore. Most guys he arrested ended up back out on the streets in a few days or months without the faintest idea of how to turn their lives around. But his friends were still convicted about their careers, showing up to work each day ready to play action hero and rid the world of marijuana users and guys who got in knife fights.

One day when they were seniors, Jude had flagged John down after practice. Jude was QB, John was left tackle, and neither was getting scouted. As their embarrassment of a season dragged on, John sank deeper into a state of silent panic, realizing his plan for a college scholarship had only ever been a foolish dream. But Jude, as usual, was pivoting. Jude's hair was plastered to his head in a helmet shape and his eyes crinkled up in excitement as he said the words that would shape both of their lives: "We should join the Marines."

John was often unenthusiastic about Jude's ideas, but this one lit a fire in his soul. He wanted to get out of Conrad, sure, but more than that, he wanted to protect his country and the people in it. That was why Jude said they should join. But as time went on, John thought the real reason Jude wanted to be a Marine was that he might get an excuse to hurt someone.

When his enlistment was up, John became a police officer because he thought it was a way he could still protect people without leaving his family all the time. He'd met Lily during year three and the long distance was killing him. But it turned out that even though he now lived under the same roof as his girls, he occupied a desert island they could never visit. And a lot of the other cops were like Jude. They weren't there to serve. They were there to dominate.

And there was Jude walking through the door.

"Hey buddy!" he said. "Already got going huh? Next one's on me!" He motioned to Owen at the bar for two more beers. "And get me a shot of Jack, I gotta catch up!"

John bristled in annoyance. This wasn't a high school party. They went through this pantomime of grabbing a casual beer together every few weeks, but no beer was casual for Jude. Not that that was any of John's business.

"How's the family?" said Jude.

"Fine," said John. "Yours?"

"Oh, fine. Kids are crazy like always."

John supplied a chuckle.

"I took the school kids to DC on Thursday for the March. Did Mel's school set up a trip?"

"Nope," said John, taking a sip.

"Figures. Well, we had a good time, really powerful experience to be using our first amendment rights. I gave Dom the money and he nearly fuckin' lost it, but it's all good, we got it back."

"The money?"

"Oh, I charged the kids some money for gas and food. Plus a little extra, haha!"

John had once been a good cop because his instincts were powerful. His gut never lied to him. People revealed so much without realizing it, and John had always been good at snatching up these hints. But once he was a cop, this ability brought him much more work and sometimes put him in danger. So he had stopped pushing. And now he pursued a different line of questioning.

"How's Tammy?"

Jude snorted. "Same as ever. We had hot dogs or chicken nuggets for dinner every night this week. Meanwhile she and Karen and our neighbor have this little walking club going that they do every fucking day."

John was always dismayed at the way Jude never wanted Tammy to enjoy herself. John thought the way Tammy handled their lives was rather impressive. When he'd first met her, he had been surprised that Jude had pursued such an intelligent and thoughtful girl—all throughout high school he'd dated one vapid bimbo after another. John had been glad, thinking Tammy would get along with Lily. They'd gotten along famously at first, but Jude didn't like that, and Lily didn't like Jude. Over time, Tammy and Lily's friendship had faded away, and Jude had launched a steady and successful campaign to dim Tammy's light. With each passing year John and Jude spent less time with each other's families and more time next to each other at this bar.

Jude was already on his second beer. "So now we're getting ready to plan a dance for the school. It's good to give the kids something wholesome to do, keep them out of trouble."

It was hard to reconcile Jude in his new role as the upstanding Catholic school leader with the boy who'd once professed a goal of nailing every girl in their high school. Then a pair of younger ladies came up to order, and Jude took a long sip of his beer while staring openly at their boobs. Now *that* was the Jude he knew.

Jude tried to call John's attention to the ladies, but he changed the subject. "Business good?"

Jude moved his head noncommittally. "'S fine. I've got Dom and Isaac working for us sometimes. Abe keeps trying to 'differentiate our model' because he thinks the housing crash is going to fuck us up."

John took a sip of his beer and searched his sieve brain for an answer to this. Abe had been an emotional kid who grew up to be a blustering man. He'd never stopped trying to prove himself to Jude, but when John looked back on their lives, the way they'd treated Abe at times was appalling. He felt like such a dick about some of that stuff now. John and Lily had spent a few painful nights with their calculator since the housing crash, and he thought it was probably wise of Abe to consider how it might affect them.

Every time he met Jude for a beer, he was annoyed with his attitude and troubled by the continued presence of that unshakable sneakiness. But he kept coming back because this was the ugly truth: No matter how bad John felt about his own shortcomings as a father and husband, he always thought he was doing a better job than Jude.

John pushed back his beer bottle and finished his water. He stood up and patted Jude on the shoulder. "Gotta go," he said.

"Are you serious?" said Jude. "I just got here, man!" But he was already walking out the door. Jude would keep drinking and drinking and then drive himself home, and John didn't want to know about that.

Spring 2009

1

From: icanseeclearynow@aol.com
Hey I just got off the phone with Chris and I have some questions.

1. *Are you really having a school dance?*
2. *Is it really a fundraiser? Or is it a FUN raiser*
3. *Is it really Christian music only.*
4. *Who are you taking!?!*

From: bluebirdy@aol.com
The real question is why are you and Chris talking about my school dance??

1. *Yes, except the adults refer to it as a "ball."*
2. *It will definitely not be a FUN raiser. I don't know how many funds it will raise either. A bunch of the adults are annoyed with each other because some of them want the school to be parochial and some want it to be independent. So I think they're distracting themselves from that by going crazy over the ball instead.*
3. *Country music is also allowed. But the music must be between 30 and 50 beats per minute, I kid you not.*
4. *I'm not taking anyone. Even if I knew anyone outside of school I wanted to bring, all guests must be homeschooled and willing to pay an extra $50 on top of the regular ticket price!!! Dad was like "Oh, are they trying to make money off new recruits?" and Mom was like "no!!! they just want to make sure any guests are nice!!"*

Tomorrow, we have an assembly to learn how to dance. Can't wait!!!

DURING LAST PERIOD THE next day, Birdy went to the lunch room to find all the tables pushed to the side and Mrs. Strabinski and Mrs. Amon standing eagerly in the empty space.

"We really want you all to have the best time at the ball," said Mrs. Strabinski, tossing her long, sweaty grey ponytail behind her back. "So we thought we'd teach you a few dance moves before the big night!" She smiled at Olivia like this was great news. Olivia looked worried.

Some parents saw the dance not only as a fundraiser, but also as an opportunity to orchestrate a dozen chaste relationships that would appreciate into marriages within 5-8 years. To give the relationships pure origins, circumstances had to be perfect. There must be dancing, and it must be classy. Music must be slow, but not *that* slow. Girls must be properly covered, yet sufficiently feminine—no pants, but also no dresses that reminded anyone about breasts or thighs. Parents must provide snacks that were not too wasteful, not too commercial, and did not create choking or caffeination hazards. Boys, apparently, just had to get there.

"Oh and before I forget, as a special treat, we decided to go ahead and include rock music at the ball!" said Mrs. Strabinski.

"Christian rock only," Mrs. Amon added quickly. Dominic and Birdy exchanged pained glances.

The ladies had not brought their Christian rock music along with them, so they proceeded to demonstrate several ballroom dancing styles in silence. Then it was the kids' turn to mimic them, partnerless. After forty minutes, Mrs. Strabinski put them out of their misery.

"Practice these moves at home so you'll be all ready for the ball!" she said, yanking at the neck of her pink floral turtleneck. "We just want you all to have a great time! At the dance, you can try these moves out with each other!"

"But make sure to leave room for the Holy Spirit," said Mrs. Amon.

"Can't the Holy Spirit be any size he wants?" Birdy asked innocently.

Mrs. Strabinski looked startled and Mrs. Amon looked scandalized, but Dominic laughed and held out his hand for a high five. Birdy grinned and gave it. Helpfully, the school bell rang at this moment, and Dominic tilted his head towards the door. "Come on, Birdy, you can help me get the kids in the car."

They walked down the hall together. "How's the new job?" Dominic asked.

"It's okay," said Birdy. "My boss is really mean." In February, she had been hired at a newly-built restaurant that was determined to convince its guests they were dining at a Zagat favorite, rather than a fast-food establishment. When responding to thanks, Birdy and her colleagues were required to use the phrase "my pleasure" in place of the gauche "you're welcome." This response soon solidified into a reflex that haunted Birdy's private life, elevating her manners to an incongruent fanciness for the next five years. In the not-too-distant future, this quick service chain would gain widespread notoriety for being either pro- or anti-families, depending on your perspective. For now, it was notorious merely for its polite employees and delicious chicken sandwiches.

"What does he do?"

"He yells at me if I don't smile. Which makes me feel even less like smiling."

"Well, he shouldn't yell at you! But you do have a nice smile."

Birdy's insides did something that resembled Mrs. Strabinski's cha-cha, but she ignored it. "It's all good," she said, "I get a free meal every shift, and it'll help me pay for college. And a dress." She stepped onto the curb and balanced along it. It was the first day she had gone jacketless in months, and the sun was warm on her arms.

"So you're going to the ball?" Dominic asked.

"Yeah, I'm not sure how fun it'll be, but I might as well go."

"Why don't you think it'll be fun?" he said.

"Um... there isn't really anyone I want to go with, and the music sounds like it will be very stupid? It'll be fun to see everyone all dressed up though."

He stopped and looked at her. "You're funny," he said.

"How so?" She didn't stop her journey along the narrow curb.

"There's no one you want to go with? No one? You must like someone."

"Nope." She kept her eyes in front of her. "And are you bringing Rachel?"

Dominic smiled. "Unofficially, yes."

"What does that mean?"

"Well... you know my parents. I'd rather not make a big deal of it. I really like her though. So we're going to meet there."

Birdy smiled at him, stumbling off the curb. "That's great!"

Dominic kept staring. "Yeah?"

"Yeah!" Her smile hurt. She racked her brains for something to say. "You can ask her to slow dance to "Shout to the North!""

He laughed. "I have a plan to get some better music in. Don't tell."

"I won't," she said, more resignedly than she'd intended.

Dominic stepped closer. "I know you won't. You're good at keeping a secret. Thanks."

Just then, a bloodcurdling howl rose from the graveyard. Dominic and Birdy said "Hannah," and rushed over. Hannah had scraped her knee on the headstone of a woman who had died in 1898. Dominic pulled a Band-aid and a cleaning pad from his wallet and got to work. Birdy watched him patch up Hannah's wound as her sweet giggle tinkled through the air. *He can be so good sometimes. Maybe someday—*she didn't let herself finish the thought. For there was Rachel, looking at Dominic with an adoration Birdy prayed had never graced her own face. Dominic looked at Rachel and winked, and Birdy turned her attention to the resting place of George McDonough, b. 1830, d. 1864. She contemplated his short lifespan as Dominic's wink replayed in her head. *Not for me,* she reminded herself. *Not mine.*

The next day, Birdy hid in a bathroom stall fielding texts from Mel. At their most recent sleepover, under the influence of the Admiral, Mel confessed she was having a crisis. She had realized she liked Vince, shocking no one but herself. Mel was not one to hold her tongue, but she was worried she would ruin their friendship if she told him how she felt. As a result, she was now bombarding Birdy with texts outlining reasons why Vince may or may not feel the same. Birdy was laughing and typing a reply about how positive she was that Vince did like Mel, when the bathroom door opened.

"Okay," said Rachel's voice, "I'm so excited. Last night, my dad and Mr. Doppelski talked on the phone."

"Ooh, what did they talk about?" squealed Margaret.

"Well, they agreed to let me and Dominic court! My dad invited Mr. Doppelski over for a beer but he can't make it for a few weekends, he's so busy. But sometime over the summer, we're going to all get together and really talk about our intentions for each other. I can just feel God's hand in this, it's so powerful."

"Oooh, I'm so excited for youuu!" moaned Margaret.

"And he said he would be okay with Dominic and me meeting each other at the ball and spending a lot of time together there."

"Ooooh, how romantic!" sighed Margaret.

"Dominic is so sweet. He says he's so happy just holding my hand. He says he's always wanted his first kiss to be really special and he hopes it'll be with me someday!"

"Oooooh, he's the nicest guy!" cheered Margaret.

Birdy eyed the toilet, wondering if it could hold all the vomit she thought she might produce.

SAT prep class was on hiatus while Mrs. Strabinski was planning the ball, which left Thursdays free for soccer. Birdy arrived at the field that afternoon to find Michael, Isaac, and Dominic doing backflips off Michael's Corolla. The spring league was pitifully small, and despite the good weather, almost no one showed up. After half an hour, Beth biked off to her new job at the movie theater, and the boys left to get snacks at 7-Eleven. Kelly had just gotten her driver's license and had brought Mel with her.

"Want a ride home, Birdy?" said Kelly, wagging her keys.

"That's okay," said Birdy, "It's so nice out I actually want to walk."

"There might be some fireflies out for you to collect!" said Mel in mock excitement.

"Well, actually, most fireflies are nocturnal," said Birdy in a nerdy voice, pushing imaginary glasses up the bridge of her nose. From the corner of her eye, she saw Dominic wandering over to them.

"What happened to getting snacks?" called Mel.

"It's so nice out, I decided to just walk home," said Dominic, smiling at Birdy. "What's everyone up to now?"

"Well, we have a history project due tomorrow, so we need to go finish that," said Kelly, gesturing at herself and Mel. "How about you guys?"

"I have to go dress shopping with my mom. Should be real fun," said Birdy.

"Ooooh, for the ball?" said Mel poshly.

"Yeah," said Birdy. "Do you have your prom dress yet?"

"Not yet," said Mel, "I think we're going shopping sometime this weekend if you want to come! Do you know if you can come to prom yet?"

St. Monica's "prom" was another generously named dance taking place in the springtime. St. Monica's was trying to raise money for a new library, so like Divine Mercy it was desperate for outside paying guests.

"Beth's coming," Mel continued, "and so is Dominic!"

"Yeah, he asked Angela Prune," Kelly snickered. "She told us all about it the next day in English class. She's very into you."

What?

Birdy looked at Dominic, who did not betray one hint of concern. "Oh yeah, I know she is."

"So," said Mel, "it's going to be really fun. Well, actually, it might suck, so you should come so it can be more fun."

Birdy considered. "Well, I will already have a dress, I guess..."

"Tell Birdy she needs to come!" said Kelly to Dominic.

Dominic just shrugged. Kelly's phone buzzed. She flipped it open and started walking backwards as she read. "Oh, Mel, we need to stop at Food Lion on the way home, my mom desperately needs more lemons apparently...." Mel and Kelly left to acquire their citruses, and Birdy looked at Dominic, who was sizing up the tree in front of him.

"Dom?"

He made no sign of having heard, and instead leapt up onto a limb.

"Dom."

He flipped upside down, hooking his legs onto the branch.

"Dominic!"

"What?" he said from upside down.

"Are you... are you going to St. Monica's prom with Angela?"

"Yeah, you just heard about that, didn't you?"

"Does..." her stomach ached. "Does... Rachel know about that?"

"Why does that matter?"

"Well..."

"Look, I'm 17. I don't want to tie myself down to one girl."

"Yeah, it's just..."

He dismounted from the tree, an ugly look on his face.

"Not everyone is a saint like you, Birdy. Some people like to have fun. Besides, the whole point of courtship is so things don't get too serious. And it's none of your business anyway. Don't you have to go shopping now?" He shoved his hands in his pockets and stalked away to the path.

Birdy turned her back on him and faced the empty fields, kicking herself. Maybe she had been out of line. She was catching on to the fact that not everyone got as dedicated to their crushes as she did. And Dominic had asked Angela to the dance, not to marry him. But she had heard Rachel's rapture in the bathroom. Dominic may not take their relationship seriously, but Rachel certainly did.

Now she had the words to explain why the whole courtship thing had always irked her so deeply. "It's a trap," she said to the empty field. For an innocent minded person like Rachel, courtship was a safe and romantic pathway to marriage. But someone as unbothered and opportunistic as Dominic could easily compartmentalize it, turning it not into an alternative, but an addition, to regular dating. It didn't seem right to tout ideals of respect and mutual goodwill, only to then use it as an excuse for duplicitous behavior.

But the last time she had gotten involved in Dominic's love life, she had lost her best friend. She could see now that Mary's family had been even more dysfunctional than she'd realized. Birdy had been on a mission to help her friends, but she'd brought her own baggage along for the ride, and in the end, her help had made everything worse. So she decided to let Dominic suffer his consequences alone this time.

Stay out of it, she told herself as she turned and headed for the path. *This is not your problem.*

Birdy had never yet enjoyed a shopping trip whose objective was to acquire formal attire, and preparing for the dance was no exception. She and Mom took a brief but agonizing trip to Goodwill in search of the mythical thrift store find that was both affordable and dazzling. Mom was a dedicated subscriber to this legend, while Birdy was a staunch skeptic. Within moments it was apparent that there were no diamonds to be found in the rough. Mom would have made them stay longer on principle, but the smell of cigarette smoke in the air was bothering her, so Birdy won that round. They left and drove 45 minutes to the nearest Kohls. Birdy tried on a handful of options and found one that was that was modest enough, flattering enough, and cheap enough. It was dark green, its straps were wide but not in a weird way, and it would look fine with a bra and shoes she already had. Mom kept calling it a cocktail dress. Birdy internally recoiled at this phrase, but knew better than to insult Mom's dress terminology at this tense point in the game.

Once they had found the dress, Mom remembered she needed to shop for some new underwear and insisted that Birdy allow her to do this in privacy. Birdy was happy for some moments alone and brought a few more things to the dressing room. Most were too big or too small or too much exactly like clothes she already had. Then she tried on a blue tank top. It would not have passed muster at the dance. It didn't conceal her bra straps, it didn't hide her cleavage. And she wanted it.

Mom looked at it in the checkout line and sighed, but said nothing. For once, the fight had gone out of her, and besides, Birdy was paying. They went to McDonald's and instituted a cease-fire over fries, hamburgers, and chocolate chip cookies.

When they got home, Mom grabbed a quilt and a book in one motion and crashed on the couch beside Dad. Birdy went upstairs. Chris was shut in his room. Birdy logged onto Facebook to find it had once again updated its format. Every time this happened, she got an invitation from someone imploring her to join a group protesting the change. Birdy rejected Margaret's latest appeal and fiddled with her toenail polish as she scrolled the new timeline.

Pop. Isaac's name flashed in a chat window at the bottom of the screen.

Isaac: hey beautiful

Her stomach dropped in alarm, but before she could respond with a casual "lol ok" he wrote back again

Isaac: haha jk

Isaac: so what's up?

Birdy: Haha nothing much, how were your snacks?

Isaac: good haha

Isaac: we went hiking after, it was fun

Birdy: Cool, where did you go?

Isaac: rosehill mountain

Birdy: Oh I love it there!

Isaac: Yeah Dom came with us and brought Angela the slut lol

Okay... don't acknowledge that.

Isaac: he tripped got a huge gash on his arm and was bleeding everywhere lol

It was tempting to join in disparaging Dominic, but Birdy opted for redirection.

Birdy: Well I had to go shopping with my mom, I think hiking would be better

Isaac: oh right dress shopping right?

Isaac: do you want to go to the ball with me?

Birdy: Yeah haha

Oh, fuck. Oh fuck. Fuck fuck fuck. She'd sent her response about dress shopping one terrible second too late. Birdy's face flamed as she stared at the screen, her mistake blazing back at her.

It wasn't that she didn't want to go with Isaac. It was just that she didn't want to *go with him.* Dominic hadn't teased them in so long that she'd almost forgotten about his supposed crush, but if Isaac also carried the wound of unreturned feelings, she didn't want to dump salt in it.

Isaac: Awesome

Shit shit shit. Her heart hammered so hard it made her fingers shake. They exchanged a few more messages before she made an excuse and signed off. Then she threw herself into bed.

You have to tell him you just want to go as friends, she told herself sternly. *You can't treat him like Dominic treats people. But he probably doesn't even like you anyway! He probably likes Olivia or something!* She nodded and burritoed herself into her blankets. Tomorrow she would catch Isaac first thing and make sure they were on the same page.

She was finally drifting off when a horrid thought yanked her back awake.

I never told Isaac I was going dress shopping.

2

BIRDY'S HEART POUNDED ALL night. Though she applied a copious helping of deodorant in the morning, she could smell her sweat as she got out of the car at Divine Mercy. Her knees shook as she walked up to the building. *Please, God, just let me see Isaac first.*

She saw Dominic first. He was waiting by the door. "Birdy!" he practically sang as he leapt in her path, "I heard Isaac finally made a move!" He swept her up and swung her around in a circle as though congratulating her for a lifetime achievement. Her cheek mushed against his, and her arms hung limp by her sides. She drew away from him and looked at his arms, straining against the sleeves of his polo. No gashes.

Fred, Josh, and Michael clustered behind Dominic, snickering. Birdy registered her hatred for them in an empty way, then turned her attention back to Dominic. Dominic's knucklehead groupies thought it was just a joke, it *seemed* like just a joke. But ever since the March for Life, things had been happy between them, not just friendly but warm and close. And then yesterday, she'd ventured an admonishment, and he'd been angry at her. His little joke felt like a betrayal, or worse, a punishment.

Everything she wanted to say to Dominic felt stuck inside her, blocked by a preemptive lump in her throat. If she said anything serious it would come out angry and wet, seemingly disproportionate to the situation. Instead, she pinned a small smile on her face.

"You're hilarious. Look how hard I'm laughing."

"Did you get a nice dress? Isaac is *really* looking forward to seeing what you wear." The glee on Dominic's face was appropriate for birthdays, weddings, and Christmas only.

"Shut up, I know it was you," she said, stepping around him.

"She said yes! Oh, it's so beautiful," she heard him saying to the other guys as she walked down to the locker room.

Isaac was already in there, flipping his phone open and shut.

Shit. Birdy's carefully worded speech vanished from her mind. "Isaac, um, I'm really sorry, um, so Dominic did something, he pretended to be you and asked me to the dance, and then I said yes because I was trying to say yes about something else you said, I mean that he said, and it's not that I wouldn't go with you to the dance, I still would, but like, as friends? But you didn't actually ask me so we don't have to go together—like we could, if you wanted to, but as friends, but—"

Isaac smiled and motioned his hand to cut off her babble. "Don't worry," he said, "I found out like two minutes after it happened. Let's not make it a weird date thing. Let's just hang out at the dance like we would have anyway."

Birdy nearly fainted with relief. "That sounds perfect." Then she sighed and leaned against the wall next to Isaac. With him, she was able to ask the question that was stuck inside her before. "What did he *do* that for?" She couldn't keep the anguish from her voice.

Isaac ground his toe against the linoleum. "Well, I know he was pissed you found out he's going to the St. Monica's dance with Angela while he's also stringing Rachel along. And on top of that he hates me and likes to fuck with my life."

"He hates you? I mean I know he can be a jerk to you but I didn't think..."

She trailed off at the sight of Isaac's solemn face. He glanced out the door; the hallway was now empty. His next words tore out of him.

"Well, you two have all kinds of weirdness between you. And he hates me because he thinks either I like you... or that I... don't... don't like girls at all."

Birdy swallowed. "Which one is it?"

Isaac's voice sounded like his throat was raw. "I wish I liked you, Birdy. I'd give anything to like you. But I think..." His eyes were huge, willing her to understand.

She'd been afraid to ever do it before, but now Birdy put her arm around his shoulder. "It's okay, it's okay. I won't tell. It doesn't matter to me. I love you. It's okay," she murmured, as Isaac steadied himself with shaking breaths.

BIRDY TALKED AS LITTLE as possible for the rest of the day. She had often wondered if Dominic secretly despised her, and this felt like proof he did. She could feel his eyes on her every time their paths crossed, but she didn't look at him once.

At the end of the day, he grabbed her shoulder. "Birdy, hey—"

She wrenched away from him. "We need to talk soon." She could see it had dawned upon him that she did not, in fact, think he was hilarious.

"What is it?" he said, "You can talk to me." Fred, apparently Dominic's best friend now, giggled beside him.

"No, I can't," Birdy said. "Not now. Later."

"Ooooooh," said Fred. Dominic glanced at him, perhaps re-thinking his choice of crony.

"See ya," said Birdy.

Birdy's stomach was so full of butterflies she couldn't eat much of her dinner. All through that evening, she made her plan. Dominic clearly had a problem recognizing how he made other people feel. This was fascinating to Birdy, who felt like almost everything she did, or didn't do, was filtered through her desire not to hurt anyone. Paradoxically, Dominic was also capable of making people so happy—here she avoided acknowledging that she was people—so maybe he just needed a nudge in the right direction.

There was no way the parents could find out about what had happened. Hers would freak out, for sure, and she knew by now that despite their saintlike status, the Doppelskis were covering up a lot of weird shit, Mr. Doppelski himself being the primary secret. With a dad like that, who wouldn't be a little confused about kindness? She didn't want to let Mr. Doppelski's unpredictable temper into the situation. And she didn't want Isaac to get dragged into it either.

Mom and Dad left early Saturday morning to get lunch with Peter, a conveniently timed milestone that had kept Mom distracted during the past 24 hours. Birdy lay awake listening to the Doppelskis' lawn mower. It always took Dominic an hour to get through the mowing before he switched to the weedwhacker. Birdy knew he took out-sized pleasure in conquering the ancient weedwhacker each week, that there was always a long space between when the lawn mower shut off and the weedwhacker finally started buzzing. When 55 minutes had passed, Birdy left her house. She was wearing her new, bright blue tank top.

He was shutting off the lawn mower when she walked up behind him. Never one to miss an opportunity to be shirtless, he was wiping his bare chest with the discarded garment. Then he shoved it in his back pocket and stretched. For once he was going through these motions without trying to impress anyone, but Birdy was watching. She gulped, then spoke.

"Dominic."

He whirled around, and his eyes flashed up and down her body. He went slackjawed. "Birdy!" Then he remembered he was supposed to be penitent. "Birdy. I'm so sorry. For everything that I've done."

Birdy couldn't make herself smile back at him, hated him for the earnest hand he had placed on his heart.

"I need to talk to you." Her voice lost steam with every word.

Something flashed on his face—concern for her, or maybe just annoyance that this wasn't over already. "Sure, sure, of course."

"You... you can't do things like this."

Birdy was determined to deliver a magnificent speech that would change him forever. He would be transformed by her intelligence, ferocity, and possibly even her beauty. He would understand how wrong he had been, he would apologize, and she could continue to give him a place in her life. But her plan hit an immediate snag. She'd forgotten that she wasn't a powerful orator, she was just a stupid sixteen-year-old girl, desperately in love with the idiot next door.

Dominic's expression was so solemn and sincere that it had to be fake. The absurdity of this registered as amusing somewhere in her brain, but her throat ached. In the sunlight, his brown eyes glowed gold.

"When you do things... things have consequences. You can't just... do whatever you want and hurt people."

"You're right, Birdy, I'm so sorry. Thank you for setting me straight." His words were polished, but the plain boredom on his face cut her parachute strings, because there it was. He didn't give a shit. He didn't want her advice or guidance. That was why he had pulled his stupid prank in the first place.

In spite of, as he put it, everything he'd done, Birdy still thought of Dominic as her friend. She'd kept his secrets, smiled by as he loved other girls, even helped him study, arranging herself so even if she couldn't have him, she would still matter to him. Now, in a thunderclap of humiliation, she saw that for all her endless analysis and devotion, she barely knew him, and he had never returned a fraction of her caring.

Why would it be so funny for someone to like me? Why do you care so much who Isaac is into? Why can't you just leave me alone? Why?

Her questions zipped around her brain, but she couldn't talk. Her windpipe crumpled and heat prickled behind her eyes. If she said one more word, she would cry, and that would sever the final fraying threads of her pride. She was never going to be with Dominic. She preferred he didn't know how just how deeply he'd hurt her.

"Okay," she croaked. He reached out an arm to hug her, and she lamely accepted.

"Sorry I'm kinda sweaty," he said, and she chuckled like there was nothing remarkable about being so close to his muscular torso. She didn't look at him as she pivoted for the street.

"Have a nice weekend," he called as she walked away. She couldn't answer over the huge lump in her throat.

The blacktop radiated heat as she walked back up Victoria Street. The thick air made it hard to breathe and she could feel her hair expanding from her scalp like her mounting hatred for herself. She'd had a chance to tell him off for everything, and he'd turned her into jelly. He was probably back to thinking about the weed-whacker, as if that was his biggest problem. But although the tears were now pouring down her face, a small, evil part inside of her smiled. He had liked her shirt.

3

TWO WEEKS LATER, Birdy was ready for the dance. The dress was fine. She didn't love it, she didn't hate it, and it wouldn't get her kicked out of the dance, although that might be nice. After curling her hair badly, she sat on her bed to gather herself.

Birdy had spent the past fortnight playing back her conversation with Dominic, then responding to each replay with visions of how it could have been so much better:

Dominic, it's really hard when you like someone who doesn't like you back. I don't like Isaac that way, but I really care about him as a friend and don't want to be part of hurting him like that.

Oh, Birdy, that makes so much sense, you're right. But... who do you like that doesn't like you back?

It doesn't matter... because I don't trust him.

Then she would turn away, and the truth would dawn on him, and he would realize how foolish he'd been...

Ugh. She shoved her face into her pillow in an attempt to suffocate her irritating imagination. Then she sprang out of bed, fixed the makeup she'd just ruined, and pounded downstairs, trying to leave all her stupidity back in her room.

Mom squealed about how her baby had grown up, hoisted her neckline higher, and told her to have an absolute blast. Dad told her she looked beautiful, drove her to St. Paul's, and mercifully asked nothing about who she would be dancing with. Full of equal parts dread and hope, Birdy walked into the church hall for her first dance.

Between Beth's atheism and the disaster surrounding Mary's move, Birdy had stopped attending both Songs and Teens and Praise Night, so she had not seen the church hall in some time. The Divine Mercy parents had outdone themselves, which is to say, they had erected a single balloon arch in the school colors of navy and khaki. Never had there ever been a more solemn balloon arch. Birdy deposited a bag of popcorn on the snack table, which appeared to be the same one they used at Songs and Teens. The popcorn wasn't technically allowed, but it had cost one dollar, and she knew people would eat it.

George Strait crooned from the speakers. A crowd was already amassing—a crowd by Divine Mercy standards, anyway. The Faduccis and Herons had tapped into a vein of Pennsylvanian homeschoolers who were eager for a night out. Dominic stood in the far corner holding Rachel's hand, talking animatedly to a group of her enchanted friends. Rachel's hair was piled high and she wore a sky blue gown and long white gloves that made her look like Cinderella. On someone else it would have looked cheesy, but Rachel was gorgeous.

Birdy looked around the rest of the room. Margaret and Polly were comparing their dresses. They had also gone for the old-fashioned look, but their style was more colonial than regal. Gabby stood beside them looking pretty in a knee-length pink dress—possibly another cocktail dress. Her short hair was curled and a touch of makeup brought her brown eyes to life. Birdy started walking over, but Fred cut in front of her wearing a proud smile and a stiff tie.

"Good evening," he said.

"Hi Fred," said Birdy. Fred's hair was parted severely down the middle. He extended a grand hand and opened his mouth, but Isaac appeared beside him.

"Wanna dance?"

"Yes," Birdy said gratefully, and they hurried off to the dance floor.

Isaac was wearing a red tie and had combed his hair. "You look nice," he said.

"Thanks, so do you!" Birdy answered.

"You must really like me to have gotten so dressed up for our date," Isaac said.

Birdy laughed. "Only the best for you!"

Fred managed to ask her to dance to the next song, which was fast enough to be fun. She was still grateful when it was over. She finally found Gabby, who had just escaped from a dance with Josh, and they pledged to stick together, hoping their numbers would discourage additional approaches by their classmates.

The collective enthusiasm soon waned. The hordes of girls began segregating from the few boys. Birdy saw Rachel go to the bathroom with her purse and her group of friends, probably to get five sets of the same mirror pictures on five separate digital cameras. When she was gone, Dominic took something out of his pocket and strolled over to the table where the speakers were. Isaac left in pursuit of cookies, and Birdy and Gabby stood talking to Michael and Gabby's friend Sophie.

Acoustic guitar interrupted the peppy praise song, and heads perked up in confusion or recognition. "You and Me" by Lifehouse was coming over the speakers.

"I love this song!" said Birdy.

"Me too," said Gabby.

"It was only supposed to be country and Christian!" Margaret whined from somewhere behind them.

Birdy craned around to observe the muted pandemonium. Someone must have alerted Mrs. Amon that the singer's lyrics were not directed at Jesus, because she was charging toward the speaker table, determined to halt this rubbish as soon as she could figure out where it was coming from.

When Birdy turned back around, Dominic was in front of her.

They had avoided each other at school, so she hadn't been this near him since that morning at his house. He seemed taller already. His shoulders pushed at the seams of his white church shirt. It was too small, but he had compensated by rolling up his sleeves. Dominic didn't greet her with his usual easy grin, or even with the empty stare he had drilled her with for the past two weeks. Instead, he smiled gently and held out his hand. She took it, and he led her to the floor.

He turned to face her and put his free hand on her waist, pulling her to his chest. Her hand shook as she placed it on his firm shoulder and willed herself not to drench him in sweat. He held still for a moment, then started in a confident box step. He had been paying attention to the lessons.

Dominic's hand was rough, and holding it felt like a victory. She hated herself for that, but she didn't fully believe she was holding it at all. This was exactly the sort of scenario she would create in her head as she lay alone at night, or scribble in one of her secret notebooks; invented proof that he felt something romantic for her, that he had ever spent an ounce of forethought on her. In fact, it was eerily similar to an episode of *Smallville* she and Chris had watched last week. *Am I making this up?*

Reality inserted itself when she stepped on his foot. No, unless she was so masochistic that even the fantasy version of herself was a complete spaz, this was actually happening. Dominic lifted her arm, and her nerves ignited, but his confidence told her what to do. Her skirt twirled around her as she spun, and then she was facing him again.

They kept repeating the routine, box-step-box-step-box-step-twirl, and Birdy never looked at him because she thought it might finally kill her. Instead, she concentrated on his chest, so close she yearned to rest her cheek on it, and hoped he couldn't feel how hard she was shaking. They remained alone on the floor. The song was about feelings the teenagers were supposed to be too young and holy to have. The lyrics articulated her desire and confusion so perfectly it was annoying. Was he making peace, or twisting the knife? And where was Rachel?

Come on, Birdy told herself. *It's just a dance.* If only she could believe her own lie.

Mrs. Amon had had no luck with the speakers and was now scooching on her knees around the perimeter of the table, hunting for clues. Birdy thought if she could muster some friendly banter, then this would stop being so weird. She glanced up to make a crack about Mrs. Amon, but the joke died in her throat. His gaze was pointed above her head, his smile mean. Was she a prize, or a joke? The traitorous burn rose behind her eyes, and she swallowed it away.

The song ended and their eyes met at last. She stared at him as he smiled, bowed and left without one word.

Birdy scurried back to her friends. Isaac's mission had been successful. "Um... Here's some cookies," he said, holding out an entire tray. She took three so she wouldn't have to talk. Her hands still shook. Mrs. Amon finally disconnected the rogue iPod responsible for the secular disruption, and Matt Maher interrupted Rihanna's request that she please not stop the music.

On the other side of the room, Dominic embraced the radiant Rachel, who had just returned from the bathroom.

4

ON WEDNESDAY, MOM DROPPED Birdy at Mel's house after school. They changed out of their uniforms and then stretched out on the side porch hammock, eating Cheetos and drinking Pepsi.

"So, how was the ball? Any cute boys?" Mel asked.

"Um, no," Birdy laughed.

"Ready for St. Monica's?"

"Yes!" said Birdy. "Will there be any cute boys?"

"No," said Mel.

Birdy waited until Mel was taking a sip of her soda before saying "I kissed Isaac." She cracked up as Mel spluttered her soda out of her nose and shrieked.

"WHAT HAPPENED?!"

Birdy kept laughing. "It was dumb. We don't actually like each other. We were just outside at the dance and decided to try it."

As Birdy had scarfed cookies after her weird dance with Dominic, Michael had tapped Isaac on the shoulder. "Pink dress or green dress?" he said, pointing to a cluster of girls on the other side of the room. Isaac sized them up and said "Green." Michael sauntered forward, perhaps emboldened by his new backflipping skills, and was soon dancing with the girl in green. Dominic and Rachel waltzed chastely beside them, and Birdy left to catch her breath outside. Isaac joined her on the balcony a few minutes later.

"You okay?" he said.

"Yeah, fine, why?" she said at lightspeed. He gave her a knowing glance.

"Look, we've established we definitely don't like each other, right?" said Isaac.

Birdy snorted. "Yes, I think I'm clear on that.

"Well...do you want me to kiss you?"

Birdy gasped and then choked on her own spit and was grateful for the subsequent coughing fit as she tried to think of what to say. Isaac shot her a half grin and patted her on the back, edging closer.

"Just hear me out. We could piss Dominic off and get a practice round out of the way for... when we actually... like someone."

The thought of kissing Isaac was unappealing. But she did love to check outstanding items off her list. And she did want to piss Dominic off.

"He was watching you when you left just now," Isaac added. His hand was now on her shoulder, the one further from him. Birdy grimaced and pressed a fingernail into the balcony.

"I dare you," he said, as though playing his trump card. Which he was. In the last sixteen years, Birdy had had no better chance at kissing a boy, and had no better prospects in sight. If she went through with this, it would be absolutely nothing like the way she had imagined her first kiss. But, having tried to murder her imagination mere hours ago, she was okay with that. She felt reckless, and was also sick of being someone who considered it reckless to kiss a friend on a dare.

Birdy shrugged. "Well... okay. Sure." *Just what you always wanted to say before your first kiss.*

They leaned toward each other. Isaac had also been growing lately; Birdy could see straight up his nostrils and figured this was why people closed their eyes. They were both tilting their heads the same way, and she corrected course before their lips met. Their teeth knocked together. He tasted like freezing cold Sprite. They bounced apart, magnets of the same pole.

He extended his hand in a comradely sort of way and they shook, laughing. "That was so romantic," said Birdy.

"I knew you wouldn't turn down a dare."

Back on the porch, Mel was still awestruck. "I'm honestly shocked at you," Mel said. "I thought you were going to like wait for marriage to kiss or something."

This stung, but in truth, Birdy did feel a bit guilty about the whole thing. She kept telling herself kissing was no big deal and it was better to practice on someone she didn't care about that way. But what she really wanted was a guy who would be happy just to kiss her and wouldn't be poised to criticize her technique. It was disappointing to lower a standard that seemed so basic.

Birdy made a face. "I only did it because I'm positive he isn't into me. He likes someone from school who likes someone else. I would rather kiss someone I actually liked. It's kind of a weird thing to do with someone you don't like."

Mel tilted her head. "That's fair. It's a lot of germs to toss around with someone who might not even care if they got you sick."

Uncaringness brought Dominic to mind. Birdy told Mel how he'd changed out the music, then explained how on Monday, Mrs. Amon had assembled everyone to inform them she was holding the iPod in custody until someone owned up to it. There would be no consequences, she assured them, she just wanted to know the truth. The iPod was Damian's, but he didn't fall for the bait, and no one snitched on Dominic. Mrs. Amon was annoyed at their silence and revoked everyone's lunchtime speaking privileges.

"She would be outraged if she knew I was going to your dance. You should hear the way she goes on about St. Monica's. She thinks everyone there is basically possessed."

Mel considered this. "She's not totally wrong, though. People at St. Monica's are kinda shitty. It's just that I think they're kinda shitty everywhere else, too."

They sat with this nugget of wisdom for a moment. At first, Mom had been hesitant to allow Birdy to go to the St. Monica's prom, but Chris had saved the day.

"Come on, Mom, Winston's girlfriend goes there. He said they're using the money for a new library. It's falling apart and they haven't bought new books in years." Mom was rather taken with Chris's friend Winston, a tall, rich, and pleasantly dumb soccer player who they'd met at a game. "Plus, can you imagine Mrs. Amon's face when she finds out?" Mom was a sucker for children in literary poverty, and she wasn't opposed to being spiteful to Mrs.

Amon, who was now the villain of Mom's dinnertime board meeting recaps, so she had agreed to let Birdy go.

Mel took another sip of her soda.

"So, what's up with you and Vince?" said Birdy.

Mel snorted and coughed again. Things were very good with her and Vince. Mel had finally gotten up the courage to ask him to her prom, and he not only accepted but had produced a card he had made inviting her to his prom. Ever since, they had spent even more time than usual together, but nothing amorous had happened yet. Mel finished her soda and sighed. "I think it would be really, really nice to kiss Vince. And I think if he got me sick, he'd bring me hot chocolate."

On Friday, Chris and the freshly returned Patrick dropped Birdy off at Mel's to get ready.

"Have fun," said Patrick. "I hope you meet your prince!"

"Be smart," said Chris from the passenger's seat. "Don't hang out with Winston, he'll try to share his weed."

"I don't smoke!" said Birdy.

"Still," said Chris.

Kelly arrived shortly after Birdy with her parents, Beth, and a duffel bag full of supplies. Mr. and Mrs. Merryman were jolly Pennsylvania transplants, and they would be watching Bailey and Jessie while Mr. and Mrs. Holloway drove the kids to the prom. The adults chatted downstairs while Kelly worked her magic. She gave Beth an intricate braid over one shoulder, Mel cascading waves, Birdy long curls, and herself a regal updo. They filed downstairs, and Mrs. Merryman clasped her hands over her mouth.

"Ooooh, you girls look like a clutch of *jewels!*" She bounced a coral index finger along their row. "Ruby, amethyst, emerald, *sapphire,*" she declared, finishing with Beth. Bailey and Jessie squealed and Mrs. Holloway descended upon them with her camera, alternating between saying how cute they all looked and saying that Dad would be home soon. Then the doorbell rang, Mel shrieked, and Mrs. Holloway let Vince inside.

"Ohhh, you look so handsome, sweetie!" they heard her say. She stepped aside and Vince followed, looking lost without a hat to protect him. Birdy, Beth, and Kelly all said "Awww!" but Mel just beamed at him, silent for a moment.

But not for long. "I told you we'd look good in red!" she said, yanking his vest. He blushed and cleared his throat.

"You look beautiful," he murmured.

"Awww!" said Birdy, Beth, and Kelly. He smiled at them. "You guys look nice too."

Mel looked at the clock. "Mom, is Dad coming or not? We need to go."

"Oh, sweetie, he'll be here soon. I think he was just..." but Mrs. Holloway didn't really seem to know what Mr. Holloway was.

Mel crossed her arms. "We just need to go. He can see us when we get home."

Mrs. Holloway turned away, tucking her hair behind her ears. Then she grabbed her keys.

St. Monica's looked like St. Paul's awkward little sister—squat, stone, and asymmetric. Its prom committee had erected not one, but five balloon arches. They'd also put up streamers and, for some reason, a piñata. Rihanna pounded from the speakers, and the gym smelled like shoes. Kids stood around the perimeter of the room, clutching cups of punch for dear life. Beth led them over to the punch bowl and started doling out cups.

"You're so good at that," said Kelly. "Do you work in the food service industry?"

"Oh, I do, thank you for noticing," said Beth. She sipped the punch. "Ugh. We should have brought something to spike this."

"How does it feel to be back at St. Monica's?" asked Birdy.

"It's fine," said Beth. "This gym looks almost the same as the one at Conrad."

"Yeah," said Vince, "I wonder if there's gonna be a piñata at our prom."

The Cha-Cha Slide started playing and Mel dragged Vince to the dance floor. Kelly and Birdy looked at each other in trepidation.

"Come on guys, it's really easy," said Beth. She waved a beckoning hand and they obediently followed.

As they cha-cha slid, a familiar pair entered the gym. Dominic and Angela came out swinging, turning the line dance into something slightly obscene even though they weren't touching. They drew closer with each passing song, and by the first play of "Gold Digger" they were full on grinding. Dominic fist-bumped Vince in passing, but otherwise did not acknowledge his friends. Instead, he shmoozed, smiled, and stumbled his way to the center of every other group in what seemed like an imitation of drunkenness. When Angela went to the bathroom, Dominic grew lonely and found someone else to grind with. When she returned and looked upset, he grabbed her and whispered in her ear. After he had transmitted his secret message, they started making out like their lives depended on it.

Mel and Vince's sweet happiness was contagious, lending a sheen of delight to everything. Birdy got to put names to faces after tons of St. Monica's stories. They each got to take a swing at the piñata, but were at the back of the line when it finally broke and only scrounged an Almond Joy and a Peppermint Patty between the five of them. A few boys asked Kelly and Birdy to dance, but God in his divine consistency did not send any winners their way. In between bouts of painful small talk and awkward dance moves, they regrouped to eat snacks and take pictures. Beth was invited to dance more frequently and stayed busy chatting with the masses of people who were excited to see her again.

"Beth, I thought you hated it here," said Birdy.

"I did," said Beth, "But I guess a lot of people liked me." Another friend came by for a quick exchange. When she left, Beth said "I think it's just because I'm tall. Highly visible."

"Beth is irresistible," said Kelly.

"BETH!" squealed a voice right on cue. A tall girl with a long blond braid threw her arms around Beth. They looked like mirror images of each other as they hugged. "Great to see you again!"

"Jen!" said Beth. She looked at Birdy. "This is Jen, she's a senior, she was my big last year."

"Hey," said Jen to Birdy. "This is my boyfriend, Winston," she said as though presenting a grand prize.

"Little Cleary!" said Winston. Birdy waved at him. He misinterpreted the wave as a high five but was unperturbed by the awkward angle of their slapping hands. Jen smirked by his side. "You should have brought Big Cleary! We're all going to the bathroom if you wanna come!"

"Thanks! I think I'm fine in here."

"Cool!" said Winston, exactly as enthusiastically as if she'd accepted.

Beth pointed at him. "See you there!" Winston smiled and pointed back, and Jen gave a thumbs up as she steered him away.

"Are you going with them?" said Birdy.

"No way," said Beth. "I'm still not over the last time I tried smoking weed."

At 10:30, Angela staggered up to them. "Dominic is soooo hot right?" she said, swaying. "He drove me over here! We're about to go back to his car," she added, wiggling her eyebrows.

"Sounds cozy," said Mel.

At 11:00, Officer Holloway stood waving in the gym entrance. Vince, who had been holding Mel close during a slow dance, stood ramrod straight and strode over to him, leaving the confused Mel in his wake.

Birdy went over to Mel. "You're dad's here."

Mel rolled her eyes. "Oh, *now* he shows up?"

Officer Holloway was releasing Vince from an iron handshake when Birdy and Mel walked up to them. Officer Holloway looked stunned for a moment; then he reached for Mel.

"I'm so sorry I didn't make it to see you off, Melly," he said. Sorrow shone through his usual wooden demeanor. "You look so beautiful."

Mel's irritation melted into a happy smile. "Vince looks pretty good too, right?"

"Uh, sure," said Officer Holloway.

He herded them all back to the minivan, pointedly seating Mel up front and Vince in the back row, where his long frame shunted Birdy into the window. They dropped him off, went back to Mel's, changed into pajamas, and took three shots each of some rum Kelly had smuggled in her bag of hair tools. Kelly moaned in disgust when Beth took a fourth. Then they settled in to rehash the night.

They looked through all the pictures on Kelly's camera, and then Mel's, and then Beth's, but as soon as Birdy turned on hers, its lens retracted with a pitiful whine.

"Oh no, my battery died!"

Beth sprawled backwards on the bed and said "Good because I'm so comfyyyy right now I just want to sleep."

Kelly said "WAIT!" and sprang up to get them glasses of water, which they dutifully consumed. Beth fell asleep in the middle of complaining that now she was going to have to go pee. Kelly muscled Beth to the left half of the bed and then settled in beside her. Mel turned out the lights and lolled on the floor next to Birdy.

"Sleep tight," said Kelly. Birdy smiled, flipped to the cold side of her pillow, and dropped into sleep.

Summer 2009

1

THE SMITH BARN HAD never held animals. Rather, it held a peeling fishing boat, three dirt bikes, a lawn mower, and an assembly of broken tools. On occasions such as these, it also held a horde of drunk teenagers.

Vince had told his parents he was hosting a bonfire, and it was true. Kids brought backpacks full of marshmallows, graham crackers, and Hershey chocolate bars. Under the s'mores supplies, they stashed whatever alcohol they had filched from their parents or paid their older siblings and questionable older friends to get for them.

Birdy had been to Vince's a few times before. Like her, he was the youngest of four, but unlike her, his three brothers were ten, twelve, and fifteen years older than him. His parents were only a few years from retirement and were more interested in grandchildren and travel than in teenage occupations. Vince had gravitated to Mel's house since he was small, but his place was reliably quiet and often empty, traits that were growing more useful as they got older.

On Conrad High's prom night, Mel and Vince finally had their first kiss and became Facebook Official the next day. Now it was time to blend their social circles, which were already pretty well blended. The Facebook Event was called "S'mores and Shots." The students of St. Monica's and Conrad High were eager to mingle with each other. Both student populations had minimal school pride; each felt the kids from the other school were getting things they lacked. There was no posturing about whose school was better; only competition about whose school was worse.

It had taken a week for the stress of being at Divine Mercy to dissipate from Birdy's chest, but ever since, it had been her best summer yet. She was working 30 hours a week, leaving her in the happy position of having extra money and time to spend with her friends. She had her learner's permit and was steadily accruing driving hours through terrifying commutes to and from work. Chris and Patrick were also working more than ever, but when they were all home, they watched *The Office* or went to the movies as usual. If Beth was working, she pumped extra butter on their popcorn, to Chris's outsized gratitude. Beth had also gotten to meet Peter when he was home for another visit that had spawned a cloud of passive aggression so noxious it drove them to go see *The Ugly Truth*. Now, Beth was out by the fire chatting with a group of girls from Conrad High. Kelly and Birdy stood next to one of the dirt bikes.

"Your hair looks fabulous tonight," said Kelly.

"All thanks to you," said Birdy.

The morning after the prom, Birdy had taken a shower while everyone else was sleeping. Afterwards, she stood trying to pick from Mel's bookshelf, and Kelly sat straight up in bed. "Birdy," she said accusingly, "you have curly hair."

"I know that," said Birdy, "It looks kind of cool when it's wet. But there's no way to make it stay nice."

Kelly had stared at her, sighed, and flopped out of bed to pull a bottle of mousse from her duffle bag.

Now, Birdy's hair hung crunchy curls. Kelly had also bought her a hair straightener as an alternative styling resource. Birdy had protested that none of this was necessary, but she did enjoy having at least some control of how her hair looked.

At the bonfire, Kelly was continuing her role as the keeper of crucial bottles. There was rarely any alcohol in Birdy's house to sneak out of it, but Kelly's parents had an abundance because they had fine tastes and liked to be prepared. She didn't want to take too much from any one bottle in case they noticed, so she had mixed a little bit from several types all into one plastic water bottle, from which she and Birdy now sipped.

"Pleaahh, oh that's horrible," said Kelly.

"Thanks for sharing," said Birdy, eyes watering.

"My pleasure," said Kelly.

"What's even in there?" said Birdy.

"Let's see there's gin, whiskey, vodka, tequila, and spiced rum... and something I'm forgetting."

"There was some really sweet taste in there."

"Oooh, peach schnapps!" said Kelly, snapping her finger and pointing at Birdy.

Birdy laughed. "I don't even know what all of those taste like on their own. My parents don't really drink. That's probably a good thing for them though."

"My parents don't drink that much, but they get so excited when people come over, and they want to be able to make any guest whatever cocktail their heart desires. So we have all this alcohol and tons of snacks and food and drinks all the time."

"That's so nice," said Birdy. "My house is like, Old Mother Hubbard's house."

"What?"

"You know, like Old Mother Hubbard, whose cupboard is bare."

"What is that even from?"

"It's a nursery rhyme!"

"Oh," said Kelly, giggling. She sighed. "I know I'm lucky," she said. "It's sad too, though. They wanted to have a huge family. But all they could have was me."

"Well, thank God for that!" said Birdy. "Your parents are so nice."

Kelly smiled at her. "They can be annoying sometimes. They're so hung up on every single thing I do. But then at least it's better than Beth's parents."

"I've still never even met them."

"I haven't seen them in forever either. Beth doesn't like having people over. But you're not missing anything. Her dad will be crazy happy for weeks and then just suddenly hate everyone. And then her mom just hates everyone all the time." Kelly glared at the floor. "You'd never know it, because Beth is so happy and nice. But that's why she's always spent so much time at me and Mel's houses."

"That's so sad," said Birdy, peering out at the fire. Beth was no longer there. "Where is she anyway?"

"Looking for someone?" said a male voice.

Birdy turned around to find a sweaty blond guy leering at her.

"Oh, no. I mean yes, but not you, I wasn't looking for you. Sorry. I mean."

He continued to smile and reached out his hand. "I'm Kevin."

Birdy gingerly shook it. "Kevin, hi, nice to meet you."

"This is Birdy," said Kelly.

"Bernie! Cool name." Birdy didn't bother to correct him. "Weren't you in Geometry with Mr. Brooks?"

"No, I don't go to Conrad," said Birdy.

"No, I know I recognize you from Geometry," said Kevin.

"Well, I took Geometry with Mrs. Hart, two years ago, at Divine Mercy," said Birdy.

"Divine Mercy? Where's that?" said Kevin.

"Conrad."

He squinted at her. "So you're sure you weren't in Geometry with Mr. Brooks?"

Birdy looked over at Kelly, who was observing this exchange with an elated smile. She widened her eyes for help, but Kelly only smiled wider. Fortunately, Beth swooped in just then.

"Hey guys," she said, expertly boxing Kevin out. Beth wore a tiny, hot pink tank and jean shorts. Kevin stared for a second, looking more confused than annoyed, then melted away.

"Thank you for saving me," said Birdy, "Kelly was no help."

Kelly cackled evilly and Beth snorted along with her. "Kevin's a douche," she said. "He doesn't deserve you. But to pay me back, you have to promise me to go up and talk to any nice guys that do show up. You too, Kelly."

"How are we supposed to know if they're nice if we don't know them?" said Kelly.

"Oh, my God," said Beth, rolling her eyes. "You just talk to them! Then if you aren't feeling it you pretend to wave to someone and you leave."

"Where have you been, anyway?" said Kelly, eager to change the subject.

"Oh, I was just talking to Fiona. I'll introduce you when she gets back, she's smoking now."

Kelly held up her bottle. "Need a drink?"

"Don't mind if I do," said Beth.

Kelly gave her an appraising glance. "Did you smoke too?"

"Just a tiny bit," said Beth, pinching her fingers together. "Baby steps." She looked between Kelly and Birdy. "Are you guys ever going to try it?"

"I'm never inhaling anything other than oxygen," Kelly said immediately. Birdy had found drinking to be enjoyable so far, but being high didn't seem like any fun. The red eyes and eerie smiles of the recently baked were off-putting, plus Beth had told them an awful story about getting high and then completely freaking out and crying around a bunch of strangers.

"Probably not," said Birdy. "I really don't want to get arrested or something, you know? I don't want to mess up college."

"Oh well," said Beth, who was used to Kelly's health-oriented and Birdy's college-oriented trepidations. "I bet I can get Mel to do it. Can I have that drink?"

Kelly handed over the bottle to Beth, who then offered more to Birdy, who took another disgusting swig.

"Bernadette Cecelia Cleary, I am very disappointed in you!"

Birdy looked around in alarm, only to see Dominic approaching with his hands in his pockets and a mischievous smile on his face.

Crap. As hurt as she'd been about Dominic's prank, he'd poked a hole in his own magnitude by acting so stupid at prom, and she'd been having so much fun recently that her personal disasters had faded from her focus. Lately, she was thinking about Dominic less than she had in years. But she had not been at all prepared for his eyes to crinkle at her while she was drunk. She felt a goofy grin spilling all over her own face.

"Bernadette Cecelia?" said Beth.

"Yes, *Elizabeth...*" Birdy paused.

"Jessica," supplied Kelly.

"Your middle name is *Jessica?*" said Birdy.

"Yes," said Beth.

"That seems more like a first name," said Birdy.

"Shut up," said Beth.

"The point is, Birdy is *drinking* like some kind of *public schooler,*" said Dominic, putting an arm around her.

"I'm just a heathen, can't help it," said Birdy. She peered up at him. "I didn't know you were coming."

"Oh yeah, Vince invited me earlier today."

Thanks a lot, Vince.

"Hey man!" Vince and Mel were approaching, hand in hand. Vince and Dominic had recently discovered they were both members of the Church of Natural Light, and their shared devotion had rekindled their friendship. Vince let go of Mel's hand for a moment to welcome him in the greeting of the faithful, a simultaneous handshake and back pat. Then he put his arm around Mel. Dominic reached to put his arm back around Birdy, but she'd conquered her initial flusterment and stepped out of range. This was not lost upon him, and he said to her, "Isaac's here too, don't worry."

"Cool," said Birdy.

"I heard you had fun at the ball." He was doing that deliberate asshole thing, but with Kelly's brew in her veins it was easy to stare him down. She only shrugged, and he tried again.

"He's going to love your outfit." He looked her up and down. "*I* love your outfit." Birdy had gone back for five more colors of the blue tank top. This one was white.

"Oh yeah? Hey, is Angela coming, or did you invite Rachel this time?" Kelly's brew was powerful stuff.

Dominic winced and held up his hands. "Yikes, sorry. I was just saying you look nice."

Isaac materialized, looking almost unfamiliar to Birdy. He wore a tight black t-shirt and backwards baseball cap and seemed broader than last time she'd seen him. "Hey Dom, did you know Angela is here?"

Dom flinched. "What the hell, Vince? You said she wasn't coming!"

"She's not... I didn't think she was," said Vince, taking off his cap and scratching the back of his head.

"Kidding," said Isaac. "Can't you take a little joke?"

Dominic shot him a look of pure venom, but Birdy couldn't stop laughing. Dominic gave her another obvious once over. "Well, someone's feeling sassy tonight."

"Wait," said Mel, "I keep meaning to tell you what Bailey did on her last day of school."

Mel's story carried them to friendly shores, as there was no shortage of ridiculous sibling stories to swap. Everyone was laughing at one of Isaac's when a voice trilled through the air.

"Dommy!"

Angela Prune had found the bonfire after all. Isaac smiled beatifically at Dominic and then she was upon them. Her pink lace cami was scooched just low enough to reveal the top of her neon green bra. A Playboy bunny dangled from a chain around her neck and nestled in her cleavage.

Dominic snapped into a posture of excitement. "Hey baby!" he said, picking her up and spinning her around.

"I didn't know you would be here!" she squealed. "You said you were babysitting tonight!"

"I came to surprise you!" said Dominic.

"Ohhh, Dom! How did you even know I was coming here?" She was excited, not suspicious. Mel smacked herself in the forehead.

"I just had a feeling," he said, and then kissed her passionately. Birdy stepped away, unable to bear it. She wasn't jealous, she was just overwhelmed by the stupidity of the situation. She also felt sorry for

Angela, who was shallow and annoying but who was also clearly operating on a deficit of logic and self-regard.

Birdy and Isaac paired up for beer pong against Kevin, the sweaty blond guy, and Logan, another sweaty blond guy.

"Ohhh, I get it, this is your boyfriend?" said Kevin.

"Nope," said Birdy.

Isaac gasped. "I thought we had something special!"

Birdy woke up the next day on Mel's floor, wrapped in a soft blanket. She opened her eyes. Sunlight streamed through the window, but the other girls were still asleep. Kelly's brows were furrowed in what looked like a serious slumber. Mel was curled up beside her and wore a little smile. Beth was next to Birdy on the floor. Her limbs were all askew and her hair buried her face like an exploded hay bale. Birdy smiled and rolled onto her back.

As soon as she changed position an ache jolted behind her eyes. She was pretty sure she had disregarded Kelly's usual imperative to drink her water. She'd been too busy drinking new combinations of alcohol. She'd met some people, played a lot of games, and had the satisfaction of watching Dominic live the results of his own stupidity. Her feelings might be annoyingly persistent, but she had finally come to a freeing realization. *He's just one very dumb fish in a pond full of them. And he's not my problem to solve.* The ache behind her eyes was pulsing now, but Birdy felt peaceful. She rolled back over and dozed.

2

ONE THURSDAY IN LATE JULY, Birdy rummaged around her room for her work belt. She spotted it under her bed, and when she pulled it out, the USB cable for her digital camera came with it. After she got dressed she uploaded her pictures to Facebook, entitling the album "Spring Things Because I Lost My USB Cord For a Few Months."

At work, her first customer fished a baggie of pennies from his pocket to pay for his meal. Birdy counted them out and handed back the extras.

"You look stressed," said the customer.

Mr. Breech, her boss, was bagging the man's order, and Birdy felt his head snap toward her at these condemning words.

"Oh, I'm not!" she exclaimed, a crazed smile on her face as she handed the customer his drink. "I love it here!" Mr. Breech appeared by her side with a steaming tray. The customer was unnerved by her enthusiasm and took his meal from Mr. Breech without looking at him.

"Well... okay. Thanks," he said, backing away.

"My pleasure!" she called after him. Mr. Breech glared at her but went back to the kitchen with no comment.

When Birdy got home, she checked to see if there were any notifications from her new album. Rachel Faducci had granted her a few likes, commenting "Aw, u r sooo pretty! :)" on a picture of her, Mel, Beth, and Kelly at the St. Monica's prom. Margaret Amon commented on a picture of Birdy and Gabby at the Divine Mercy Formal, "oh em gee it's meee back there!!!!" On a picture of Mel sporting a mustache made from a strand of her hair, Vince had commented, "Gorgeous."

On Saturday, Birdy was eating cereal and reading Dear Abby when Mom burst inside from her morning walk.

"BIRDY!" Her footsteps barreled back to the kitchen. "Wait till you hear this!" she erupted. "Tammy and I were talking just now. Did you know about DOMINIC and RACHEL FADUCCI?"

Uh oh. "No! What? What about them?"

"Rachel thought they were courting! But then she saw a picture of him with some girl at the St. Monica's prom on someone's Facebook! And her parents called Jude and Tammy to tell them the courtship was off, but apparently they never even knew about it! Dominic had pretended to be his dad on the phone to Mr. Faducci and he set the whole courtship thing up himself without them knowing! So I told Tammy about the time that Peter had been dating a girl for WEEKS without telling us and how everything ended up okay! Boys just want a little privacy sometimes! She was like 'Okay, thank you so much, that makes me feel so much better!'"

Birdy opted to remain casual so Mom wouldn't realize she wanted to get out of this conversation as soon as possible. "Wow! That's so crazy!"

"I just can't believe he'd do something like that! I mean, can you?"

"It's crazy!" said Birdy again. "Whose picture did they see him in?" *Was it mine?*

"Oh, I don't know, she didn't say! She was just so stressed out about it, I felt so sorry for her!" For Mom, the true excitement was the opportunity to administer life advice.

"But I told her, look at Peter, he went through a hard time, but he's coming back to us, you just have to pray and give it time! I said, Dominic is going to be fine!" Mom finished her water with a satisfied sigh. "I'm going to go shower."

As soon as Mom left, Birdy dashed up the back stairs to the computer nook. Chris was busy with his own Facebook business and was cranky when she asked him to look through her album. He scrolled through Spring Things Because I Lost My USB Cord For A Few Months while she hung over his shoulder, gnawing her finger-nails. And there—in the background of the picture of her and Kelly making peace signs, there was Dominic, making out with Angela Prune.

Now that she noticed, it was unmistakable. *Rachel could have seen it.*

She anxiously explained the situation to Chris, who on a different day might have been interested, but today was not.

"Okay, that's terrible that Dominic was being a dick and is now in trouble. Now let me finish what I was doing," he snapped. At 10:30 he drove her to work in the spiky silence of angry siblings. Saturday lunch shift was the busiest of the week, but between every tray of food she handed over and every fake smile she flashed, Birdy wondered again—*Did Rachel see* my *picture?*

She almost ran a red light on the drive home. "Careful, honey," said Dad, throwing an arm out to shield her. He settled back in the passenger seat. "Chris is staying over at his buddy's house tonight after work. Mom and I are watching *Gone With the Wind.* Do you want to join us?" He must have been worried by her near traffic violation.

"No thanks," said Birdy. "I wanted to read." This was always an acceptable excuse for Dad, who nodded in approval. At home, Birdy showered the smell of fast food off herself, put on shorts and a t-shirt, and headed to the backyard with the rainbow quilt. She spread it next to the maple tree and pulled out *A Wrinkle in Time,* an old favorite she could slip right into.

"So," said Dominic.

Birdy leapt a mile and turned around. He stood next to the blanket. His head was blocking the sun. She scrambled to her feet.

Dominic looked calm. "Rachel saw me in the background of one of your pictures from St. Monica's prom."

Oh, shit. "Oh my gosh, I am so sorry. I did not mean for that to happen, I'm so sorry. Are you okay?"

He smiled. His lips were swollen; a bruise blossomed around his right eye. "I guess it makes sense you're not trying to cover up for me anymore."

Birdy clutched her hands to her face. "Dominic, I'm so sorry, I know how it looks, but I swear to God I didn't mean for that to happen. I didn't mean for her to see you in that picture or anything. I didn't know you were behind me in that picture at all."

"Yeah, yeah" he replied, with a smile that said he didn't believe her. "That's more something I would do. I didn't think you were like that."

"I'm not!" She wasn't, but she was uncomfortably aware of the part of herself that sometimes wished she was. She felt as responsible and awful as if she had ratted Dominic out on purpose.

He took a step closer, amused now. "Maybe I've been a bad influence."

Neither of them spoke for a moment, and just like that, the air changed. She turned away, pretending the maple tree was a fascinating sight. He stepped in front of her and smiled gently.

"Yes?" she said, trying to sound sardonic.

He didn't answer, just kept looking down at her. The painful butterflies again.

"Hey, Birdy" he said. His voice was soft. He moved a transparent strand of frizz out of her eyes and tucked it behind her ear. "You know what?"

"What?" she said, sounding more wobbly than sardonic this time.

He moved his hand through her damp hair down to the small of her back. "My dad got really pissed at me. As you can see. Not so much because I broke his rules, more because he thinks I made him look stupid. I saw my mom filling your mom in on the whole thing, but I'm sure she left out the part about my dad beating the shit out of me. And I was thinking how you keep on ending up in my personal business. I turn around and you're always right there. And it made me realize something."

His other hand now landed on her hip and he drew her close. He brought his lips within an inch of hers. She didn't pull away.

"I hate you."

The butterflies burst into flame as she jerked back. He dug his fingers into her skin.

"You think it's your job to make sure everyone is doing the right thing, and you can't stand to even look like you did something wrong. You'll never admit when you *want* something, but you won't leave me—the fuck—alone," he snarled, shaking her slightly for emphasis. He blurred in front of her as her eyes filled with tears. He stayed in her face until they fell. Only then did he release her, laughing like it was the funniest thing in the world.

"It was just a joke. I just wanted to see what you'd do. You always take things so seriously! God, you should see your face right now."

She stumbled back, mortally wounded. He smiled viciously and stalked out of the yard.

Fall 2009

1

From: michael.faducci@yahoo.com
To the Divine Mercy Board Members,

 I pray you are well on this, the feast of the Assumption. Just one year ago, my family was on the cusp of a new stage in life. We prepared for my eldest daughter to attend Divine Mercy School, feeling God was calling us to explore a new path.

 But He did not make this path a smooth one. Though my cherished daughter, Rachel, had a wonderful first year at school, her heart was shattered by none other than Dominic Doppelski. I have generously donated my time and books to share with the students my passion for godly courtship at no cost to the school. This young man used my own subject matter to deceive me and my precious daughter, only to be discovered through my daughter's own careful observation. I encourage all board members to cultivate thoughtful Facebook usage among their children, as I have with mine.

 I am appalled that this happened at all, but especially that it happened under the very nose of Jude Doppelski, Divine Mercy's driving force and supposed shining light. For someone who claims to be such a family man, it is concerning that he never noticed the amount of sneaking his son would have had to do to uphold not one, but two romantic relationships. And perhaps more. In light of these findings, I question his ability to balance his duties as a business owner, board member, husband, and father. My family and our friends will not be returning to Divine Mercy unless Dominic's extreme disrespect is rectified.

BIRDY READ MR. FADUCCI'S damning email over Mom's astonished shoulder just before they left for Mass.

"This is so rude," said Mom. "What does he mean, *thoughtful Facebook usage*?" Birdy thought this might be directed at Mom, but wasn't about to explain about her fateful album. Despite the early hour, the email had already made the rounds by the time they made it to church, where Mr. Doppelski cornered Dad.

"I'm not backing down from the school I broke my back to build just because some new family got their feelings hurt. They're gonna see more of me than ever. I'm taking on the Algebra 1 class this year. What are they gonna do about that?" Dad had no idea, especially considering he had not read the email.

Still, the hurt feelings of the new family were a force to be reckoned with. The ball had worked its magic, convincing twelve new families to come to Divine Mercy, and nine of them were friends of the Faduccis and Herons. They sent their deposits in May, the board scrounged up three new teachers in June, and by the time the shit hit the fan in the last days of July, the school was financially dependent on their continued tuition payments. It was clear that for Divine Mercy to stay afloat, something was going to have to give. So, like God Himself, Jude Doppelski sacrificed his son for the good of his creation.

Dominic would be taking all his senior year classes at The Community College of Conrad, earning college credit and high school credit at the same time. Mrs. Doppelski talked up this decision big time to Mom, saying it would save so much money in the long run and that Dominic had blown away the admissions people with his math test scores. But it was only because Abe Doppelski had connections in the administrative department that Dominic had been able to snag a full course load when he signed up in mid-August.

Birdy learned all this information in snatches, as Mom repeated the scoop from her morning walks, as Abe accosted Dad in the church parking lot, as she and Isaac crossed paths during their respective workouts. The person she heard nothing from was Dominic.

Up until that moment under the maple tree, she had convinced herself that though her feelings for Dominic were doomed, they were sufficiently guarded. His flirtations were careless, centered on his own experience because he was blind to everyone else. An unrelenting sucker for a mission, she'd imagined she could travel undetected along her stark and solitary path until she found someone else to love. But Dominic had seen right through her all along. He'd thrown down scraps for her to see what she'd do, then laid a feast before her just to snatch it away. He hated her. And that feeling, at least, was mutual.

From: petercleary@hotmail.com
Hey Birdy,
As you can see, I got a new email address. I needed something more professional for job applications. I promise it really is me though and not some weirdo. It was good to see you all last week. How are you holding up without Chris? What's it like being an only child? I know how much you always want to be the center of attention.

From: bluebirdy@aol.com
Hey Peter,
Wow, your new email address is very professional. Where are you applying? Make sure to tell them in your interviews that your greatest weaknesses are actually your greatest strengths!

It's okay without Chris. It's like I'm a prisoner and my cellmate's sentence is up. It's a little lonely, but I'm happy for him and now I get his rations. It helps that I'm not actually a prisoner and I finally got my license. Now I'm the one driving the Spirit. Its spirit is a little broken but it gets me to work and to see my friends, so I haven't even really been home much since Chris left. School starts in two more days and I think it's going to suck. But at least I don't have to drive with Mom anymore.

On August 30, Birdy got in the dispirited Spirit alone. She stood in the threshold of Divine Mercy, the familiar scent of mold waking those stupid butterflies in her gut. This year couldn't get any worse than the previous two, could it? *Don't ask that,* she warned herself. *God might answer.*

She spotted Gabby on the way to the locker room and her knees shuddered. They hadn't really talked over the summer other than Facebook-level exchanges. Surely Rachel would have told her about Birdy's picture—surely Gabby would have seen it herself. Was Gabby mad at her? Was Rachel?

But Gabby turned around and smiled. "Hi!" she said, reaching out for a hug. "I missed you! How was your summer?"

"Pretty good," Birdy lied. *I discovered I'm a pathetic piece of shit. I think I ruined your cousin's life by accident. It was so fun.* "How was your summer?"

"Good," said Gabby, "I've got so much to tell you!"

Isaac walked up to them, trailed by a slight girl with straight red hair and big brown eyes. "I found someone," he said, touching the girl lightly on the shoulder. The girl glanced at him and smiled shyly.

"Hi!" said Gabby, hugging the girl. She drew back and pointed at Birdy.

"This is Birdy," she said, "And this is Maddie!"

"I've heard a lot about you," said Maddie.

"You too!" said Birdy. Maddie was Gabby's lifelong best friend. "Welcome to Divine Mercy."

"Thanks! Gabby says it's so much fun," Maddie said breathlessly. Her teeth were very straight; she pursed her lips like she was used to having braces behind them.

"We have a good time," said Birdy, feeling like an actress in one of Mary's cheesy movies.

"I'm really glad you joined us," said Isaac, grinning down at Maddie from his new height with his new haircut. Isaac's impeccable grooming set him apart from the other formerly homeschooled boys wandering the halls.

Maddie smiled back at him. "Me, too."

Birdy's first class was Pre-Calculus with Mrs. Hart. Polly, Fred, and Olivia were her classmates, along with a hunching set of twins in thick glasses named Sean and Liam. Mrs. Hart was giddier than Birdy thought was strictly necessary about Pre-Calc and gave them an overview of her expectations before launching into a shockingly impassioned review of SOHCAHTOA.

Thanks to the school's growth, the grades were more separate than they'd ever been before. Halfway through the day, Birdy realized she would not have any classes with Rachel. That was a relief. Her brain used to teem with principled, imaginary scenes in which she cleverly solved whatever pickle she found herself in. There used to be an entire alternate reality where she was strong and brave. But her final confrontation with Dominic had burned that part of her away. Thoughts of herself standing in front of Rachel led nowhere at all.

At lunch, Birdy saw Rachel sitting surrounded by friends, some of whom she recognized from the ball. Rachel's perpetual smile was gone. Birdy sat at a table with Isaac, Gabby, Maddie, and Michael. Michael had spent the summer in California and was now so freckled he was almost tan.

"Holy shit, what is all that?" he said, craning over as Isaac unpacked his lunchbox.

"Look at this," said Isaac, unpacking a veritable picnic. "My mom keeps getting paid to do these product reviews for her blog, and then we get to eat the extra food. So first she reviewed these baggies—" he opened a sturdy looking Ziploc printed with pumpkins, a far cry from his and Birdy's usual foldover, poor-people sandwich bags— "and then she reviewed this lunchmeat—" he held up a sandwich stacked an inch thick with turkey "—and then we got these baked chips and this apple sauce."

"*Organic* apple sauce?" said Michael, reading the label as Isaac started slurping what was apparently a drinkable pouch of the stuff. "What are you, gay?"

Birdy's heart wrenched for Isaac, but he didn't need her sympathy. "Only for you, baby," he said, pointing at Michael with a limp wrist. Gabby and Maddie giggled shrilly while Michael shook his head, laughing.

"Whatever happened with Anna?" Isaac asked Michael.

"We kinda lost touch when I went to California. I did hang out with this one cute girl there though. Blond," he said, with a poorly delivered wink at Gabby.

Gabby sat up straight and leaned across the table. "That reminds me. I hung out with a guy this summer too." She filled them in on her brief relationship with Mark, a boy from 4H camp. Maddie had had an equally brief relationship with his best friend, Tyler.

"We both had our first kiss on the same day," said Maddie, glancing from Gabby to Isaac and pink with pride. Birdy wondered listlessly why she herself was seemingly incapable of meeting a boy she wanted to kiss who also wasn't a dirtbag. *Should I join 4H?*

"Wow, Tyler's a really lucky guy," said Isaac, lavishing Maddie with his ice-blue eyes. Her smile grew ten sizes. Birdy took a huge bite of her sandwich.

"Birdy and I kissed once," he went on.

Maddie's smile slipped, but she slapped it back on fast. "No way!" she said, sounding totally enthusiastic, "When was this?"

Birdy was grateful her mouth was full. She chewed carefully and turned her eyes on Isaac, willing him to stop talking.

"It was back in the springtime, it was kind of a dare," he said. "Kinda gross, really."

Birdy swallowed and chuckled mechanically. Isaac was doing what Dominic used to do, emphasizing how platonic this one female friendship was to make himself a more appealing catch. It was still annoying when he did it, but it hurt much less. Plus, Maddie was now giggling uncontrollably, so it seemed to be working.

But then—

"We all know Birdy's more into my cousin," said Isaac. "You put up those pictures of the St. Monica's prom just to get Dominic in trouble, didn't you?"

His tone was teasing, but she felt like he'd pushed her off a skyscraper.

"No, I didn't," said Birdy, spewing a wet sandwich crumb.

Gabby snorted, eyebrows raised, to indicate her disbelief. Birdy's ears got hot.

"He was all over the place at that dance. It's not my fault he ended up in the background of one of my pictures." Dominic had left fingertip bruises on her back; her skin now throbbed in memory of them.

"Okay, okay," said Isaac, eyeing Gabby and Maddie, who were both smirking now. "Someone's feeling sensitive today. It was just a joke."

I am really sick of this type of joke. Birdy gathered up her trash, shoved it in her lunchbox, and left the room.

The next day, Isaac caught her in the parking lot before school started.

"Hey, I was just kidding yesterday. I can tell I upset you. Can you please forgive me?"

Birdy looked into his earnest blue eyes. Many reasons why she was angry passed through her mind, but the one that came out of her mouth surprised her. "You threw me under the bus so you'd look good for Maddie. That's just what Dominic always does. I thought you were different from him."

To her surprise, Isaac looked furious. "Why the *hell* does everything I do have to be compared to what Dominic does? I'm not him. I'm just me. I'm going to do what I'm going to do, regardless of what he does or doesn't do."

Birdy was still angry, but felt he made a fair point. Everyone was always making Dominic into the measuring stick for Isaac. Everyone except Isaac.

He sighed. "Look, you know I'm not actually into Maddie. But I need to get through two more years in my house before I can go away somewhere else. My life will be a lot easier if I have a girlfriend, believe me."

He softened further. "I shouldn't have said that about you though. Sorry."

His apology seemed genuine enough, but it was also apparent that he wasn't about to publicly take back what he'd said. And Birdy couldn't unsee the way Gabby had so readily agreed so with his joke. She'd expected better from both of them. She was always expecting better. Why was she such a chump?

Good thing I kissed Isaac, she thought. *Really prevented me from getting embarrassed.*

That day at lunch, Isaac refrained from mining Birdy's private pain for social credit and focused on charming the socks off Maddie. Gabby fell all over Birdy and then began an uncomfortable flirtation with Michael, in which she held the upper hand and sporadically experimented with her power. Birdy settled into her familiar role as the extra wheel. Before long, she didn't even feel the hurt. She simply carried a dull awareness that she didn't trust a single person in her school.

Birdy's hopes for a good year were ghostly at best, and over the course of the week they nailed themselves into the coffin. On Thursday, Margaret kept sidetracking Religion class by arguing with her mother about veiling, so Birdy left to text Beth in the bathroom. She left the stall still texting and found Rachel staring at her, looking stricken.

"Hi Birdy," she said.

"Rachel," said Birdy, pocketing her phone. "How are you?"

"I'm okay," said Rachel. Her eyes were watery.

With Beth still in mind, Birdy decided to just be direct. "Rachel, that whole thing with the picture and Dominic—I didn't mean for that to happen, you shouldn't have had to find out like that." *Yeah, that was good.*

"Did you notice him at the dance?"

"I... I saw him there, I didn't know he was in the picture I took though."

"So you saw him with that girl?"

"Yeah... but..."

"Why didn't you tell me?" said Rachel, blinking back tears. "I thought we were friends."

Seeing Rachel moping around school had added some comfortable padding to Birdy's hatred for Dominic, but now her loathing was all for herself.

"I don't know," she said, tears filling her own eyes. "I was trying not to get involved."

Rachel looked bewildered. "But you should always stand up for your friends."

The unfairness of it all was swallowing her like quicksand. *I did stand up for you and he embarrassed me and you laughed along with everyone else. He kept showing you how mean he was and you couldn't see it because you're so fucking nice you would think a rattlesnake was a pretty new necklace.*

"Rachel—I actually did try but, Dominic—you just can't trust him and—"

"Well, I realize that," said Rachel with a rueful little roll of her eyes. "I've been so upset about it all. But," she took a deep breath, "I've been praying a lot about it, and I forgive you. Friends?"

"Uh, yeah, of course," Birdy said, whiplashed.

Rachel of the unquenchable sweetness now gave a watery, beautiful smile. "And I know you two are friends, so—would you tell him I forgive him too?"

Rachel looked at her expectantly and Birdy shook her head, feeling like the victim of the world's kindest con job. "I can't," she whispered, in a tone like it was obvious, and maybe that was rude but why was it not obvious to Rachel how weird that was?

Rachel gasped a little and her face crumpled. "Oh," she said sadly. "Okay." She drifted to the door, then turned back to give Birdy a brave hug. "That's fine." She finally left and Birdy stared after her, gripping the cold porcelain sink. Then she went back to the stall and cried, because even though she was six weeks into her plan to never speak to Dominic again, she didn't see how she would ever escape him.

2

MEL PACED THE ROOM, her cheeks painted with a red C and a blue H. Kelly was braiding blue and red ribbons through her hair. Beth was curled in the corner of Mel's bed, scrawling something in a notebook and wearing a tight red t-shirt, short blue shorts, and tall knee socks with blue and red stripes. Birdy had missed the colors memo but was relieved to be here after her terrible week. It was Friday night, and they were going to watch Vince play.

Or so they hoped. Vince had put in three loyal years with Conrad High's unreliable and unheroic team. Now he was a senior and rumor had it that Coach Potter, the man who had once sprained his ankle stepping over his dog, was going to start him tonight, their first home game of the season.

"He's gonna do great," said Mel. "He's so fast!" She threw herself on her bed and then leapt up again. "I think they're really going to have a good season."

Beth shut her notebook and put it in her backpack. "Did he ever say if he's going to get any of his friends to play with us?"

The Conrad Rec League had finally remembered the existence of its 12 and up teams and had officially discontinued them. This had no bearing on their usage of the field, but Mel had proposed that they simply hold pickup soccer games in her yard. All four girls now had jobs with irregular hours, so it made more sense to fit their games in around work and school from week to week.

"He said a few guys are interested. It would be good to play with some more people who actually like to play," said Mel.

"Yeah, plus some of those guys might be cool," said Kelly.

Beth shook her head. "It's just the uniform, Kelly. They're just like St. Monica's boys with shoulder pads."

Kelly made a disgruntled noise and turned back to her braid.

"But that doesn't mean you shouldn't talk to them!" said Beth in a rush. "I'm sure they'd be thrilled if you'd talk to them!"

"Nice save," said Kelly.

Beth laughed and addressed Birdy. "Dominic and Isaac would probably come too, right?"

Birdy pretended like she didn't hear. She had never explained to them what had happened with her Facebook album. Mel's suggestion of soccer at her house had been a relief; it simplified her avoidance of Dominic.

"Right?" said Beth. "Were they trying to sign up for soccer this year?"

"Well," said Birdy. "Well, it's just, you know that album I put on Facebook that had the pictures of the St. Monica's prom?"

"Yeah," said Beth.

"Well, you know my friend Gabby? Well her cousin, Rachel, also goes to Divine Mercy and, well... apparently, he had tricked Rachel's parents into thinking they were courting, but his parents never knew about it. And so Dominic and Angela ended up in the background of one of my Facebook pictures, and I didn't realize it, but then Rachel saw it and her family got really upset because they thought Dominic and Rachel were like promised to each other. So then Dominic thought I put the picture of him and Angela up on purpose. And he came over and basically told me he hated me."

She was trying to act casual, but she was shaking like a dead leaf on a twig.

Beth watched Birdy, then crossed her arms. "Well, it sounds like we don't need that fucker in our soccer games then."

Birdy laughed. "I'm pretty sick of Isaac at the moment too."

"Got it," said Beth. "No Doppelskis at our pickup games." She put on her backpack. "Ready to go?"

"Ready!" said Mel, bouncing to her feet. "Wait," she said. "Birdy, just borrow this." She tossed Birdy a red t-shirt so she could match the color scheme. As she changed, Kelly finished her braid and turned to face them with a smile.

"You know, I changed my mind. I think we should go to Songs and Teens tonight instead." Birdy snorted.

Mel drove them over to the game in her mom's Camry. Kelly and Birdy happily gave Beth the front seat. Mel's driving was terrifying, but unlike Kelly and Birdy, Beth had neither a driver's license nor an inborn sense of impending doom. Conrad High was a tall, crumbling brick building with no air conditioning and poor heating. Mel parked in front of it with a jerk and they joined the trickle of kids walking to the dull green field. A pair of girls, dressed aspirationally for fall in Ugg boots and red scarves, shrieked as mosquitos divebombed them. In the distance, the marching band played something cheery but unrecognizable.

The sharp, rusty bleachers bounced ominously as they found their seats. Just before kickoff, a massive man sat right in front of Mel.

"Shit," Mel muttered, "I can't see at all!" She looked around wildly for somewhere else to sit.

"Take my spot," said Birdy, standing up.

"Thank you so much," said Mel desperately. Birdy shuffled into her spot and stared at the man's flabby, hairy neck. They rose and put their hands over their hearts while Fiona Dawson, who they'd met at S'mores and Shots, sang an embellished version of *The Star Spangled Banner*. Then the game began, along with Mel's running commentary.

"What the hell, he's not on the field! Oh, there he is, okay good."

"Henry's gonna throw it now, I think this play is called Catfish—oh no, it's not Catfish, maybe this is Salmon Spawn—"

"Okay he caught it! Oh no, he dropped it!"

"Oh no. Oh no. Oh no."

"Okay, that was good."

"Okay, he's off the field now, defense is on."

"Okay, that was good—no—okay—that wasn't the best block but—"

"Oh, interception!"

"Okay, Vince is back up, Henry's setting up, I think this is Salmon Spawn again but it might be Bow Season—"

"Okay he—OH MY GOD VINCE!!!! OH MY GOD!!!"

Mel was on her feet and cheering. Bow Season was apparently effective, because Vince had brought the ball to the end zone. Birdy hadn't seen the play but jumped up with her, swept into a united joy she'd never felt at Divine Mercy.

A few minutes into the second quarter, Beth rummaged in her backpack and checked her phone. "I'll be back in a bit, I'm going to go see Amanda!" Birdy watched her loud socks retreating down the bleachers and turned back to the game.

The score steadily rose as the teams traded touchdowns. At halftime, Fiona Dawson, apparently a multitalented individual, led the cheerleaders in a booty-shaking routine. Birdy saw a lot of vaguely familiar faces in the crowd. There was Kevin and Logan, who she'd met at Vince's house, Regina, a former conscript of CRL, and Sam, the creepy soccer player who she and Beth had once worked together to defeat.

At the beginning of the fourth quarter, the man in front of Birdy got a phone call, snapped his phone shut, and lumbered down the bleachers in a huff. By squinting just right and listening to Mel's explanations, Birdy was able to piece together what was happening on the field. Finally, with 15 seconds to go and the score tied, Henry, Vince and their teammates settled into position. "I think they might do Sweet Corn, not sure though, no I think it's Bow Season again it—"

They later found out the play was called Atomic Crab. Henry caught the snap, jogged from side to side, and sent the ball flying just before getting tackled by a gorilla-shaped individual. Vince sprinted 20 yards, plucked the ball from the sky above, and loped into the end zone as Conrad went nuts.

Mel charged down the bleachers, Birdy and Kelly scrambling after her. The man with the hairy neck stood at the bottom. "That was the best game of football I've seen here in 30 years!" he wailed to Birdy, apparently feeling they had bonded during their time together.

Beth jogged up and Mel grabbed her arm. "Oh my God Beth!" she screamed. "Did you see that? Did you see that?"

"Yeah!" said Beth, smiling. "Crazy!" Mel grabbed Kelly and marched onward, while Birdy fell into step with Beth.

"How's Amanda?" said Birdy.

"I don't know," said Beth. Birdy looked at her quizzically and Beth shook her head rapidly. "I mean, wait, she's good, she's good, she wanted to tell me about her trip to Deep Creek, sounded really fun."

At that moment they found Vince on the field. Mel jumped forward and hugged him, then stepped back to a less romantic distance. "Well played, well played."

Vince beamed down at her. "Thanks. Thanks for coming." He looked at the rest of them. "Thanks, guys!" He seemed to be addressing a wider audience, so Birdy turned around to find they'd been joined by a pack of Conrad kids.

"Hi Birdy," said someone in her ear. Birdy turned to find a petite girl with spikey black hair smiling at her. "Amanda! How are you?"

"Oh my gosh, this game was so good! Where were you all sitting?"

"We were close to the front, but this huge guy was in front of me for a lot of it and I couldn't see very well."

"Oh man, that sucks! You should have had Beth kick him out!" She tossed her head toward Beth, who was plodding around in imitation of the guy who'd tackled Henry.

Kevin barreled into their midst. His Conrad Wrestling t-shirt was drenched in sweat. "Dude, that game was so badass," he said to Vince, clasping his hand. "This is our year, the Minutemen are gonna kill it. Wrestling is throwing football a party tonight, skipping is not an option."

"Aw, thanks man," said Vince, grinning.

"No problem, I know you'd do the same for us." Doubt flitted across Vince's face as Kevin turned to Kelly. "You coming, girl?" He gave her what he thought was a manly smile.

Kelly looked taken aback while Birdy smiled at her in revenge.

"Uhhh," said Kelly.

"You've got to come," said Amanda, "I'm coming! Oh, my gosh Beth! Hi!"

"Hey girl!" said Beth, throwing an arm around her.

"You need to bring Mel and Birdy and Kelly tonight, I miss them! Plus, you and me really need to catch up too. I still need to tell you about when I went to Deep Creek with Tommy, okay?"

"Okay, can't wait!" said Beth.

Amanda waved and called "See you soon!" as she left.

Birdy looked at Beth, but Beth looked away, tightening her backpack straps. "Come on guys!" She pointed to Kevin. "See you soon, Kev!" She strode back in the direction of the parking lot, socks flashing. Kevin left too after hinting mightily that he was picking up some alcohol, and Mel smiled over at Kelly as he walked away.

"You know, Kevin and Kelly has a really nice ring to it..."

"No, it doesn't," snapped Kelly.

3

ONE CRISP SEPTEMBER EVENING, Maddie's dad came to Victoria Street to share a beer with Mr. Abe. The next day, Isaac and Maddie were officially courting. There was no Facebook designation for their brand of relationship status, so Isaac and Maddie opted for, "It's Complicated."

Mr. Abe was only too happy to differentiate his rules from Mr. Doppelski's. He stopped Birdy and Dad in the St. Ann's parking lot as Doppelskis of all shades trailed into church behind him. Birdy tracked Dominic's brisk walk up the steps as Abe blabbed.

"Jude's so strict about no dating till age eighteen, but that just doesn't work out too good. I think it just pushed Dominic harder to break the rules, you know? Better just let it happen, make it a good situation for them. Your boys have girlfriends, right?"

"They've had them," said Dad, who remained fuzzy on what courtship was, what Jude's rules on dating were, and how Dominic had broken them. Jude peeled off from his family and stood silently behind Abe, holding Rebecca in one arm.

"Hey, I had a few girlfriends in high school too, it's just part of growing up," Abe continued. It seemed important to him that Dad agreed with him. "He's just a real standup kid, any girl would be lucky to court him. Or date him." He threw Birdy a look that was both smug and admonishing, and with that, he breached the limits of Dad's patience.

Dad inflated himself and crossed his arms. "Just like any boy would be lucky to go out with Birdy. If any boy was good enough for Birdy." Dad may not have been entirely sure what Abe was driving at, but he was on Birdy's side. Birdy was grateful for his loyalty but still wanted to evaporate.

Mr. Doppelski couldn't resist joining the fun any longer. "Are we talking about Isaac's little girlfriend?" he said, making Abe flinch. "Didn't think the kid had it in him! Say, good job Isaac!" he said to Rebecca, nuzzling her nose.

"Dood dob Isaac!" Rebecca squealed back, giddy to be in on her dad's joke. They laughed together while Abe turned purple. Dad looked down at Birdy to see if she knew what the hell was happening right now. Mr. Doppelski flicked his smirk at Birdy, and her stomach backflipped. She stole away from the merry men and into church.

Birdy still didn't know what the adults knew or thought of her role in exposing Dominic. But even though he was no longer at Divine Mercy, his indiscretion seemed to have unleashed something within its student body. The faithful teens were testing boundaries, with embarrassing results. On Monday, Margaret sat next to Birdy in English class and confessed her obsession with Katy Perry. "I know you like some really secular music so I knew you wouldn't judge me." Fred dipped his toes in the waters of cursing by occasionally saying things like "That damn Obama," or "I don't know what the hell those Democrats think they're doing." Josh tried to get in with Isaac and Michael by replicating what he must have perceived as their edginess. He started sitting at their lunch table and laughing loudly at all their jokes. One day, Maddie and Gabby went to the bathroom together, and Michael watched Gabby walk away, emitting a faint, gross whistle as he turned back to the rest of them.

"Hate to see 'em leave, but you love to watch 'em go," he said. Birdy had nothing to say to that, but Josh leapt to respond.

"Yeah, I love girls' butts."

Birdy choked on nothing while Isaac and Michael looked suddenly delighted. Josh had no idea it was at his expense.

"Oh yeah?" said Michael.

"Yeah, and their boobs too."

Birdy instinctively hunched forward, but Josh's attempt at lechery was so stupid that she didn't actually feel threatened.

"Well, sounds like we have some common interests, Josh," said Michael.

"Yeah, boobs are so nice," said Josh, emboldened. "Fred and I were talking about them. At church this weekend, there was this one girl dressed really immodestly, and her"—his voice cracked— "cleavage was really amazing."

"Shut up," Birdy snapped.

"Why?" said Josh, trying to look tough.

"Because Mrs. Amon's standing behind you," said Isaac.

Josh yelped and turned around to see if it was true, which it wasn't. Isaac and Michael cracked up as Gabby and Maddie returned.

"What's so funny?" said Maddie.

"We were just talking about modesty," said Michael. Gabby raised an eyebrow at him, but Maddie did not compute the evilness of his grin. Instead, she smiled at Isaac and spastically patted his arm.

Did I die without noticing? Am I in hell right now?

Isaac and Maddie's courtship managed to both neatly prove Isaac's prowess with females and prevent any funny business from happening between them, as fifty minutes separated their houses. They rarely saw each other outside of school. But Isaac's achievements were not limited to the romantic and spiritual realms. Awkward moments with Josh notwithstanding, Isaac was steadily reinventing the social fabric of Divine Mercy. Whereas Dominic had built flocks of admirers, Isaac wove a web of equals. He popped in and out of every group, leaving trails of friendships in his wake.

It didn't hurt that Isaac's punishing daily workouts had begun to pay off. He shared his mother's penchant for photography, and his favorite subject was himself, shirtless. He kept sharing pictures of himself flexing in the back field at sunset, at dawn, before storms, you name it. The young ladies of Divine Mercy boldly wore out their Like buttons on these snapshots. Maddie accepted this state of affairs gracefully.

"I know all these other girls probably like him too, but he's so committed to purity," she confided to Gabby and Birdy one day. "He would never do anything unfaithful to me."

Birdy admired Isaac's social acumen but hated watching the charade between him and Maddie, just as she hated being subject to Divine Mercy's milquetoast style of teenage rebellion. As the miseries of school compounded upon themselves, she was ever more grateful for Mel, Beth, and Kelly. On Friday nights, whoever wasn't working went to Vince's games. Away games required them to travel 40 minutes or more, and Kelly firmly designated herself as the driver on these road trips.

Some weekends there were parties, which consisted of drinking dubiously sourced alcohol in fields that vaguely qualified as someone's backyard. Vince hosted an early one of these gatherings—"Touchdowns and Tequila"—but as the Minutemen continued to perform uncommonly well, he grew conflicted and tried to rise to his accidental position of leadership. After their third game and third win, Vince resolved not to drink for the rest of the season and implored his teammates to follow suit. On the invite for "Bros in the Barn" he wrote "BYOB, I'm not providing anything but water and if you are on the football team, please DO NOT bring alcohol. I'm not drinking for the rest of the season, I want to be on point." The Minutemen didn't listen to Vince, but they accepted his decision with affection.

Where they did listen to him was his insistence that they show up to every practice, leaving them unable to join in the games of pickup soccer at Mel's. Fortunately, Beth had plenty of people to invite. Along with nice girls like Amanda White and Katie Foster, there was also Kevin and a seemingly endless rotation of his neckless teammates. One of them, Evan Wharton, annoyed Birdy from the first sentence he ever spoke to her, which was "I wrestle 165."

"Oh, wow," Birdy had said.

"Yeah, it's kind of a tough weight class. But me and the boys have each other's back, we make it work. Like last week we snuck into a strip club together, that was cool." Birdy could not figure out which of these inane non sequiturs to respond to, but Kevin saved the day.

"Dude, that wasn't cool," said Kevin loudly, glancing over at Kelly, "That was so stupid. We shouldn't have done that." Sober Kevin was no less sweaty but occasionally less creepy than drunk Kevin.

On the last Saturday in September, their game ended early when it started pouring. Amanda and Katie ran to Katie's car, and Kevin's gang piled into his Jeep while Kevin hastily put up its top and windows. Birdy made for the front porch with Mel, Beth, and Kelly.

"Well, shit," said Beth, who had ridden her bike as usual.

"Beth, you're not riding your bike all the way to the theater in this," said Mel, wiping rain out of her eyes. "We'll give you a ride to work and then we'll pick you back up for the sleepover."

"Okay, I just need to stop home really quick for my uniform and my sleepover stuff," said Beth. "You don't have to come in or anything, I'll be really quick." They drove to Beth's squat rancher, which would have looked depressing even without the rain.

"Gosh, I haven't been here in forever," said Mel, shutting off the engine and opening the car door. "Birdy's gotta see it! Do you still have your hermit crab?"

Beth glanced at Mel, lips pressed shut, and sped off to the front door.

"Jeez, slow down," Mel said to Beth's back. Kelly and Birdy hurried after her, eager to get out of the downpour. The girls burst through the door into a dark living room. A weird stench assaulted Birdy's nostrils. *Ugh. It smells like...*

"Oh my God, Beth, did a skunk die in here or something?" said Mel.

Beth, normally immune to Mel's big mouth, flinched. "Oh, I think my dad just forgot to take the trash out or something," she said, sounding distracted. "Come back to my room!"

Beth's room smelled like Sweet Pea by Bath and Body Works. It was covered in clothes, books, notebooks, CDs, cosmetics, and an unoccupied hermit crab tank. Beth put on her uniform and rushed around with her duffel bag, collecting shoes, sweatpants, and shirts like a tornado. "Just a minute!" she kept saying. "I just need my..." Halfway through packing her duffel, she grabbed her backpack instead and shoved a stack of notebooks inside.

"Just need to grab my toothbrush! I'll be right back!" Still holding her backpack, she dashed into the bathroom across the hall and slammed the door shut.

"Oh man, I actually really need to pee," said Birdy.

"I think there's another bathroom down the hall," said Mel. "One of those doors right by the entrance?"

Birdy wandered down the dim hall and back into the dark living room. A peeling white door stood out from the brown wood paneling. There was a latch on the outside, but it was unhooked. Birdy pushed the door open, smelling a putrid waft of air as she fumbled for the light switch.

"BIRDY!" Beth shrieked from down the hall, "Don't go in there!"

The shrill fear in Beth's voice was lightning in Birdy's spine. But she'd already flipped the switch.

It was a bathroom. And it was a garden.

On the far wall, a splintery square of wood covered the window. Rickety shelves rose from the tile floor, wide, bright lamps perched precariously on them. And on each shelf, green plants with skinny, jagged leaves reached up toward the lamps.

Beth was growing weed.

4

BIRDY TURNED AROUND TO SEE BETH, who stood with her hands clapped over her cheeks.

"Birdy, please, listen, just listen, okay—"

"Guys, are you—" said Kelly, coming up behind Beth, but she stopped, speechless. Mel, looking over the top of Kelly's head, said "Holy. Absolute. Shit. *What?*"

Beth wrung her hands, her blue eyes darting, her words jumbled. "My parents are gone. Like *gone*. My mom left 10 months ago. My dad left before that. This was all his stuff. I don't know where they went and I don't even want them to come back, I just need a way to make it two more years till I can get out of here and I have two jobs already and I just needed something else to cover all the shit I have to pay for and this helps. Please don't tell, I don't want to have to go to foster care or like *jail* or something."

"Beth, what is going on though? What do you mean your parents are gone? We need to slow down," said Kelly.

"Okay, but let's get out of here. The lights are supposed to be off right now," said Beth.

Birdy made a detour in the other bathroom and then joined the rest of them on Beth's bed. "Okay," said Beth, some of her poise returning. "My dad lost his job a long time ago—you guys know that. That's why I had to leave St. Monica's. But nobody's hiring and after a while he just gave up and I guess he was bored or something but he started trying to grow weed. He spent a bunch of money on all that crap," she said, gesturing in the direction of the weed bathroom. "But he was really impatient and before anything even sprouted I guess he decided it wasn't worth it because he took off entirely."

"Where did he go?" said Mel, sounding pissed.

"I don't know, but he has this friend he met when he was in the Army who lives in West Virginia, so he might be there. With her." Kelly gasped, and Beth nodded. "Yeah. That's what my mom thought. So then after a few weeks my mom said she— needed a break." She looked at them with a mockery of a smile. "She said she was going to visit her sister for a few days. But while she was gone she called me in the middle of the night." Beth's nose started running. "She goes 'Beth, I'll be back in a few weeks, I just need to clear my head a bit more. But you'll be fine holding things together for a little while.'" She sniffed and rose angrily to her feet. "So that was over Thanksgiving break."

"Beth!" cried Birdy. "That's terrible!"

"Yeah," said Beth.

"What if something happened to her?" said Kelly. "She wouldn't just leave you like that."

Beth gave her a pitying look. "She would, Kelly. She did."

Kelly struggled for a moment. "Well...Does your aunt know about this?"

"I have no idea," Beth said, "I guess probably not, but I haven't even seen her since I was like ten. She and my mom don't get along that well, so it's kinda weird that she went there. But, so, right after my dad left, I found this." She dug into her backpack and pulled out a dogeared pamphlet entitled *How to Grow Marijuana At Home*. "He left it in the bathroom. And, well, when I'm not with you guys... it's just really, really boring and lonely here." She sounded sheepish at admitting her loneliness and started talking faster. "So I thought it might be interesting to see what happened if I did what the pamphlet said. And it worked really well."

"So," said Birdy, thinking over her family's financial woes, "So, what, you've been selling this and—it's been enough to pay for *rent*—or your mortgage—and food and *everything?*"

"Not exactly," said Beth. "My dad grew up in this house and my grandparents paid the mortgage forever ago. So that's a big expense I don't have. I pay for electricity, water, cable, phone, internet, my phone, and food." She ticked off her bills on her fingers, manicured purple this week. "I already worked at the theater when she left, and I got the job at Waffle King after she left, and I get a ton of tips there. But it's not always quite enough for everything. So I used the pamphlet and some stuff on the internet to get the plants growing and—it wasn't really hard to find people to sell to, you know?"

"Because you're irresistible," said Kelly.

"Highly visible," corrected Beth with a smile. "But I try to be picky about who I sell to. I only sell to people if they promise to keep it quiet. I really don't want to get caught, obviously, and I don't want the whole world to find out about it."

"Beth," said Birdy, failing to conceal her panic, "How is the whole world *not* going to find out about it? I mean how are you staying safe, what if someone doesn't keep it quiet, what if kids are talking about you and their teachers or parents overhear or something, what if you get caught?"

Beth sat back down on her bed, businesslike. "Well for starters, most of the teachers at my school don't give a shit. I've had maybe one or two who cared, and everyone else is just trying to avoid being bullied by some fifteen-year-old. And most of the parents also don't give a shit, which is why we get to have all these fun parties and no one ever gets in trouble. And no offense to Mr. Holloway, but the Conrad Police don't give a shit either."

"Accurate," said Mel.

"They're worrying more about their own problems than what all the kids are up to," said Kelly.

"Right, and none of them are looking for me to be a drug dealer. And I try to cover my tracks. I got a TracFone from Walmart that I use only for weed stuff. I never have people at my house, I try to meet up with them in public but hidden areas."

"Like football games?" said Birdy shrewdly.

"Yeah, sorry, I know you realized I didn't really go talk to Amanda at the opening game," said Beth apologetically. Birdy had to giggle at that.

"Oh, or the time when we were looking for t-shirts to decorate and you disappeared for twenty minutes!" said Mel.

"And when you kept leaving at S'mores and Shots?" guessed Kelly.

"Yeah," sighed Beth.

"You've been at this for a while," said Mel.

"I have," said Beth. "This is my fourth crop." She grinned. "The last two sold like hotcakes." Her smile dropped from her face and she turned to Mel, pleading. "Please Mel, don't tell your dad."

Mel looked at Beth like she was crazy. "Are you kidding? I would never do that to you!"

Beth laughed, but her eyes got shiny wet.

Birdy gnawed her thumbnail. *You can't stand to even look like you're doing something wrong.* Dominic had hurled this observation at Birdy, and it was at least half-true, and it was why she was so worried right now. Images flashed through her mind—Beth in handcuffs, Beth in a jail cell, *herself* in a jail cell. *This is all very, very illegal, you can't just go on knowing this is happening, you should tell someone.*

But who would that be? And it was illegal, but how wrong was it, really? Why was it legal to let alcohol make you act stupid, but not weed? How was it fair that Beth's parents could leave her and Beth could get in trouble just for trying to survive? And come on, would they *really* end up in jail?

Maybe, she told herself, but she shoved the thought away. The point was that whatever the consequences might be, she could never turn Beth in. Beth, adored by the masses, had been cast aside by her parents and was scrabbling alone in fear. To Birdy, that was the real crime. Beth cheered her on when she talked to cute boys and protected her from weird ones. She drove her bike like it was a motorcycle, she was fearless on the soccer field. She was a sunflower of a girl, strong, bright, and lovable, and she needed someone to shelter her now.

Birdy looked at Beth. "I'm so sorry your parents left you here. We'll take care of you instead."

Mel and Kelly started talking at the same time.

"We can help cover some of the bills, we can give you rides, we can help take care of the house—" said Kelly.

"We can help if you need clothes or a permission slip or school supplies or whatever—" said Mel.

"We can help with your budget and homework and food!" said Birdy.

Beth sunk into her pillows with an exhausted smile. Mel leaned forward and plucked Beth's phone out of her pocket. Birdy watched over Mel's shoulder as she changed her name in Beth's contacts from "Melicious" to "Mom."

"Just call me if you need anything, sweetie," she said in a New Jerseyish accent as she handed it back, making Beth laugh. Then she did a double take at her phone.

"Oh, fuck, I'm so late, I still need to pack, I need to get to work, I need to—"

"Okay, don't worry about packing, just get whatever you need for work. We'll come back here for the rest of it after we pick you up, okay?" said Kelly in a calming voice.

"Okay," Beth said, nodding rapidly and charging for the front door.

In the movie theater parking lot they watched Beth's blond braid fly behind her as she sprinted inside.

"So what we need to do," said Kelly, putting the car in drive, "is go back to Beth's house and clean it up a little bit."

"Or a lot," said Mel.

"And get her some food," said Birdy.

"And make a plan for how we're going to help her," said Kelly.

"Like a schedule or something," said Birdy.

"Her parents suck," said Mel.

They went back to the house, which felt even gloomier now. "Probably should have locked this behind us," Mel commented as they went through the door. Kelly immediately set to attacking the crusty mess in the kitchen, muttering "Ew, ew, ew, ew." After a minute she pulled a notebook and pen from her purse. "We need a broom, some dish soap, more sponges, *gloves*, and OH, NO!" She dropped her pen and jumped a foot in the air. "Okay," she said, getting her pen from the floor, "and mouse traps."

Birdy looked in the fridge, which was empty except for a box of baking soda lying on its side, some shriveled apples, and a hardened block of cheese. "What has she even been eating?"

"Come write what she needs on my list."

"Her favorite cereal is Lucky Charms," called Mel from the living room.

They went to Walmart to pick up dinner supplies and the cleaning stuff Kelly wanted. Under the tutelage of a food blog called Dinner on a Dime, Birdy had recently figured out how to make edible chicken. Once they got back to Beth's, she helped get the kitchen up to Kelly's standards and then started working on the food.

Mel went to get Beth while Kelly and Birdy finished dinner. Kelly found some candles in Beth's room, put them on the table, and lit them. Beth walked in a minute later.

"Oh my gosh," she said, "it smells SO GOOD in here!" They gathered at the table and Kelly brought out the plates. Beth was exuberant in her gratitude and regaled them with stories about work. Most of the teachers at Conrad High were either very young or very old, and Beth had seen two of the young ones on a date.

"So then they walked out together, and I guess they wanted a snack for the road or something, so they got back in line. So Marcus is helping them and they're standing there not paying attention at all, and Mr. Grove totally went for it and put his hand on her butt. And Ms. Hopkins was totally into it, she was giggling and snuggling and basically humping him. So then after Marcus tried to hand them their candy three times, they finally looked up and then they saw me and they both made a face like this –" Beth pulled a grimace of shame "— so I just gave them a thumbs up and kept working!" They all laughed, and Beth leaned back contentedly in her seat. "This was a good idea. It's really nice to have someone make dinner for me. And the house looks so clean. And it's so nice to tell someone about – you know. Thanks."

"It's our pleasure," said Mel.

"It's a good thing Birdy's a professional chicken servant," said Kelly.

"I'd rather serve it to Beth than anyone else," said Birdy.

"Well that's good, because Beth's probably exhausted from running a secret business," said Kelly.

Beth laughed. "I'm really happy I told you. There are obviously a few people who know about the weed side of it, but it felt so weird not to tell you about my parents and everything."

Birdy put her chin in her hand "I'm sorry you've been dealing with all that alone. It's like you had to suddenly grow up and you couldn't tell anyone. Your parents ran away and left you with all this responsibility and then you have the plants on top of it and it's like they're your kids."

"I guess that makes us aunts," said Mel.

"Ohhh, yay, this is the only chance I'll ever get to be an aunt," said Kelly.

"I never thought I'd be a plant aunt," said Mel.

This turned into a discussion of what the children's names were, who Beth's favorite child was, and how it was kind of weird that she was selling her children. After a few minutes Mel faded from the conversation and started scraping her knife across her empty plate, making a horrible noise.

"Stop!" said Kelly.

"Sorry," said Mel, looking serious. "I was just thinking... I'm obviously not going to tell my dad. But I kind of think we need to tell Vince."

Mel texted Vince before they went home, and they met up with him at the watering hole. He sat on a log as he listened, elbows balanced on his knees, chin balanced on his thumbs. When they were finished explaining, he took off his hat and banged it on his knee a few times, then put it back on. His pale eyes were sorrowful.

"Beth, your parents suck, I can't believe they did that to you. I'm really sorry, I'm totally here to help you out."

"Thanks," sighed Beth.

"I just have one request." He clasped his hands in supplication.

"What?"

"Please don't let Henry buy anything from you, it'll destroy our season."

5

From: petercleary@hotmail.com
Good news: I got a job through a temp agency at this refrigeration company and even though I feel like Ryan from the Office, the good news is that the company is actually closed on Christmas! Still don't think I can make it home for Thanksgiving because it's for some reason open then—I guess Thanksgiving has a lot of refrigeration disasters so they need to be prepared.

You sound like you're staying busy. That's cool about the new soccer arrangement, how's that been going? How's the football season going? How do Mom and Dad feel about you zipping all over town? I hope you're bringing your pepper spray. Kidding. But stay safe.

From: bluebirdy@aol.com
Congratulations on the job!! Is your boss Bob Vance? I'm so glad you might be able to come for Christmas, hope it works out! Should I mention the job to mom and dad or keep it quiet?

The football season is still going really well. Soccer has been fun too. Mel is always looking up different plays or trying to come up with new ones on her own and she always makes us do them. It's fun and would be somewhat more fun if we were playing against people who didn't already know all the plays. But we have a good time. And afterwards either Mel or Kelly's mom will usually feed us something— they LOVE feeding people. They don't have Dutch ovens though, serious disadvantage.

Mom and Dad seem accepting of my zipping around. Dad is excited I'm getting to experience the fun of high school football. He always asks really detailed questions about the games which I am unable to answer. He likes when Mel comes over because she has better information for him. He wants to come to a game sometime but he's always too tired at the end of the week. Mom is good with it too I think—after Chris left she would come up to me every day saying "Honey—you just seem so lonely." Now she has stopped saying that so I guess she's not worried about me being lonely anymore. Plus I think it makes her feel cool to let me go to the PUBLIC SCHOOL games because a few of the moms at my school think that is insane and we know Mom likes to be different. This time it's working to my advantage!

I'm being very safe and bringing a dagger and pepper spray with me wherever I go.

BIRDY ASSUMED PETER WOULD not think assisting a drug dealer qualified as staying safe. But the practicalities of doing so didn't seem dangerous at all. Birdy, Mel, and Kelly soon fell into a routine of feeding, transporting, and bankrolling Beth, and it felt only right.

The Clearys had at least five books with titles along the lines of "100 Essential Ways to Stretch Your Pennies." Birdy had grown up browsing these and was therefore baffled to discover that Beth ate almost every meal out of the house. She got a free meal every time she worked at Waffle King, and supplemented these meals with Chipotle, McDonald's, and snacks from 7-Eleven. No one had ever told her how much more expensive it was to eat out than to cook, and she didn't know how to cook anyway. Birdy figured out how to feed her for $15 dollars per week and taught her how to make pasta. They started making weekly dinners at the Clearys' house in addition to getting food from Mrs. Holloway and Mrs. Merryman, which first confused and then excited Mom and Dad.

Birdy secretly hoped that if Beth knew more about how to save money, she wouldn't feel the need to keep growing weed. Instead, Beth enthusiastically accepted Birdy's cooking lessons and used the cost savings as an opportunity to update her wardrobe. Birdy realized with apprehension that Beth's plants—her kids, as they now called them— weren't just her income source. They were her hobby. She loved poking around in the dirt and experimenting with ways to improve growth. And contrary to the old adage, Beth did occasionally get high on her own supply.

Beth had smoked weed eight times. Four of those times, she had completely freaked. For this reason, she was not a dedicated pot user. Beth did not like to risk the possibility of anyone seeing her anxiety, a personality trait she worked desperately to hide. But the other four times she'd smoked, she'd enjoyed the way it unlocked her brain. In her dad's pamphlet, there was a throwaway sentence about how curing the buds for longer could lead to a more potent high. One night while high and alone, Beth had contemplated this idea and figured if it worked, she could raise her prices. She drew a diagram that made no sense the next morning, but inspired her nonetheless. With her next crop she had cured the buds for longer, tested the results herself, charged more money on a better-high guarantee, and made bank.

After Beth told them this tale, Mel was intrigued and begged Beth to let her try the upcoming batch. On the night it was ready, the two of them went out into the dark woods, leaving Birdy and Kelly in the dark house.

"If they're going to get high, we're going to drink," said Kelly, producing Yuenglings for herself and Birdy. They went to drink them in Beth's room, where it smelled good.

"Are you ever going to try weed?" said Kelly.

"I don't know," said Birdy. "I really hate the smell."

"Me too," said Kelly. "Then again, I also hate the taste of alcohol."

Birdy laughed.

"You know, it's funny," Kelly continued. "I would never, ever sell weed. But if I *did* ever sell weed, then I'd never experiment the way Beth does. If curing the buds went fine the first time, then I wouldn't risk messing them up by doing something different the next time. But Beth's willing to take the risk."

"That's true," said Birdy, who'd had similar thoughts. "She's so brave." She wavered. "Sometimes I wish she was less brave."

"I wish that all the time," said Kelly, and Birdy smiled. "But it also feels like we're the only people who care about her enough to notice what's going on. So I don't really think she'll get caught." She looked at Birdy like she was hoping for reassurance.

"Yeah," said Birdy, trying to hush her doubts. *Stop being so paranoid.*

Beth and Mel wandered in sometime later wearing vacant grins. Beth went to the kitchen and loudly consumed the entire week's groceries. Mel sat beside Birdy on the ground. The whites of her eyes were red, making her green eyes vibrant. "Birdy," she said lazily, "The pattern on your sweatshirt is really charming."

As the weather grew colder and darker, Kelly constantly offered to drive Beth around. But just as she truly enjoyed nurturing her kids, she also truly enjoyed riding her bike and frequently rejected Kelly's offers.

To Birdy, the time spent with Mel, Beth, and Kelly was her real life, and the time spent at Divine Mercy was an unpleasant performance. Birdy took her tests, ate her lunch, occasionally laughed at jokes, and texted her real friends from the bathroom. Mr. Doppelski dropped by almost every day to teach his Algebra 1 class, which was right after Birdy's Pre-Calc class. He always burst into the room with some variation of "Well, if it isn't the finest mathematical minds at Divine Mercy!" Everyone laughed, but Birdy always stuck close to the group as she made her way out of the room.

Mom was still on the board, which was how Birdy knew Mr. Doppelski was still touchy about Dominic's fall from grace. In deference to his touchiness, the independent vs. parochial debate had quieted. Instead, the board's sole occupation was planning a spring event that would do double duty as a student activity and community fundraiser. Mom was keeping gleefully silent about what it was. All she would say was that it wasn't a dance. That would have been an awkward topic to navigate around Mr. Doppelski, and the students were pairing off quite easily these days anyway.

On the Friday before Halloween, Mrs. Amon discovered Gabby and Michael squeezed behind the desk of shame, making out. Gabby and Michael proudly bore both her verbal assault and the rumors that proceeded to fly around the school. Maddy went home with Gabby for a sleepover that afternoon, their bodies already hunched in the gossip position as they hustled to Gabby's van. Birdy stood with Michael and Isaac in the parking lot.

"What are you wearing Monday?" Isaac asked Birdy. The students were allowed to dress up as saints in observance of All Saints Day, which was on Sunday.

Birdy didn't want to dress as a saint, but was enticed by the opportunity to skip her uniform. "I'm just going to wear regular clothes and say I'm St. Alexis, a girl who just died and went to heaven recently."

Michael laughed. "Mrs. Amon will hate that."

"Exactly," grinned Birdy.

"Are you going to the youth Mass tomorrow night?" asked Isaac. St. Paul's had recently introduced Saturday evening youth Masses, in case the Songs and Teens crowd wanted to spend more of its weekend at church.

"No, I'm working," said Birdy. *And I don't want to go.*

"We're going," he said, gesturing to Michael and himself. "You know Fiona Dawson right?"

"Yeah," said Birdy. "How do you know her?

"We met in Driver's Ed and she goes to Songs and Teens when it's not football season. She's singing in the youth Mass, so we're going to see her sing and then to her friend Evan's Halloween party after."

"Oh," said Birdy, slightly annoyed. "I think I'm going to that same Halloween party after work."

"Maybe we'll see you," said Isaac. "What are you wearing to that?"

"My work uniform."

"Sexy waitress! I love it!" said Michael.

"I'm not a waitress, and it's not sexy. Trust me," said Birdy.

"Well why are you wearing it?" said Michael.

"Because I'm broke," said Birdy. She was also trying to repel Evan. When he invited them to the Halloween party, he'd said "I can't wait to see your costume," in a way that made her instantly resolve to wear a shapeless sack. Her work uniform, a black polo and black pants, was close enough. Furthermore, she'd blown her budget buying things for Beth. She decided to save money and confuse Evan with one stroke, bringing her passive aggressive costume count up to two for that year.

"Well that's interesting," said Michael, looking skeptical. "I think this is going to be a really big party because his parents aren't going to be home. Do you know if Dom's going?"

Isaac and Birdy shrugged.

Birdy had not seen Isaac and Dominic in one place in a while. Now that they could both drive, their social paths had diverged. Not content with ruling Divine Mercy, Isaac was busy expanding his influence to a wider circle. When Birdy got off work on Saturday, she went to Evan's house, where a sexy angel kept watch by the front door.

"Hey girl!" said Fiona, her halo scraping Birdy's cheek as they hugged. "What are you supposed to be?"

"I'm a fast food worker," said Birdy.

"Okay," said Fiona brightly, not sorry to be the better dressed of the two of them. "So I had no idea you knew Isaac Doppelski." She pointed a glittery finger to where Isaac stood holding court in his Sean Taylor jersey. A few feet away, Michael demonstrated a backflip to a lukewarm audience.

"Oh yeah, he's my neighbor and he goes to my school," said Birdy.

"Your school sounds fucking weird," said Fiona. "No offense," she added halfheartedly.

"You have no idea," said Birdy.

"But you're sweet," Fiona reassured her. "And Isaac is sooooo nice." She wavered on her stilettos. "Sooooo many girls I know are into him. But he's really, really faithful to his girlfriend, even though she lives really, really, far away so he only sees her at school. It's soooo sweet." Fiona's face was in fact rather sour at this statement.

Fiona was not the first Conrad girl from whom Birdy had heard rave reviews of Isaac. Dominic, meanwhile, had long since dumped

Angela Prune, but—as Angela had mournfully informed Mel and Kelly at school—he had made plenty of friends through her that he got to keep in the breakup. He spent more time with the St. Monica's crowd, from which Mel and Kelly were eager to extricate themselves.

Birdy had the misfortune of being saddled with an overly enthusiastic memory and thus associated nearly everything about her house with Dominic, from the maple tree to a shirt he had once complimented. Still, the distractions of keeping Beth afloat had recently shoved him to the periphery of her mind. He lurked in her feelings but not in her daily occupations. They had turned into parallel lines. If she just kept going, she'd never touch him.

Though she was touching a lot of other people at the moment. The room was lit only with purple string lights and was packed with Redskins, Ravens, Minutemen of various teams, celebrities, and a zoo of scantily clad animals. Birdy picked her way through the crowd, brushing against glitter and sweat.

"Birdy! *Petrificus totalis!*" someone yelled in her ear. Birdy turned and laughed. Mel was wearing round glasses frames and had drawn a lightning shaped scar on her forehead. Her St. Monica's uniform was doubling as a Hogwarts uniform tonight, though she had rolled the skirt up several inches.

"It's the Girl Who Lived!" said Birdy.

"There you are!" said Beth. She'd rummaged through her mom's mountains of abandoned clothes and come up with a neon Jazzerciser ensemble. "What the hell are you wearing?"

"Remember, she's scaring away Evan," said Mel. "And I'm sorry, but you're still beautiful."

"I can't believe you both wore uniforms," said Kelly, stomping her foot. "This is Halloween!" Kelly was a much shorter Taylor Swift. She wore a silvery dress, had her hair in a curly updo, and had painstakingly crafted an enclosure for her water bottle that looked like a VMA.

"My math teacher always says you just gotta go with what you got," said Mel, "And that is exactly what me and Birdy did."

"Okay, but I'm taking your hair down," said Kelly, and she gently unfastened Birdy's ponytail and brushed her hair out with her fingers.

Evan trudged up to them, the odor of his wrestling singlet preceding him. "Beth," he yelled. "When are you going to have more weed?"

"What are you talking about?" said Beth with a nervous giggle.

Evan yelled louder. "I heard from Fiona, you grow it? Can you hook me up? I tried some of hers a couple weeks ago, it was so—"

"Shhh, I know, I was kidding," said Beth, her voice rising into a shriek. "Trying to be subtle. You know?"

Evan didn't know. He noticed Birdy and squinted harder. "Hey, Birdy, you—didn't I tell you this was a Halloween party?"

"Yeah, this is my costume."

"Oh," he said, looking confused. Then he sniffed the air. "Does anyone smell chicken or something?"

Beth anxiously watched Evan as he was swallowed into the costumed melee. "Well, I think we all need a drink after that conversation," she said, with a fake smile.

Birdy accepted a nasty cup of beer, heart pounding. Of course it was never going to be true that high schoolers would stay quiet about Beth's weed business, but it was unsettling to see how casually Evan had blown her cover. Beth pounded down a beer and started demonstrating Jazzercise moves. After a beer of her own and a few nips from Kelly's VMA, Birdy went upstairs to look for a bathroom. She opened a door and found Dominic, wearing a cowboy hat, jeans, suspenders, and no shirt, his arms tightly wrapped around a Tinkerbell.

So much for parallel lines. *Why the hell did I wear this?* Dominic paused his consumption of Tinkerbell's face and looked up. "Aw Birdy, what's the matter? Are you feeling lonely?" Tinkerbell placed a proprietary claw on his arm and shot Birdy a death stare with her black rimmed eyes. The front of her hair towered from her scalp in a ferocious bump. Birdy turned on her heel and walked away. The girl didn't scare her, but Dominic did.

"Where's the bathroom?" said Beth when Birdy found her again. "I need to go too!"

"I don't know, I ran into Dominic and some Tinkerbell bitch." *Shit.* Birdy hadn't meant to say it like she was about to cry.

"So did you ever go?" said Beth, smoothing over Birdy's uncouth emotional outburst.

"Uh, no," said Birdy.

"Okay, so first we're going to find us a bathroom. And then we're going to find you and Kelly some boys to talk to."

Despite her disparaging assessment of the boys of Conrad, Beth was still dedicated to helping Kelly and Birdy access their inner flirts. It was a tedious process, but Beth was nothing if not determined. In the weeks since they'd learned her secret, she'd increased her efforts, bent on repaying them in some way. Birdy suspected tonight's nudge was also an effort to distract herself from the conversation with Evan.

Vince walked up wearing a long red wig, his tight yellow and red striped sweater making him look like a scarecrow. "Ello! I'm Ginny Weasley!" he said in a British accent. Mel cracked up and Vince grinned down at her. They did this sometimes, entering their own little world for a fraction of a second before snapping back to the group.

This was Birdy's issue, which Beth was sure she could get over—she wanted a relationship like Mel and Vince's that was built on a foundation of real friendship. And you couldn't exactly go hit on a guy because he looked like he might be best friend material. But with both Beth's feelings and Dominic's mean smile fresh in her mind, Birdy struck up a conversation with a boy named Aiden, who was dressed as a Ravens player. They chatted for a few minutes until she lost him to a passing cowgirl.

"That's okay," said Beth. During Birdy's time with Aiden, she'd acquired a can of Four Loko. "I heard he has herpes. Look, Danny's here!"

Birdy's stomach butterflies fluttered weakly. Danny was a Conrad baseball player with a torn meniscus who she had talked to a few times. He was sweet, in an empty sort of way. Birdy waved to him and he approached her, flattening the top of his soft brown hair.

"Hi," he stammered when he reached her. "Cool costume."

"Hi" said Birdy. "I like yours too." He was a lumberjack, or something. "How's Nala?" Nala was Danny's golden retriever puppy. His kind eyes lit up at the sound of her name and he launched into some tales of her antics. His love for her was endearing, but as in their previous conversations, some of the things he said left Birdy uncertain about his intelligence level.

"She's so naughty sometimes. I have no idea how people get their dogs to do what they say."

"Oh, I think you can give them treats when they do what you want them to do." Birdy's uncertainty was an act, not that she was an expert on dog training. When she was ten, she had consulted *Dog Training for Dummies* in an attempt to teach some manners to the Clearys' long-gone puppy, Galahad. He had learned to shake hands, but had still clawed both their couch and their cat, Lancelot.

"Oh, that's cool! I think my dad said something about that!" Danny's mind was truly blown. Birdy smiled but didn't know what else to say.

"Well—" he said. He held his mouth open and clenched his fists. "I—I—I gotta go find my friend." He sighed and looked at her helplessly.

"Okay," said Birdy, just as helpless. Danny wandered away. Birdy looked to Beth for advice, but Beth was busy chatting up one of Danny's teammates, her empty Four Loko dangling from her fingertips. Then Evan appeared by Birdy's side. *Come back, Danny!*

Evan hooked a thumb under the strap of his singlet. "You know, that's actually a cool costume. It's like, a secret agent or something."

"Um, it's just my work uniform," said Birdy, now thoroughly regretting the decision to wear it. "I just didn't come up with something better in time."

"That's so cool how you're not trying so hard like all these other girls. You're so cute for that." Evan attempted a charming smile just as Fiona fluttered by, missing her halo.

"You lost your halo, angel!" said Evan.

"I guess I'm a devil now!" said Fiona.

"Oh, no, angel! Don't be bad!"

"I'm so bad now, Evan! I lost my halo!"

"Aw, angel! You can still be good without your halo!"

"I don't think so, Evan! I'm feeling naughty!"

Interested though she was in the eternal battle of good versus evil, Birdy left them to their debate on the subject and made her way back to the loud living room, where Henry held a beer bong for Amanda. Kevin, wearing his singlet, was leaning into Kelly and yelling something, while Kelly leaned away, holding her VMA like a shield. Isaac and Michael were doing handstand pushups. Dominic and Tinkerbell were making out on a chair. Angela Prune, dressed as a sexy bunny, stood crying in the arms of a sexy squirrel. Birdy felt a hand on her shoulder.

"This is getting stupid," yelled Mel, "Let's get out of here. I'll bring us back for our cars in the morning." Birdy gave a thumbs up, and Mel charged back through the crowd. She returned dragging a stumbling Beth behind her.

"I'm still having fun!" said Beth angrily, but Mel ignored her. Birdy linked an arm through Kelly's and told Kevin they were leaving. They burst out the front door into the chilly night, their ears ringing in the sudden quiet. They piled into Mel's car and Vince drove them home, while Beth muttered that she was having fun and she was about to do a danceoff and did anyone try that Four Loko stuff, it comes in a really tall can? Then she said she felt weird, grabbed Kelly's purse from Birdy's lap, and puked into it.

They pulled up to Mel's house, where five jack o' lanterns glowed on the front porch. Officer Holloway's car was not in the driveway, as he was guarding the streets of Conrad from costumed vagrants. Vince and Mel turned to the backseat to see Beth dangling her head above Kelly's purse, Birdy shoving herself into Kelly, and Kelly fuming.

"Okay, we're running Hollywood."

Mel liked expanding her playmaking hobby to other areas of their lives, such as sneaking around. Hollywood meant their cover story was going to the movies. It was their main play.

"Why would I have worn this to the movies?" said Kelly, still pissed about her purse.

"It's Halloween," said Mel. "Plus, she'll probably be asleep anyway."

"What movie did we see?" said Birdy.

"Don't worry, you didn't go. I told her you were coming over after work."

"Well, what did *we* see?" said Vince.

"You're not even coming in! But let's go with *Paranormal Activity.*"

"We saw that last time," said Kelly.

"It was so good we saw it again," said Mel.

"Fuck that movie," said Beth from inside the purse.

Vince snickered. "Good luck." He kissed Mel and set off through the woods. The girls crept up the walkway. "My dad didn't even carve a pumpkin this year, did I tell you that? My mom made his," whispered Mel as they reached the front porch. "Okay, this time let's do Birdy first, then me and Beth, then Kelly,"

"I don't need a babysitter!" snapped Beth.

"Yes you do, now shut up," said Mel. "Let's go."

The lights were on inside. Mrs. Holloway was asleep on the couch, *The Shining* and an emptied wine glass and bottle on the coffee table beside her. Birdy crept for the stairs until Mrs. Holloway sat up.

"Birdy," she said, shoving strands of hair from her eyes. "How was work?"

"Good," said Birdy.

"Good," said Mrs. Holloway, nodding blearily "Glad you made it here safe, the other girls must be upstairs, there's lasagna if you..." She fell back on her pillows, fast asleep.

6

TWO WEEKS LATER, the Minutemen made it to their first playoff game in fifteen years, and Dad finally agreed to brave three hours beside Abe in the stands. This put Birdy in the annoying position of riding over to Conrad High with the two of them in Abe's precious truck.

"Jude said he had somewhere else to be, but didn't say where. He's always doing stuff like that, says it's for the business, but he forgets I know just as much about the business as he does and he never has anything to show for it. I think he's just mad it's not him playing out there. We went to states my senior year, you know," said Abe as he parked on a frosty patch of grass. Dad, who had come to watch football and not to gripe about Jude's whereabouts, nodded absently while his eyes drifted to the field glistening in the distance.

Birdy, Mel and Kelly huddled together, envious of Beth in her warm movie theater. Dad and Abe sat in front of them. The Minutemen won the coin toss and proceeded to be crushingly, devastatingly, humiliatingly defeated over the next two hours. Henry got sacked countless times, Vince fumbled most of the passes Henry managed to throw, and the defense was Swiss cheese. Dad went from eager silence to dejected silence. Mel went from endless hype talk to whispering, "Oh, no, Vince." Even Abe stopped talking eventually; there was nothing left to say.

When the game finally ended, Dad stood and nodded regretfully at Mel. "Mel. Tell your fella I've been there. It's rough. But it'll pass."

"Thanks, Mr. Cleary," sighed Mel, a grizzled war veteran.

Birdy parted ways with her father, and the girls got snacks at 7-Eleven before heading to Kevin's victory-turned-consolation party. This time it was indoors because his parents were gone to wherever

Conrad parents went on fall weekends. Vince threw his season-long discipline to the winds and drowned himself and his sorrows in jungle juice. He passed out on a flowery couch, misery etched on his features, the bill of his hat wedged under his neck at an awkward angle. Mel righted it and covered him with a flowery blanket.

"It's probably for the best anyway," she said. "He likes to sleep when he's sad." She plopped down on the couch and hooked an arm around the floral lump of his feet. "Guess I'm driving tonight."

Mel had had the foresight not to drink any jungle juice, but Birdy and Kelly were each two cups deep by the time Beth arrived from work, her skin flushed and crisp.

"I can't believe you biked here, you're insane!" Kelly yelled into her ear.

"Oooo, Beth," said Birdy, "I have something for you before I forget!" She dragged Beth to the hallway where she'd left a shopping bag full of peanut butter, jelly, and boxed mac and cheese.

"Thanks!" said Beth, putting it in her backpack.

"You just need butter and milk for the mac and cheese," said Birdy.

"Oh," said Beth, "I don't think I have those."

"Oh," said Birdy, feeling dumb. "Well, I'll bring you some next time I come over. How are the kids?"

"They're growing up so fast! Really, they're only this tall," she said, making a tiny space with her fingers. "But I've got my ways to stay busy while I wait." She withdrew a bottle of Jagermeister and two cans of Red Bull from her backpack. "Want to do a Jagerbomb?"

"Where'd you get the Jager?" Birdy asked when they'd finished.

"Oh, Logan used it to pay me one time, instead of cash. I was fine with that part, but ever since then he always comes up and talks to me like something *happened* between us, so that's weird."

"Oh," said Birdy, "Well he completely sucked tonight,"

"Hope it's not my fault," said Beth.

"Hmmm," said Birdy, "I actually saw him around here some-where..."

"There," said Beth, pointing, which Logan unfortunately noticed.

"Eyy Beth!" said Logan, wandering over. "Where'd you get that bottle, girl?"

"Hey Logan," called Beth, her smile splendid as always.

"She got that from me," Logan told Birdy.

"Oh," said Birdy yet again.

"Thanks again, Beth," said Logan, "Looking forward to next time."

"Uh, yeah," said Beth.

"So do you know when next time will be?" he asked.

"It's gonna be a few months," said Beth.

Logan stepped even closer. "I can't wait," he said, placing a hand on Beth's back.

"You got your answer, now back off, and pay her in real money next time instead of stealing Jager from your dad or your creepy uncle or whoever" said Birdy, finding herself with her hands on her hips.

Beth burst out laughing and Logan blinked several times. "It was my brother's! But, yeah, okay... sorry..." he said, and left fast.

"If only he'd moved that quick during the game," Birdy muttered after him as Beth kept laughing.

"Oh, wow, this is good," she said. "We need to give you Jagerbombs more often." She took another long sip from the bottle. Then she punched Birdy's arm. "Look!" Mel was still on the couch reading Better Homes and Gardens. Danny was in a corner talking to Henry. And Kelly—Kelly was entering her number in a guy's phone, while Kevin pouted some distance away.

"Who's that? He looks cute from here!" said Birdy.

"That's Nick Everett," said Beth, "I've been trying to get him to come to soccer forever, he's really nice."

"Good for her!" said Birdy.

"Birdy," Beth said aggressively, grabbing Birdy by the shoulders, "I don't want to see you and Danny waiting around for one more second. You're hot, you're beautiful, you're brilliant as fuck, you're funny as hell, you're amazing as shit, and this is your! Night!"

Perhaps Henry had given Danny a similar hype speech, because he was already approaching when Birdy turned around. "I was really hoping you would be here tonight," he yelled into her ear. She looked at him and he was smiling, his eyes unfocused. *Wow, you look drunk,* she thought. *And that's saying something because* I'm *drunk.*

She smiled back and said, "Me too," which didn't totally make sense, but that was immaterial to Danny. She watched herself fully face him and place a hand on his arm. His lips were right there. *Might as well.* With a stumble over her mental cliff, she kissed him.

Birdy didn't love the taste of beer; she really didn't love it after it had been hanging out in Danny's gums for a while. He responded with great and slobbery enthusiasm. The thinking part of her brain generated an image of Galahad attacking Nala with puppy kisses. But the drunk part of her enjoyed herself. She burped in his mouth, but he didn't react. *I'm one of those people who makes out in a random corner now,* she thought. After a few minutes, Danny pulled away and took her hand. "Come on, let's find somewhere."

They tripped down a hallway, past a portrait of Kevin in a kindergarten cap and gown, into an empty bedroom. The floral bedspread on the queen-sized bed indicated it belonged to Kevin's parents *Oh, weird.* Danny plopped down on the bed. The floral carpet tilted beneath Birdy's feet. Danny gestured to Birdy, forming words with his mouth but saying nothing. *No.* A bed, where the main idea was to lie down, no, that was not a place she wanted to go with Danny. Now that they'd broken apart, she had no desire to consume any additional secondhand beer. She was trying to figure out how to say that nicely when Danny closed his eyes and keeled backwards, asleep.

With some effort, Birdy rolled him onto his side so he wouldn't choke on any puke that might be forthcoming. On her way back down the hall, Birdy heard someone else dispensing puke into the toilet. When she got to the living room, Beth was dancing with one of Kevin's neckless friends and Kelly was making out with Nick. Mel looked bored with her magazine but leapt to attention when she saw Birdy.

"What happened?" she yelled in Birdy's ear. "He's really cute!"

"He is cute, he was really cute but it was just so slobbery," Birdy said. "And I wanted us to stop because there was a bed there and— Kevin's mom must reeeally like flowers by the way— and then I was trying to figure out what to say when he fell asleep!"

"Oh my God nooooooo!" moaned Mel.

"No, no it's okay, because here's the thing. It's never going to work. The problem with Danny is that he's so nice but I still don't really think he would bring me hot chocolate you know?"

Mel laughed so hard that tears came to her eyes. She hugged Birdy fiercely and Birdy hugged her back, their legs forming an unsteady A-frame. "I just love you so much," Mel yelled. Birdy smiled into Mel's shoulder, happy despite the pathetic endings of the football season and her meager flirtation, buoyed by the pounding of music and the swirl of alcohol and the joy of friends.

Winter 2010

1

"BIRDY! RIGHT NOW!"

Birdy groaned and slunk down the stairs. The sounds of a Barry Manilow Christmas album grew louder as she descended. Mom was planted in the living room, clutching dusting supplies, eyes wild.

"Start getting the stuff out."

The boys were coming home for Christmas. Dad was picking up Chris tonight, Patrick would drive in tomorrow morning, and Peter was set to arrive shortly after Patrick. Mom had been hyper with anticipation for weeks, but now the day had arrived, and they still hadn't decorated.

Birdy hauled the last box down from the attic. As soon as it hit the top of the stack, Mom shook her head. "Wait, I need you to put it in the kitchen first. We have to declutter and vacuum before we put all this up."

Birdy bit back a sigh. It wouldn't do to display discontent before a single Santa had been unwrapped. Decluttering was easier these days with only Birdy around to leave her socks in the wrong location, so she got through that task quickly. Then she vacuumed the downstairs, stopping occasionally to listen to Mom's constructive criticism.

When Chris got home, he was mad they had decorated without him. When Patrick got home, he couldn't believe they had only decorated the day before. "I mean, I can *believe* it," he added. As the initial excitement of Patrick's arrival settled, the nervous anticipation mounted. They busied themselves by slicing sugar cookies, and Peter snuck in without them noticing.

"Hey guys," he said from the kitchen doorway. He'd shaved off his bun but kept the beard.

"OH", said Mom, rushing to him, "You're finally home for Christmas! It's like the prodigal son!"

All parties concerned were catechized enough to be offended at this comparison, but as Peter put down his bag, kicked off his shoes, and settled on the couch, Mom kept referencing it. After the fifth mention of Jesus's parable, they'd had enough.

"Well, I wasn't exactly away spending my inheritance," said Peter.

"Peter! You know what I mean!" said Mom, stomping her foot.

Please shut up, Peter. Patrick glanced over at Birdy chewing her thumbnail and smiled.

"Birdy's like the son who stayed home and she's about to get really mad because she's just been hanging around being good this whole time," said Patrick. Birdy smiled at this, although the being good part was a bit questionable these days.

"You know what that makes you in this parable?" said Chris

"Helpful servant?" said Patrick.

"Fatted calf," said Chris.

"Guys!" said Mom. "I was just saying it just reminds me of the story!"

"I'm sorry Mom," said Peter, putting his arm around her. "I meant to tell you, it looks really nice in here. When are we going to do the tree?"

"Oh, I don't think we'll do one this year," said Mom. "Dad's knees are really hurting him, plus they're just a waste of money."

Peter's face didn't change, but his shoulders sagged. Birdy braced herself for angry commentary from Chris, but Chris only said, "Well, how about the four of us go get one?"

Mom frowned, deciding if she was losing control of the situation and if she was okay with that.

Chris grinned and put an arm around her other side. "For behold, thy son was lost, and now is found, and the Lord sayeth we must get a tree." Mom rolled her eyes and smiled, so the kids found their coats and got into Peter's Subaru.

On Christmas Eve they got all dressed up and headed to St. Ann's. "Kind of an ugly church," Peter whispered to her as they walked inside, and Birdy realized with a pang it was his first time there. Father Bill wore white and gold vestments, the altar was decorated with matching linens, and the advent wreath was fitted with all new white candles. Three small pots of poinsettias and a Christmas tree completed the decorations. Birdy knew Ms. Karen was responsible for church's finery, as she had documented her handiwork in today's blog post, "Liturgical Living at Church and at Home." The Clearys sat in their usual pew, now more crowded with the addition of Peter.

Dominic had graduated from altar serving to lectoring. The candles illuminated him through his crisp delivery of the first and second readings. He had spiked up the front of his hair with gel, an ill attempt at fanciness that Birdy viewed with smug dislike. Despite the loathsome lector, it was a nice Mass because Ms. Karen had asked one of the St. Paul's cantors to cover for Mrs. Fitzgerald, who was having her hip replaced.

After Mass, Mom flagged down Ms. Karen to take a family picture for the Clearys. She had probably envisioned it being a quick snap, but she had forgotten who they were dealing with. Karen took lighting and posing very seriously, so it was ten minutes before she was satisfied with her work. Then she pulled out her own camera to take a few backup shots before she released them.

Thoroughly disgruntled, the Clearys finally made it to the minivan.

"The music has gotten surprisingly good," said Patrick as they pulled away.

"This is the first time that lady's been there," said Birdy.

"Bet she doesn't stick around," said Chris.

"Oh, I bet she will! Her name's Lucy Knight, she's such a sweet-heart. She's supposed to just help out while Mrs. Fitzgerald is getting better, but I bet she'll love it at St. Ann's decide to stay!" said Mom.

"Sure she will," said Chris.

"Man, that kid doing the readings seemed like a total douche," said Peter.

"Oh, he—WHAT did you just CALL him?" said Mom.

"A douche. Short for douchebag."

"I KNOW what—Peter, that is—do you know what a douchebag *is*?" Mom looked like she was being tortured.

By now the other Cleary kids were snorting.

"Yeah, it's that kid who was doing the readings."

The minivan veered to the shoulder and screeched to a stop. In the driver's seat, Dad howled with laughter, tears of joy rolling down his cheeks.

2

VINCE'S TEAMMATES HAD MADE many claims that they would go just as hard for the wrestlers as the wrestlers had for them. But the reality was that while it was fun to drink outside on a chilly night, it was miserable to drink outside on a freezing night, especially once there was snow on the ground. Recently, Birdy and her friends had spent Friday nights at Mel's, Kelly's, or her own house. Tonight was a special occasion, so they were at Beth's.

Birdy was in the kitchen, having just filled a pot of water for spaghetti. When she'd tried to shut off the faucet, she'd found it wouldn't stop dripping. Mel came in holding a basket of folded laun-dry and observed Birdy's efforts.

"That sound's going to drive Kelly crazy," said Birdy.

"And it'll waste water," said Mel. "Here." She took a hair elastic off her wrist and wrapped it around the handle and faucet so to squeeze them shut. The dripping stopped, and Birdy shrugged.

"Works for me."

Mel had somehow acquired a bottle of wine for the occasion, and Beth lit some candles. The girls wrapped in blankets and sat down to eat in the chilly kitchen, slowly warming as they drank their wine. Mel raised her glass.

"I would like to make a toast to Beth, on this very special day. Now that you're seventeen, you don't have any extra privileges, but you're one year closer to being able to gamble and buy tobacco. Now open your presents!"

Mel gave Beth a new Adidas shirt, Kelly gave her a basket of her favorite snacks, and Birdy had written her a story called The Adventures of Beth the Bong.

Beth put down her empty wine glass. "Something funny happened at school today," she said. "You know Sam Purcell?"

"Wasn't he on the boys' CRL team?" said Kelly.

"Yeah," said Beth. "And this now he's in my history class."

"He sucked at running," recalled Mel.

"Right," agreed Beth, "Probably because he smokes a ton." She emptied the rest of the wine bottle and stared into her glass for a moment. "Today in class he asked if I would want to like... partner up with him."

They all looked at her blankly.

"Like, business-wise," she clarified. "He sells too. But some people really liked my stuff last time I had it and they told him about it."

"Wait, this is the same guy who touched us excessively during scrimmages?" said Kelly.

"He asked you about this *in class?*" said Birdy.

Beth chuckled. "Yeah, he's that guy. I said no. But still, kinda cool that people liked my last batch." She drained her glass in a few gulps.

Kelly said, "My mom always says that word-of-mouth advertising is a key part of any successful marketing campaign."

"Beth's Little Buds," said Mel, blocking letters on an imaginary sign in front of her. "Reaching new heights every day."

The wine made them all sleepy. Beth's bedroom floor was too messy to sleep on, so they made a nest in the living room, where they were surrounded by the skunky weed smell from the bathroom. Birdy tried to get comfortable, but the hard, freezing tile under her blanket kept her wide awake and buzzing with thoughts.

Beth is getting a reputation for this. That can't be good.

Beth's had a reputation for it all along. That's how she sells to people.

But that's so risky. That Sam guy was so creepy. If he knows, that means the wrong people are finding out.

Really? What are the idiots of Conrad going to do? Beth's amazing. I'll stand by her through anything. I'll do anything to help her.

That's what you said about Mary.

And?

And Mary ended up moving away and hating you.

But this isn't like that at all. Beth and Mary are completely different, the circumstances are completely different.

Girl with crazy family coping in an unhealthy way. Totally different.

Well, that describes me too. So shut up.

They went to Mel's in the morning, arriving home a few minutes before Officer Holloway. He stopped in Mel's bedroom in his usual zombie state, gave Mel a squeeze, and kissed the top of her head. Then his demeanor shifted, and he took a big sniff. Mel hopped away from him, and he looked around at them suspiciously. Mel smiled wide and started chattering about her day, not an unusual state of being for her. The rest of them became statues of innocence. Cowed and tired, Officer Holloway gave them one last glower before dragging himself to the shower.

Beth immediately freaked out. "You guys can never come over to my house again. We can't all smell like it! He'll figure it out!"

"You're giving my dad too much credit," Mel snapped. "He's not Sherlock Holmes. He doesn't care about his job or any of us enough to get to the bottom of that smell."

Birdy and Kelly stayed quiet as this complicated moment hung between the other two girls. Beth's jaw was set and skeptical, Mel's face was flushed and on the point of tears.

"Well, he still lives with you, that counts for something," said Beth, her words dripping with disdain. They looked at each other in fury for another few seconds and then they were both crying.

"I'm sorry, I'm sorry," sobbed Mel.

"It's okay, it's okay, I'm sorry too," wailed Beth.

Birdy fished a bag of chocolate espresso trail mix out of her backpack. "Who needs a snack?"

Mel and Beth snuffled and took some, and they all sat around eating while the crying settled down. Twenty minutes later, Officer Holloway appeared in the doorway again, freshly showered and shaved. "Is everything okay in here? I thought I heard someone crying a little bit ago." All four girls burst out laughing, and he edged away from the door, desperate for sleep.

3

"AFTER MUCH DEBATE, I am excited to announce that the Divine Mercy board has settled on its spring fundraiser event." Mrs. Amon adjusted her glasses and leaned forward over the podium on her tippy toes. "I have written a stage adaptation of *Beauty and the Beast*!"

The faithful teens looked back at Mrs. Amon, the implications of this development dawning on them with varying degrees of speed.

"Now ideally we would have started rehearsals a while ago, so from now till April 30, we'll be having practice every single school day. And we want to avoid hurt feelings, so instead of holding auditions, I've assigned the roles based on everyone's personal strengths. Luckily we all know each other pretty well, don't we?" Mrs. Amon winked horrendously.

Margaret, with her stage presence and confident singing, naturally got the lead role. Isaac got the part of the Beast. Michael confidently told Gabby he would be Gaston, the strong and devilishly handsome villain from the Disney movie, but this role did not exist in Mrs. Amon's version. Instead, he was "Townsperson Number 3." Fred was Margaret's father, Polly and Maddie were her sisters, and Gabby was the hag who cursed the Beast. Birdy was put on stage crew.

From: petercleary1@hotmail.com
Hey Birdy,
Mom said you're in a play? First, are you actually in a play or did you just mention that a play existed and mom ran with it? Second, what is the play, if it is real? Third, when is the play, if it is real? Fourth, how's that guy from church with the hair gel?
Love Peter

From: bluebirdy@aol.com
The tales are true, I am in a play. Well, I'm not actually in the play, I'm a stage hand. I was a little disappointed about that for a second, but it turns out it's much better than being in the play, which is Beauty and the Beast. Now you may think you know this tale, but you would be wrong. It has been revamped to prevent its cast or audience from smiling, laughing, or enjoying themselves.

In this version of the story, Belle's name is Beauty, so as not to confuse anyone with French. But don't worry, the song "Belle" from the Disney movie is still the opening number, for some reason. Beauty has two sisters, and the dad goes on a journey and asks his daughters what they want him to bring back for them. The two bitchy daughters want basic bitch things like clothes, but sweet and thoughtful Beauty requests a simple rose— clearly she isn't superficial like her sisters. Except this is winter, so it's actually a really inconvenient request. So the dad buys the basic bitch stuff easily, but he has to go out of his way to find the rose for Beauty and whoops—the only place he can find the rose is in the courtyard of a slightly enchanted looking castle. When he steals the rose, he really pisses off the monster who lives there. The monster demands that he give him something in exchange for the rose he stole. Dad, a powerful thinker, says "I have nothing but my three daughters." Well, you know the predator latches on to this and says okay, give me one of them. And after some weak protesting on Dad's part, Beauty ends up back at the castle, having made the courageous and yet totally unnecessary choice to cover her dad's ass. Instead of being witty household objects, the servants in this story are for some reason invisible. As we do not have the budget for 10 invisibility cloaks, the servants will wear black clothes to represent their invisibleness. But don't worry, we are still using the Disney "Be Our Guest" song in the play, with all its puns pertaining to household objects. Eventually the beast falls in love with Beauty, for unknown reasons, and he becomes nice and all the servants stop being invisible. Allegedly, the citizens of Conrad will be willing to pay to watch a bunch of kids pretending to be invisible, and that will give the school money to grow.

Oh, and I will also wear all black clothes as a member of the stage crew. This works for me because I would rather be an actual invisible servant than a pretend invisible servant.

Love,
Birdy

From: petercleary1@hotmail.com
This play sounds horrible, but you did not tell me when it is. You also did not tell me how hair gel boy is. Tell me or I will have to ask my other sources.

From: bluebirdy@aol.com
Don't worry, I'm sure the other sources will tell you when the play is soon enough. As for hair gel boy, he is, as you correctly stated, a total douche and we do not talk.

The weird thing is, I remember reading a book a long time ago that was a retelling of Beauty and the Beast that had almost the exact same plot as this play. But I can't remember the name of the book or anything.

From: petercleary1@hotmail.com
Is this it?

Peter attached a link to Amazon.com, which had ten copies of an old book for sale. He had one shipped to her, and a few days later Birdy confirmed her hunch—Mrs. Amon's "original" retelling was not only ripped from this obscure paperback, but it also lifted entire passages from it as transitional narration.

Untroubled by her plagiarism, Mrs. Amon stepped into power like it was her birthright. Rehearsals were held in the church, requiring the students to operate under an awkward mixture of reverence and drama. Mrs. Amon did not take kindly to complainers and dished out harsh punishments to anyone who goofed off, performed poorly, or otherwise defiled the source material. Mr. Doppelski, who seemed to have endless hours to spend away from his day job, popped in to help on a regular basis. One day Birdy was reviewing notes with Mrs. Amon and Mrs. Strabinski before practice when he came strolling up the aisle.

"Afternoon, ladies, I'm ready for you to put me to work." He stood so close to Birdy that their arms brushed, making her stomach hurt.

"It is so nice of you to take so much time out of your busy schedule to come help us," gushed Mrs. Amon.

"Ahh, it's no trouble," said Mr. Doppelski, "When you're trying to build something good you gotta put in the work!" He produced a pair of dimples. "I'm just here to keep an eye on things anyhow, you're the ones putting in the real effort."

"Abe's probably glad to have a little break from you," teased Mrs. Strabinski.

"He probably is!" said Mr. Doppelski. "We'll let him run the show a little bit. And I'll help you run this show!"

Birdy was hoping the adults had forgotten she was there, but now Mr. Doppelski took a step back and looked at her. "You're on the stage crew?" Birdy nodded. "What, you bad at acting?"

She demonstrated her bad acting skills by laughing at his joke. He laughed back like they were old pals, giving her a tap on the shoulder that awoke a legion of goosebumps across her skin.

Mr. Doppelski was not quite the humble helper he made himself out to be. Instead, he seemed to fancy himself the producer, not running the play directly but still having say over the money and anything else that struck his fancy. Today he was in one of his goofy moods, and he kept singling people out with compliments and constructive criticism. When practice wound down that afternoon, he bid them all to sit in the pews so they could have a little chat. He assumed the Friendly Pastor Position, preaching to them as he paced back and forth in front of the pews.

"Listen, I know it's not always fun to do what us adults say. But you know, this school has a mission. We're here to show our town what it means to be real Catholics. We may be small, but we've got God on our side, right? So we're gonna do this play, and we're gonna get people from all over Conrad to come see it, and they're gonna see what we're all about here. And maybe some of our old CHOC friends will feel inspired to join our school and help us grow. Just keep that in mind on those days when you wanna complain about practice." He gave them all a teasing look, like he knew some of them were big complainers. Then he shooed them all with his hands.

"All right, time's up, everyone can go home. Go do what you need to do. Do your homework, make your bed, clean out your ears. Put your pictures on Facebook." Everyone was chuckling along at his silliness, so no one noticed him glare at Birdy with this last instruction.

Birdy's ears hummed with panic under his contemptuous gaze. Then he smiled at Margaret and kept yammering. Birdy's panic remained, but she also felt the satisfaction of finding a missing puzzle piece. *So that's how it is.*

Birdy's ears resumed their humming at Mass on Sunday, as Mr. Doppelski took the podium. She kept her eyes on her missal.

"A reading from the first letter of St. Paul to the Corinthians. Brothers," he began, omitting the "and sisters" printed in the missal,

"If I speak in human and angelic tongues, but do not have love, I am a resounding gong or a crashing cymbal."

How did it feel for him to read that? Probably like nothing. Mr. Doppelski was remorseless, as far as Birdy knew. She had heard the reading many times, so she already knew what was coming next—love is patient, love is kind, love doesn't steal your favorite snacks, something like that. It was one of the most popular parts of the good old book. In the two thousand years since Paul wrote his letter, had there always been a Jude Doppelski to read it, explaining love to a congregation whose trust in him was entirely misplaced? The thought was depressing.

Her parents justified hardship by saying their faith required more from them. Birdy had always respected this tenet, even if she didn't appreciate how it played out on the ground. She'd held herself up with the martyrs who could bear all things, endure all things, because if they could die for God, the least she could do was suffer in silence.

What a sucker she was. From what she could tell, building a life around God's whims was at best foolish and at worst a clever excuse to step on people. And that was assuming there was even really a God in the first place. Birdy never missed a question on a religion test, but after three years at Divine Mercy, her faith was all but dead.

The readings and homily passed, and Mr. Abe and Joseph rose to fetch their collection baskets. Birdy's eyes wandered to the back of Dominic's head, but even looking at him from behind was painful. She landed on Mr. Doppelski instead and marveled at the amount of gel he'd managed to cake into his short hair. Did he have his own supply, or did he share Dominic's?

Birdy phone buzzed in her pocket. It would be Mel, offering up her mom's lasagna tonight, or Kelly, offering to bring everyone to Walmart later, or Beth, reporting how many tips she'd gotten so far on the breakfast shift. She watched Mr. Doppelski deposit a bill into Abe's basket and remembered Mel's diagnosis of his affliction: *Creepy weirdo.* She smiled to herself, and a wave of affection for her friends washed through her, settling the panic.

She kept thinking of them as she rolled through the stand-kneel-stand portion of Mass. Mel, Beth, and Kelly had healed and fortified her in so many ways. What drove them to take care of each other was what Paul claimed was the essential ingredient for all the rest of it—good deeds and profound knowledge, powerful faith and the songs of angels. Birdy had this greatest of gifts, and it whispered to her now, nudging her to believe there was something else out there beyond her pathetic existence. Love, like music, was how Birdy glimpsed the divine. She ceded enough to the hypocrites who ran her life. She refused to let them ruin that too.

God. Hi. What's up?

This felt awkward. It was hard to take the Hail Marys out of a scrupulous Catholic girl, so while Birdy still ground out a few whenever she had to merge lanes, it had been a while since she'd addressed God directly.

I know we don't talk much anymore. Sorry. But please, help me. I want to be a good person, but I'm so tired of all this bullshit.

It seemed rude to come in with requests after months of silence. But recent events had spooked her, and if God was really up there, there was one thing she wanted from him more than anything else.

Please protect Beth. I'm really scared for her. I'm scared about everything.

Mrs. Knight spoke from the choir loft. "For our communion hymn, please turn to number 631, 'Be Not Afraid.'"

"Oh," Mom said plaintively. The choir usually butchered this song, but Mrs. Knight's voice was like water spilling over sun-washed rocks, refreshing the words Birdy had heard a hundred times. Trials and terror, loss and confusion, they were all part of the journey, the music claimed, but God would protect her through it all. Foolish as it would have seemed five minutes ago, it felt like an answer to her prayer.

The communion line was a single loop of advancers and retreaters. Mom snuffled as they filed into it. Mom would have loved Praise Night. She had a direct line to God, which he used to flood her with miracles and signs. He wasn't so clear with Birdy. All she got were whispers, and music that grounded her soul.

Birdy took the Eucharist from Father Bill's doughy hand. She ached for it to mean something to her, for it to feel like the miracle it was supposed to be, but it just tasted like old man cologne. She turned around, prepared to march past the Dark Doppelskis, but Mom stopped. Rebecca had tangled a hand disastrously deep into Mrs. Doppelski's long dark waves, and both of them were now staring in silent alarm.

"Oh my gosh, here," said Mom, and she reached to free Rebecca's chubby fingers.

"Thank you," Mrs. Doppelski whispered back. Mr. Doppelski looked over his shoulder at the muted commotion behind him, then turned back to Birdy, who stood inches away. He fixed her with that odious smirk, a smile only they knew was laced with hate. This was where she would smile back as she always did, because they were in church, because she went to his school, because he ruled her world.

Do not be afraid. The phrase was so frequent in the Bible as to be meaningless, but as Mr. Doppelski gazed at her, it filled her up, a battle cry. If God was there, then he knew all of it; her doubts, her drinking, her deceits, but that meant he knew the truth of the man in front of her, too. So Birdy clasped her hands reverently beneath her chin, looked Mr. Doppelski in the eye, and glared.

Mr. Doppelski started, squinted, and then Rebecca was free and Birdy was on the move back to her pew. Her clasped hands shook, her mean glare crumpled, and tears welled in her eyes. She felt how she always did after Peter's painful visits, hope draining from her body, despair flooding its place. *Do not be afraid?* Impossible. She was always afraid.

More words came to her then. If she were Mom, she would say God was speaking to her.

Hold on. Just hold on.

Spring 2010

1

"DOMINIC DOPPELSKI TRIED TO hit on me the other night," said Beth. They were in Kelly's car, driving to the rec fields. It was their first pickup game of the spring, and rain had flooded Mel's yard.

"Oh, God," said Birdy, ignoring the stampede his name sent through her body.

"Yeah, he put his hand on my back and said, 'Beth, I feel like we've never spent enough time together."

"Gross," groaned Mel.

"And do you know what I said?" said Beth.

"What!" said Kelly.

"I said, 'Aw, Dominic, that's because you're always too busy trying to keep your girlfriend and your booty call from running into each other!' And then he just kinda looked at me like—" she crossed her eyes and opened her mouth wide and slack "—and then I got myself away from him."

Birdy joined the others in derisive laughter, but a silent wail of mourning blew through her chest. Just last week, she had gotten a friend request from none other than Mary Vespa. Curiosity won, and Birdy accepted. The next day, she logged in and saw Mary had written on her wall: "Hey!!! howve you been?? miss u so much!!"

Birdy couldn't believe her eyes. Was this the right Mary? She gave some polite but unenthusiastic response. After that, Mary constantly liked her posts. Even more noteworthy, she had also friended Dominic and liked all his posts too. Birdy wished she could go back and tell her younger self to stay out of their business.

As they walked through the muddy grass, Birdy saw an unexpected figure swinging from a goal crossbar. "Oh by the way, I asked Sam to come play, is that okay?" said Beth. She sped away from them, waving to her guest.

Weedy was too apt of a descriptor for Sam Purcell. His slenderly muscled arms hung from his woven tank top, bracelets of braided hemp and colorful embroidery floss climbing his thin wrists. A Rastafarian hat covered his limp, ash-blond curls, and he was high so frequently that even when he wasn't, his eyes settled into a permanent squint.

"Greetings, women," said Sam.

Vince, Henry, Kevin, Logan, Amanda, and Katie arrived, and Vince divided them into teams. Sam's footwork was incredible, but his cardio was shit. He was impossible to tackle, for about five minutes. After that he was too tired to carry on and they ran right over him. Even aside from the Sam disturbance, it was a sad return to soccer. The ground wasn't much drier than Mel's yard, and frigid water seeped into their cleats. Wind muffled their calls and blew the ball off course. They soon threw in the towel.

Kelly offered Birdy a ride home, but Birdy decided to walk. She wanted to think. It was the first day of spring, but the cold wind assaulted her face and the only new life to be seen was the occasional premature daffodil. She kept her eyes on her squelching feet as she passed the Doppelskis', but she wasn't even thinking about Dominic anymore. She was trying to decide why Beth was acting so weird. She was always pulling new friends to play with them, but when Beth's breeziness turned fake, it was a portent of trouble.

Her questions were answered a few days later. Birdy was at Mel's house after school when Vince arrived and flopped onto the bed where they were sitting.

"There's no room," said Mel, trying to shove him off with her foot. Vince just spread his arms and legs out wider. Then he flipped over onto his back. Despite his goofing, he looked troubled.

"Something funny happened at school today," he said.

"Nothing good ever starts with that statement," said Mel.

"Well... you know Sam Purcell?"

"Yes..." said Birdy, locking eyes with Mel over Vince's sprawled form.

"I think he and Beth are like... into each other."

The girls digested this tidbit.

"I know she said he was trying to partner up with her... like for the weed... but..." Birdy said.

"I think he wants to partner up with her for more than that," said Vince with a snort. "And the weird thing is... well, the surprising thing is... she seems into him too."

"What makes you say that?" Mel demanded.

"Um. Well she was sitting on his lap before class. And then after class, they were holding hands in the hallway. So."

"I don't like the idea of her hanging out with him," said Birdy, hugging Mel's blue throw pillow.

"You sound like someone's dad," said Mel. "But, yeah, neither do I."

"Yeah, they're kind of a weird match," said Vince. "Sam's a creep, and he tries to have that drug dealer look. And Beth—"

"Looks like a Barbie," said Mel.

"Drug dealer Barbie," said Birdy.

"I never had that one growing up," said Mel.

"It only came in Happy Meals," said Birdy, and they laughed. Then Mel looked sad. "She must be lonely."

"She must be *really* lonely," said Vince.

Mel put her hand on top of his head. "Can you keep an eye on her for us?" Birdy had never known it was possible to convey a look of utter devotion from upside down and while sprawling obnoxiously, but Vince did then.

Footsteps pounded up the stairs, and Kelly burst into the room.

"Hey Birdy," she called out with delight, "How's play practice?"

"Ugh," said Birdy, slapping both hands over her face.

"What play?" demanded Mel.

"It's *Beauty and the Beast*," said Birdy, "and I'm only in it because I have to be, and I'm not even really *in* it because they put me on stage crew."

"You're so sneaky! Why do you never tell us anything?" demanded Mel, who was doing a lot of demanding that afternoon. She whacked Birdy on the head with a dogeared *Seventeen* magazine.

Birdy batted Mel's weapon away. "How did you find out?" she moaned.

"Margaret Amon tagged you in a picture," Kelly beamed.

As the lead actress, Margaret was dedicated to documenting the entire production. She had been taking pictures of everybody, stage hands included, and had even begged Birdy to take some of her rehearsing.

"It might look good on college applications," said Vince.

"Yeah, I'll be sure to record it so you can send it in some footage with your applications," Mel offered gleefully.

"When is it?" said Kelly.

"April 30 and May 1," sighed Birdy.

Kelly rushed over to the calendar on Mel's wall and penciled in the performances.

Beth bowed out of their usual Friday night sleepover, saying she was too tired from work and would see them at soccer the next day. On Saturday morning she arrived at Kelly's, not by bike but by an unsavory chauffeur.

"Oh, hi Sam," said Kelly. "Didn't know you were coming."

A smile oozed across his face. "I slept over with Beth last night."

Beth smiled too, but didn't dwell on his statement. "I figured we could always use another player, and Sam's so good." To demonstrate, Sam flicked the ball up from the ground with his toe and started juggling.

Mel was not impressed. "Hey, Mia Hamm, we're using that to play."

He glanced at her, gave the ball a few more touches, and let it settle as Vince walked up with Kevin and Henry. Unbelievably, Angela Prune pulled up in a sagging VW Beetle as they were dividing into teams, though Mel and Kelly both looked bewildered at her presence.

"I heard these games are really fun," said Angela.

"From who?" Mel mouthed to Birdy.

For all Sam's impressive ball handling, it did not translate to fortitude on the field. Every time someone tackled him, he yelped in pain and clutched his ankles. Birdy knew faking injuries was part of the pro-soccer toolkit, but she considered it low to do during a pickup game. Even Angela looked tough by comparison.

Beth did not take it easy on him, and when the game was over, she stood in front of him with a huge grin. "Hey, nice job," she said patronizingly. Sam sized her up, grabbed her butt, and planted a moist kiss on her mouth. Birdy immediately began picking up cones, trying to expunge that image from her mind.

Officer Holloway trudged out to the yard. "Mel," he called, "Mom wants me to remind you, you can't go anywhere until home-work's done." Mel waved and ran in the opposite direction.

Beth picked up a cone and brought it to Birdy. "You missed one, Bird!" she said, putting it on top of Birdy's cone stack. "Hi Mr. Holloway," she beamed, but then she glanced back over her shoul-der because Sam was hot on her tail.

"Hi Beth," said Officer Holloway. He inspected Sam. "Hello there." He put out his hand to shake, but Sam just smirked.

"Sup, Officer." He dragged Beth away by the hand, unhelpfully leaving a whiff of weed scent behind him.

Birdy watched Officer Holloway from the corner of her eye, calculating how soon she could walk away without being rude. Nor-mally, he seemed as intent as she was to avoid small talk, so she was surprised when he spoke.

"Who is that guy again?"

"Sam Purcell. He used to play CRL soccer with us."

"He's not at St. Monica's is he?"

"No, he's at Conrad."

"With Beth?" Officer Holloway's posture was now charged, his arms crossed tight. Birdy nodded, and Officer Holloway scowled in

Sam and Beth's direction. "They're going out?" Sam answered the question himself by making another grab for Beth's butt. Birdy and Officer Holloway both turned away in embarrassment, which left them directly facing each other.

Birdy had never been sure how much she could trust Officer Holloway, who had maintained decades of friendship with Mr. Doppelski and who was a colossal disappointment to Mel. But when their eyes met, she saw a man who was just as anxious as she was at the thought of Beth with Sam. In his protective energy and smothered worry, she sensed something of her own father. She threw out a line she knew would have caused one of Dad's delightful armor cracks.

"Don't worry, I'm pretty sure she could kill him with a single kick."

The effect was brief but instantaneous—he flashed a luminous smile that flushed the sad lines of his face with life. "Ha!" He cocked his head at Birdy, the smile already fading as if the effort had exhausted and confused him. He looked back at Beth, who was now doing cartwheels with Angela while Sam watched. Officer Holloway sunk back into himself. "Take care," he said to Birdy. Then he put his hands in his pockets and wandered away.

2

MARYLAND IS KNOWN FOR its unique flag, its tasty crabs, its Old Bay to put on the crabs and everything else, and its sport of lacrosse, which was invented by Native Americans and is now played mostly by rich WASPs. At least these are the things that Marylanders know Maryland for, often to an obnoxious degree. Maryland also has its less widely known cultural touchstones. For example, certain Marylanders identify as Southerners because Maryland rests a smidge below the Mason-Dixon line. Despite its pockets of country music love and latent racism, Maryland remains a solidly mid-Atlantic region that stretches from coastline to mountain ranges. As such, it boasts all four seasons, often within the same week.

That year, there were flurries on the first Monday in April, and by Friday, Birdy was digging out shorts. At times like these, she imagined some heavenly body standing by the thermostat and turning the dial left, right, left, right, left, right, while the earthlings scrambled for proper attire. With this sudden temperature shift came a sucker punch of humidity. Local girls who had straightened their hair sighed as it doubled in volume, and morning commuters scrambled to remember if it was hot or cold air that would defog their windshields. Birdy enjoyed the change in weather, but it ushered the destruction of Beth's kids.

It started with a storm. On April 8, the humidity built to its breaking point and the heavens unleashed their first thunderstorm of the year. Leaves and branches poured down along with the rain, and half of Conrad's residents lost power. The electric company was not prepared to address such an event, and it took them hours to start restoring the grid. Birdy was at home, bemoaning her family's septic tank and doomed to a camp toilet and bottled water, but Beth was sleeping over at Kelly's house, which had a backup generator. Mrs. Merryman asked if Beth would please stay with them until the power was back on at her house. Beth said her parents wouldn't mind at all.

Beth was somewhat worried about her kids, but the allure of Mr. Merryman's chicken parm was stronger than her maternal instinct. She decided to let them skip a day or two of water, forgetting that they were also without their grow lights. When she finally went home on April 12, the kids were suffering.

The humidity spikes continued, ruining more than hairstyles. Days after Beth discovered the stunted growth of her plants, she found a new problem—they had a weird fungus, and it was spreading. The pamphlet didn't address this turn of events. She consulted an internet message board called "r/homegrow," which advised her to try feeding the plants with a mixture of Coke and vinegar. "The extra sugars kickstart chlorophyll production, while the acid in the vinegar will help kill the fungus," explained the confident poster. This winning combo turned the plants black and left the fungus very much alive. In desperation, Beth checked her curing jars, only to find they were overrun with mold.

She finally broke the news to everyone on a Friday night.

"God, I'm sorry!" said Mel. "Stupid weather!"

Beth shrugged. "It's all good."

"You don't seem that upset," said Birdy.

"Well... I was kind of upset at first, but it's also been stressing me out really bad lately. More people keep coming up to me and asking me about it and I didn't want to be *known* for this, you know? It was supposed to be a secret. Plus I noticed my electricity bill was way higher whenever I had the lights on so that takes away some of the profit anyway. And I do get a ton of tips when I work at Waffle King, so I think I could change up my hours there this summer and probably make way more money without all the work."

"And lawbreaking," said Mel, clutching imaginary pearls. Beth snorted.

"Did you tell Sam yet?" asked Kelly, scraping designs into Mel's bedroom carpet with her finger.

"No actually..." said Beth. "I think I need to dump him. To-morrow."

The others remained stock-still, trying not to show how happy this news was.

"What makes you say that?" asked Birdy.

"Stop being so polite, Birdy, I know he's horrible!" groaned Beth, covering her face. No one could keep a straight face after that.

"I, for one, think his hats are really tasteful," said Mel.

Beth threw a dilapidated Beanie Baby at her.

"Do you know what you're going to say? Do you need to re-hearse?" said Kelly.

Beth shook her head. "I'm not going to say anything too groundbreaking. I just need to tell him I don't think we're a good fit and I don't want to date anymore." She picked at her pink nail polish. "I can't tell if he liked me just for the weed or just for what I look like, but he sure doesn't like my actual personality."

Birdy smiled, admiring the way Beth could face a breakup without spending hours worrying over every possible emotional and social outcome.

"We're staying at your house tomorrow night, right?" Beth said to Kelly.

"Yeah," said Kelly, "We're gonna watch the Penguins game and my mom is making wings, fries, salsa, guacamole, and this cheese bread thingy."

"I love your house," Birdy sighed.

"I think you mean the *Caps* game," said Mel.

"My dad really wants Vince to come watch, speaking of," said Kelly.

"He is," said Mel.

"Well, maybe after the game we can sneak some wine again and toast to Beth's newfound freedoms," said Birdy.

"I think the Lord is really opening up a new pathway for you, Elizabeth," said Mel.

"Amen!" said Beth, waving her praise hands.

3

BIRDY WORKED THE LUNCH shift the next day, which flew by in the usual whirlwind of ketchup and steaming paper bags. When she went to get her phone at the end of the shift, she had a text from Beth.

Elizabeth Jessica: just got off work, im gonna go have a chat with sam and then ill be over to kellabell's!
Birdy: Good luck!!!

Birdy stopped at home, where Dad was grading tests and Mom was stressing her way through a favor for Ms. Karen that involved sorting papers into colorful stacks. Then she drove over to Kelly's, where Mel and Vince were already waiting. It was the ad break, and Vince and Mr. Merryman were having a passionate yet amicable argument about Ovie vs. Crosby. Mr. Merryman was always amicable. He stood to greet Birdy.

"Come on in, hon! Ooh, can you leave your shoes by the door?" Birdy backtracked to fulfill his request. Mr. and Mrs. Merryman were both successful salespeople who worked in Baltimore. They would welcome anyone into their home, provided they removed their shoes first. Their house was larger and newer than any other one Birdy had been to in Conrad. Sparkling light fixtures hung from high, white ceilings, and every surface was clear and gleaming. All the furniture was vast and soft, and the carpet was thick beneath her socks. The walls were dressed with professional family portraits, plus many more portraits of just Kelly. Overall, the Merryman home had the air of having been beautifully cared for out of pride, love, and a smidge of germaphobia.

"It smells delicious in here," said Birdy.

"Thanks, sweetie!" said Mrs. Merryman. She beamed from the kitchen island, a fixture that always seemed dazzlingly fancy to Birdy. Mrs. Merryman walked Birdy through her clumsy first time making salsa, instructing her to add plenty of salt and squeeze in a fresh lime. Then she scooped some up on a chip so Birdy could taste it.

"Oh my gosh, it's delicious!" she said. "I can't believe I did that! Thank you!"

"You're welcome, sweetheart! Oh—" she said as Birdy reached for a second chip. "Go wash your hands before you eat another!" She called over her shoulder to Kelly. "When did you say Beth is getting here?"

The food was all ready and the game was more than halfway over, but Beth still wasn't there. Kelly looked down at her phone. "It's supposed to be pretty soon," she said in a perky voice, but when her mom left the room she leaned in to Birdy. "Do you think she's okay?"

"Maybe it was a longer conversation than she thought," Birdy murmured back. She ate her way through the next hour, which ended with the Caps victorious and no Beth. Kelly flipped her phone open for the hundredth time.

"She's on her way now!" Kelly announced.

"Sorry she couldn't make the game! Tell her to help herself to anything in the fridge when she gets here!" said Mrs. Merryman. "I know she loves my guacamole!"

"Thanks, Mom," said Kelly, "I guess she got stuck at work or something." Mel and Birdy exchanged a glance.

"We're heading downstairs for a movie night," said Mr. Merryman in his booming voice. "Couples only. You two coming?" Mel and Vince were emphatically declining when Beth walked through the door.

Normally Beth arrived a bit flushed, but in good spirits. Today her eyes were puffy and smeared with makeup. She hadn't changed out of her work uniform and she didn't seem to know that huge loops of hair were sticking out of her braid.

"Oh sweetie!" said Mrs. Merryman. "Tough night at work?"

Beth nodded. In the blink of an eye, Mrs. Merryman assembled a plate of appetizers, warmed it up, and set it on the island with a Pepsi. Birdy, Kelly, and Mel tried to catch Beth's eye as this went on, but Beth stared at the floor.

"Have a seat, Bethy," said Mr. Merryman, leading her to a seat at the island. His immense kindness overrode his immense cleanliness, and he didn't ask her to remove her shoes.

"Thanks," said Beth, flashing her dazzling smile at Mr. and Mrs. Merryman. She dropped it when they went to the basement. She shoveled food in her mouth while everyone else waited. Finally she scrubbed the wing sauce from her hands with the napkin and tossed it on the island.

"So... how did it go with Sam?" said Birdy.

Beth looked at her empty plate. "Bad."

They waited again. Then they watched in shock as Beth got up, opened the fridge, grabbed one of Mr. Merryman's Yuenglings, and chugged it.

Kelly snatched the empty can and buried it deep in the trashcan. Beth didn't even look up. The ticking of the clock on the wall was deafening.

"What happened?" begged Mel.

Beth finally looked at them, her anguished blue eyes darting between their frightened faces.

"He didn't—he didn't like that I—wanted to break up." Her voice was thin and hesitant, nothing like usual. Birdy had never seen her this way, not when she was sad and drunk, not even on the day they had discovered the weed.

"He said he'd turn me in if I didn't... didn't sleep with him," said Beth.

There was yet another horrified silence in the kitchen. Birdy felt a banner of rage unfurling inside her, but she couldn't find any words. Then Kelly asked the question on all their minds. "Didn't you already...?"

"I hadn't yet," said Beth. "I told him I wasn't ready, and he always acted like he was doing me a big favor by waiting, but I knew I was never going to with him because he always talked about how he doesn't use condoms, so... like I'm not trying to get pregnant or some gross disease on top of everything else. But tonight, he said, I had to... so I told him I was on my period." Her eyes, fixed on the island, twitched apologetically toward Vince, who kept still. "So he said... I could do some other stuff. Instead." She closed her eyes and her chin wobbled. "He acted like that was a big favor too. But right after he f-finished, he goes 'That wasn't good enough to keep me quiet.'"

"What a piece of shit," whispered Mel.

"So he said he wouldn't turn me in if I gave him all my plants. And I wouldn't give them to him anyway, but they all died. I told him that but he doesn't believe me." She went limp and sunk to the ground. "I wish I'd never started any of this." The despair that so often overtook her when she drank clouded her eyes. "Oh, Jesus help me."

Birdy sat down to hug Beth. *Jesus, really please help us.*

Vince straightened up. "I'm gonna go find him."

Mel sprang to her feet too. "Why?" she shrieked.

"He can't do that shit. Not to Beth."

"What are you going to do?" asked Mel, shaking his arm.

"I'm just going to talk to him," he said, gently freeing himself. "Don't worry, you've seen him play soccer, he has no balls."

"And we're going to get rid of the kids," said Birdy.

Everyone looked at her. Then Beth nodded. "Yeah. Let's do it."

It was fortunate that they were already at Kelly's house, because hers was both the least densely occupied and the best stocked with cleaning supplies. Kelly took four pairs of rubber gloves, a roll of paper towels, a bottle of cleaning spray, and entire box of garbage bags and still barely made a dent in her parents' inventory. The pantry was vast and leagues away from the basement, where Mr. and Mrs. Merryman were watching *Love Actually.* Kelly went down to tell her parents they were going out, and the girls left.

On the car ride, Birdy sat in the backseat with Beth, who stared out the window the whole time. In the light from passing cars, her expression was strange, like someone had erased her face and re-drawn it incorrectly. At Beth's house, Kelly distributed the supplies with military precision. They went in the bathroom and stared at the shelves of blackened plants.

"Well, I sure wouldn't want to smoke that," said Mel.

"Maybe we shouldn't put them all in the regular garbage," said Kelly. "Someone could find them if..."

"We can tear up the plants as we go and then bring them to the woods and mix them in with the regular leaves," said Birdy. She'd disposed of the plants a hundred times already in her mind; now the moment was upon them.

They pulled and crumpled plant after dying plant, spilling dirt everywhere. Beth unplugged the lamps and shoved them in the trash bags, then threw in some extra junk from around the house. "This is actually perfect," she said, "trash day is tomorrow." Kelly dragged the planters to the dark yard and emptied the dirt into the neglected flower beds. Then she stacked them and put them in the junk palace of the garage.

Birdy brought the trashcan out to the curb and came back to the house, where Mel waited by the front door. Together, they took the remains of the plants to the woods and buried them in the damp earth. When they went back inside, they helped Beth and Kelly move the shelves into the garage. Then they all scrubbed the bathroom, kitchen and living room, four cyclones of evidence destruction. It was 11pm when they finally stood basking in the glow of Beth's sparkling house.

"It's never looked better," Beth chuckled.

Then they looked at the state of each other, streaked with dirt and sweat. "I guess we tell my parents we were playing soccer?" said Kelly.

"No," said Mel, "just—" her phone buzzed and she stopped to flip it open.

"Vince," she said. Birdy looked at the screen.

Boyfriend: dont worry about sam. he wont bother beth again.

Kelly's parents never fell asleep if the girls were still out. Mel instructed Kelly to borrow some shorts and a sweatshirt from Beth and say she'd spilled a Slurpee all over her clothes when they were out. While Kelly said goodnight in the basement, the rest of them booked it upstairs to shower. When they were all clean, they climbed into Kelly's two queen beds, but their nerves were still too haywire to sleep.

"Well, we've done a lot of weird stuff," said Mel, "But that might have been the weirdest."

"All the other weird stuff we've done prepared us for that weird stuff," said Kelly.

"I've been meaning to do some spring cleaning," said Beth from under layers of blankets.

"There's nothing Sam can do now," said Mel. "He can't prove anything. Not that he would do something anyway, I know he's scared of Vince."

Birdy just listened. All she could think was that they had just crossed some kind of threshold from which there would be no turning back. But she couldn't tell where they had crossed to yet. And that was kind of weird sleepover talk, even from her.

Eventually Mel and Kelly dropped off to sleep. A little while after that, Birdy heard Beth's breathing grow wetter beside her.

"Are you okay, Beth?" whispered Birdy.

Beth sniffed. "I'm glad the kids are gone. But I feel so gross. It was so gross."

"With Sam?"

Birdy felt Beth nod. "But I don't know why I feel so bad. I mean he didn't actually *do* anything to me. Like he didn't force me to or anything..."

Birdy sat up straight. "What are you talking about? Yes he did force you!"

"Shhh! Birdy! I mean like he didn't—grab me or touch me or hurt me."

"But he threatened you!"

"But... I was so scared at the time it seemed like it was my only choice, but now I wonder why I didn't just leave. I could have just left."

"You were scared. He liked scaring you, and that's messed up." Birdy's voice shook. "He loved getting the chance to upset you and make you feel less than him. He is such a piece of shit and you're so spectacular that the only way he could hope to get close to you was to get at you when you were vulnerable. It's like you said. He saw these things on the surface about you that were exciting to him, but he didn't even care about the real you. But he thought he had a right to you anyway."

Birdy wanted to sound comforting, but she was unhinged, furious that Sam, too weak to match Beth's brilliance, had been bold enough for this.

"It's okay, Birdy. Don't worry about it so much," said Beth, rolling over to end the conversation.

4

THE NEXT DAY WAS Sunday, Birdy's day off but nobody else's. She went to Mass with her parents, then sat down at her desk, flipping through her planner. During the last week of April, practices would move to the stage at St. Paul's, culminating in three nights of questionable glory: a dress rehearsal on April 29, opening night on April 30, and the finale on May 1.

Though the content and company were less than ideal, Birdy had come to enjoy certain aspects of stage management. There was something fundamentally satisfying about providing the support that kept things moving. It was fun to sneak around in her dark clothes, working against the clock to create order behind the scenes. It was like evidence destruction in reverse.

Beth and Vince reported that Sam was totally avoiding them and everyone else at school. Beth had so many friends that she could easily travel in packs, further shielding herself from him. She acted sunny as always, as though the crying girl from the sleepover had never existed.

April 30 arrived, and Birdy peeped out from behind the curtain with 20 minutes to go. Her stomach clenched at the buzz of voices. Beth and Kelly were in the third row from the back, laughing with Mom. Kelly would be coming again tomorrow with Mel, who was working tonight. Then Dominic stepped through the door.

He had grown taller and stronger, his hair freshly cut. Better looking than ever. Tonight, there was a new facet to her feelings when she looked at him, something that tempered the shame, sadness and anger.

He liked scaring you, and that's messed up. Birdy's own words came back to her as she watched Dominic worm his way around the room. They took the edge off his power and turned him into a specimen, an attacking virus not to fear, but to study.

"Birdy," snapped Mrs. Amon, "It's time."

Birdy pulled back as Mrs. Amon stepped in front of the curtain. "Friends, I just wanted to welcome you all to our humble little production. We're so excited to pour out our gifts for the Lord, and we're so happy to have you join us this evening. God bless."

The best that could be said of the play was that it was over fast. Margaret left behind a critical rose during the big romance scene, but Isaac improvised beautifully and moved the plot forward without it. On Saturday, she remembered the rose, but Isaac, who could barely see out of the enormous Beast mask, tripped to the ground while approaching their embrace. Margaret dove to her knees and delivered an adlibbed, passionate monologue about how though he may fall, she would always be by his side, helping him rise again. Mrs. Amon wept in the wings.

After the Saturday night show, the cast and crew came out for bows. Out in the audience, Peter sat beside Dad. When he caught sight of Birdy he leapt to his feet and cheered raucously. Birdy smiled back, feeling a little bit proud and overwhelmingly pleased to be finished.

After Birdy was released, she found Mel and Kelly by the snack table, Kelly in a pink tee shirt and pink plaid Bermuda shorts, Mel in a purple sundress that looked beautiful against her pale skin and dark hair.

"That was the clunkiest dialogue I've ever heard," Mel exclaimed as Birdy approached.

Kelly crossed her arms. "Did you skip over an entire scene tonight?"

"We sure did," said Birdy.

"Well, you were better off for it," said Kelly.

Half-costumed kids sprinted around the reception area, fueled by freedom and illicit sugar. Birdy hadn't seen Dominic tonight, but Mr. Doppelski was working the crowd at an aggressive pace. Despite the happy atmosphere, he seemed agitated. He went up to Mr. Faducci with a belligerent smile and struck up an uncomfortable-looking conversation that ended with Mr. Doppelski slapping Mr. Faducci on the arm and cackling, while Mr. Faducci stepped back stiffly.

Mr. Doppelski turned to the snack table, and an eager look came to his face.

"Well, if it isn't Ms. Melissa Holloway!" he said, prowling their way.

"Hi, Mr. Doppelski," said Mel.

"Dad couldn't make it out tonight?"

"No, he's working," said Mel.

Mr. Doppelski's voice took on that jokey tone that made Birdy see red. "Well, I'm guessing he never would have let you leave the house dressed like that!"

Mel's face fell in confusion. She glanced down at her outfit, then looked back at Mr. Doppelski.

"Or maybe he's just too chicken to tell you to cover up for once! I'm gonna have to have a talk with him!"

"That is a really strange thing for a grown man to say to a teen-age girl," said Birdy.

Everyone looked at her.

"Excuse me?" sneered Mr. Doppelski.

"You heard me," said Birdy. He gaped at her, red with loathing and for once speechless, but she stood her ground. She'd had enough.

Finally, he jabbed his finger into her shoulder. "You're a real piece of work. This young lady is practically my daughter and I'm just looking out for her, and you're getting all upset over nothing. You know, I'm glad Dominic doesn't hang around you anymore. You better stay away from my boys."

"No problem," she laughed. He turned away looking furious and stalked right out the door.

Birdy looked at Mel, whose jaw hung wide. She put her arms around Birdy. "My little firecracker," she said, rubbing Birdy's head obnoxiously. "That was amazing!"

Kelly was laughing uncontrollably. "Oh my gosh," she said, crossing her legs, "I'm gonna wet my pants!"

Peter waited back at the Clearys' to hang out with Birdy when she got home, but he turned down Mom's offer for him to stay over.

"That's okay," he said, "Chris probably snuck in there for a midnight snack and left popcorn kernels in the bed." Birdy went to bed, thankful for all her people, and dropped fast into sleep.

Something was shaking her arm. It was making her whole body bounce.

"Birdy. Birdy, honey."

There was light on the other side of her eyelids, but she didn't want to open them because then it would be morning.

Wait. Why is Mom in here?

Birdy opened one eye. Mom sat on the edge of her bed, looking scared.

"Honey, I'm so sorry, but there's been a terrible accident."

Birdy sat up straight in bed. *Peter?* But no, Mom would be beside herself. It couldn't be him.

"Who?"

5

BETH GREW UP KNOWING her parents would never move because they didn't have to pay a mortgage. What they had never mentioned, and what Beth had never realized, was that the house still accrued property taxes. Not being an adult homeowner, Beth didn't know property taxes existed.

In the weeks after the incident with Sam, Beth walked a tightrope through life. She was this close to shattering, but if she just put one foot in front of the other, she wouldn't. True to Vince's promise, Sam stayed away from her at school, and Beth, the expert at looking happy, forged onward.

On April 30 she went to Birdy's play and giggled through it with Kelly and Mrs. Cleary. On May 1, the beautiful weather finally invigorated her. She would start the new month fresh, she thought. She opened all the windows and let the sunshine pour into the dank brown house. It had only been a few weeks since the mega clean, but the clutter was already piling up, and she would be like Kelly and do some organizing.

Normally Beth plucked out the electricity bill and ignored the rest of the mail, so she decided to sort through the pile. There were catalogues, credit card offers, contractor advertisements, and something that said "Final Notice." She opened it with sweating hands. Crucial words popped out at her— "Maryland Property Tax Bill" and "FINAL NOTICE OF DELINQUENCY" and "LEGAL ACTION WILL BE TAKEN." Beth didn't know exactly what it all meant, but the main idea was there on the bottom of the page— she was on the hook for two thousand, three hundred and forty-two dollars.

Beth tumbled off her tightrope. She didn't have that money, had no way to get that money, didn't know what would happen if she didn't get the money. $2,342 was incomprehensible. Beth abandoned her organizing and sat weak on the couch until it was time to leave. She worked her shift at the movie theater in a daze, at one point pumping soap onto the popcorn instead of butter. Fortunately, her friend Marcus noticed and intervened.

"You okay, Bethy?" he said.

"Fine," said Beth.

Her friend Donna smiled. "Come out back with us after," she said.

Beth did. After they finished closing, she put her nametag in her pocket and followed them outside. That late at night, no one ever cared what went on behind the movie theater. Beth knew there was a 50 percent chance that smoking would upset her even more, but the prospect of even potentially quelling the panic inside her was intoxicating in itself.

After a few minutes out back with Marcus and Donna, Beth did begin to feel better. She could figure out the money. She could figure out anything. She might not even need the money. They probably might not come looking for it or anything.

"You fucking bitch!" screamed Sam.

Beth recoiled, whipping her head around for him, hoping it was just her imagination. But there he was, a growing figure emerging from the shadows across the parking lot. Where had he come from? What was he doing here?

"I knew you were lying! You're high!" He skidded to a stop in front of them, hacking, his pale eyes ablaze.

"Hey man, calm down," said Marcus, who was about three times Sam's size. Sam tried to move towards Beth, but Marcus stepped between them. Beth staggered around the front of the building and fumbled with her bike lock. She could hear Sam pounding up the sidewalk—he had somehow broken free of Marcus and was coming her way. She hopped on her bike and pedaled, her heart lightning fast, her mind and legs nightmare slow. She pulled out of the parking lot, away from Sam, into the cover of the dark streets. It was 11:58 pm.

Her bike's reflector piece was long gone. Her uniform was black. There was no moon.

6

JUDE STORMED AWAY FROM Birdy and out to his car. Who the fuck did she think she was? She was conniving, that's what he'd never liked about her. Sneaking around, sneering at him, after she'd spent years drooling over his son, when he was the reason she had a school to go to at all. Ungrateful little bitch.

It made him think of Tammy this morning in the bathroom. She just kept sitting there, frozen like an idiot, but for just a second she'd looked at him like *he* was the idiot. He'd slammed his hand louder on the counter and she'd flinched back into herself. But the memory had been eating at him all day.

Jude pulled into Green Dog to get a quick drink before going home. He needed to take the edge off. But he kept thinking of what Tammy had said and that one moment of hatred on her face. One quick drink turned into a few more. Rob made noises about taking his keys, so Jude waited till his back was turned to go to his car. Then he poured himself into the driver's seat and started the engine.

He pulled onto Baker Street, empty at this hour, rolled down his windows, and took off. He'd always loved that feeling of wind whipping his face. It was like being nine years old, flying down hills on his bike, flying just because it was fun and not because he was outrunning anything. The faster he drove, the better he felt. The air buffeted through the car, refreshing his mind. Washing away the iniquities. No responsibilities. No fears. Just wind.

7

AT 1:09 AM, OFFICER John Holloway was dispatched to the site of a car accident. A white male, mid-forties, had hit a tree at high speed on Houser Lane. His airbags had deployed. Substance use was suspected. As John pulled up to the site of the accident and stepped out of the car, his heart started pounding. For there rested a wrecked blue Ford Escort, the beloved car of his old friend, Jude Doppelski.

Jude was semi-conscious and utterly shitfaced, but otherwise appeared to be free of serious injuries. Brian and Gary, an EMT duo, had gotten him out of the car and were administering first aid. Officer Nicholson was scribbling notes in his pad as he spoke to the homeowner who had heard the impact and made the call. Nicholson was twenty-five, still quite passionate about the job.

Once he confirmed his friend was alive, John shone his flashlight around the rest of the scene. Jude had tried to turn too fast, spun out of control, and hit a tree with the driver's side corner of his bumper. So why was there a dented scrape all along the passenger's side? John wondered if he had hit a deer or something before running into the tree, but he didn't see one nearby. He bent closer. Was that red paint?

He stood and shrugged to himself. With 9 kids at the house, half of whom were confirmed daredevils, anything could have made that dent. He looked around. No one had seen him inspecting Jude's car. Nicholson clicked his pen shut with satisfaction and exchanged a few words with Brian and Gary before coming to stand beside Officer Holloway. Nicholson looked like a cartoon strongman. He folded his arms across his impossibly broad chest and his embarrassingly slick mustache quivered in indignation. "Sucks he got so fucked up, but luckily no one else got hurt." John nodded in agreement, zipping his mind shut on the thought of Tammy, who he knew would somehow absorb all the consequences of this night.

John went home two hours after sunrise. Lily was drinking coffee and reading at the kitchen table, wrapped in her pink bathrobe. He gave her a tired kiss before trudging upstairs, where the girls were still sleeping. He scalded himself in the shower and managed to fall asleep quickly despite the night having been purely terrible.

He woke to the sound of hysterical crying and sat bolt upright, wildly alert. He had already jumped out of bed when Mel burst through the door.

"Dad," she sobbed, crumpling into his arms. "Somebody hit Beth last night. On her bike. Somebody hit Beth with a car and then just left her there in a ditch. And her parents aren't around Dad, they're gone, they left her, I'm sorry, I should have told someone, I should have told you!"

Officer John Holloway was a miserable man who was afraid to be one bit more miserable than he already was. He had known something was wrong at Beth's house, anybody could see that, but he hadn't investigated. He had known Jude was cruel and sneaky and drove drunk, but he still met up with him for a beer every few weeks because he didn't want to upset the balance with his old friend. He had turned away from his questions at the site of Jude's accident because he didn't want to get involved in something complicated. But as his daughter bawled in his arms, John Holloway remembered the flavor of duty.

8

ALL THOSE MONTHS AGO when Mel had put herself in Beth's phone as Mom, she had unwittingly set herself up to experience every parent's worst nightmare. Brian and Gary, who were having an eventful shift, couldn't find a wallet on the bicyclist who was unconscious in the ditch on route 346, but she had a nametag and a cellphone in her pocket. That was enough to tell them that the girl was Beth, and to call her mom.

Mel could barely form a coherent sentence, so Mrs. Holloway had called everyone's parents to tell them what happened to Beth. Birdy practically rolled from her bed into the car, and Mom drove her to Mel's house. Kelly was already there, and Vince was jogging through the woods. They gathered on the porch, the perfect sky mocking their terror.

Officer Holloway had left to go help even though it was his day off. Mrs. Cleary and Mrs. Holloway were practically strangers, but they bonded quickly over their love of gossip and each other's daughters. They spoke tearfully at the kitchen table, piecing together what they knew or suspected.

Finally, Mom went home and told Birdy that Dad would get her when she was ready. The four kids, all of whom felt ancient, sat in agonized silence on the porch. Bailey timidly brought them a tray of snacks, which Birdy and Vince couldn't stop eating. Kelly and Mel couldn't eat anything. It was mid-afternoon before they all realized they had skipped church, but Birdy thought she had prayed more in the last 5 hours than she had in the last year. They were still gathered when purple began to streak the sky and Officer Holloway came home.

He trudged across the porch and pulled up a chair to face them. He sat with his elbows on his knees, hands kneading his hat. "Quite a day," he began.

Mel looked like she was going to kill him for the inadequacy of this statement. Sensing this, he cleared his throat and shared the important part first.

"Beth is going to be okay," he said. "I d-didn't think it was possible" he said, and Birdy's eyes welled up in response to the tears in his voice. "He was going way too fast, didn't even stop when he hit her, and she was in that ditch for hours before she was found." His voice broke again on the last word.

He cleared his throat again. "They took her to Shock Trauma. Her vitals are good, even though she broke a bunch of bones. Good brain activity. She was wearing her helmet, thank God—but—you should see it. Or maybe not. Anyway, she woke up. They put her back to sleep just for the pain. You all can go see her tomorrow."

Then he shifted. They could all see he was holding back something unpleasant.

"And it turns out she may have been safer in that ditch than at her house."

They looked around at each other. This would be the part where he rebuked them for not telling anyone that Beth's parents were gone. Birdy was ready to confess anything, as if ample truth now could undo her silence, erase what had led to Beth lying shattered in a ditch. But that wasn't what Officer Holloway meant at all.

"We knew something was up with her parents, but were a little confused about what was going on because Melly—" he glanced at her—

"Was crying her eyes out and couldn't think or talk straight," Mel finished for him.

"Right," he said. "I brought a group to her house to figure out what was going on. And it turned out someone was already in there."

Sam had not tried to pursue Beth on her bike. Instead, he wrested himself from Marcus's grasp and turned his attention elsewhere. When Officer Holloway and his colleagues showed up at Beth's house, they found him inside, having broken through the back door moments earlier. His presence in Beth's house was troubling, but more troubling still was the switchblade he pointed at the cops.

Mel whimpered at this, but Officer Holloway waved his hand and continued. After finding three large and angry men pointing their bigger weapons and bigger voices at him, he lost his nerve and surrendered his backpack. No one patted him down.

"When we searched his backpack—" Officer Holloway had to pause again to collect himself. The man who had rediscovered love this morning couldn't stop crying now. "He had some items of concern in his backpack. Some scissors. A bunch of baggies. A—another knife. Vials of—something, and a needle. Duct tape and—and zip ties."

"Beth had just broken up with him," whispered Mel. Officer Holloway nodded and cleared his throat. "We figured there was some sort of half-baked kidnapping scheme going on. So Nicholson goes 'What the fuck is all this?'" He swallowed. "And he just went nuts."

Vince had said Sam had no balls, but he mustered a single testicle long enough to kick Officer Burns, draw a gun from inside his waistband, fire at the cops, and miss entirely.

Nicholson shot back, but he didn't miss.

Officer Holloway fixed his daughter and her friends with his bloodshot eyes as he enunciated the news. "Sam Purcell is dead."

They stared back at him, horrified. He cleared his throat again.

"None of this should have happened. I'm so sorry, kids. There shouldn't be a kid hurt, there shouldn't be a kid dead. But it's not going to end here, I promise." He looked at them. "I promise. We're gonna track down Beth's parents, we're gonna get her somewhere safe, and we're gonna make sure Mr. Doppelski—Jude—" he pressed his lips together and looked at the ground a minute. "Jude Doppelski shouldn't have been on that road. We're gonna make sure he doesn't have the chance to do that again. We'll make sure Beth gets justice."

Mel gazed at him in concentration and he gazed back, weaving a promise in the air between them. Then he patted her on the shoulder and went inside to see his patient wife.

As soon as he was gone, Mel glared at Vince with animal ferocity. He looked up from his trance at the floor.

"What?" he said.

"I thought you said he wasn't going to bother Beth," said Mel.

Birdy wished Mel would please, sometimes, save her bluntness for private conversations.

"I did. I talked to him. I told him that was bullshit, and she didn't owe him anything and plus all her stuff was dead anyway."

"You—*talked* to him? I thought you—beat him up or something."

Vince shifted around to look at her. "Well, I *told* you I was just going to talk to him."

"But I thought you were going to really make a point."

"What, and have your dad show up and arrest me?"

"Maybe that would have been better than what ended up happening!"

"Are you kidding?" said Vince, hurt and fury streaking his voice. "How was I supposed to know all *this* would happen?"

"No I just mean—" said Mel, who was starting to cry. "I just thought you had done something more—effective."

Vince looked like he was going to cry for a second too. Then he stormed away to the woods.

Mel kicked a headless Barbie across the porch. "God, I didn't mean for it all to come out that way! I just—I thought he'd done something that would really work!"

Kelly agreed. "I get it. I was under the impression something different had happened between him and Sam too."

"That's how he made it sound!" said Mel.

Birdy said nothing. The other girls looked at her expectantly.

She sighed. "I assumed he did more too. But maybe that's just because I wanted that to be true. I wanted Sam to"—her voice crumbled—"go away. But—we were all trying to protect Beth. And it turns out, we all did a pretty shitty job."

Mel slunk down on her chair. "Yeah," she murmured. "I just wanted Vince to be better than me."

9

DEAREST DIVINE MERCY FAMILIES,

Congratulations again on a spectacular, frenetic performance of Beauty and the Beast this weekend!!! Sadly, I must write to you with upsetting news. Mr. Doppelski was in a bad car accident this weekend. By the grace of God, he is okay!!! However, as he and his family is such an important part of our school, we will be closing school until Wednesday to give us more time to shower him and his family in our prayers and support. Contact me to join the meal train!!

Yours in Christ,

Roberta Amon

BETH HAD SURGERY ON MONDAY, so they didn't get to go see her until Tuesday. Mrs. Merryman drove the girls to Shock Trauma in Baltimore and led them through the bleached halls to Beth's room. They found her with casts on her arm and leg and her ribs wrapped in bandages. Her hair was stringy, her face scraped and swollen, but she was awake.

"I'm ready for prom," she said.

Mrs. Merryman fussed over Beth for ten minutes, then abruptly turned for the door. "I'm going to find you all some treats," she said, fanning a hand near her eyes.

Mel plunked on the edge of Beth's bed. "Beth," she whispered. "I just can't believe it. It's crazy."

Beth straightened up, then winced. "You don't even know how crazy." She told them everything that had happened since she opened the property tax bill, her energy waning as she went on. She sunk back into her pillows as her tale came to its end, then listened in subdued surprise when Mel filled her in with their information.

"Wow, shouldn't have got in Creepy Weirdo's way, I guess. But I'll take all this over Sam trying to kidnap me and the kids." Birdy smiled through a blur of tears as Beth went on. "These drugs feel really good. But I think I'm going out of business for good."

Mel leaned in closer. "Did they—you know. Did they like... check on you? Like the cops or hospital people or whatever? To see if you were high?"

"Yeah," said Beth, "they had to test my blood before surgery. There was a doctor in here like right before you came who said they could offer me drug counseling."

"What?" Birdy whispered in panic. "Are they going to report you?"

Beth looked annoyingly relaxed. "There's like this law that they don't have to. I think the doctor kinda felt sorry for me. And the law also says they don't have to tell my guardian. And I don't even have a guardian, so that's nice."

Birdy thought "nice" was a stretch, but Mel looked pleased. "Well luckily Mr. Doppelski got tested right where he crashed, so he's already been charged with a DUI."

Kelly shook her head. "I can't believe Sam tried to—" she broke off and turned to Birdy. "Do you think people at Divine Mercy know what Mr. Doppelski did?"

Birdy snorted. "My mom says they're all just praying for his quick recovery right now and they haven't told anyone what exactly he's recovering from yet."

On Wednesday Maddie threw her arms around Isaac the moment he stepped in the building. "You poor thing," she cried, "I've been so worried about your uncle! Are you okay?"

Isaac met Birdy's eyes over Maddie's back as he patted it. "I'm fine," he said.

Maddie drew back. "God will take care of him, I know it. I've been praying for him."

Isaac again looked to Birdy first. "He needs it."

Mr. Doppelski's Algebra 1 class was left to fend for itself, and Mrs. Doppelski kept gunning out of the parking lot before the other Divine Mercy ladies could shower her in prayers and support. On Saturday morning, as Birdy was eating her frosted mini-wheats, Mom burst through the door, fresh from her morning walk, and slammed her sweaty palms on the table.

"You will not believe the story Tammy just told me."

10

AT 4:30 AM ON MAY 1, Tammy Doppelski sat on the toilet, holding a positive pregnancy test for the 10th time. The house was as silent as it ever was, though she knew at any moment Rebecca would be roused from her slumber by the instinct that her mother was awake without her.

Far from viewing her period as the curse of womankind, Tammy welcomed it as her dear friend. So when it didn't show up when it was supposed to, she sought the answer immediately. An old campaigner, she woke early to test with the first urine of the morning. She was exhausted, but she hadn't slept well at all. As she watched that second line appear on the white plastic stick in her hand, she felt like she was floating on the ceiling, watching her pathetic life unfold like it belonged to someone else.

She loved the baby already, she couldn't help that. Her sister had yelled at her once saying Jude had brainwashed her and she just kept popping them out like a machine without even caring about them. But that wasn't true at all. Things got completely overwhelming about 5 kids ago, yes. She was chronically spread too thin, and even though she spent every waking and sleeping moment in service to her children, she suspected more than one of them had major issues unfolding right under her nose.

But still, every day her children amazed her. Dominic had once built her a birdhouse that looked exactly like their home. Damien had memorized his times tables at age 5, and really understood them. Sarah drew remarkable caricatures that made Jude howl with laughter, even when they were of him. She delighted in watching who they were becoming, even though they made her so very, very tired. And every time she cuddled a clean, soft, milky baby against her neck, she thought she would do it all ten more times just for a moment like this.

Yes, she already loved this baby. The poppy seed sized person nestled within her would grow into a unique and irreplaceable soul, with its own cares and worries. It would have its own ways of delighting her, its own ways of frightening her. Before long, it would leave the safety of her womb and enter a world of hurt and suffering. A world where her husband was its father.

And that was a terrible thought.

Take this one back, she begged of God. *Take it back.*

Dominic was two the first time Jude had hit him. Not the first time he spanked him, all kids needed spankings sometimes, especially Dominic, who was a wild child. No, when Dominic was two he had deliberately poured milk on Jude's work papers, and Jude had clocked him in the face. Twice. Tammy had held him and given him M&Ms until it was all better. Dominic was much bigger and angrier now, so that tactic didn't exactly work anymore. Now she was waiting for the day Dominic would hit back. She was surprised he hadn't already. Now she could see that the actual way to fix things would have been to get out way back then, to have taken Dominic and left, before they were so firmly rooted in the life they led, before there was no way out. But she hadn't wanted another broken family. She wanted hers to work.

After that first time, Jude had been so remorseful. He'd sobbed, practically groveled. And soon thereafter, he found God again. He was Catholic but had conveniently cooled on his faith from ages 14-25, the prime years for amusing debaucheries. Tammy was Christian, and he sometimes went to church with her, but after he had lost control at Dominic Jude did a bunch of soul searching and seemed to fall back in love with God. It delighted her, and she joined the Catholic Church to support him on his journey. She wanted the same things he said he did, and she thought that meant she could keep him happy. But it didn't work.

The hitting wasn't even the worst thing. It had only happened a handful of times, and only to a few of the kids, as far as she knew, anyway. Until the last few years he had always been so, so sorry afterwards. The biggest problem with Jude was that his family never knew which dad and husband they were going to get that day. It was the way his jokes veered from funny to cruel without warning. It was the way he raged at and insulted them for minor infractions. It was the way he would seem to be paying no attention to the kids at all, only to turn around and use their private worries and fears against them.

Tammy was rehearsing how she would break the news to him when the bathroom door burst open. She'd been so absorbed in her thoughts that she hadn't heard footsteps approaching. It wasn't Rebecca, as she'd thought it would be. It was Jude.

He snatched the test from her hand and yelled at her, kicking the wall and the vanity and slamming his fist on the countertop, but not her, thankfully. He had never hit her, or any of the girls. This was his idea of chivalry. Until recently, she had always bought it when he said she should be grateful for that. But the other day, on Sarah's 8th birthday, Jude had cut Sarah a giant slice of cake and placed it in front of her. After her fifth happy bite, he'd chuckled, "Now don't eat too much, boys don't like fat girls!" The memory of Sarah's little body freezing up still haunted Tammy.

Jude was angry, even though it had been Jude who insisted, 16 days ago, that he needed her right then, even though she told him she could get pregnant right then. She had told him no. As she watched his tantrum now in the bathroom, a spark of anger lit some-where down deep within her, next to the baby maybe, keeping it warm. But fear snuffed it out fast. How old would this child be before he hurt it?

Please take this baby, she begged of God. *Take it back.*

Jude managed one of his eerie mood shifts until about halfway through breakfast time, but when Frankie upended his cereal bowl, he lost his mind. Tammy was grateful it was the final day of the play. She left the house with the kids minus Dominic at 11 and bought them all McDonald's, a rare treat. Jude might yell at her for that too, but she knew there was enough money in the food budget, and fur-thermore, hot, salty, greasy fries were all she could fathom eating at the moment. And she felt oddly reckless.

Jude arrived soon before the play began, sitting on the opposite end of their row from her. After the play, she saw him lurching through the crowd, yukking it up with this person, antagonizing that person. Making a scene with Mr. Faducci, as if enough awkwardness hadn't passed between them already. The spark of anger returned. Tammy saw Jude talk to Birdy and Mel and their friend. Then he stormed away from them and out the door.

Dominic never showed up to the play, so Tammy got the kids home and the twins helped her get the younger kids to bed. Then she laid down in her own bed, fighting nausea that could have been from the baby or could have been from the fear of what would hap-pen when Jude came home. But he never did.

The call came at 2 am. Dominic still wasn't home, so when the phone rang, her first thoughts went to him, but it turned out that Jude was in trouble. She left the kids under Karen's supervision, and she and Abe drove over to the hospital together. The halls smelled like soup and antiseptic, and she had to stop in the bathroom to throw up. Abe eyed her questioningly when she returned. He felt he had a right to an explanation, and normally she would give him one, but that spark within her was growing, and she ignored him.

A tentative doctor and a vaguely familiar policeman stood guard in Jude's room, but Tammy didn't need them to tell her he'd been drinking when he had his accident. Abe gasped and cursed behind her as she approached the bed. Jude's eyes were shut, his eyelashes curled on his swollen cheeks, a bandage across his forehead. She took his hand, fitting her thumb into the perfectly round scar on the back of it. She thought this was where a good wife would cry, maybe caress his hair, but she didn't do that. All she did was look down at him and think, *You can just stay right there.*

In the morning, the house was quiet. Karen and Abe mercifully brought all the kids with them to church, though someone would likely pop back home soon. Tammy found some insurance paperwork she needed and then walked out to the mailbox. Jude normally took the first pass of the mail, but they were out most of the day on Saturday and he'd never done it. It was mostly junk, except for one thing—an envelope from M&T Bank. *Important Information Regarding Your Account,* it said. But their family didn't use M&T. They used Bank of America.

Open it.

The nudge, Tammy told Mom, came from the Holy Spirit. With her husband safely unconscious in a hospital bed, she had the courage to listen. The letter inside ironically confirmed that he had now moved to paperless statements and billing. This was an odd choice for Jude, a man who normally thumbed his nose at any form of environmental protection, no matter how much clutter he incurred as a result.

Tammy went to the M&T website and logged into his account using his email address and his usual password: r3d$kinf@n1234.

Tammy had met Jude in Differential Equations, where she had tutored him to the B that helped him scrape his way into the engineering program. It hadn't even been a required class for her accounting major—she was just curious about it. She managed the finances of her teeming household with ease, mentally subtracting every cent that left their bank account in the form of shoes, toys, food, and electricity. It took no time at all to notice that this secret account was getting regular check deposits.

Check the school account. Again, she would tell Mom later, it was the Holy Spirit nudging her. She pulled up the Divine Mercy account, typed in the same stupid password, and confirmed her suspicions. The Divine Mercy account balance was remarkably low, because someone was making regular withdrawals that correlated precisely with the deposits in Jude's secret account.

And the credit card linked to his secret account? Well, it was making purchases at secret clubs and secret stores.

Couldn't her husband even have had the decency to use his secret money on his secret alcohol problem, instead of pouring their family budget down his lying throat?

The spark of anger ignited into an inferno. But somewhere inside that incandescent rage was a flicker of triumph.

Thank you, she told God, *Thank you.*

Summer 2010

1

Conrad Sun, Guest Column

I Am Not a Hero

Officer John Holloway, Conrad Police Department

Last month, I was part of an operation that ended in the death of a Conrad High School junior, Sam Purcell. He fired at myself and my colleagues, and evidence suggested that he planned further violence. Because of this, people say my colleagues and I are heroes. My colleagues acted bravely, but I know that I was not a hero.

In August 1969, I met my friend Jude Doppelski. We were kindergartners at St. Ann's School. We played football together from backyard pickup all the way through high school. We enlisted in the Marines after high school together and ended up back home in Conrad together when our service was through. We were in each other's weddings. We were part of the same faith community. We met for a beer every two weeks.

It's that last part that haunts me. Because in May, my old friend got drunk and then got behind the wheel of a car, a nasty old habit of his. I knew about this habit, but I pretended not to. I didn't want to complicate my life, a desire that now seems very foolish. That night, Jude spun out of control and hit a tree, totaling his car. My colleague arrived at the scene just before me and charged him with driving under the influence.

Sometime during the same night Jude was driving drunk, a girl on a bicycle was hit by a car that kept on driving. Bad enough, but this girl happens to have been a guest in my home more times than I can count. My daughter met her in kindergarten, just like I met Jude in kindergarten. She is strong, smart, and braver than I have ever been. Over a year ago, her parents abandoned her. She was sick of the excuses and failings of the adults in her life, so she took matters into her own hands. She supported and cared for herself without parents for over a year, with the help of a few dedicated friends, my daughter among them.

The morning after Jude was driving drunk and the girl was injured in a hit and run, Sam Purcell tried to break into the girl's home. She was at the hospital by that time, but Sam didn't know that. She had recently dumped him, and he didn't like that. So he broke into her house, bringing with him materials that indicated intent to hurt her. When we discovered the contents of his bag, he fired at us. My colleague fired back, and now Sam Purcell is dead.

Now my colleague acted within the law. He stopped the offender. But I was connected to these cases at multiple points. If I had had more courage in my personal life, then maybe no one would have ended up hurt or dead that night. Jude Doppelski may not have been driving drunk. The girl may not have been biking from her second job to her empty house at midnight. Sam Purcell might not have pegged her as the victim who would have no parents at home. He might have had a chance to mature into a man who took responsibility for his actions, instead of dying a boy who tried to punish a girl who hurt his feelings.

My daughter's friend had been suffering in an unsafe situation for quite some time. My daughter and her friends took it upon themselves to help her through this situation, but it wasn't enough. They were only trying to do the work that we adults should have done. They saw a suffering friend, and they met her with open arms. But they didn't know they could do more than that. That was my job, and I failed.

If I had done my duty instead of going through the motions, if I had stepped forward instead of turning away again and again and again, things could have been different. My colleagues and I were the last line of defense for our community, but we could have been the first line of defense too.

Unfortunately, sometimes it takes tragedy for us to open our eyes. So let's keep them open. I beg the citizens of Conrad to think about what our responsibilities are, and what we want our community to value. Do we want justice? Mercy? Do we want to merely punish, or do we want to protect? Do we want this all to be a neat story we can forget in three weeks, or will we acknowledge how complicated it is? And will we let those complications change the way we do things?

This community is full of people in pain. If you're reading this, reach out to a friend in need. Use your resources, whether that means time or money or food or merely love. Next time you are a witness to suffering, please, don't look away.

THE *CONRAD SUN* HAD a moderate paper readership, but its website exploded with the publication of Officer Holloway's op-ed. Birdy had already visited the computer room five times today to read it, and every time she found herself glued to the comments section, which was alive and nasty.

Pig cops dont give a shit about us

omg wait do u think the jude guy actually hit the chick!!!!??

I heard the Doppelski guy is getting charged with vehicular assault. His brothers my cousins landlord

Why was this young girl out so late at night? And hanging out with a bad kid? There must have been warning signs, she should have known better than this

Jude Doppelski is a good man with many children! God will provide and save him!!

Heard sam purcell was a drug dealer. Maybe its best hes gone... just saying

This guys a pussy he clearly didnt have the stones to pull teh trigger

Birdy scrolled away, face blazing, and printed the article.

The previous summer, packed with fun and parties, seemed like a hundred years ago. The teenagers of Conrad were in a holding pattern, quietly exchanging information when possible and avoiding large gatherings and illicit substances of any kind.

Sam had had a small and pitiful funeral—Kevin, Amanda, Katie, and Angela had attended and reported—and after that, no one appeared to miss him. He had lived with his grandfather and uncle, both of whom accepted the news of his death with resignation bordering on apathy. They had guns, but the one Sam had used wasn't registered to them. Birdy had seen TV shows where police shootings resulted in some kind of consequence or inquiry, but according to Mel's sources, that rarely happened in Conrad.

Instead, for the first time in years, the Conrad County Police Department had a real investigation on its hands. The attitude around the station was energetic, even though almost all the cops knew Jude personally and about half of them remembered Beth Nolan's dad from somewhere along the line.

While Jude was undeniably guilty of the DUI, he was pleading innocent to vehicular assault. He didn't remember it and said there was no proof. According to Mel, the CCPD had—much to its excitement—collaborated with a forensics lab to match the paint on Jude's car to the paint on Beth's bike. Jude was also pleading not guilty to embezzlement charges.

According to Mom, Tammy viewed all this as the perfect opportunity to get Jude out of their lives without dragging the children into it. She had opted not to press charges for domestic violence, but she had also declined to bail him out of jail. Due to the glacial pace and revolving door of the Conrad legal system, Jude would remain in custody until his trial, which, Officer Nicholson vowed to Tammy, would be held sometime in the fall, winter, or spring.

By the Wednesday after the accident, the CCPD had located Beth's aunt. Beth's mom really had gone to visit her sister all those months ago, but then she had said she was going back home. With a few phone calls, the CCPD determined she was really in Florida, and that her husband was in California. Both were charged with neglect, the house went into foreclosure, and after years of worrying, Aunt Meg welcomed Beth home.

Mrs. Merryman became the point of contact for Aunt Meg as they worked out the details of Beth's new life. But as Kelly reported miserably to Birdy one day, Aunt Meg's attitude toward her parents was shifting from gratitude to admonishment. Beth's best friend's dad is a cop, asked Aunt Meg? And he didn't figure this out? Why didn't *you* figure this out? And that drug dealer guy who broke into her house—what was with that? None of her teachers thought something was off? Those two coworkers who saw Sam come at her—why didn't they call the cops right then?

Mrs. Merryman had done what she could with these questions, but the girls knew the real answers, which ranged in flavor from embarrassing to devastating. Officer Holloway was totally checked out until recently, Mr. and Mrs. Merryman were simply delighted to have extra kids around to love, Sam wanted to steal the weed he thought Beth had, the teachers at the school were also checked out, the coworkers and Beth were blazed. Now that their deception had blown up in their faces, it all felt so stupid. But the kids held their silence on the remaining lies, terrified of ruining Beth's salvation at the last minute.

Beth spent an interminable two weeks in the hospital, but the two weeks after her release flew by. Papers were signed, arrangements were made, and before they knew it, Beth's things were packed and waiting in six big boxes in Mr. Merryman's spotless garage. Mr. and Mrs. Merryman implored Aunt Meg to give Beth one more week to stay with her friends. She had agreed to one day. Now they were down to the wire, spending their last hour together in Kelly's room.

Birdy had said many goodbyes to many friends over the years, but none that felt quite like this one. Mel wouldn't stop bouncing on her butt on Kelly's extra bed, even after Kelly told her irritably to stop. Kelly was reorganizing the top of her dresser, which was already pristine. And Beth sat on Kelly's bed, right arm and leg in casts, left foot encased in a neon green sock and jiggling.

"Well, Columbia's not too far away," said Mel in response to no one.

Beth's Aunt Meg and her family lived in Columbia, an ultra-planned community in a nearby county that was consistently ranked as one of the best places to live in the nation. The school district where Beth would be spending her senior year was rumored to provide laptops for each student.

The front door opened and shut, and Mel dashed to the window. "There's no car here," she said. "It's probably Vince." She said "Vince" the way Abe Doppelski might say "Ronald Reagan."

He appeared in the doorway a minute later, looking ill. He took off his hat, squeezed it, and put it on again backwards. "Beth, just wanted to say bye." He went to the left side of the bed and bent over to give her an awkward hug.

"Thanks for everything, Vince." Beth kept thanking all of them for everything.

"No problem. I'm sure we'll see you all the time. Columbia's not that far right?"

They kept saying things like this because the thought of not seeing Beth after everything—such a hard-working word— was unfathomable. Yet Birdy knew all too well what it felt like to lie to herself. She knew she would never stop loving Beth, and she knew just as certainly that something had shifted in the bedrock of their group's friendship. Beth's aunt and uncle had already taken a protective stance against them, and that was distressing but maybe not unjustified. Things weren't going to be the same again.

Mel was still standing by the window. Deep shadows fell across her exhausted face. Vince looked at her like she was the best thing he'd ever seen. He crossed the room in four long strides and embraced her. "I'll be home later if you need me," he murmured into her hair. For some reason, this was the thing that sent a stab of emotion into Birdy's throat. She swallowed as Vince waved to the rest of them and left.

Kelly shot a shrewd look at Mel, who gave her a trembling but happy smile in return. Birdy filed this away and turned her attention to Beth.

"How was that doctor's appointment, Beth?" Beth and Aunt Meg had taken a day trip to Columbia the day before so she could meet the new doctor she would be seeing.

Beth shifted. "It was pretty good. I start physical therapy next week. It seems like the doctor is really good. Since I was already in good shape and I'm young, I have a better chance of healing well. I'm probably not going to be ready for soccer this fall," she continued, fighting to keep her face from crumpling, "but they do have some spring soccer leagues around there, and he said I might be ready for that. And there's an indoor soccer place too if I'm ready by winter. Plus maybe I can try another sport at school too. Maybe track."

"Yeah, show Howard County what your gazelle legs can do," said Kelly.

Beth snorted. "Crippled gazelle legs."

They all laughed too hard at this, desperate to squeeze out one more inside joke as they surged towards the event horizon. Birdy tried to soak in the image of Beth, her blond braid and her pink pre-wrap headband, her Coca-Cola T-shirt, her scarred but strong leg extending from her black Adidas shorts. Her casts that were covered with the names of her masses of friends, including the three in this room who had tried and failed to take care of her. Her blue eyes that Birdy had seen sparkling with sass, emptied by pain, brimming with love.

They all jumped when they heard a door slam outside. Mel swirled around. "They're here." Two minutes early. Birdy's stomach liquified as she and Kelly each grabbed one of Beth's colorfully taped crutches. Beth used her good side to rotate her legs off the edge of the bed and stood up. Mel came over from the window, and the four of them stood in a huddle, the light of their love enclosed within. This was their last moment to hold onto what it had been. When they broke apart, it would go forth and be changed.

Beth looked around at them with that cheerful determination Birdy had loved since the first day of CRL soccer. "Well, I'm not gonna lie, I'm looking forward to not working three jobs and not having to ride my bike everywhere. And getting my license. Although ironically there are a metric fuck ton of walking and biking trails in Columbia." This made them smile, but they were all on the verge of sobbing.

"I just wanted to tell you that... just that I could never find friends like you guys anywhere else," Beth's voice shook as they held each other and finally succumbed to tears. "No matter where I go. Thank you for everything."

"You mean thanks for letting you get run over by a drunk creepy weirdo?" Mel shot back, and then they were all laughing and crying and laughing and crying again.

Mrs. Merryman tapped on the door. "It's time, girls." They led Beth down the stairs, hearing Mr. Merryman's voice as they descended.

"I got a pot of coffee going, can you have a cup before you hit the road?"

"No, thank you," came Uncle Gus's chilly response, and a wave of panic electrified Birdy's heart because now it was real. Beth was no longer subject to the rhythms of their world; she was already halfway to belonging somewhere else. Beth's shy ten-year-old cousin Brayden helped the parents load the U-Haul trailer attached to the shining white Tahoe. The girls didn't help; instead, they fussed over Beth. They had already fussed over her all morning, so the remaining tasks were pointless. Birdy helped her put on her flip flop; Mel retied the bottom of her braid; Kelly disentangled wisps of hair from her beaded hemp necklace. One last flurry of hugs, and then Aunt Meg helped Beth into the SUV and shut the door. Beth, their fierce and free and fragile spirit, disappeared over the hill, and her friends stood in the road wondering where on earth to go from here.

2

AFTER THE ACCIDENT AND its fallout, Mom and Dad had
gone into crisis mode. The Doppelskis needed help, the boys were
due home from school, and there was so much information flying
around that it was weeks before the full narrative emerged, especially
because Birdy took her time volunteering what she knew.

The day Beth moved away, Birdy went home and sat on her
bed. An early summer thunderstorm was starting. There was a knock
on her door, and Mom and Dad both stepped in. *Here it comes.*

They settled in carefully, Mom on the edge of her bed, Dad on
her wooden chair. They had heard, now, about Beth's year of neglect
and how Sam had tried to hurt her, how Mr. Doppelski had done it
first. They knew Birdy and her friends had tried to help Beth.
Thanks to Tammy's revelations, they also knew the full truth of Mr.
Doppelski, but Birdy didn't think they realized she'd had her suspicions all along. She hoped they'd never get there. They reacted so
destructively to shame.

"We know you've been through so much lately," Mom said to
Birdy. "So we haven't wanted to bother you. But honey. Lily Holloway told me you all had been helping take care of Beth for a year!"

"We weren't taking care of her for a year," said Birdy, knowing
precision on this point was irrelevant, but hairsplitting anyway. "We
found out in September that her parents were gone. But they'd been
gone for almost a year before that."

She expected them to be disappointed in her, and they were,
but it seemed their most potent emotion was hurt feelings.

"Why didn't you tell us, honey?" said Dad. "We could have
done something before it got so bad."

"We've always raised you to know you can tell us anything and
we won't get mad," said Mom.

Birdy looked at the steady drip of water falling from her ceiling
to the bucket. From the moment she met Beth's plants, it had never
seemed like an option to tell them any of it. *You seriously don't know*

why I thought you couldn't fix it? But Birdy had to live with her own shame. She had said nothing, and Beth had come to harm.

On Tuesday, she met up with Mel and Kelly after work at Woods Crossing Shops. They drank milkshakes at the stone tables, the movie theater looming behind them like a haunted house.

"So," said Kelly. "Has anyone heard anything new about any of it?"

"No," said Birdy.

"No," said Mel.

They slurped their milkshakes.

"There were some crazy comments on your dad's article online," said Birdy.

Mel didn't answer.

"Do you think anyone's going to say anything about Beth's kids?" said Birdy.

"Vince says no one liked Sam and no one wants their parents to know they got drugs from him," said Mel. "And that everyone liked Beth so no one wants their parents to know they got drugs from her. I mean, no one wants their parents to know they got drugs from anywhere."

Birdy felt a blaze of dissatisfaction with this answer. How could Vince possibly know what everyone thought and what everyone would do?

"But what about the baggies that were in his backpack? Don't people wonder why he brought those?" said Birdy. She'd kept the lid on her worries for a month and now they were spilling everywhere.

"Most people don't even know about that. We just know because my dad told us."

"But doesn't your dad wonder about it?"

Mel looked uncomfortable. "Probably. But it doesn't matter. The plants are gone. The police know he was mad she broke up with him. My dad already knew that, and then Beth told them that again when she was in the hospital. So that's his motive, and he can't say anything about it because he's dead."

Birdy's clenched cold fingers around her milkshake. She remembered freezing them off at the March for Life and observed that death was at times extremely convenient. Kelly stared off in the distance, looking distressed. Then a crease appeared between her carefully plucked eyebrows. "Don't look Birdy, but I think that's—"

"Oh my goodness, is that Birdy Cleary?" said Mrs. Amon. The sound of her voice about curdled Birdy's milkshake. "Just got off work, I see!"

"Yeah."

"Best restaurant ever!" She tilted her chin to an angle of extreme sympathy. "And how are you *doing*?"

"Fine," said Birdy.

"How is your poor friend?" said Mrs. Amon. "Your mom's sent out a few emails about her and we have just been *praying*. How's she doing?"

"She's okay," said Birdy.

"Well, The Lord works so mysteriously sometimes," said Mrs. Amon, shaking her head. "Maybe this will be a conversion experience for her."

"Why do you think she needs a conversion experience?" said Kelly with surprising hostility.

Mrs. Amon looked startled Kelly was there. "Oh, I don't think we've met, hon? We've all heard so much about Birdy's friends from St. Monica's. Are you one of them?" Mrs. Amon looked pleased with her social wiles.

"Yes," said Kelly.

"And your friend who was injured—she went there too?"

"Beth went to Conrad," said Birdy. Mrs. Amon gave little *Well, there you have it* jerk of her head.

"Maybe this will be a conversion experience for Mr. Doppelski," said Mel as though struck by divine inspiration. "Maybe he'll stop getting drunk and running people over."

"That hasn't been *proven*—"Mrs. Amon huffed.

"That's where the evidence points," said Mel.

"Well, even if he *did* do it—by accident—that would mean God put him right where he needed to be. To save your friend from that boy. She was clearly mixed up with the wrong company. You all could have gotten hurt too. Thank God for those brave police officers."

Sam's death was convenient even for Mrs. Amon; it made Mr. Doppelski's situation look better by comparison.

"Beth wasn't mixed up with the wrong company," said Birdy. "She was just trying to get home from work."

With this, Birdy felt something detach inside her. She'd told many lies to cover up for Beth, and it seemed she was now married to the lies forever. If truth was something real to be found, it followed that breaking the truth would have real internal consequences. But how could Birdy speak truth to Mrs. Amon, when Mrs. Amon would insist on contorting it into a falsehood of her own?

"Well, lovely as always to see you, Birdy," said Mrs. Amon. "I'll be praying for you *all*."

"God bless you," said Mel, waving as Mrs. Amon walked away. Then she turned back to Birdy and Kelly. "For our next crime, how about we plant some drugs in her Bible?"

In Mrs. Amon's eagerness to dunk on other schools, she failed to acknowledge a key point about her own. Divine Mercy was finished. Once word got out that Mr. Doppelski was not only suspected of a drunk hit and run, but had also been stealing from his friends and family for years, no one had the heart to try to keep the school afloat. The academic year had ended two weeks early, and the students had scattered to new educational bases.

The Herons, Faduccis, and all their associates were starting a school of their own, closer to their homes in Pennsylvania. Margaret was returning to regular homeschooling. Michael was too, but first his family was moving to California. The Doppelskis and Olivia were going to public school. Polly was off to college in Ohio, and Josh was headed to St. Monica's, throwing everyone for a loop. Fred managed to snag a spot at Bosco. There was an interval, horrendous to Birdy, where Mom wanted Fred to carpool with Dad, but Dad avoided the idea until it died.

Birdy would earn her final high school credits at the Community College of Conrad. She didn't know why her parents were, even now, basing their decisions off things the Doppelskis did, but the promises of reduced college debt and a new environment were enticing. Just as he'd done for Dominic the year previously, Mr. Abe pulled a few strings to help Birdy get a full course load despite her low priority enrollment status.

"No problem at all, no problem at all," Mr. Abe said in response to Mom's profuse gratitude in the St. Ann's parking lot. "She's such a bright young lady, she deserves a good opportunity."

Isaac wiggled his eyebrows at Birdy from behind his dad's back and Birdy looked away to hide her snort. She assumed Abe's desire to help her was at least partly influenced by his guilt that his brother had run over Beth, but she never said thank you. It felt a little late for him to be trying to support her.

By now, Birdy and Dominic were experts at avoiding one another. With the Doppelskis' new situation, they were given the chance to flex this expertise so extensively that Birdy found it almost comical. Mom sent Birdy over at least once a week to deliver meals and play with the kids. More than once, Dominic drove past her house the instant she stepped outside to go to his. He was taking as many credits and working as many hours as he could, trying to fill in some of the gaps his dad had left.

Mr. Abe was attempting the same, with enthusiasm. He continued to use his newly professional and kindly manner with Birdy, as though he had not, on several occasions, implied that she was actively attempting to seduce his sons and nephews. Abe whipped around Jude's house, finding things to fix. He thrived under his new responsibility as his brother's placeholder in their community, but he had a major assist from his wife. Birdy opened Facebook one day to find a link to Karen's latest blog post.

A Mama of Homeschool Dropouts Tells All

No, your eyes did not deceive you. The big news at the Hallowed Home this week is that the Lord has brought some major changes to our lives. Ready to hear more? Read on.

There was an ominous picture of an empty pair of kids' tennis shoes.

You all know how dedicated I am to educating our children at home and raising them to know the Lord. Gosh, that's the whole reason I started this little corner of the internet in the first place! Even when my oldest two sweeties started school a few years ago, I still considered myself a homeschool mama. They were going to a school that my family helped start, after all. And I still had my other littles at home, exploring and learning together every day.

But the Lord sometimes has plans we don't understand. For privacy's sake, I can't share all the details. I just have to say that someone very close to me and the school has been very selfish. His or her actions have weakened the school finances so much that it can't keep going. Its not opening again this fall.

I know you're saying Karen! This is when you get down on your knees and PRAY!! But trust me friends, I have. I just ask that you don't judge me too hard for the next piece of the news.

Now there was a picture of an empty cereal bowl.

My oldest five kids will be attending public school this fall.

I know, I know! Yes, I have all the same questions as you. Will they be safe? Will they be corrupted by bad influences? Will they be tempted by drugs, alcohol, and other bad behaviors? Will they still love the Lord?

Remember when I said I prayed about this? Well I put all those very questions before the Lord. And do you know what he said to me?

He said Karen, I'm watching over them. Don't you know that by now?

So now I'm asking you for help. Not for me, but for my dear sister in law, Tammy.

Now there was a picture of an empty laundry basket, which Birdy felt hinted more at orderliness than devastation.

Tammy's husband has been severely injured in a car accident. He is not going to be able to work for a long time.

Picture of an abandoned pencil.

As you know, our husbands are brothers, and they run several businesses together. They live right next door. This family involvement has always brought us such an uplifting and supportive family culture, but right now it is the source of a lot of fear and uncertainty.

Like me, Tammy has many children. In fact she has one more than I do and another on the way! Go Tammy! Ha!!

Tammy is now getting ready to go back to work to support her family. That means all of her kids are going to public school and yes— even daycare.

Cue a picture of a bare pink tricycle.

Feeding and clothing all the children she has joyfully accepted is quite a tall order. Will you please consider contributing to the fundraiser I have set up on their behalf? This faithful family is suffering greatly due to their father's emergency situation. This website, Go-FundMe, makes it easy to raise money for good causes. Please prayerfully consider making a donation using this amazing resource.

And don't worry, I'm not going anywhere! With my bigs in school, I will have more time at home with my littles, and for my blog! Keep your eyes here for more ideas about homeschooling, homemaking, and having fun.

The story of the homeschooling family next door, now father-less, was catnip to the Catholic internet. The post was re-pinned on Pinterest 10,000 times within the first day. The donations came roll-ing into GoFundMe. Karen got offers to endorse diapers, clothes, shampoo, and toothpaste, and she did so with gusto, churning out new posts five days a week. Strangers from all over the world stepped up to support the Doppelskis on very little information other than that they were a big, Catholic homeschooling family in need. Com-ments sections alluded that they were personal friends of Mike Fa-ducci, well-known Catholic author.

Abe was awestruck by Karen's viral moment and told anyone who would listen how impressed he was by her. He was inspired to tell Birdy one day, "You know, I've got to hand it to you ladies, you can come up with some great ideas we men would never think of." He even starred in a highly shared Q&A blog post, entitled "Inter-view With My Husband: All Your Big Questions Answered," in which he explained how he believed in God's mercy and was grateful for God's blessings that allowed him to lend a hand to a family in need.

Tammy accepted the donations with pragmatism, enrolled her children in the Conrad County school system, and renewed her CPA license. Her old vacant giggle developed a seething edge.

One Friday evening, Birdy brought over a giant bag of apples and five boxes of macaroni and cheese. Steve, Sarah, and Frankie were throwing a Frisbee in the front yard. As usual, Dominic's car was not in the driveway. She picked her way back through to the kitchen and started working on dinner. Tammy came out to get a drink of water.

"Oh, you know the kids love mac and cheese! Thanks so much Birdy."

"My pl—no problem!" said Birdy, ripping open the powdered cheese packet.

Tammy smiled absently. "When Dominic was six or seven he snuck an extra scoop of mac and cheese. Jude caught him and made him keep eating more until he threw up." Birdy's hand shook, spilling some of the yellow dust on the counter. Tammy drifted out of the room.

It was hard to hate Dominic after what had happened in his family. It didn't make his own behavior okay. Birdy just couldn't say she would be any less fucked up in his place. When dinner was ready, she walked through the house picking up toys and calling the kids to eat. She felt haunted by the ghost of a younger Birdy, who had walked these halls convinced that she'd hidden her heart in an impenetrable fortress, never noticing it was bleeding all over her sleeve.

And who had the younger Dominic been, back before she'd ever met him? A scared little kid who grew up trying to make everything fun because everything actually sucked so bad, who thought the way to love people was to treat them like dirt.

3

AMIDST THE REORDERING OF his family structures, Isaac continued to pose shirtless in fields. One day Birdy ran past him while he was flexing with his hands in his pockets and staring into the road. She waved, but he didn't wave back. The next time she passed, he waved her over.

"I don't want to disturb your photo shoot," said Birdy.

Isaac laughed and took a drink from his soda. "Don't worry, I'm done."

"Okay, good." She stretched a quad. "Are you excited to go to Conrad?"

Isaac sighed. "Yeah, I am. It'll be nice to be around more people. And I already know a lot of people there anyway."

Birdy hesitated, then said, "I saw about you and Maddie." Just that morning, she had seen the telltale broken heart on her newsfeed informing her that their complicated relationship had ended.

"Yeah," sighed Isaac again. "Everything that happened with the school and Jude totally sucks. But for a second there I thought, well at least now I have a way to end things with Maddie and it'll be easy." He looked like his stomach hurt. "But she didn't feel that way at all, she kept saying it was okay, we'd still see each other, we'd still make it work, we could make it through anything." He shook his head. "So I still ended it, but it was awful. I feel so bad about it. I didn't realize how seriously she was taking it all."

Birdy found this exasperating but said nothing. He looked at her. "I'm guessing you saw that coming." She feigned innocence and he snorted. "Don't rub it in." He started packing up his camera. "What about you? Any boys in your life?"

"No. I'm too picky."

"You? Picky? Dominic's pretty average, don't you think?"

"Shut up."

"You hate that you fell for the guy that every other girl also liked, don't you?"

"Yes, I do. Don't rub it in." Isaac laughed and sat on the stump where his camera had been, and Birdy sat beside him. "How's he— how are things between you two?"

Isaac shrugged. "Well— I've kind of been feeling like shit because I knew all along the stuff Uncle Jude did to him, and the rest of them. The stuff he's actually in legal trouble for wasn't surprising at all either. But Dom— remember how he used to tease me and you?"

"Uh, yeah, think so."

"Well there was this one day me and Michael and Dominic went to work with my dad, and Dom was making those same kind of comments all day—but about Michael."

"Oh, no."

"Yeah. Michael is clueless so he just thought he was being funny, and my dad acted like he didn't get it, but—you know how excited he was when I started dating Maddie. Anyway, things had been weird between me and Dom for a while, but after that it felt like anything good that was still left between us died."

"That makes sense," said Birdy.

He looked at her. "You know what I think?"

"What?"

"I think you're really good at making people feel noticed. And Dominic *loves* feeling noticed, it's like a drug to him. But he thinks if a girl likes him then she's just going to give him what he wants, and you never really went along with what he wanted. And he couldn't stand that."

"Well, he always had multiple girlfriends! I wasn't going to get mixed up in that!"

Isaac laughed. "I know that, but he didn't know that. He's so self-centered and he thinks everyone will act like he does."

Birdy put her head on her knees. "Maybe that's everyone's problem. Let's just stop thinking people will react like we would." She checked her phone. "I need to go get ready for work," she said. "See you at church tomorrow?"

"Unfortunately," said Isaac, looking bitter now. "It's really not the time for me to have my major rebellion. But I can't wait to get out of Conrad and never go to St. Ann's again."

"Sorry," said Birdy, which felt wildly insufficient to address Isaac's troubles.

Isaac shrugged. "Me, too."

The next morning, Birdy sat in the pew with her parents and Chris, listening to Mrs. Fitzgerald squawk. She thought bitterly of the day been so moved by Mrs. Knight's singing, when it felt just for a moment like God had lent her his own strength. A lot of good it had done.

The sick timing of Beth's wreckage and salvation indicated, to Birdy anyway, that there was indeed something out there driving the universe. It was all too specific to be random, wasn't it? But if God was out there, then why did he make it so complicated? Why did Beth have to be abused, abandoned, severely injured and then rescued only via a Rube Goldberg machine of failures? Beth got justice only as the accidental result of multiple fuckups by every single person who was supposed to be helping her.

"The Lord be with you."

Birdy looked up. That was not Father Bill. An energetic priest with a gray crew cut stood on the altar, looking brightly around the church from behind rectangular glasses. He led them through the prayers, even singing some of them in a clear, strong voice. There was no explanation of his presence until they sat down for the homily.

"Good morning everyone, and thank you for having me at your parish today. I'm Father Nicholas Martin and I'm with the St. Martin de Porres Society over in Baltimore. I thank you for giving me the opportunity to see so much of God's creation this morning; it was a lovely drive out here." Birdy assumed he was warming them up for donations, and thought he was barking up the wrong tree.

"We know that sacrifice is central to our faith. It's all right there," he said, gesturing to the crucifix hanging behind him. "God can and absolutely does use our suffering to teach us, and to build us. We can unite our pain to his, share in his suffering, and hopefully transform that suffering into powerful love."

He straightened his glasses and pierced them with his stare. "The problem begins when we start trying to interpret and control the suffering of others. And especially here in America, we tend to do this. Something bad happens and we hear about it, we pray, maybe we even donate to the cause when a priest asks for money." He paused and leaned into the microphone. "As I plan to do shortly." This brought a sprinkle of weak laughter.

He stood tall again. "But then we take that suffering we heard about, and we twist it so it doesn't change our lives. 'Oh, this happened for a reason. Oh, those people wouldn't have been killed in that natural disaster if they'd prepared themselves better. Oh, that cop wouldn't have killed that innocent guy if he hadn't been dressed like a gangster. Oh, that woman wouldn't have been assaulted if she hadn't dressed immodestly." Father Martin's voice turned sharp, and the laughter froze.

"And then there those other tricky problems, like abortion, or gay marriage. Now sometimes we think we know how to solve those problems. The solutions are don't get an abortion and don't be gay." Father Martin's face told them he didn't think these were adequate solutions. The congregation was silent. Birdy looked at the back of Isaac's head, six pews in front of her, perfectly still.

"We Catholics in the United States get so worked up about these things. Lately a lot of us are afraid our tax dollars will go to someone else's health insurance and pay for someone else's birth control. Or they'll fund a school that teaches something we disagree with. Or they'll fund a program that gives someone a free pass, gives them help they didn't earn. Sometimes we think the pinnacle of our duties as American Catholics is voting. Voting. Filling in the bubble, hoping it all comes out the way we wanted, and saying that's the best we can do. We think voting against a certain somebody is enough. We pray that certain laws will get passed or overturned, but we don't think so much about why those laws exist. We don't think about why it is that people feel the need for abortion, or can't buy what they need. So we vote and say our prayers, and we think our votes and our prayers absolve us from any additional obligations.

"It's fun to get worked up about these issues, we feel good and strong when we do it, and that's because they're ten steps removed from us. After all, maybe *we've* struggled to pay for our food and education and healthcare, but we've found a way. Why can't other people find a way? If they would just be more like us, then they wouldn't have these problems.

"Sometimes we send a few pennies overseas to poor people in villages that look quaint and deserving. But when the poverty is closer to home, we don't feel as bad about that. We close our eyes to our neighbors just 45 miles away." He pointed in what Birdy assumed was a Baltimorely direction. "Neighbors who live in houses that were built to fall apart. Neighbors whose ancestors arrived here as slaves and have never been welcome except as scapegoats. Or neighbors who fled awful conditions to come to America because they heard it was better here. They heard we would welcome them here.

"But Jesus didn't tell us to help only those who look like us, or only those who are worthy. Which is good news for every single one of us in this room, because none of us are worthy. You, me, your great aunt Sally, we're all sinners. And we're not getting anywhere by refusing to engage with people who think differently than us, whose lives look nothing like ours. If you can sit there and your biggest worry is whether or not the poor people deserve your taxes, then you're sitting at the end of a series of tremendous blessings. It's time to thank God for that grace and share it with others.

"Money is of course important, suffering people need material help. But Jesus does ask that we be like him, and Jesus was out there actually doing the work. Giving help that cost him something. And it is uncomfortable, oh yes it is. Sometimes it's uncomfortable because suffering people can be jerks. Sometimes the work conditions are physically uncomfortable. Sometimes it's uncomfortable because you find out you were wrong and you now need to change your mind. You might find that your eternal and all-knowing church has serious flaws and it's up to you to step up and fix them."

His voice softened now. "So today, yes, I ask for your financial support. But more than that, I also ask you to look into your heart and ask whose problems you think you've already solved. And then ask yourself how much you've ever listened to someone with that problem. And then I ask you to try to relieve that suffering, not merely by praying, not merely by donating, but by doing something. We always pray, we always need to pray and give God the chance to tell us what we didn't want to hear. But we don't let it end there. We pray and we listen to what He tells us to do when we get up."

Father Martin sat down. Birdy looked over at Chris, who placed primly scandalized fingertips over his lips and blinked cartoonishly at her. On her other side, her parents looked more authentically stricken.

Mrs. Fitzgerald said, in a tone of distaste, "Our second collection today will be for the... St. Martin de Porres Society of Baltimore." Then she began the offertory hymn, which Birdy immediately tuned out. She thought of the $20 sitting in her wallet, which she'd been planning to use for new running shoes. Abe came around with the collection basket, catching Birdy's eye with a fatherly nod that made her want to hurl. She considered giving to the second collection just to piss him off, but she figured that was not in the spirit of charity.

Mr. and Mrs. Cleary left while the closing hymn was still play-ing, a sign of true unrest. Chris tracked them closely, aiming to beat Birdy to the car for old time's sake, but Birdy trailed behind them, planning to hand her money to Father Martin on her way out. When she spotted him, he was chatting with Dominic, who was now the primary lector. Birdy's courage failed her and she rushed past, twenty dollars still sweating in her palm.

Birdy reached the van, where Chris was stretched out on the backseat, looking smug. Birdy smiled at him and turned over this new development in her mind. It was like she'd spent her entire life in a dark house, and Father Martin had just flipped a switch and re-vealed rooms she'd never seen before. The way he told it, being Christian had nothing to do with reveling in your own sacrifices, and everything to do with getting off your ass.

It solved none of her problems, but it was something to think about.

Fall 2010

1

Congratulations on the promotion!! And I'm so excited you'll have off for Thanksgiving! It can't get here soon enough. Maybe you could make us some thanksgiving steak? How's the new apartment? Is it weird to live alone for the first time in your entire life?

Dad seems to be enjoying the school year. Mom is helping Mrs. Doppelski a lot and it makes her very tired. She says she feels like she's the pregnant one.

My first few weeks of classes have been fine. I just finished Statistics. My English class starts in a minute and then I have Psychology. On Tuesdays and Thursdays I have Astronomy and Communications. I'm learning some interesting stuff but basically all my professors seem bitter to be teaching at CCC. Vince and Henry and a few of the other soccer people are here too so I eat lunch with them sometimes.

Beth seems to be doing okay, but it's been a little hard to get in touch with her. We haven't started soccer up again. It just feels wrong without Beth. But guess what, there's a boxing gym in Conrad! Can you believe it? Apparently in the spring, there is a 1-credit class there. My psych professor told us about it, but then she seemed to regret saying anything. She works out there, and she not-so-secretly hates all of us so I bet she doesn't want us to disturb her. I thought it sounded kind of cool so I might try it. Just call me Apollo Creed.

DR. GERPEL CLEARED HIS THROAT to begin class. "After great Pain, a formal feeling comes/The Nerves sit ceremonious, like Tombs." He looked at them through his large glasses frames. "Any thoughts?"

The students drooled back at him. Birdy's thought was that Dr. Gerpel looked like a hipster hobbit—short, hairy, and slightly portly, with a beanie, tight flannel, and skinny jeans.

A guy with long, shaggy hair raised his hand. "Does it mean pain makes you feel fancy?"

Dr. Gerpel sighed. Privately, Birdy thought Emily Dickinson made a great point. After the upheaval of the past few months, she felt stiff inside, like she was both resting and bracing herself for whatever might come next. But she didn't want to share that with the class.

Dr. Gerpel released them, disappointment in his every cell, and Birdy went to Psychology. Professor Kline opened a Power Point as Birdy took her seat. She flicked a hand through the air under her blond bob, like she was used to having longer hair. Then she crossed her arms and faced them.

"When you think about psychology, your first thought might be about people lying on couches talking about their problems. And we'll get to that, but first we need to talk about the stuff that puts you on the couch in the first place. And you might think that's all in your head, but remember that your head is part of your body. Okay? Your head has your brain inside, pretty important body part. When you think about any psychological ailment, remember to look at the body."

Professor Kline was coming alive a little bit. She seemed to have taken pleasure in delivering that last line.

"Here's one of the fundamental examples of what I'm talking about. You may have heard of what we call the fight or flight response. This is an ancient evolutionary mechanism. When your body perceives danger, it gets itself ready to either flee from that danger or attack it. So your pulse quickens, and your pupils dilate. Your breath shortens, you might even get a stomachache. This is called physiological arousal, and it's a useful state of being when there's really a threat. *Physiological* arousal, okay?" she snarled at the boys snickering behind Birdy.

"If your fight or flight response is very sensitive, it might react to danger in situations that aren't really that dangerous. Your body has the reaction, and your thoughts are paired with this response. Regular worries can seem to inflate in significance when they are paired with physiological arousal."

Birdy thought about how often she experienced what Professor Kline described. Her pounding heart, her aching head, her churning guts. The pressure in her chest that stole her words sometimes. These were her constant companions, but she didn't feel fear now. She was fascinated.

Professor Kline tapped her keyboard and the screen switched to a diagram of arrows pointing to each other in a loop. "Cortisol is the stress response hormone. Your body releases it under stress and ideally, it should dissipate when the threat has diminished. But sometimes the feedback loop gets disrupted, and you keep releasing cortisol when you don't need it. So you take what could be a neutral experience, okay? And you turn it into more stress. You do this all the time, in a way that interferes with normal functioning, and you might just be experiencing an anxiety disorder.

"Take your person who's got all the cortisol buzzing around, for example. That person might have irrational outbursts, lash out at the people around them, and be very controlling. Or they might feel frozen and unable to do anything at all. Or they might hold tightly to certain rituals, either their own or someone else's, in order to soothe themselves. Anxiety has a strong genetic component as well, so you might see it really wreak havoc in a family system."

Professor Kline tapped her keyboard again, but no new slide appeared. She pounded it a few more times before bending to her laptop and glaring. "My third grader used this last night and I *told* him not to touch my PowerPoint but—" She vengefully shut her laptop and blew on her forehead. "Did anyone even do the reading?" she asked with an angry tilt of her chin.

Professor Kline proceeded to adlib a lecture that managed to be both boring and passive aggressive, but Birdy felt like her whole life had changed in that chair. She wanted to know more, but Professor Kline was in no mood to assist. When class ended, Birdy was the first one to the door. She held it open for the guy behind her, who said "Thanks."

"My pleasure," she responded. The guy, who was at least ten years older and had distractingly blue eyes, looked confused.

"I mean...well, uh." Birdy speedwalked away down the hall, noting that embarrassment was apparently the type of threat that triggered her stress response. She was headed the opposite direction of where she needed to go, but she couldn't turn back now. Trying to look purposeful, she maintained her course, decisively rounded a corner, and walked smack into Dominic.

"Oh," she said, bouncing off him. Her already pounding heart went crazy. People milled around them as they stood frozen in place. The last time Birdy and Dominic had touched, he was tormenting her in her backyard. He'd been malicious then; he was petrified now. For all her recent empathetic reflections, a vindictive, consuming hatred roared to life when she saw the fear in his eyes.

She'd met this panicked Dominic before. She'd lived a lifetime since they'd been this close, and now she had everything she needed to step on him. All it would take would be a nasty look, an ugly word. That's what he would do. That's what his father would do.

His father had hurled Beth inches from death; this fact hung between them now, tangible as the ground beneath their feet. But something, whether a fluke or a miracle, had lifted Beth from her terror to a new life where she might have a chance to heal. And Mr. Doppelski's destruction ranged far beyond that night in May.

Dominic's hair was longer than usual and flat with grease. His lips were chapped to bleeding even without Mr. Doppelski around to bloody them. Birdy studied the eyes that had so consumed her and found a stye in one, yellow crust in both. The former nucleus of her existence was just an ordinary, neglected boy.

Beth was neglected, abandoned, and abused; saved only by a miraculous series of fuckups, but she had friends who loved her. Their love was foolish and immature, but it was also boundless, generous, eager to shoulder what little of her burden it could, and she loved them in return. Dominic, for all his admirers and charm, had no such luck.

The hate settled; only pity remained. Birdy would never be the hero in his story. She knew now that she couldn't fix him, but neither would she break him. Fool though she might be, she chose mercy.

"Hey, Dominic" she said softly. Then she stepped around him and walked away.

"HERE WE ARE AGAIN," said Kelly.

"Off the hook," said Mel.

"We're just getting started," said Evan.

Birdy said nothing. It was the first party in months, but Vince, fearing Officer Holloway's new vigilance, had only asked a few people to come. The night was surprisingly chilly, and Mel, Birdy, and Kelly were drinking Mike's Hard Lemonades by the fire.

"How's school?" said Birdy, frustrated this was all she had to say.

"It's hard," said Mel. "AP U.S. History is really hard."

"You'd probably be good at it," Kelly offered to Birdy.

"Maybe," said Birdy. Things had been strange since Beth left, and Birdy was hoping tonight would give them a boost. She wished Evan would go away so they could really talk.

"Oh look, it's everyone's favorite slut," said Evan, who had not gone away. Angela Prune was approaching fast.

"Come on, man," said Kevin, who was also annoyingly present and sweating through his 3OH!3 t-shirt.

"What, she— hey, girl," Evan said to Angela as she walked up. "I was about to get a drink, want something?"

"Get me anything!" said Angela.

"Let's go," said Evan. Kevin went with him, but now they were stuck with Angela.

"Oh my gosh, it totally sucks that you guys are in APUSH," she said. "Civics is so boring without you! I miss soccer too! When are we going to start soccer again?"

Stop. You're not Beth. Just shut up. Birdy was suddenly furious to be standing with Mel, Kelly, and the wrong fourth member of their quartet.

"No idea," said Mel, gazing stubbornly at a smoldering twig.

Angela set her sights on Kelly. "How are things with Derrick?"

Who's Derrick?

"Fine," said Kelly, glancing at Birdy like she'd heard her thoughts.

"He's not your first boyfriend, is he?" said Angela.

"He's not my boyfriend, we're just talking. But I hung out with this other guy for a little while. Nick."

"Oh, Nick Everett? Did you sleep with him?"

"No!" said Kelly.

"Well, that's smart. Take it from me, if you really like him, don't have sex for at least three weeks," said Angela, holding up three fingers decisively. "I've learned my lesson. If you want it to last longer, you can't do it too soon, or they'll get bored." Her pride in this hard-earned wisdom was depressing enough to deflate Birdy's rage, but Angela seemed thrilled to have shoved them into bonding mode. "How long did you wait with Vince?" she asked Mel.

Mel went redder than the bonfire. "Uh—"

"I'm back," Evan called from the dark.

"Me too," said Kevin, proffering a cup of something.

"Oh my god, love that band!" said Angela, tugging Kevin's shirt. "Don't trust a ho!"

"Guess we can't trust you," said Evan, maneuvering a different cup of something into Angela's hand before Kevin could close the deal.

"Oh my god, you're so bad," she shrieked, slapping his arm. "Let's go play flip cup!"

They made for the barn, and the three girls stood in silence. Mel and Kelly looked at each other, then at Birdy, who was fighting to keep her face from morphing into a giant question mark.

"Let's go to the watering hole," said Mel.

The path to the creek was charged with autumn sounds. They sat down at the clearing, Kelly and Mel making two points of a triangle with Birdy as the distant third. In two swift motions, Mel finished her Mike's and tightened her ponytail.

"Birdy, something happened, but I don't want you to be mad."

Birdy had a guess. "What is it?"

"Well—you know Vince and I are dating."

"Um. Yeah," said Birdy.

"Well, you remember how I was kind of mean to him when we found out about Sam Purcell and Beth and everything."

"Yeah."

"Well you know how everything's fine now?"

"Yeah?"

"Well, that's because... when I went over to talk to him about it I thought we might break up. But instead... instead we started making out and... well, his parents weren't home and... you know." Mel widened her eyes significantly.

"You... had sex?" said Birdy.

"Yeah." Mel narrowed her eyes at Birdy's underwhelmed reaction. "Did you already know somehow?"

"Um, I just kind of figured it out."

"What? Before Angela said that just now?"

"Well, you clearly made up and you seemed to make up really suddenly and now you seem closer than ever."

"Oh," said Mel.

"Plus Vince seems really... pleased with himself whenever we have lunch," Birdy added, amused.

Kelly smirked. "I told you she would have figured it out already."

Birdy fidgeted with a dry tulip poplar leaf. "You thought I was going to be mad?"

Mel squirmed. "I just, I know you take your faith seriously, different than I do anyway, and...I don't know. Like I remember back when you were telling us about Mary and Dominic, you were like"—she put on a sobbing voice— "I just can't believe they abandoned their principles"—Birdy slapped her hands over her face in embarrassment— "and I just didn't want you to be upset."

Birdy shook her head. "I'm not! I mean, I don't want you to get pregnant or something. But Vince is a good person, and I know he adores you. I don't think you're going to hell or anything like that."

"Phew!" Mel wiped imaginary sweat from her forehead. Then she got serious again. "Do you want to wait till you're married?"

Birdy braided the strands of a stray pine needle. "I don't know. Kinda seems impossible. I want it to be with someone I love, anyway. But really, I'm not too sure about my faith at the moment. The church has all this stuff to say about sex, but it doesn't seem to match what I see in real life. You have terrible people who follow all the rules, but then you have decent people like—" she bit Isaac's name back from her lips.

"Angela," said Kelly.

"Angela's a decent person?" said Mel incredulously.

"I mean, she's pretty dumb and annoying," said Kelly, "but she's also had a really sad life. Her parents are kind of like Beth's, but... well she's not Beth, so."

"How do you know?" said Mel.

"Well, ever since everything with Sam and Beth I think she feels like we're really close, and she always catches me in the bathroom when I'm fixing my makeup and tells me all this stuff."

"That's brilliant," said Mel. "She knows you'll never run when you're fixing your makeup!"

"I know!" said Kelly. "It's awful!" She was laughing, but then she looked sad. "But actually, it is awful."

"And is God really going to send her to hell for being—dumb and unlucky?" said Birdy. "It's embarrassing that I said *that* about Mary and Dominic, but I was mad that they were so mean about people who didn't act as Catholic as them when they were secretly going against this teaching that they acted like was the most important thing about being Catholic in the first place. Plus Dominic didn't respect Mary at all, and it makes me so sad that she gave it up for *him,* and then the consequences for doing that were so insane. I mean, she was a bitch to me—"

"I still hate her," said Mel.

"—but I'm pretty sure she thought it was okay to break the rules with him because she thought they could just get married or something if she got pregnant. But instead her whole life got uprooted and meanwhile nothing happened to him at all."

She sighed and looked up at Mel, who was thoughtful. "Is that why you've been acting weird?"

"Yeah," said Mel.

"I thought you were mad at me about something, like something about Beth and Sam and your dad or something."

"No, no, it wasn't that at all. Well, it kind of was, in a way. It was like, we've trusted each other with so much that it seems stupid to not be talking about this, but I was just worried about it."

"Well, you could be a stripper, and I'd still love you."

"Oh good, because I got this new job..."

Now Birdy turned to Kelly. "Now who the hell is Derrick?"

Kelly blushed. "I'm sorry, I wasn't trying to hide it from you or anything. He's a guy from St. Monica's. He started working at Chipotle with me this summer and we've been hanging out since school started, and Angela freaking followed us in the bathroom when I was telling Mel about him."

"Well, have you slept with *him*?" said Mel.

"No," said Kelly. She took a deep breath. "But I probably will."

"Gee, you sound thrilled," said Mel.

Kelly put her chin on her hand. "Well, I used to feel the same way as you, Birdy. About waiting for someone I loved. But... something happened."

"And you didn't want me to be mad?"

Kelly laughed. "Not that, exactly. It just got lost in everything else that was going on. Nick and I started texting a lot after that one party. And every once in a while we would hang out. I didn't talk to you guys about it too much because it was kind of a nice escape. Everything with Beth was so stressful, and I liked just going off with Nick. He didn't know anything about Beth's kids.

"I was waiting for him to ask me out on a real date, but it was always just us meeting up to hike and then making out in his car. So one day he texted me and said his parents and sister were gone, so I should come watch a movie. *The Hangover,*" she added, knowing Birdy would be wondering. "So it had barely started, and we started fooling around, and he asked if I wanted to have sex and... I chickened out. I liked him so much, but I was stressed out about being on his parents' couch, and he was really sweet, so I thought he'd understand." She rolled her eyes angrily. "And he wasn't mean about it exactly, but he was pretty disappointed. And then he never talked to me again."

"Kelly, that sucks! I'm so sorry I didn't know!"

"Well the thing is, that happened in April, literally the day before the storm. Beth came to my house that night, but I didn't tell her about it because I was so embarrassed. It didn't seem like something that would happen to her. And then I told Mel about it at school, but then everything went crazy and I never got the chance to tell you. But it still hurts.

"So now I think if I get another opportunity, I should just take it. Derrick's been pretty nice, and guys can't wait forever. And if I get some practice it won't be embarrassing when someone I really do like comes along."

Birdy felt a pang for Kelly. "But you deserve more than *pretty nice*. It seems like doing it with someone you really like is what makes it fun. Not that I would know."

Kelly looked at Mel. "Mel? Thoughts?"

Mel nodded sagely. "That is what I like about it."

Kelly tilted her head. "I don't know. Some of the other stuff is pretty fun on its own."

Mel and Kelly started giggling like crazy and Birdy snorted. "I just, I don't know why Angela's a slut for sleeping around, but guys apparently can't help themselves and no one cares. And then, I believe it could just be fun, but then I don't get how it can be no big deal but also something worth getting at any cost. Worth stealing." She remembered Beth's ruined braid that night, and her throat burned.

"Like Sam," whispered Kelly.

"Yeah," whispered Mel.

Birdy couldn't abide the CHOC brand of sexual ethics, where straight men were clandestinely accommodated and everyone else was torpedoed, but its secular alternative didn't feel better. In both circles, she had at some point found herself in a crowded room, trying to feel something.

"It's like Praise Night," Birdy said.

"*What?*" Mel gasped.

"It's like, music is one of the things that makes me *feel* like I believe in God, instead of just thinking of it. And I think a lot of people are like that, which is why Praise Night exists in the first place. They know music has that power, but they start in the wrong place. It's like when you have to dilute your juice."

"*What?*" said Kelly.

"Okay, when I was little, we would buy apple juice, but then my parents would make us put water in it, so there would be more juice and it would last longer. But then it didn't taste like juice, and it wasn't the thing we liked anymore. So I'm saying at Praise Night or Songs and Teens, you take this good thing, this music that can make you feel connected to God. And then you just—make more of it, nonstop, and be like look, isn't this amazing? We're talking about Jesus, don't you love it? And it loses the meaning it could have had. It's like they're taking this true, beautiful thing and just—"

"Forcing it," said Kelly.

"Exactly!" said Birdy. "So I think that's what I don't like about hookups. I hate when I have to act like something is incredible when it's just okay, if I know it could be something great. Whether it's watery juice or crappy music or just some random guy who's not actually going to care about me."

Mel stretched out on the leaves and called to the sky, "Lord, send Birdy a beautiful man who will play her beautiful music and bring her hot chocolate and full-strength juice!"

Birdy laughed. "That would be nice." She stretched out beside Mel and looked up at Kelly. "I love you both."

"Really?" said Mel. "It's hard to tell with you, you're always so shallow."

Kelly smiled. "I love you both, too."

2

KELLY WOULD HAVE BEEN able to make the jumble of decorations on the table beautiful, but she wasn't there, and Birdy was nervous. Isaac walked up beside her.

"I don't know why my mom gave you this job," he said. "For someone who's good at so many other things, you really aren't the best at stuff like this."

"Um, that is the meanest compliment I've ever received."

"I meant it more as a nice insult."

"Well, can you help me instead of standing around insulting me?"

Isaac picked up a blue fabric banner reading *Welcome Baby Noah!* and taped it on the wall above an elaborate fake cake Ms. Karen had constructed out of diapers, ribbons, and paper. He arranged some infant-themed tchotchkes, told Birdy which objects to place in which decorative baskets, and finally topped off their efforts with glittery confetti.

"I'm glad I won't be the only sane person at this party," Birdy said as they inspected their results.

Isaac snorted. "Are you kidding me? I'm covering for my dad at work, thank God. I don't want to be at this shit show. But feel free to tell me the highlights."

Ms. Karen charged into the room bearing a tower of blue-frosted cupcakes. Isaac stepped over to try to take it from her. "No!" she barked. "I'm in the zone!"

Oh, God. Isaac took this as his cue to leave. After putting down the cupcake tower, Ms. Karen grabbed her camera from the sideboard and snapped a few shots of the room. She smiled over at Birdy. "This looks great, hon!" Then she pulled out her new iPhone and snapped a few more. "I think I can use these for Instagram!" Birdy made a mental note to ask Isaac what Instagram was and Ms. Karen went back into the kitchen, where Mom and Mrs. Strabinski were perspiring through the assembly of a veggie platter.

Mrs. Doppelski came in the front door and thudded into a hard gray chair. She looked ready to pop, which was a term Mom had nearly killed Chris for using at the end of her pregnancy with Rebecca. She still had over two months to go before Noah would be born—ten weeks, to use the terminology of the moms. Thanks to all the previous CHOC babies, there was no need for one more scrap of clothing or equipment to be purchased. The objectives of the shower were to drown her with diapers, stuff her with cupcakes, and ignore the subject of her imprisoned husband.

Mrs. Amon waltzed in, ready to blow the third objective, with Margaret slouching behind her.

"Birdy! I miss you so much!" Margaret squealed, her shiny hair flying as she threw her arms around Birdy. Birdy hadn't realized they had this type of relationship, and she patted Margaret carefully on the back. "Hey! How's everything going?"

"Oh, I miss Divine Mercy SO much," she pouted. "It's so boring being just at home." She glared over in her mom's direction. Mrs. Amon had a hand on Mrs. Doppelski's belly and was crouched down talking to it. "What's it like at CCC? Do you ever get to see Dominic?"

"Um, I run into him sometimes," said Birdy, privately finding her pun hilarious. She didn't want to talk to Margaret about Dominic though. "What have you been up to?"

"Well, I'm making this new dress, and I started working at this restaurant that my dad's friend owns and it's so fun, I get to bring out all the drinks and menus and stuff, and I'm writing my own play!"

"Wow, sounds busy," said Birdy, glancing around for a way out of the conversation. Nancy Vespa glided into the room. Suddenly Margaret seemed like a much more desirable companion. "What's your play about?"

"Oh, it's about this girl and this boy in Victorian England who are in love and he's a little bit mean but she's really good and kind and it just changes him into a better person."

Sounds fictional. "Oh, kinda like *Beauty and the Beast?*"

Margaret recoiled. "No! I made it up myself! It's called *Glory in the Garden!*"

Birdy was saved from learning more about Margaret's work of art by Ms. Karen, who called the shower to an opening. "Welcome, friends," she said, in her group voice, "As you all know, Tammy is getting close to meeting her little one, and we are so glad to have you all here!"

The proceedings began with a guessing game about what day Baby Noah would be born. Then there was a guessing game about how many Hershey Kisses were in a jar, and then they all wrote their "best wishes for baby" on scraps of paper. Mrs. Amon tried to give hers directly to Mrs. Doppelski, but at a glance from Ms. Karen, Mrs. Strabinski stood and collected all the papers. Birdy surmised that the wishes would be vetted before they were given to baby.

"My favorite baby shower game is when we guess how many pounds Mama has gained! Are we doing that one?" said Mrs. Amon.

"No!" snapped Ms. Karen, her blogger veneer dropping for a moment. She smiled again. "That would just make the rest of us feel bad about ourselves, wouldn't it? Tammy looks like a million bucks!"

Mrs. Doppelski shifted in her seat and smiled gratefully at Ms. Karen. In truth, she looked more like a lost penny. Her skin was doughy, her eyes were sunken and puffy, and every movement looked uncomfortable.

"Oh, of course she does!" said Mrs. Amon.

"That's a lovely name you've chosen," said Mrs. Vespa, apropos of nothing.

Tammy glanced up at the banner. "Oh, thank you," she said, seeming surprised it was there at all.

"It is lovely!" Mrs. Amon agreed. "Did you and Jude pick it together?"

There would have been a shocked silence, except that Mom burst out with an immediate "Ah!" of fury. Birdy clicked her pen a few times. Margaret, on her left, looked at her mom with her hands over her mouth.

Karen looked helplessly at Mrs. Doppelski, who answered with a simple, "No."

"Oh!" said Mrs. Amon. "I was just wondering. You know, we have all been praying for him so much."

Mrs. Doppelski looked like she was drowning. Mom got up and glued her fists to her hips.

"You know, Carly and I got here *early*—" here she looked right at Mrs. Amon, who with a brittle smile showed that being excluded from party prep did not offend her, not at all "—and we made some really delicious refreshments. Shall we have a little snack break?"

There was a relieved rush to the snack table. Birdy piled Chex mix, French onion dip, and some disturbingly wet carrots on her plate. Ms. Karen brought a plate of food to Mrs. Doppelski just as Maria Doppelski ran inside. She was helping her dad watch all the little kids next door. "Uhhhh, Mom, we kinda need you for a second..." Her stiff blond braids framed a nervous face.

Ms. Karen wavered in irritation before jogging out of the house, calling, "Be right back!" Birdy slathered a carrot in dip.

Unlike a toddler, Mrs. Amon could not be distracted from her schemes by snacks. She struck while Mom and Mrs. Strabinski were gossiping behind the cupcakes.

"Tammy," she said, sitting beside her and placing her hand on Tammy's stomach again. "Tammy, I just wanted to tell you."

Birdy stopped eating her carrot; it was too wet, and its crunch would impair her listening.

"I just want to tell you, we have all been praying for Jude." She waited for Tammy to melt with gratitude, but all she got was ice. She tried again. "Some of the ladies and I, we decided to pray novenas for him from now until the trial is over. We're really hoping the judge will be merciful to him, and he can come back to being part of our community soon. It's just not the same without his presence."

Mrs. Doppelski moved her lips into a smile shape. "That's true, Roberta. It's not the same without his presence."

"I can only imagine how difficult it must be to uphold a marriage when your husband is away for so long. I'm sure you're getting many graces for this suffering." Mrs. Amon wore a tragic expression.

Mrs. Doppelski looked back at her like she was stupid. "I'm not upholding our marriage. I'm filing for divorce."

Mrs. Amon drew back slowly, settling into her indignation with relish. "Tammy, I'm surprised to hear you say that! I mean I wondered of course but—honey, we are called to remain faithful to our spouses no matter what! He made a mistake, but is that enough to break your vows? Your *vows*, Tammy. It's your responsibility to get him into heaven."

Mrs. Doppelski snapped her plastic fork in two, and Mrs. Amon flinched. "First of all, Roberta, civil divorce is permitted by the Church. Second, I will be seeking an annulment, as per my priest's recommendation. And third of all, even if the Church didn't allow those things, I would still divorce him. I never want to see that man again. Everyone in this room has suffered terribly because of him— except maybe you, I guess. You always liked having him around."

Mrs. Amon took on the expression of a catfish on a hook. Margaret looked at Birdy, a mixture of horror and glee on her face. Now there was a thrum of genuine delight in Mrs. Doppelski's tired eyes. "Would you like a cupcake? Karen made them. They're to die for."

Mrs. Amon made a big show of removing herself from the chair and selecting a cupcake in a dignified fashion. Ms. Karen came back in and took stock of the room. "Ahh, Roberta, we can always count on you to find the dessert! Everyone else, be sure to get a cupcake too before they're all gone!" Margaret, who had apparently received the thrill of her life, breathed hot French onion breath into Birdy's ear, "Oh my gosh, oh my— *GOD*—did you SEE that?" Birdy nodded back, carefully chewing a damp carrot and thinking Mrs. Amon should have known better than to mess with a scorned and pregnant woman.

3

THE EVENINGS GOT DARKER, Mrs. Doppelski grew rounder, and in a flash, Thanksgiving was upon them again. This year, Chris would be with his new girlfriend's family and Patrick would be with friends at the Jets game, leaving only Peter and Birdy at home. Birdy expected Mom's usual holiday devastation at their diminished numbers, but two late arriving uncles changed the game.

Mom's brother Jerry and Dad's brother Jimmy were both bachelors who had made individual appearances on past holidays. This year they were both coming. With shocking prudence, Mom and Dad acknowledged that neither their kitchen nor Conrad's offerings could accommodate both Jerry's veganism and Jimmy's enthusiasm for turkey slathered in butter, so they went out to eat near Bosco.

Peter and Birdy were placing bets on the ways Jerry and Jimmy's dietary preferences, and corresponding personality traits, would collide, but they had yet another surprise. Both uncles liked nothing better than roasting their siblings and had endless jokes to make about their quirks. Lunch passed in a haze of hilarity. Back at home, Jerry immediately opened a bottle of port, and Jimmy grunted his approval and pulled out a merlot. Mom had one glass and fell asleep instantly; Dad had two glasses and began giggling in an unseemly fashion. When talk turned to the 1980 Olympics, Peter motioned Birdy to come out front.

They sat on the porch steps in crisp air. Birdy saw a plume of dark smoke billowing into the darkening sky and wondered how Abe's first pass at operating the turkey fryer was going. Peter pulled a beer out from his jacket, cracked it, and handed it to Birdy.

"Careful," he said.

"I've had beer before," said Birdy. She sipped it. "Oh wow, that's actually pretty good!"

Peter laughed. "That's because I bought it legally and for more than two dollars."

Birdy made a face. "Come on, you just turned 21 this year."

"That's long enough to stop buying shitty beer."

Despite her protests she felt loose and warm by the time she reached the bottom of the can. "I'm really glad you came home," she told Peter, her voice wobbling. "I was kind of worried you wouldn't want to since Chris and Patrick weren't here."

Peter's face fell. "Birdy, I missed all of you. The last few Thanksgivings have totally sucked."

"Yeah, they have," said Birdy. Stupid tears came to her eyes. "I know Mom and Dad are crazy, but why did you have to hurt their feelings so bad?" *What was in that beer?*

Peter sighed. "I know I never really explained it. I was trying to protect you guys. I didn't want to, like, be the one to make Mom and Dad less in your eyes, somehow. Even though I know you already know how they are." He straightened his legs in front of him and stretched out his fingers.

"Do you remember when I was taking that creative writing class when I was a junior?"

"Yeah," said Birdy, "we had a lot of fun when you took that class."

"Yeah," said Peter. "So for one unit we had to write a fantasy story. This was right after Christmas break. I wrote this story called 'The Gno-homes' and it was about a colony of hairy gnomes, and every time the queen gets upset they get poofed to a new settlement and their stuff always gets left behind and they always have to start all over again. So they all bend over backwards all the time to make the queen happy so they don't have to get moved away, but it never works. And it went in a different direction from there, but you can guess where I got the inspiration from. I didn't even realize all the way where I got the idea until I was finished writing it." He took a sip. "And it was actually a funny story, like it wasn't meant to be tragic or profound or anything, I just had fun with it. And Mr. Brinks loved it."

Birdy felt apprehensive.

"Mom and Dad both made it in for parent teacher conferences in March, and Mr. Brinks thought this story was so good he decided to show them at the conference. An example of my excellent work." Bitterness shaded his face for a moment. "Well, obviously Mom had ideas about where the inspiration came from, and she lost her shit. They took me out to lunch a few days later, and I thought it was going to be something good, but we never even made it into the restaurant because Mom was so angry about the story. She said Mr. Brinks was her colleague and now he would know it was about her and think less of her."

"So that's why Mom didn't want to go back there the next year," said Birdy.

"Yeah. And she kept pushing me to admit that the story was about her, and I wouldn't admit it, but she wouldn't buy it. They made me quit the paper as punishment."

"Oh, Peter. And she acted like you just quit for no reason."

He nodded. "And that... it just broke me. It's hard enough growing up the way we did, but then to have that thrown in my face, that not even my private thoughts could be mine, that they had to be okayed by Mom, I just couldn't take it anymore."

A lump grew in Birdy's throat. Peter had explained perfectly the thing that had dogged her and her siblings for their whole lives, this constant and total violation of their internal agency.

"Did Chris and Patrick know about all this?" Birdy croaked.

"Patrick knew. But I made him keep it from you and Chris, because I was even more mad at Dad."

"Why?" said Birdy.

"Because he just let all that happen. He tried to mediate and be so calm and nice, but I needed something different that time, and he didn't do it. He eventually convinced me to just apologize to calm her down, but I was so mad at myself afterwards for doing it."

The lump in her throat instantly gave way to tears and anger at Peter. How dare he find their father less than heroic? But just as quickly, despair rushed in to drown her ire, because of course Peter was exactly right.

"Things settled down for a little while, but then they started looking at moving again and also started trying to get me to apply to colleges. And it wasn't even like I decided not to go—I just couldn't go. Not to college or to wherever they were going to move. And then Mom's like, 'Peter, you're ignoring your potential. You're such a talented writer, you could be an English major!' And then Dad wanted me to join the Marines! I was just like, can you hear yourselves? Have you looked at your lives at all?" Peter made an incredulous gesture.

"So... you know the rest. I just didn't come. And that sucked, but it was the right thing for me. I needed to cut the cord, and I hoped it might wake them up a little." He glanced at Birdy hopefully. She made a "sorta" motion with her hand. He half smiled.

"I needed to get away from them. But I really missed you guys. You're the only people who really get any of it. I wish I'd told you about it sooner," said Peter.

Birdy shook her head. "I can see why you didn't. I think I would have had a harder time understanding before." She put her arm through his. "You must have been terrified going through all that. Mom would always act like you were out living this life of hedonism."

He laughed and swiped tears out of his stubble. "I know, the whole prodigal son thing! Yeah, it was mainly just really stressful. But in a good way. It was stress that I caused and that I could fix." He put his hand on top of hers. "If I get you another beer, will you please explain to me what the deal is with Mom and the Catholic settlement up the street?"

She laughed, her breath making a fog between them.

Winter 2011

1

NOAH ANDREW DOPPELSKI WAS born on January 6, 2011, at exactly 9:00 AM. His mother slept like the dead the night before his birth, awoke to crushing labor pains, and pushed him earthside three hours later. His aunt Karen held his mother's hand in the hospital where all his siblings were born and where his father was arrested one spring night. His uncle, cousins, brothers, and sisters sweated, prayed, and slept at home, and his father stared at a wall in jail.

A week later Noah was clothed in white, and Father Bill's shaking hands doused him in holy water and slathered chrism all over his forehead and his fine brown hair. Arthur and Maggie Cleary stood by as godparents, bringing their usual combination of gravity and enthusiasm to the task. For the rest of the day he was passed from one set of arms to the next, as a multitude of siblings, cousins, and friends praised the smell of a brand-new Catholic.

Being both the godmother and the church secretary, Mom had the task of filing paperwork with her own name on it, which tickled her deeply. In her eagerness to get it done fast, she went to work on Sunday and made an unpleasant discovery.

Mom had a voice message from Jane Watson, a rather chatty secretary for the archdiocese, regarding Father Gerard Tooley, the pastor of St. Ann's from 1970-1975. At long last, the archdiocese was cracking down on the sex offenders in its midst, and Father Gerard was being charged with abusing an altar server sometime in the 90s. The archdiocese, having previously taken pains not to build a paper trail, was now demanding documentation from his prior positions.

At the dinner table that night, Birdy and Dad chewed Hamburger Helper while Mom relayed this development. She was not her usual gushing gossip geyser. Instead, she sounded miserable. She put her elbow on the table and scooched her food around with her fork like a dejected little kid. "You know, Tammy always used to say how the boys are serving at the parish just like their dad... they were always so proud of that."

Dad leaned toward her, alert. "Jude told me that priest was transferred because of something that happened with a nun. Not a kid."

Her parents stared at each other, but Birdy didn't know why they were acting so surprised. Jude was, after all, not exactly an honest man.

After dinner, Mom drifted into a state of silent contemplation, which was unusual for her—normally she contemplated out loud. A few days later, Birdy was rereading *Harry Potter and the Order of the Phoenix* on her bed, when Mom knocked on the door.

"Can I come in?"

Mom seemed conciliatory, cautious. She perched on the edge of the bed.

"Honey, I want to talk to you."

"What's up, Mom? Are you okay?" asked Birdy.

"Honey I—I've been thinking about everything that has gone on with Jude and Tammy. She's told me so much about him and about their relationship. All these things that... that she told me before, but now seem so much worse. It's not like he changed, but how I see him changed. He was always so boisterous and not always that nice to Tammy, but I just thought... I just thought... I don't know."

Birdy waited.

Mom made a helpless gesture. "It was just that your dad and I have arranged our whole lives around bringing you guys up in our faith. And that's brought us so much difficulty at times."

At times?

"You know, money is a little tight for us and we kept having to move to find schools we could send you to. And then we moved here and there's this whole community of people who seemed just as convicted as we did. It seemed like it was working, and so much of that was because of Jude that that was what I focused on. I saw him being so rude sometimes but that almost helped. It was like, you don't have to be this weird stick in the mud like Roberta Amon." Birdy snickered and Mom smiled a little as she went on. "You can still be a normal and fun person and still choose this very different life." Mom's face crumpled to misery for a moment. Then she took Birdy's hand.

"What I wanted to say is that Tammy told me that when they met, she didn't even want to date him at first. She thought he was condescending to her, and he wasn't supportive of what she wanted. He was always trying to change her into someone else. And then eventually she did change into someone else. Because it felt so good to have that attention from someone who was so strong. She didn't have a great family, and his wasn't the best either but he still had this really strong community connection back home. He had all these big visions for the future, and they both wanted something better for their kids than they'd had, and he just knew she would be the perfect person to go along with him.

"But he never really respected her. And he never really listened to her. And he just never saw her as an equal, and she did all this work in support of his vision, and then there he was having this big secret side life without her."

Mom was at times livid, desolate, joyful, and ecstatic, but never solemn. She was solemn now.

"And it just made me think—your dad and I aren't perfect, and there are things about our family that are hard."

To put it lightly.

"But I always know that I made the right pick with him. He doesn't put me down. He didn't have to wear me down. He sticks with me and... he's helped me more than you'll ever know. And when a man doesn't respect you, you'll know it. And you'll know it if you don't respect him. And I want you to know that if you ever feel like a man isn't there for you, but just some idea of you, shut it down. You're too amazing to waste your time like that. Just walk away."

Mom liked these moments where she could reveal the secrets of the universe to her children. Birdy's miserable attachment to Dominic had already taught her the folly of waiting for a guy to transform into someone who valued her when he had no map for the journey, and no desire for one. So maybe it wasn't the revelation Mom thought it was, but Birdy was still touched, and grateful.

She knew Mom wanted her to give something back now. She could see the hopeful glint in her eye, that maybe Birdy would spill all the beans about Beth's situation or reveal whatever the hell had happened between her and Dominic. She didn't do that, but she did hug her. For a minute, she inhaled Mom's sweetness and melted into her softness, feeling the same comfort she must have when she was small.

"Thanks, Mom."

2

BIRDY, KELLY AND MEL were huddled around Kelly's computer, stalking Beth's Facebook. Predictably, Beth already had quite a social life. There was a picture of her decked out in blue and orange, crowded in with some friends at a pep rally, and another of herself after finishing her first run since the accident. As they clicked through the photos, the green dot appeared next to Beth's name in the chat menu.

Kelly: BETHYYYYY
Beth: KELLLYYYYY
Kelly: How the hell are you!
Beth: im amazing! but i miss you guys so much!
Kelly: WE MISS YOU TOOO
Kelly: we're all here right now lol
Beth: i shoulda known lol
Beth: guess what im doing tonight
Kelly: going to the movies?

Beth: noooo. i never want to smell buttered popcorn again haha

Kelly: lol

Kelly: okay are you studying?

Beth: ugh no

Kelly: hahaha

Kelly: going out with your cool new friends?

Beth: ding ding ding!

Kelly: Yay! Who are they? Are they nice? Are they smart? Are they good at soccer???

Beth: cant right now i gtg! Ttyl lylas!!!

Her green dot disappeared.

"Well, okay then," said Mel.

"Well, that's Beth for you," said Kelly, chewing a fingernail. She scrolled down Beth's profile for a few more minutes, then clicked to the main news feed to see that Katie had just changed her profile picture. "Aww, she looks so cute!" said Kelly. She clicked on the picture, poised to leave a comment, but there was one there already—"Dayuuum giiiirl" by Beth Nolan, 1 minute ago.

With a swoop of her stomach, Birdy realized that Beth had ended their chat conversation but hadn't actually signed off Facebook. They all stared at the screen, but no one said anything. Instead, Kelly clicked randomly until she ended up on Vince's profile page. She wrote a taunting message about the Penguins' recent victory over the Caps, liked a cute picture of Mel and Vince and paused at a post by someone named Lucas Grant.

The accompanying text said, "Hey man, here's my latest, hope you like it."

"What's this?" asked Kelly.

"Oh that's Vince's friend who graduated the year before him. He was the starting wide receiver before Vince, but he's also this amazing singer and has like ten thousand subscribers on Youtube. Watch!"

Kelly clicked play. The video opened on a good-looking guy holding a shiny guitar.

"Hey everyone, glad to have you back at my channel." He smiled at the camera and—*whoa*—his eyes cocked toward his mouth at an intriguing slant that cut right through all Birdy's pickiness. "I really like this song," he said, strumming something familiar. "It makes me think of family and how we're all connected to each other." His heavy eyebrows knitted in concentration, and he started singing.

"Oh wow, I love this song!" said Birdy.

"Oh, do you now?" said Mel.

It was "Daughters" by John Mayer, but Birdy thought Lucas sang it better. His voice was deeper and stronger than John Mayer's emphysemic rasp. She noticed he actually had 16,000 subscribers, and he deserved it. He was a gifted performer. He seemed to be looking right at her through the screen....

"Birdy. Do you need to be alone for a minute?" said Mel.

"Ewwww!!" shrieked Birdy as Kelly and Mel died laughing.

"Should I play it again?" Kelly offered sweetly.

"It was just a good song okay?" Birdy said.

"Yeah, just a really fantastic song," said Mel.

Still smiling, Birdy checked the time. "Are you guys ready to go?"

Though she hoped she would not run into Professor Kline, Birdy had indeed signed up for the boxing class that semester. It hadn't been a hard sell to her parents—because of what had happened to Beth, they were enthusiastic about Birdy learning to defend herself. The class was on Monday evenings and was open to the community beyond CCC, so Kelly and Mel signed up too. They still didn't have much heart for soccer without Beth, and they were all attracted to the idea of punching things.

In the parking lot, they lingered in Kelly's car. They stared across the vast and unevenly paved asphalt at the gym, which was between a Chinese restaurant and a pawn shop. Mel soon had enough of Kelly and Birdy's hesitation. "Well, I'm going in." She hopped out of the car, and they followed.

They pushed open the door and inhaled sweat solidifying on leather, a stench that Birdy would come to know as the aroma of hope. A rhythm that went WHAPWHAPWHAPWHAP BEEEEP played around her as she took in the sights. Punching bags hung from the ceiling in the left third of the gym. A small one ricocheted as a tall man pummeled it with the sides of his fists; a long one thudded as a stocky woman slammed it with her shins. A boxing ring rose from the center of the room, and two skinny guys in leather headgear pounded each other inside it.

"Look, they look lost, they must be our classmates." Mel led them over to a group of people who mostly looked a few years older than them, except for one middle-aged man with a tonsure. Birdy was trying to think of something to say to one of them when a forceful voice filled the gym.

"Allright, college kiddos, let's get down to it!" A tall man in a grubby baseball cap was striding toward them. His entire presence was loud and a gappy grin consumed his face. "I'm Coach Hatch, this is my gym, and today we're going to mix some life lessons in with your higher learning. This is Ryan, terror of the East Coast," he said, pointing at the man standing quietly by his side. Ryan was younger and trimmer than Hatch. Tattoos wound down from the left sleeve of his black t-shirt, ending in coils around his fingers. Coach Hatch waved a long arm and the tonsured man flinched backwards. "Let's head over to the mat."

The mat was a large area to the right of the boxing ring where a huge cardboard box waited. Ryan dug into the box and started passing out hand wraps, long rolls of woven cloth meant to protect the bones in their hands when they punched. Ryan demonstrated how to put them on while the class struggled along.

"I don't see why I need to do this," said a guy whose red hair and unmerited bravado reminded Birdy of Michael. "I hit the bag in my basement all the time and my hands have always been fine."

"That's cute," said Hatch. "Guess you can't hit very hard. We'll help you get stronger, don't worry." The guy blushed and busied himself with his wraps. Birdy ended up with a loopy mess on her hands that looked nothing like Ryan's neat arrangement.

"Right so now that your hands are protected, *now* we pass out those gloves you're all dying for," said Hatch, reaching back into the box and extracting rectangular mesh bags. Birdy unzipped hers and found a pair of gleaming black boxing gloves. Their fresh smell made her smile, but putting them on over her wrapped hands was a struggle. Beside her, Mel muttered a curse through her teeth, which she was attempting to use to secure her right glove's Velcro strap.

"Now the last thing you need to box is your mouthguard, but I'll hand those out as you're leaving because you need to fit them at home. Normally, you want to always have your mouthguard in when you're boxing, because you don't want to lose any teeth. And trust me, I know a few guys who've lost some teeth," said Coach Hatch.

"*You're* a guy who's lost some teeth," said Ryan. Coach Hatch smiled and flashed his missing canine. "Yeah, but that wasn't from boxing, that was from a street fight," he said. A nearby girl gasped in disapproval. "And I wasn't wearing my mouth guard for that! Just goes to show you! So anyway, that means today we aren't doing any contact drills. You aren't ready for that anyway. We're just gonna start by learning how to throw a punch. And before you can throw a punch, you need to get in your fighting stance.

"If you're right-handed, put your left foot in front. If you're left-handed, put your right foot in front. Then do the hokey pokey and turn yourself around." Hatch snickered at their confusion and went on. "Now get up on the balls of your feet, like this."

Coach Hatch showed them how to balance their weight and how to step while maintaining the correct distance between their feet. The class wobbled around like baby giraffes.

"Okay, your feet are in place so let's get to those hands. When you're boxing, number one rule is keep your hands up. That means any hand that isn't punching is glued to your face at all times. That's because you can hit as hard as you want, but if someone hits you as hard as *they* want then you're toast. So you're gonna protect yourself. I know you see Floyd Mayweather waving his hands down by his waist like crouching tiger kung fu panda or whatever, but I guarantee you're slower than him and he's an idiot anyway. When you're in my gym, you're gonna be a badass but you're going to protect yourself too. I don't want stupid heroes in my gym, only smart ones," he said, raising an eyebrow at the redheaded guy, who pouted.

"All the punches are numbered. I'm pretty sure you all know your evens from your odds, but you're from CCC so who knows? Anyway, your odd number punches come from your front side, and your even number punches come from your dominant side. So Blondie here," he said, stopping in front of Kelly, who about died, "She's righthanded, so her odd numbered punches will come from her left side. But Blackie here"—now it was Mel's turn to die—"she's a southpaw, she's lefthanded, so her odds will come from her right side, evens from the left. Got it?"

Ryan smirked at Mel and Kelly's blushing faces and Birdy beamed like it was the last day of school, but it was all in a day's work for Hatch, who continued with the lesson.

"So your fists are glued to your face like this, elbows tucked in, we're not flapping them like chicken wings right, we're tucking them in to protect our ribs, and we're not sticking out our chins like cavemen, we're keeping them tucked in too so that when a punch comes in"—" he motioned to Ryan, who threw a slow-motion punch at Hatch's face—"I'm safe. I just tuck into my little turtle shell, I take all he can throw at me, and then— WHAP!" Hatch threw a punch over top of Ryan's, and Ryan mimed stumbling backwards in pain. They looked like they were having the time of their lives.

There were only a few minutes left in class by the time they were allowed to punch for real. Ryan put on mitts and waited in front of Birdy while she got in her stance.

"Okay," said Ryan in his measured voice, "So remember, you're in your stance, bend your knees a little more, and your hands are tight on your face, and you've gotta imagine you're taking the skin off your face when you throw the punch, then you're gonna snap it 90 degrees just before you hit me. Ready?" Birdy nodded and he held out the mitt.

WHAP.

The smack of leather sent a vibration straight up her arm to her brain, where it lit a new world on fire. She needed to do it again.

"Nice one," said Ryan. "Let's try it again, remember to step into it with your left foot when you throw it."

She tried, but she tripped off balance and her next jab glanced off the target. "You want your step to land at the same moment as your punch," said Ryan. "Remember to keep your knees bent so you stay in control. If your legs are straight, you aren't ready for your next move."

She threw her third jab and her shoulder was already tired, but there was another satisfying smack, louder than the first. "Yes! Do you remember how to throw the two? This is a power punch, you're going to turn your hips hard and use your legs to put all your weight into it."

For three minutes, the gloves and mitts were her whole world. Then the round timer blared and she dropped her hands, panting. "Looking good," said Ryan. "Now just do some shadowboxing to loosen back up." He moved on to Mel, and Birdy looked at Kelly to see if she had any idea how to shadowbox. Kelly shrugged.

They learned more each week, but they weren't allowed to try sparring until the very last class. Birdy's sparring partner, Meghan, kept coming at her violently for 5 seconds at a time and then shrinking away. Birdy threw a lot of punches but didn't land anything good. Her shoulders screamed in fatigue. Then Meghan threw a punch so wild that Birdy saw it coming and ducked. As she rose, she slammed a good hard two into Meghan's face.

"MMMMM" said Meghan. She staggered back to the sagging ropes of the ring, where Coach Hatch stood in her corner. Ryan waved Birdy over to their side.

"Looks like she needs a second," said Ryan.

Over in the opposing corner, Meghan had ripped off her gloves, yanked off her headgear, and was now rapidly unwinding her hand wraps. "I am DONE," she declared, "I am SO DONE." She gathered her things in a huff and climbed out of the ring. Coach

Hatch removed his ballcap, scratched his scalp, and winced over at Ryan. "Wasn't for her, I guess," he called.

"Mumymph," said Birdy.

"What was that now?" said Ryan.

Birdy spat her mouthguard into her glove. "I said, 'sorry!'"

Ryan narrowed his eyes at her and then grinned. "No, you're not. You're not sorry at all. You loved that, admit it!"

Birdy studied the sagging ropes and threadbare canvas of the ring. "Okay, yeah. I loved that."

3

JOHN INCHED HIS CRUISER down Victoria Street, watching for any kids playing in the road on this gray day. It was his eighth or ninth visit since Jude's arrest. The first one had felt uncomfortably similar to the time his mom found out he and Jude put dog poop into Abe's bag of Halloween candy, and she made John invite just Abe over to play.

But they'd both grown up. Abe seemed sobered and deepened by the circumstances. Without Jude around, he wasn't trying to seem bigger and better than he really was. He had too many real problems to solve. And he really did want to differentiate DBC's model, which was why John was here today.

When John pulled up, Abe was standing in the driveway next to a rented Dumpster. Their goal today was to rearrange the garage to throw out some junk, put aside some equipment to sell, and make room for a CNC router and accompanying work station. Karen was pretty sure she could capitalize on her recent viral status and start an Etsy shop where she could sell statues, crosses, and wood cuttings of her own design. Lily had informed John that Etsy was a website where you could buy "cute stuff." John could only imagine the roasting Jude would have given Abe over this development.

"I wasn't sure at first, but Karen convinced me," Abe had said on the phone. "She said Conrad is small, but there's this whole world of people online and a lot of them will pay for anything if you take a good enough picture of it."

John shook hands with Abe as he entered the garage. He had contributed a single hour of labor to its building several years back. Dominic and Isaac were installing a pegboard and shelving all along one wall, wearing shorts and t-shirts despite the snow outside. They looked like men, almost. Both had grown full muscles around their knotty joints and floppy feet. They worked perfectly in sync, but aside from the occasional muted communication, they seemed unaware of each other, missing the laughter and banter John remembered from when they were younger. What was that about?

A man with a high and tight knocked on the garage wall.

"Abe, need a hand?"

Abe the hero worshipper returned for a moment as he gaped at the man in the doorway. "Yeah, s-sure man, I mean, you sure man?" His eyes flicked down to the man's knees and then back up to his face.

The man smiled. "The rest of me still works." All three of them had nursed enough forty-something injuries to know that this was a polite fiction. If something was up with his knees, then he would surely be hurting later—the idea that he could avoid using them in a moving job was laughable. But Abe chuckled. "We could definitely use the help." Then he looked back and forth between the man and John. "You two must know each other—right?"

"Never officially met—" the man stretched out his hand, but John had already seen it in the way the man's face had flashed from earnest attention to wry humor on a dime—this had to be Birdy's dad.

"You must be Arthur Cleary," said John as they shook.

"And you must be Officer Holloway. Pleased to finally meet you."

"John. Great to meet you too. I think I'm normally asleep when you bring Birdy over."

"Nowadays she can get there by herself anyway."

"Mel said she's coming over tonight."

Arthur nodded. "Yet again. We'll have to start paying rent for her."

John smiled. "She's a good girl. Mel's lucky to have her."

"Birdy's lucky to have Mel. I can see how much they mean to each other and build each other up. That's a real gift."

"They're loyal to each other, that's for sure," said John with a sigh. The thought of Beth hung over him like a black cloud.

Lacking a teenage daughter, Abe stood between them bobbing his head. "Really lovely young ladies, great girls, both of them." Arthur nodded back at Abe, expressionless, another Birdyism. John had reason to suspect that crushing thoughts lurked behind her placid stare. He suspected the same of Arthur now. Uncanny.

John cleared his throat. "Well, how can I help?"

An hour into the job, Arthur lifted a heavy box from the ground. He staggered out to the Dumpster, clunked the box inside, and leaned against the red metal, looking pale. John looked at Abe, who leapt to attention.

"Hey, think it's time for a union break? David made these real good cookies, I'll grab us some." He cast about for folding chairs and set some in front of his crew. "Sit down a spell." John wondered at this strangely folksy word choice but said nothing. Abe power walked to the house.

John could see Arthur wasn't going to sit down first, so he did it. Arthur thudded down across from him and slowly straightened his legs. They sat a moment watching the boys, who were nearly done with their project. Then Arthur leaned forward.

"I read that article of yours a while back."

John's stomach flopped. He didn't know what to say and came out with a weird "Oh?"

Arthur nodded. "Terrific writing. Took a lot of courage to say all that."

John still felt embarrassed but was now grateful too. Arthur went on. "It's such a tough situation." He stared at his knees a minute, then chuckled. "I cut it out for Birdy, but when I went to give it to her she'd already printed it out for herself."

Over in the corner, one of the shelves slipped out of Dominic's grip and crashed into the box of screws. "Jesus, Dominic," said Isaac.

"Sorry," Dominic muttered, scrambling to collect the screws as they spiraled away.

Arthur glanced over at them and then turned back to John. "So I bought a few more copies and sent them to a few people I thought would be interested. Really made me think."

"I appreciate it. Not everyone liked it." Including his boss.

"Sometimes people need to get really angry before they can really listen. And make a change." Arthur sighed from somewhere deep inside himself, and John wasn't sure they were talking about the article anymore. He tried to think of something nice to say, but Abe walked in and relieved the burden.

"Got the good stuff here. Come on over here, guys," he said, waving to the boys. He plunked a plate of cookies and a six pack of beers on the remaining chair. Isaac strode to meet them and Dominic skulked behind. Dominic's hair had gotten shaggy, a contrast to the men's former-military haircuts and Isaac's precisely parted and gelled situation. The sight of him was a sucker punch to John's heart. He was the spitting image of Jude before he'd enlisted and made a lifetime switch to his own neat cut. But he didn't act like Jude. He didn't even act like Dominic.

When Dominic was twelve, he would have cheekily reached for one of the beers and opened it, maybe even gotten a sip before someone stopped him. He would have been animated, eager to ingratiate himself with the men. Now he took a stack of cookies and ate them in single bites, staring at the floor. Isaac did a similar impression of a vacuum cleaner but also initiated a friendly conversation the recent Super Bowl.

Arthur finished his cookies and checked his watch. "I'd better be going. See you soon." He nodded over at the newly constructed shelf. "Nice work, boys." The boys said thanks, and Arthur strolled back down the street, disguising the pain in his legs with a leisurely pace.

Abe said "Boys, clean up this stuff and take a bathroom break or something. Put the plate in the dishwasher." Abe had always been a fastidious one. Dominic and Isaac gathered up the minimal trash and left.

As soon as they were out of the garage, Abe turned to John. "Did you hear? They're calling me to testify against Jude." Abe had clearly been dying to say this—reserve had never been his virtue.

"I heard." Conrad's criminal justice system was entirely comprised of hometown boys. Jude's lawyer, a county appointee, had been a few years ahead of them in school. The prosecutor was the father of John's old lab partner and was on the Knights of Columbus at St. Paul's. Judge James Kettermine had been a sophomore during their senior season. One night, after John and Jude committed a series of blunders, Kettermine saved the game with two miraculous field goals. Kettermine proceeded to harp on his glory day for the next two and a half decades, even though he'd choked on every other important play that season. John and Jude still despised him.

"You're testifying too?"

John nodded. "I am."

Abe looked comforted by this in a distracted way. "I gotta tell you man, I've never been so nervous about anything in my life. But still I know I gotta do it man, I just feel so guilty, I knew how bad he could be, I had a feeling something shifty was going on with that money, and I knew he was a dick to the kids, and I knew he used to get trashed, and that poor girl—" He stopped. Dominic was back in the garage, watching them.

"Hey bud!" said Abe with artificial cheer. Isaac came to stand by them, and Abe blabbered as Dominic approached more slowly. "Now that is one hell of a shelving unit."

John thought he was laying it on a little thick, but tried to assist. "It does look good. What are you gonna put on it?"

Dominic cleared his throat. "Work stuff. We need to keep it more organized in here." John could see he was caught between not falling for their bullshit and wanting very much to have someone notice his work. He had always liked making things.

"I'm impressed you two did all that yourselves."

"Oh, the two of them have been working together since they were born!" said Abe. "They're a good team."

Neither member of the team acknowledged Abe's claim. Abe responded to their silence by laying it on even thicker.

"Although Isaac really just helped put it together this time, Dominic figured out the measurements and bought all the materials and everything. He's always been the one who's good at making stuff, just like his dad." With these words, the comradery Abe was trying to stoke suffered instant death. Everyone in the garage suddenly looked nauseous. "Ahhhh," said Abe, like he'd just stepped in dog shit. "Better put these away," he said to the floor as he swiped up the folding chairs and fled the garage. Isaac muttered something about needing to charge the drill batteries and left too. This left Dominic and John alone together, which John felt was the most awkward possible combination. Dominic started gathering scrap wood and hurling it into the wheelbarrow with the set jaw and forceful movements of a young man trying not to cry.

John gathered wood scraps too. "Abe's right though. Remember when you made those stilts for you and Mel and Vince when you were kids? They've held up! Jessie was using them the other day."

Dominic said nothing.

"You ever think about doing something with that? Going into engineering or something?" Why was talking so much? Pretending like he had any right to counsel Dominic, when he'd kept his blinders on around Jude for years, only to arrest him in the end?

Dominic apparently wondered the same. "It's funny that you're suddenly so interested in my life. Got any other great ideas for me, chief?" He tossed a piece of wood in the wheelbarrow and drew himself up, flexing his young strength against John's weathered sadness. John chuckled internally at that scathing adolescent barb—*chief,* dear God—and in the same moment he knew why he was saying these things to Dominic. Behind that mocking, piercing smile, a battle raged. There was the boy who loved to play and build, who went to school, worked almost full time, walked his baby brother every night at the witching hour, and most likely still had energy to party on the side. Then there was the boy who had learned at his father's knee how to hurt and deceive and frighten, who had maybe also learned to drown his sorrows in cheap liquor. These boys fought beneath Dominic's taut surface, clawing each other, putting that hate in his eyes. He was nineteen, a dangerous age. Which powers would he put to use in the world? Which man would he become?

In forty years of friendship with Jude, John had collected a wealth of knowledge he had mostly never divulged. Now he decided to feed a piece of his knowledge to the first boy, who was aching and scared and desperate for someone to think he was special.

"You know, there's a lot more you can do with an engineering degree than being a property manager. A hell of a lot more. And the reason your dad didn't do more is that he can't stick with things. He always makes big plans and when things get hard he finds a way to destroy whatever he's done and say it's someone else's fault. And you notice when one of his ideas does work out, it's because he got other people to do the work? He kept this company going for so long because his favorite thing to do in the world is shit on Abe, and Abe can't admit that so he just keeps jumping higher to see if he can get his brother to treat him like a real person. But you don't have to stay here and keep playing the same game. You could be better than him."

Dominic opened his mouth and shut it again. The anger drained from his face and he looked back at John with wide, shimmering eyes.

"In fact, you're already better than him. And you know, your parents gave you a real different kind of life, and you can go out and be something different. You don't have to stay and clean up your dad's mess. Take the good things he gave you and go do something with them. Go somewhere where no one knows your dad and figure out who you're going to be."

Dominic was gaping at him now. John, feeling like he'd said enough uncomfortable things for the morning, backpedaled out of the garage.

Spring 2011

1

THE SPIRIT MADE A troubling squeal the entire drive to Mel's house, but it shut up when Birdy cut the ignition. She was halfway up the path when the front door flew open.

"Birdy! Look!" Mel yelled, dragging her into the kitchen.

She turned the faucet on and then off again. Birdy looked at her, puzzled.

"It was broken," Mel explained. "It was leaking like Beth's used to. And I did the same thing with my hair tie, but then I was like, this is stupid, there are five people in this house, and we actually use the sink. So then I Googled some stuff and then I found this video on YouTube and I figured out how to fix it!"

"Wow!" said Birdy, impressed.

Officer Holloway walked in, looking exhausted and sad. "Hi honey," he said, "Hi Birdy." He took a glass out of the cabinet and filled it with water, leaning heavily against the counter as he downed it in a few gulps. Then he did a double take at the sink. "It's not leaking anymore. Where's your hair thingy?"

"I fixed it!" Mel exclaimed.

Officer Holloway's face broke into that rare and excellent smile. "Are you kidding me? How did you know how to do that?"

"YouTube," said Mel.

Officer Holloway looked momentarily appalled, then shook his head in wonder. "Well, I guess it worked," he said. "Thanks for taking care of that. I didn't know when I was going to have time to figure it out. I don't exactly want to ask for Abe's help right now," he sighed.

"Or ever," said Mel, wrinkling her nose.

Officer Holloway snorted guiltily. "He's not so bad," then amended his statement at the sight of Mel and Birdy's faces, "*Lately,* he's not quite so bad." The girls remained unconvinced as John continued. "Still, though, he's got a lot on his plate. The trial's tomorrow." And Officer Holloway once again looked so sad that Mel didn't argue.

"You girls heading to the gym?" They nodded, and Officer Holloway nodded back. "Knock 'em dead." Then he took on a wicked expression Birdy had never seen before. "You know who used to box, is Abe."

"I know," Birdy said distastefully. "He told me."

Officer Holloway continued to look rather giddy. "I heard he was pretty good, used to tear it up in the Army."

"He told me that, too," said Birdy, "And he phrased it exactly that same way. He offered to give me pointers."

"Did you take him up on it?"

"I told him my coaches are really good."

Officer Holloway snickered as Mel and Birdy headed for the door. "Tell your dad hello for me," he called after them.

Birdy, Mel and Kelly had all joined Conrad Fight Club after their CCC class ended, and they went as often as they could. Mel and Birdy walked across the parking lot that had once seemed so scary and was now scattered with pink petals from the cherry blossom trees flanking the front door.

Birdy and Mel put down their stuff, wrapped their hands, and found bags to hit while they waited. Hatch and Ryan had just finished teaching the latest group of CCC kids and were taking a water break before Mel and Birdy's class. One of the CCC kids wandered over to Birdy's bag. His smug smile put Birdy on instant alert.

"You look good," he said. "Your footwork is really good." Birdy smelled a rat, as Ryan had just told her two days earlier that her footwork needed some help. This guy either didn't know what he was talking about, or he was lying. Both unappealing characteristics.

"Thanks," said Birdy, footworking herself away from him in the method Ryan had suggested. He followed her around the bag. "I've seen you around CCC."

"Oh yeah?" said Birdy.

"Yeah, I could show you some more moves if you want."

"Oh, that's okay," Birdy began, but a hoot of laughter interrupted.

"You hear that? This white boy wants to show Birdy some moves!"

The white boy convulsed as Coach Hatch swaggered up to them smoothing his wrinkled tee. His missing tooth gaped in his joyful smile. "Now I don't mean to scare you, little man, but Birdy is mean. Don't let her fool you with her nice face, she'd kill you in that ring. So why don't you come fix up your weak-ass hook with me, and leave Birdy alone so she can tear up that bag in peace."

White Boy followed Coach Hatch with his tail between his legs. Ryan held out his mitt for a side swiping five as he passed by Birdy's bag.

"Do you know yet if we'll be losing you next year?"

"I just put in my deposit for University of Maryland," said Birdy, relief in her voice. They'd accepted all her credits, had come through with some scholarship money, and had appealing possibilities for her major. "But they have a boxing team there!"

"No shit!" said Ryan. "Hatch has a buddy with a gym in DC, we go there for sparring sometimes. We'll have to bring you."

Birdy was unable to picture herself sparring in a DC gym, but liked the thought. After a lifetime of fearing the future, lately she'd been running toward it. Each spring evening was lighter than the last, and each one brought her closer to college. This gym was one of the few things she thought she would miss. She turned back to her bag and stood on the balls of her feet. Another month of school, a carefree summer, and then she'd be gone to a life that was all hers.

2

JUDE SAT IN THE holding cell, his head shaved like some criminal, his suit and tie drenched in sweat. The trial was over, gone in a flash, and now Judge Kettermine was deliberating.

Fucking Kettermine, Jimmy Kettermine, who had kicked a football accurately two times in his entire life, was thinking over his fate.

Jude was still smarting from the trial. It had been humiliating.

To start with, his lawyer was some shit. Samuel Garmin. Garmin, Garmin, there was something about that name that rang a bell. When he'd asked, Garmin had said he was a few years ahead of Jude in school, but Jude couldn't remember him at all. Jude pled innocent to everything but the DUI because who wouldn't, and though Garmin was defending him he didn't seem to believe him. First he dragged the trial preparations on for almost a year, and in the end, he'd angled for Jude to have a bench trial, insisting a jury would only hurt Jude's chances. Jude had a story all prepared that explained away the bank accounts and the dent in his car, but Garmin didn't want to hear it.

"I'm not presenting that in court," he'd said. "You're not going to testify. We're just going to keep our heads down and maintain that there's no proof you did any of what they say you did." Garmin had tapped his pencil on his pinstriped knee. "Other than the DUI."

The prosecutor, Francis Morton, was much more enthusiastic. Jude recognized him from St. Paul's. Though stooped and balding, Morton had managed to assemble a painful parade of people Jude had never thought would betray him. First there was a vengeful stripper whose name was apparently not actually Tulips. She also wasn't just a stripper. She owned the establishment and yes, Jude was a frequent visitor to it. Yes, she was sure, she recognized him and especially the cigarette burn scar on his hand. (This part had required Jude to stand up and show the court his hand, as if any of them could see it from that distance.) Most damning, she had security footage showing his car in the parking lot on dates that correlated perfectly with the ones on his credit card statement.

If Garmin had listened to Jude, then he would have had a perfect alternative story to propose when he stood up. Instead, he had only one question for Tulips: "Ms. Huntley," he said, "Is there any chance your security system is displaying incorrect dates?"

"No," said Tulips scornfully.

"No further questions," said Garmin.

Then there was Abe, sweating like a pig in his Christmas suit as he detailed Jude's frequent absences and disappearances, how he'd said he was doing things for the business but how Abe had started to suspect that was false. "Sure you did, buddy," Jude had muttered, not that quietly. Garmin had glared at him. When it was Garmin's turn, he asked Abe if he had any proof other than speculation that Jude wasn't where he said he was going.

"Well, yeah," said Abe.

"And what was that?"

"The work he said he was doing was never done."

"How do you know?"

"Because I kept having to do it."

Jude was sure Garmin would ask Abe if he'd documented those conversations, if he had any contracts or work orders to back up this story, but he didn't. He just sat down. No wonder Jude didn't have to pay this guy.

Next came Officer Nicholson, who had joined him and John for drinks one time. Evidently, he was also the guy who first responded at the scene of Jude's accident, though Jude didn't really remember that. The guy looked like a goddamn superhero. He told the court about responding to the call, administering the breathalyzer, and how Jude had puked right next to his feet.

"But I stepped aside just in time," Nicholson reassured the court.

In his less violent moments, Jude's dad had often said Jude should have been a lawyer. He didn't mean it in a nice way, but Jude kept thinking of that during the trial. By the time John took the stand, he was seriously wishing he'd represented himself. He would have fought so much harder than Garmin, torn them all to shreds. John testified that he noticed the strange dents and the scrape of red paint on Jude's car, and when he'd heard of that girl's accident, he'd gotten suspicious. Jude would have gotten on John's ass, asking why the hell he didn't move faster on his suspicions if he was so smart, or what that girl was doing out so late anyway. He would have said his wife and son sometimes borrowed that car, maybe they'd bumped this bike in a parking lot sometime, it was a small town. But Garmin had only asked John if there was any proof the paint on Jude's car matched the paint on the girl's bike.

John had leaned into the microphone and said, "The lab showed a match, sir."

"But there's no definite proof?"

John leaned forward and repeated, "The lab showed a match, sir." John fixed him with that "Please stop being an idiot" look, and Garmin gave up.

Worst of all was Tammy, in her Easter dress, telling half the town how she'd broken into his private accounts. Instead of being by his side in the hospital, she'd been sitting at home, ruining everything. Tammy, Tammy, she had done her hair nice and she looked exhausted. She was probably still nursing half the night. And when she'd left, he'd looked back through the swinging courtroom door and caught a glimpse of her reaching out for the baby and then holding him close, Noah, his name was. Noah.

3

"WILL! HOW'S YOUR SISTER?" Kettermine said genially.

They were in the hallway outside the chambers, preparing to return to court. Garmin frowned at Kettermine and didn't answer. John didn't know Garmin had a sister. He didn't have one himself, but if he did, he wouldn't want Kettermine asking about her either.

John had gone looking for Nicholson and on his way back to court found Kettermine, looking completely relaxed. From the beginning, Kettermine had guaranteed them it would all be over in one day. John did not find his confidence reassuring.

John left the officers of the court, went in the courtroom, and took a seat behind Abe, Karen, and Tammy. All was quiet. A woman two rows ahead of him was clutching a white rosary and whispering her pleas. Jude and Garmin came in and sat at their table, and John could see Jude in profile, his head shaved closer than usual. Abe reached for Karen's hand and she grabbed his back, squeezing tight. Tammy interlocked her fingers and placed them on her lap.

Kettermine swept into position. His smarmy manner suggested he was starring in an episode of Law and Order, but his bench resembled the fake wood paneling in John's basement.

"Citizens of Conrad, I thank you for lending your time and ears to helping us carry out justice. This sacred institution of the courtroom, second only to God himself, is what makes our country so great. I am honored by the solemn duty to decipher this complicated case, that affects all of us so deeply."

For someone who was so honored by his solemn duty, Kettermine sure looked pleased with himself. Reflex made John want to look at Jude like *Can you believe this guy?*

"My decision is that Jude Doppelski... is guilty on all counts." A wave swept through the courtroom, half panic half relief. Kettermine surveyed them down his delicate nose. "However," he added ostentatiously, and the wave paused. John knew it was bad news.

"However," he repeated, "There will be no need for an additional sentencing hearing. The course forward is clear. I have decided on a sentence of time served."

The course of the wave reversed. Jude jerked his head up at Kettermine, scrutinizing him like he was making sure this wasn't a joke. Tammy, Abe, and Karen sat stock-still. Kettermine smiled paternally down at Jude. "You're free to go, Jude."

Jude sat nodding his head, most likely figuring out his next steps. Officer Nicholson leapt to his feet and strode purposefully down the aisle, giving Tammy a reassuring nod as he went. Tammy took a shaky breath and started shuddering. Karen pulled her to her feet and ushered her out of the courtroom, with Abe hot on their heels. John remained silent in the growing din, surrounded by all the courtroom visitors who were now stretching, gossiping, and deciding what was for dinner.

Fucking Kettermine. Wanting to have it both ways, never wanting to upset anyone too much. John recognized that unfortunate personality trait, being saddled with it himself.

4

BIRDY WALKED ACROSS THE CCC parking lot, wearing what was now her old blue tank top and enjoying the feel of sunshine on her arms. She'd just finished her calculus final and needed to study for her biology final, but for now she was free, and hungry.

tickticktickticktickticktick

The sound was coming from her car and growing louder as she approached.

Uh oh.

She turned the key in the ignition and was rewarded with the sound of absolutely nothing happening. Birdy put her head down on the steering wheel. From this perspective, it was easy to see that the dial for her headlights was still pointing to *On.* She tried the key again in vain hope, then slammed her head on the steering wheel in defeat.

Someone knocked on her window.

It was Dominic. That was unexpected, as he wasn't taking classes here this semester. According to both of their moms, he was working hard, saving money to move away. Nowadays, Birdy and Dominic had a polite-wave-and-smile type of relationship, but it was still startling to see him up close. She managed not to flinch in surprise, internally applauding herself for this as she opened the car door.

"Hey," she said.

"Hey," he smiled. "How's it going?"

"Um... great," said Birdy. "Living my best life here."

"Is that why you're headbutting your steering wheel?"

She couldn't help but laugh at this. "It's just my car. It's sensitive. I left the lights on for like two hours and now it won't start. I feel like such an idiot."

Dominic looked down at her. He had one arm on the roof of her car, the other on her open door. "Birdy, you are definitely not an idiot. At least not as much of one as I am." He eyed the hood. "I can help you jump it if you want."

Birdy sighed. "That would be amazing."

Dominic jogged off to get his car and pulled up next to her. He popped their hoods and took his neatly folded jumper cables from his trunk. Then he handed them to her.

He talked her through it with that confidence she'd always admired. She was grateful there was a task for them to share, a purpose to fill the first moments they had done more than exchange pleasantries in nearly two years. Her car soon coughed to life, and she slumped in relief. "Thank you so much, Dominic," she said. "I really, really appreciate it."

"It's no problem at all. I'll stay with you until you're sure it's working." He looked right at her again. "It's funny I ran into you here. I barely ever see you at home anymore. I'm just stopping by for a transcript thing. I'm moving down to North Carolina in two days. I've got an internship and a job set up and I should be able to start classes at ECU over the winter."

"Wow, congratulations!" said Birdy, feeling genuinely happy to hear he was escaping the strange kingdom his father had built.

"Thanks," he said, looking pleased. He paused, then took a deep breath. Just before he spoke, someone yelled "Birdyyyyy!" She turned her head and saw Brandon, the red-haired guy from boxing who was now in her Biology class.

"Having car trouble?" he said.

"How could you tell?" she answered.

He laughed. "Are you ready for the exam?"

"Mostly," said Birdy. "Are you going to the study group tomorrow?"

"Yeah, I think so. See you then?"

"Of course," said Birdy. Brandon and Dominic regarded each other and nodded, then Brandon walked away.

She looked back at Dominic, and he straightened and stepped back. "Well," he said, "You should be good now. Want to test it before I go?" He disconnected the cables that linked their cars. She turned her car back off and restarted it again. It protested no more than usual.

"Success!" she cried. "Seriously, thanks."

"My pleasure," smiled Dominic, an echo from a past where he'd known things about her life, where he'd teased her about them. Once upon a time, he would have punctuated this statement with a hug or some other physical offering, but today he just stood with his hands in his pockets.

"See you around," she said. "Good luck at ECU. Bring your jumper cables so you can rescue other idiots."

Dominic laughed and Birdy got back in her car. He was like a jagged precipice in her rearview mirror, a giant whose power she remembered but no longer felt. She honked her horn as she drove away. It sounded like a dying duck. Dominic answered with his horn, loud and strong.

JUDE SPLASHED WARM JIM BEAM in a faded Thrasher's cup. He swiped a dribble off the side of the bottle and licked his shaking finger. He was out of jail, but he wasn't home.

Kettermine had made sure to find him after the trial and give him a big ol' handshake and clap on the back. He acted like he was doing Jude the favor of the century by letting him out of jail, but he didn't give him his home back. Officer Nicholson was right behind him. Nicholson crossed his superhero arms and informed Jude that Tammy had a restraining order against him.

So now he was lying on Joshua's piss-stained couch in College Park, drinking Joshua's liquor from Joshua's random cup. Joshua had made noise about how Jude wouldn't drink under his roof, but he had so much it was easy to take some when he was gone. In fact, it was exactly like being fourteen and breaking into Joshua's under-the-bed stash. Now Joshua had a cabinet for his alcohol, but he still kept his extra cash in his pillowcase.

Joshua always left early to take the Metro to his job at a warehouse in Cheverly. It could have been a 15-minute drive, but his Impala needed a new battery. It was such a simple fix, and there was an Advance two blocks away, but Joshua didn't care to know that. He'd had the Impala forever and had painted it brown for some reason a while back, probably something shady. And somehow Joshua was more trustworthy than Jude.

Jude had been rotting here for a month, during which time Tammy had granted him one single conversation on the phone, moderated by yet another lawyer. She still wanted a divorce. She didn't want him to have the kids, ever, so more visits to Kettermine's courtroom were probably in their future. Her voice was so wobbly on the phone and still she had said these things, flushing their lives down the toilet.

The whiskey was hardly consolation for any of it. This was exactly the shit Jude had tried to avoid his whole life. Beholden to someone else, and his kids out there without him.

Jude grabbed Joshua's laptop off the peeling coffee table and flipped it open. When Jude got tired of taking walks along Route 1 and watching crap on TV, he dicked around online. It was new to him, but he could see the appeal, if you had nothing else to do. Which Jude didn't.

Joshua had taken to logging out of his Facebook, but his password was "password1234." Dumbass. Joshua was a member of the tiny and pathetic "Conrad High Alumni" group, which was mostly ladies trying to sell stuff. Still, Jude was surprised by how many people he knew who were on Facebook. Not John, of course, definitely not Arthur Cleary, not even Abe. But Karen, who seemed to have blocked Joshua, and Samuel Garmin, whose profile was public.

Garmin, the limp fuck, was enjoying his Memorial Day weekend with his family in St. Michael's. His chubby wife Winifred, his bratty kids, his crotchety parents, his ugly dog, his fat brother Barry, his sullen sister Ashley—

Fuck. Ashley Garmin.

Jude pulled the laptop closer, click, click, click. Ashley still had those freckles on her nose and arms, but her hair was a fake black now. She'd never gotten married, she wasn't in the Conrad High Alumni group, she'd transferred to St. Monica's after—

You know who else had Facebook, was Dominic.

Jude typed Dominic's name in the search bar. His profile said *Dominic Doppelski is still waiting to accept your friend request,* but Jude could still see all his business. Dominic didn't post frequently, which made Jude proud. It was weird the things people thought were important to write on this thing—Joshua, for example, would say things like "loving these new chips i got (bbq)." But it looked like last week, Dominic had written "See ya, MD!" Jude thought maybe he was taking a trip with friends or something, but after reading the tearful comments of about a hundred girls he determined it wasn't just a trip. Dominic was moving to North Carolina, and Jude should have been down there, helping him get set up, fixing things before he left because your first apartment was always shitty, but Jude wasn't there.

Then just a minute ago, Dominic posted a picture of himself standing on a college campus. "got word im officially a future pirate! Starting classes in winter!!" Jude didn't know what the deal was, why Dominic was down there now if he wasn't starting till winter, not even what his major was. Jude had taught Dominic everything, had built a whole fucking school for him, and Dominic hadn't said goodbye or anything else to him in a year.

Jude logged out, slammed the laptop shut, and gulped the rest of the Jim Beam, but it was about as soothing as lemon juice. The room blurred before his eyes, turned upside down. Dominic was gone, Tammy didn't want him to see the rest of the kids, and he'd never even met his youngest, his baby. Noah.

He leapt up and paced the room, the disgusting floor sticking to his feet. In his real life, his floor didn't stick, and he was in charge. All there was to do at Joshua's house was sit and be miserable. Out on the curb was a broken car, easy to fix. And right upstairs was

Joshua's bedroom, with its stinky socks and its porn magazines and its pillowcase full of cash.

5

VICTORIA STREET WAS QUIET today. Most of the Doppelski kids were at school and the others were on a field trip with Ms. Karen—all except one. Mrs. Doppelski had asked Birdy to come watch Noah while she met with her lawyer.

"Gunner's at the vet for a few days, so you don't need to worry about him. I'll probably be home in an hour, maybe two if things take longer than I thought," Mrs. Doppelski said. She looked nervous and tired, but eager too. "He said since Jude doesn't have a permanent address right now, it shouldn't be hard at all to—well, anyway. I should sneak out while he's happy." She gestured to Noah, who was happily trying to catch his foot. She smiled at him and crept out the door.

Birdy got down on the floor beside Noah and puffed out her cheeks. He looked astounded and stretched his tiny arm toward her. She leaned in so his hand was on her cheek, then released the air in a loud raspberry. Noah busted out a throaty giggle that made Birdy laugh back. He already had a little tooth growing into his otherwise gummy smile, making him look like a reverse Coach Hatch.

They spent twenty minutes on the floor before he started looking annoyed. Birdy walked Noah all over the house, read him board books, smiled with him in the mirror, and sang to him. Mrs. Doppelski had said she thought he might be getting close to rolling soon, so Birdy put him on his belly to see if he would. Noah didn't like holding his head up and immediately started screaming into his blanket. He soothed himself from the ordeal by taking a massive shit, and during the lively diaper change that followed, he demonstrated that he very much was close to rolling. Birdy heard the front door open just as she fastened the last snap of his onesie.

"Hi! We're in here!" she called, scooping Noah into her arms.

"Found you," said Jude.

No. No. Nonononono. Birdy's heart stopped, lurched, screamed to life as she cast about, looking for a safe place to put Noah. Normally he was in the sling Tammy perpetually wore; otherwise he was in his bassinet. Both were upstairs. *Couch, no, floor, no, changing table, no—* none would protect him. So she turned to face the room, clutching the baby.

Jude was leaning on the door frame. His haircut was different and he was thinner, paler, his crossed arms wirier than they had been before. Birdy wanted to be brave, but she was already shaking. *Cortisol. Real threat this time.*

"Ms. Birdy Cleary! I just came over to visit my son."

Her jaw felt so heavy. It took a moment to make it say, "You're not supposed to be here."

He snorted. "Not supposed to be here! It's my home!" He slurred the esses and his volume was too much. *Drunk.* He shoved himself off the doorframe and stood tall.

"No, I think the one who shouldn't be here is you, Ms. Birdy. See, I came here to see my house and my wife and my kids and my baby who I've never even met and all I find is you, in the middle of things. Just like you always fucking have been since you moved here."

Absurdly, the vulnerable baby in the scary situation brought to mind the climax of a cartoon superhero movie she'd watched with the little Doppelskis just last week. In the end, they defeated the bad guy by getting him to talk too much. Birdy thought of a hundred car rides, barbecues, school functions, and Masses. If Jude loved anything, it was the sound of his own voice. *Get him monologuing.*

"Why do you say that?"

He snorted again. "Oh, I don't know. You hop in to my school just when we get started, and we have to drag you along to everything. You stir up some weird shit between Dom and Isaac who were best buddies before you got here. You tried to humiliate me by getting Dominic in trouble with that Facebook dance thing or whatever. Your fucking friend was the reason I went to jail! You're all quiet half the time, but you've got all these fucking wheels turning inside your head!"

He's giving me waaay too much credit. At a time like this, the wheels inside Birdy's head could only produce snippets from kids' movies. And she still had fractured prayers. *Please, somebody, come. God, please, somebody.*

"It's not just you though, it's your whole family. You know what Tammy said to me? My *wife* said to me, she says 'You don't treat me right. I never realized how bad you treated me till I saw how Arthur Cleary treated *his* wife." He slapped the doorframe, pissed now. "She says, 'Maggie Cleary, she told me Arthur did this and that thing. Oh, he actually likes spending time with her, he watches movies with her, they read books together, one time she almost fucking *killed* herself but he supports her so good she's never had to go to the hospital again.'"

Birdy was too frozen to react to this shock as Jude picked up steam. "She says she's still filing for divorce, she said she doesn't even want me to have custody of the kids. MY! KIDS!" His face transformed, turned red, he slammed the side of his fist on the doorframe, sent a paint chip flying. Then he snapped back to a pleasant smile and plucked a flower from the shriveled bouquet on the side table.

If Dominic had ever frightened Birdy, he was an amateur. His master stood before her, tearing a daffodil to shreds.

"I said, Arthur Cleary? His wife is useless and he just lets her, he won't lay down the law with her, he just lets her keep dicking around. His wife's a pain in the ass, his house is falling apart, his knees are fucked, his son won't even talk to him, and you want to throw away all I gave you to be more like *them?"*

He brushed bits of stem from his hands and stepped into the room. He pulled a flat glass bottle from his pocket and took a few gulps. "So Ms. Birdy. I'm pretty fucking unhappy to see you right now. But you can make it better if you do a couple things for me. One is give me my son. Two is tell me where the fuck the key to my gun cabinet went."

"Why?" The word was a whisper. Birdy knew where the key was. When Jude ruled the house, it had occupied a hook high on the hallway wall, right next to the gun cabinet. Tammy had occasionally protested this location, knowing her monkey children could easily retrieve it if they wanted. Jude maintained it should be kept close by its point of use, an organization tenet wise for cleaning supplies but silly for that key. In the aftermath of Jude's arrest, Tammy had started using the key as the bookmark in her Bible, a detail Mom had found poignant enough to repeat more than once.

"Why?" Jude laughed. "Because I want my shit back, hon." He smiled as if to coax her. "And you're such a helpful girl, Tammy says. Not sure I agree, but now you got a chance to prove it."

Up until now, Birdy had felt like she was inching to the crest of a roller coaster, gripping the restraint, legs dangling in midair. Now she hung in the dizzy pause at the top. The freefall was about to begin.

"I don't know where they are," she tried. She hadn't finished speaking when Jude took another two steps in the room, shaking his head like a dog.

"No, no, no, no, honey, I know that's not true, you're so FUCKING involved here, if you didn't know you would have said right away."

Shit. At Jude's harsh voice, Noah stuck out his lower lip. "It's okay, baby, it's okay," said Birdy, bouncing him a little. Maybe she could hold him with just one arm, but he was long, and she was shaking so hard she was afraid she would drop him.

She looked up to Jude's disgusted glare. She tried again. "Okay, I know it sounds like a lie, but it's not, I swear." She took a deep breath. "They're next door at Mr. Abe and Ms. Karen's, they're in the kitchen cabinet with the cups on a—"

"NO!" Jude screamed and smashed the bottle on the ground. Birdy heard the wires inside the lightbulbs hum in response; then Noah answered his father with a scream of his own.

Birdy sidestepped into the kitchen and darted up the back stairs, but she couldn't use her arms, she was too slow. He caught up to her almost instantly, grabbed her foot and yanked. She flipped to her back as she went down so she wouldn't fall on Noah, and the twisting motion loosened her shoe. She kicked it off and scrambled backwards on her butt, feeling absurd, and when he got closer she slammed her heel into his face. A stab of victory as he stumbled back, but now he was livid. She was at the top of the stairs, her back was to the door, he lurched up after her two at a time and then—

"JUDE!"

A thundering voice from the kitchen. Birdy and Jude shared a bizarre moment, looking at each other like, *Do you know who that is? No, sorry, do you?* before Abe yanked his brother down the stairwell.

They crashed into the kitchen. Birdy tried the door, which was locked anyway, then checked on Noah. Teardrops glistened on his soft cheeks, but he was smiling again. Maybe, like his siblings, he enjoyed an adrenaline rush. "Gggoww," he said earnestly. Birdy wiped off the tears, kissed his tiny round belly, and laid her ear against it to listen to his brisk heartbeat. Then she heard Jude's voice from the kitchen.

"What're you doing here?"

"Joshua called," said Abe.

"I thought he was at work," said Jude.

"There were too many people, there wasn't enough to do, they sent him home early," said Abe.

As the brothers exchanged these mundanities, Birdy crept to the bottom of the stairs and peeked into the room. Abe and Jude were facing each other, heaving. Blood dripped out of Jude's nose, and he wiped it with the back of his hand. *Take that, asshole.*

"John's on his way over too," said Abe. "You can't be here, Jude."

"Oh, I know you don't want me to be here," said Jude. "You testified against me! You wanted me gone so you could take over my life!"

"I don't want your life. You went to jail because of what you did."

Birdy was used to seeing Abe in situations ruled by Jude. Even when Jude wasn't around, he was always rankled by Jude's shadow. Now he stood tall while Jude still panted. He pointed at his brother.

"You started that whole school, you had people believing in you, and then you stole from them. You got wasted and then drove and then hit that poor girl with your car. A girl our kids knew, by the way! But we both know that's not even the worst part. It's what you do right here in this house that's worse. I can't believe I just stood by and let you for so long. I'm not letting you anymore."

Whatever Jude had swigged from the shattered bottle was in control now. "You're such a motherfucking BITCH you've always been jealous, always trying to catch me but you CAN'T, you never WILL, I won't let you take away my life!"

"I'm not taking away your life, you blew it up yourself!"

"OH for fuck's sake, you'd have nothing without me, the businesses were me, the school was me, you can't stop tryna be me, I brought something good to Conrad, I made something better!" Birdy now wished for her own brothers because if it wasn't so scary it would be funny; Jude was pounding his chest like some pathetic, malicious peacock and sounded exactly like a villain in one of Mom's Lifetime movies.

"You made something better and then took it all for yourself." Jude blustered at this, and Abe went on. "I just ignored everything you did here, thinking hey, I'm not as bad as Jude, I actually felt good about that! I even let you be a dick to my own kids, even though you and I both know what it's like to be the scared little kid. I have to answer to God for letting this go on, and so do you."

"IT'S MY HOUSE!" Jude roared. "IT'S MY FAMILY!"

"That's why you're supposed to protect them! You think God gave you this family so you could scare them and hurt them?"

"Oh, Jesus Christ!" Jude rolled his eyes so hard it looked painful. Then he lunged.

Abe was ready. He pivoted aside, hands up, and sent a hard left to the side of Jude's face.

Oh, thought Birdy as Jude keeled stumbled sideways, windmilling his arms. He grabbed the countertop and redirected his course, throwing a wild punch at Abe, who easily dodged it and pivoted again. Jude snarled in frustration as he charged Abe harder than ever. This time Abe met him, drove his shoulder into Jude's chest and slammed him down to the floor. He rolled Jude over and sat on his back, twisting his arms. Jude made a wretched noise but seemed too confused by his new position to fight.

"You need help, Jude," said Abe.

"No one can help me," moaned Jude, sounding like a child.

"You can get help," Abe repeated. He licked his lips. "*I've* been getting help."

"Like a shrink you mean? God, you're such a bitch," said Jude, driving his forehead into the ground.

Abe grinned. "I thought you'd say that."

"You know they're just gonna tell you you're secretly a fag."

It was Abe's turn for a massive eyeroll. "I think I can handle that."

"What do you need that for anyway, nothing even happened to you!" Jude was angry again.

Abe sighed. "I know I didn't—you've been through—terrible things. Much worse than me. But we still grew up in the same house."

"You didn't get half the shit I did cuz you were such a crybaby!"

Birdy had watched Jude bait Abe like this for years, but he didn't rise to it this time. She had been disgusted with Abe's new attitude, but now it occurred to her that his attempts to change his behavior, however clunky, were genuine. Abe sighed and shook his head.

"You can't be here, Jude. You can't keep doing this. You know what it's like to be those scared kids—"

"FUCK!" wailed Jude.

"—you can't stay here and keep hurting them."

"I'm a good dad, I work my ass off, I changed all their diapers, I take them to all their stupid shit, work in their school, taught them all kinds of stuff so they can do anything, they don't know how good they have it!"

"Yeah and between all that shit you're a total asshole, treat their mom like dirt right in front of them, say horrible shit to them—"

"Oh I yell at them sometimes like a big meanie? They've NEVER had to—they've NEVER been through—"

"Shut UP," bellowed Abe, angry now. He leaned close to Jude's ear. "Shut up with the you NEVER. I know Dom and Coz *and* Frankie aren't *all* hurting their faces in skateboard accidents every few months."

"What the fuck do you—"

"Why do you think there's a restraining order you dumbass—"

"It's bullshit, I haven't been anywhere near them in a year, she just pulls this out of her ass since I didn't go back to jail—"

"She didn't want to drag them into the trial and humiliate them—"

"Oh you know so much about it, Mr. People Person, such a standup guy, well she can't prove anything, you just want to look like Mr. Friendly Guy so you're just going along with it—"

"I don't need a piece of paper to convince me," Abe cut him off, voice ringing. "Our kids talk. My kids knew, and once you were gone they told me. And the sad thing is I already knew too. I just pretended I didn't."

He leaned back again looking dejected. Far across the kitchen was a flicker of movement. Officer Holloway was lowering his gun in the hallway. He trained worried eyes on Birdy, then stared back down at Abe and Jude, who hadn't noticed anything.

Jude was undaunted. "They still have it better than me."

"It's not the same as what we went through—definitely not the same as what—what happened to you—"

"STOP!"

"—but it's still bad, Jude! Don't you see that? No one should have to go through what you did, Dad was awful to you and he totally fucked up how he handled the other stuff—"

"STOP!"

"—but you don't get credit just because you don't do all the same stuff. There's no excuse for hurting kids."

"I don't—you don't—"

Abe pressed on over Jude's spluttering.

"You can get help, there are people who really know how to help, you can get help for the drinking and you can learn to recognize when you're about to lose your shit." Then he added almost shyly, "And God can help you too, he can do anything."

"God? God doesn't give a shit about me."

"Jude," said Abe, "No."

"He fucking hates me, that's why it fucking happened, plus I was such a piece of shit kid it's no wonder." Tears gathered in Jude's voice.

Abe's forehead creased. Then he swallowed and said hoarsely, "You mean Father Gerard?"

Jude whimpered and Birdy flashed back to January in her own kitchen.

"You know, Tammy always used to say how the boys are serving at the parish just like their dad... they were always so proud of that."

"Jude told me that priest was transferred because of something that happened with a nun. Not a kid."

Her mom's face miserable, her dad's face stricken, her heart so hardened by disgust for Jude Doppelski that she refused to understand what it all meant. She felt sick.

"Jude, no. That wasn't your fault. You were just a kid. It wasn't your fault." Abe's voice was gentle like he was talking to Noah.

"How the fuck do you know about it anyway? I always knew you knew, but who told you?" Jude was all fury now. He wrenched his arms and nearly broke free from Abe's relaxed grip. Abe scrambled to recover him as he babbled his response, a dam finally opened.

"I was listening when you told them, I went up to the attic, I could hear into their room really well through that vent, I heard the whole thing, I wanted to find out if you got in trouble for burning my—"

"You're such a goddamn baby," said Jude, relishing this chance to squash Abe back down in his place. Abe looked hurt for just a second, then shook his head.

"That was so fucked up, what Dad said to you. You didn't deserve it, nothing you ever did could possibly—"

"Well, buddy, I did a lot of bad stuff, so that wasn't even the last time it happened," Jude sneered. "But you can bet I never tried to tell Dad about it again."

Birdy wished she could have gone upstairs and never heard these things. Abe looked like he was going to be sick himself, but he went on.

"And Mom too, she was too scared to do anything to stop Dad, it must have been the same with Father Gerard but she was wrong, she should have protected you, she—"

"Well she was right, wasn't she? She said I'd ruin everything if I went around talking like that and then Eddie—"

"Something must have happened to Eddie too," said Abe, nodding rapidly, "He stopped coming to school and then his mom had that freakout at the church picnic—"

"And then the school closed and his dad killed himself and the factory died and the whole fuckin town went to shit!"

"Well then it should have!" said Abe. "If that's what it took to stop him. You think the town was worth—what it did to you?" His voice crumpled.

Jude's face was screwed up tight, but he chuckled. "Well, I dunno, people kinda need jobs and I'm fucked up either way, so."

Abe wasn't laughing. "Well you could have been—you could have had—I just wish they'd shown you you were worth it to them."

"Well I wasn't, so they didn't."

"You're worth it—to me," Abe stammered. "That's why I always wanted—to stick with you."

Birdy expected Jude to laugh or tease at this, but he simply remained still, looking surprised. Abe seemed embarrassed by his confession and moved forward with his native indelicacy. "I just never really understood why you always wanted to stay here and stick around St. Ann's. Didn't that make everything worse?"

Jude's slur was growing more pronounced. "Well, lots of people like me here and we went to St. Ann's forever you know, I kinda stopped thinking about it, I'm not a big baby... it made the most sense to have the school be there... and it did start pissing me off sometimes but I thought I could... you know... just put it aside... or like offer it up..."

"Jude, that's—Mom would always say to offer it up so she wouldn't have to fix whatever bad stuff was happening, but—God didn't make us that way, the way he made us, that bad stuff sticks around, our bodies remind us, my th-therapist—" Jude snorted "—my therapist said you can't possibly pretend away something like that, you can't just close your eyes and pretend it never happened. I mean you of all people, you're the worst, you hate to just leave things alone, you"—Abe was desperate, running his hands through his tidy hair—"it's like when you moved in here and there was that leak under the floor. Right in here. And the people had just been living with it like that, and the floor was all lumpy and messed up, and you said if you just left it, it would get worse and worse, the mold would get all the kids sick, and we needed to tear it all up and put in something new. You trying to go around like nothing ever happened to you, it's just like that floor. If you ignore it, it's just gonna stay broken, it's just gonna get worse."

"No shit," Jude said, and then he was weeping, the shattered wailing of wounded drunks eternal. In his sorrow, Birdy saw Beth, and her knees buckled in grief. In the hall, Officer Holloway silently wiped his cheek with his shoulder. Abe didn't know what to do with his hands; he twisted them around each other, held his face, clasped Jude's shoulder. Jude's sobs lurched to a sudden hiccup. "Can I get on my back, my face fuckin hurts."

Abe helped Jude shift to his back but kept his legs across his chest. He stretched back, grabbed a low hanging kitchen towel, and dabbed blood, snot and tears off Jude's face. Noah had spent the conversation transfixed by the ceiling fan, his eyelids drooping ever more shut, and now he yawned loudly. Jude and Abe looked in shock at where Birdy held him.

God, please make me disappear.

Jude looked back up at the ceiling, covering his face. "I wasn't gonna hurt him, I wasn't gonna hurt anybody, just wanted to see my baby, I'm sorry, I'm so sorry, I wasn't gonna hurt anyone, I was just so mad, I'm sorry, I wasn't gonna do anything."

Abe met Birdy's eyes over Jude's sobbing heap. The devastation on his face told her he didn't believe Jude, either.

The room got quiet again. Then Jude lifted his hand.

"Finally made your tackle," he said.

Abe grasped it and buried his face in his brother's knuckles.

6

TAMMY'S PHONE WAS DEAD. She'd forgotten to charge it overnight. The meeting had gone well, but it had taken longer than she thought, and now she was rushing home, aching to feed Noah, and feeling uneasy. When she drove past the Clearys' house and around the curve, she saw three cars in her driveway instead of zero. A police car, Abe's truck, and an ugly brown Impala.

She floored it to the house, slammed to a stop, and pounded up the driveway. The front door was wide open. She sped down the hall to where John Holloway stood just inside the kitchen door, returning his gun to its holster. He looked at her wordlessly, and their heads turned together to the scene in the kitchen.

Birdy stood by the stairwell rocking Noah. Abe and Jude were huddled on the ground. Father and son were fast asleep.

Summer 2011

1

From: petercleary@hotmail.com
Hey Birdy,

How's it going? I was thinking of visiting next weekend, are you around? Anything you want to do when I'm there? Or let me know if you want to get out of town and come visit me. Anything you need, I'm here.

From: bluebirdy@aol.com
Hey! Everything's good here. Next Friday is Mel's birthday party and I'm working Saturday night but I'm currently doing nothing on Sundays. There's a new sub place that looks good, maybe we could go there

Patrick: Hey, how's everything going? Can't wait for you guys to visit. I'm here if you want to talk.
Birdy: Hey! I'm good, can't wait to visit! Not looking forward to the road trip part, I already bet Chris that dad will be listening to the rosary for the first 20 minutes of the trip and he said "that is like betting the sun will rise aka not a bet"

IT WAS SUNDAY MORNING. Mom and Dad were at church, and Birdy was wrapped in a blanket on the loveseat. She had a book open, but she was staring at the strip of light that snuck between the curtains, bisecting her.

Chris poked his head into the kitchen. "I'm making breakfast, want some?"

"Sure," said Birdy.

Thanks to the babysitting job from hell, the Cleary parents were walking on eggshells around the kids for the first time in family history. In the last few weeks, Birdy had told everyone she was fine about a thousand times, and Mom had berated herself about a thousand more times for sending Birdy to the Doppelskis' that day instead of going herself.

Birdy showered Mom with reassurance, truly grateful it had been her there and not Mom. She hadn't told anyone about Jude's cruel aside during his terrifying rant, but she assumed it was at least partially true. It seemed clear now that Mom's heat stroke incident had only ever been an alibi for something else, something that had caused Dad to spearhead 4 moves in the years before and since, attempting to help Mom find a place where she could be happy. Puzzling as it was, it seemed she'd found it.

Mom and Dad had shown up at the Doppelskis' that evening furious, but then Noah had reached for Dad and snuggled into his chest, Tammy had wailed apologies onto Mom's shoulder, and both parents had swelled with purpose. As Chris had privately noted to Birdy, even though Conrad was the most batshit crazy place they'd ever lived, there was no talk of moving away this time.

Birdy imagined her feelings on a balance scale all tangled together, relief and gratitude and pride on one side, terror and anger and sadness on the other. There were so many they cancelled each other out, leaving her numb. Jude was once again in jail, willingly this time, so nothing in the world outside her feelings had changed. Life was already moving on.

Still, her parents didn't make her go to church. They were the ones who first suggested she stay home, and they asked Chris to stay with her so she could feel safe. She appreciated the company, and she knew the arrangement was beneficial to everyone. This way, Chris didn't have to tell his parents he never went to church at school.

"It's a miracle Abe got here when he did," Mom said every few days. "A miracle."

This time, Birdy agreed. But the greater miracle was what she had seen Abe do once he arrived. She'd wanted him to beat Jude up and send him back to jail in shame. Instead, he had disarmed his brother's rage and embraced him in his suffering.

While Jude had slumbered on the floor, Noah had woken, nursed, and fallen back to sleep. A second, absurdly attractive cop had shown up to take their statements, and Birdy had to focus on his weird mustache to ground herself during their interview. Then Officer Holloway crouched down and shook Jude's shoulder.

"Jude. Bud. Come on."

Jude opened his eyes and rolled his head around at the group standing in vigil. Then he scrambled to his feet, eyes fixed on Tammy.

"Tammy, honey, I'm so sorry. You were right, I never treated you right, I never loved you the way you deserved, honey, Tammy, I'm gonna find a way to get better, so you don't have to be afraid of me. I'll never hurt you again, I promise, don't be scared." Tammy had nothing to say, and Jude looked down. He kept his head bowed as he stretched out his hands so his former best friend could arrest him.

Before Officer Holloway walked him outside, Jude looked over at Birdy, who stood frozen next to the mustached cop. Jude didn't meet her eyes, but she couldn't blame him after all she'd overheard.

"Sorry, Birdy," he said to her forehead. "Thanks for protecting my son." He swayed a little—he was still drunk—then he snorted like his normal self and shot her a crooked, bloody smile. "Nice kick."

Above all, Christianity demanded that she believe what she had seen. That a vile and foolish man occupying the murky depths could see the light, rise to it, and become a new kind of creature. She had scorned Abe's awkward transformation up to the moment he had saved her life. Then he'd swum right back into the depths for his brother. Birdy remained skeptical of Jude's redemption, but couldn't shake the conviction that something mightier than all of them was at work.

But what to make of this mighty force that abandoned Jude to its evil servant when he was a child? What to make of it swooping in with a miracle only after Jude grew into a man who terrorized his own children? When she followed this line of thought, her carefully balanced feelings shifted, opening on one side to a well of awe at God's mysterious ways, sharpening on the other to a white-hot blade of fury.

Birdy had witnessed something awful and sacred that was none of her business. The stories did not belong to her; to share them as deeply as she needed would be yet another violation. So she tried to put them away and keep her feelings in their equilibrium. In August, she'd move to college. Maybe that would help. She smelled onions frying. Maybe *that* would help. She went out to the kitchen, where Chris was stirring something delicious around in his Dutch oven.

"It's actually pretty useful," he said, pointing at it with his wooden spoon. "Want some coffee?"

"THANKS."

"My pleasure."

Tonight was Mel's 18th birthday, and Vince was proudly hosting her Boozy Birthday Bonfire. Birdy had one hour left before she could escape work and join them. It had been a madhouse all evening because someone had decided to host a child's birthday party without notifying the staff. Mr. Breech had threatened to fire every last one of them if they didn't start smiling, and Birdy had cleaned pee out of the play area's slide three times. Then the ice cream machine broke, ruining Hunter's fifth birthday dreams. Finally, the partiers had drifted home to bed, Nathan had mopped up the sea of chocolate milk, and only a few straggling guests remained.

The door opened, and Birdy got in position to announce her readiness to serve. Then she noticed who the guest was. She considered fleeing to the kitchen, but Mr. Breech was staring daggers at her from the drive-thru area, so she smiled as Mrs. Amon approached.

"Oh, Birdy! I completely forgot you worked here!"

This was an ominous beginning. "Oh," said Birdy ignoring Mrs. Amon's acute case of amnesia.

"Now, let's see here, I'll have a... chicken strip salad, and a large fry, and a large lemonade. Diet."

"Got it," said Birdy, tapping her screen. Mr. Breech cleared his throat, and Birdy repeated Mrs. Amon's order back to her Satisfied that protocol had been met, Mr. Breech went to go supervise someone else.

Birdy handed Mrs. Amon her change and scooped ice into a large cup. "It's really starting to get hot out there!" said Mrs. Amon, fanning herself dramatically. "Too hot for me!" She tilted her head as if she'd just thought of something. "Now, Birdy, don't you live just down the road from the Doppelskis?"

Again with the alleged forgetfulness. Dread churned in Birdy's stomach as she turned to the lemonade dispensers. "Yes..." She filled up the cup and handed it to Mrs. Amon, who took a big sip.

"Mmm, boy is that good! I can't believe how good y'all can make your diet lemonade. Now, did I hear correctly that you were there a few weeks back watching little Noah?"

"Yes..."

She leaned in. "Is it true, Birdy? Is it true that Mr. Doppelski showed up and had a massive conversion experience?"

What the fuck? "Um."

"It's just I heard Karen telling Carly Strabinski a little about it, but she clammed up when they saw I was there."

Go Ms. Karen.

"But I did hear her say you were involved and I just—thought you might fill me in!" She took another sip of lemonade. "And I heard her say the divorce is still happening?"

Birdy remained silent.

"Karen was acting like Abe did something so amazing, like something he said really helped Jude, but I didn't catch what? But then she said Jude was arrested again and Tammy is still doing the restraining order and everything, so I was just a little confused about that?"

"Well."

"And I'm sure Karen would have said more about it, but there were all the little kids around, you know. Did Mr. Doppelski and Noah get to meet?"

Birdy rolled a stray grain of salt under her finger. Mrs. Amon leaned in closer.

"You know, hon, sometimes when we know the details of a situation, we can direct our prayers more specifically for a good outcome."

Oh, come on. Birdy rolled her eyes at the transparency of this tactic and said, "I don't really want to talk about it."

"Well, I just thought you might want to share your testimony," Mrs. Amon sniffed and straightened her back.

"I don't."

Mrs. Amon's eyes landed on something behind Birdy's shoulder.

"This young lady was very rude to me, sir," she said to Mr. Breech.

Shit.

"I'll speak with her, ma'am, now let me bag up your order for ya, and why don't you take this coupon for a free sandwich, ma'am, that's my pleasure ma'am."

"God bless you," Mrs. Amon simpered, nestling her bag like treasured child. She took a big sip of her lemonade. "This stuff is just too delicious." *That's because I didn't give you diet, bitch.*

Mr. Breech beamed as Mrs. Amon made her slow exit from the building. Then he held up his finger at Birdy. "Last warning."

An hour later, Birdy finally dropped into the Spirit's driver's seat, head pounding. Mrs. Amon was gross. She wasn't aware of the hell Jude had endured at the hands of the institution she was so eager to preserve exactly as it was, but if she did, she would undoubtedly have some excuse, supplied by God. If Jude's conversion was sincere, then only agony had brought him to it. The whole thing was a tragedy, and Mrs. Amon was dying to devour a piece.

On the center console was a red greeting card with Big Bird on the front. The text inside said "Big Bird says happy 3ʳᵈ birthday!" but the sender had made some changes with a green pen. Now it read "Big Bird says I'll fuck you up if you mess with the babies on my street! Thanks for being you, Big Bird. Love, Isaac." She had found it under her windshield wiper a few days after the incident. Normally it made her smile, but tonight she flipped it face down. She didn't want to think about Isaac, or his family, or her family, or Mrs. Amon. She wanted to climb out of her skin.

Angry tears blinded her as she drove to Mel's. She parked and shed her uniform in the car, trading it for denim shorts and an American Eagle top. Then she followed the path down to the Smith barn. Mel and Katie sprinted to greet her with shrieks of welcome and begged her to do a birthday shot, and she immediately agreed. Then Kelly came back from going to the bathroom and was miffed she missed the birthday shot, so they did another one. Angela Prune arrived and squealed and hugged Birdy and her thoughts zipped *Angela-Dominic-Jude-Mrs. Amon* and she told Angela they should really have a shot together, how had they never had a shot together?

Several BAC points later, Birdy was talking to Katie and Angela, breathing the sawdust air and the cooling night, when someone walked into the barn. He looked around, not wondering where to go, merely picking what to do first. She knew who he was, and she decided to tell him so.

"Ooo, you're Lucas! The musician Minuteman!" Birdy called as she lunged across the space that separated them.

Her eyes were level with his broad chest, and he stepped back to look down at her in amused surprise. "That would be me.... How do you know that?"

"Oh, they all talk about you all the time and I saw your video you put on Vince's wall that one time."

He wore a flannel shirt with cut off sleeves, a garment that fascinated her. If it was too warm for sleeves, then why wear the flannel? Had he made it himself? Like actually found his mom's orange fabric scissors and turned his warm shirt into a half warm and half cold shirt? She pondered this mystery, looking him over until she found his face. His eyes were blue and clever and searching.

"I've been coming to Vince's since I was like fifteen, how come I've never seen you before?"

This sounded like a line, a secondhand line at that, but she didn't care tonight. "I don't know, I've been coming here since *I* was like fourteen, I don't know why I've never seen you before either."

"Well, you apparently already know everything about me, are you going to tell me about you?"

"Well, I'm Birdy," she said.

"Birdy?" he smirked. "Is that your real name?"

"No," she said primly, "My real name"—dramatic pause— "is Bernadette."

"Bernadette!" he grinned. "Wow, you might as well have 'I'm Catholic' stamped on your forehead."

"That's exactly what I always say!" She exclaimed. "So you can see why I call myself after avian beings instead."

A deep heartbeat passed before he spoke next. "Yeah," he said, holding her eyes as interest bloomed across his features. "Yeah, I like the avian name better."

2

"AND HE SAID YOU seemed really intelligent."

It had been a week since the birthday party, and Birdy was listening to Mel on the porch swing, confused and flattered. Just a moment ago, she had parked the screeching Spirit and crossed the yard beneath a wide July sky that made her aching heart stand up and stretch. As soon as she had thudded down beside Mel, Mel had popped to her feet and fairly exploded with her news. Lucas, the musician Minuteman, was Very Into Birdy.

Birdy searched her memories for when she may have seemed intelligent. All she thought she had seemed was drunk. Once their names were established, she had bopped in and out of Lucas's orbit for the rest of the evening. He'd challenged her to a thumb war, and she'd enthusiastically participated, perceiving that she had demolished him. When she thought now about the way his hands enveloped hers, it seemed obvious that he'd let her win.

Later, she'd ambled out of the barn and away from the fire and noise and music to observe the brilliant sky. Despite her best efforts, her mind's default setting was existential pondering. When her thoughts went in that direction, it was soothing to look into space. There were so many other stars out there, and maybe some of them were orbited by planets as fucked up as this one. Maybe some of them were better.

"Not feeling the party?" Lucas had followed her outside and was approaching her spot.

"They just have such a nice sky," she said as he sat beside her in the damp grass. "I just love how the stars look so tiny but they're so big. Did you know a million earths would fit in the sun and the earth is like the size of a period compared to a football field or something?"

Undaunted by this incomprehensible factoid, Lucas started explaining constellations to her. She listened with moderate interest while also noting that he held his solo cup in such a way that his bicep was fully flexed. He was expending far more energy than necessary to keep that cup in position. It made her roll her eyes. But it was also a nice bicep.

When "Paper Planes" came over the speakers, she gasped, interrupting his soliloquy.

"Good song," he said.

"Ew, no I hate this song," she said, "I hate when she's like 'if you catch me in the huhhh and you something something suuuuh!' But I do like that part when it's like, 'all I wanna do is'" –she produced a series of weird gun sounds— "'and take your monayyyy!' Plus I like making fun of Vince for saying it was a *thinkpiece*. Oh come on, we need to go tease him about it right now!" she said, rocketing from the grass in pursuit of her joke.

"Wow, you're fast!" he said, joining her, "Lead the way!"

And she had, quickly forgetting he was even following her.

Apparently, Lucas was impressed by the dregs of information she had retained from numerous readings of *The Usborne Book of Space,* or maybe he was just excited to find a listening ear for his own stellar knowledge. Maybe he found slurred attempts at gun noises to be intellectually stimulating. Probably he'd just liked that she was cute and drunk.

She was going to college in less than two months. She was pretty sure he'd mentioned his upcoming trip to Yosemite at least three times. There was clearly no future here. Did that have to be so bad?

Birdy stood on the edge of the cliff in her mind.

"So?" urged Mel. "Are you into him?"

Why not?

"Yeah, I think I am."

3

VINCE WAS MORE THAN happy to pass Birdy's number on to Lucas. "And don't worry, while he was telling me how amazing he thinks you are I told him you're a classy lady and he better treat you right."

"Thanks," Birdy laughed.

"But he's cool, he says he's down for whatever."

The next day, Birdy flipped her phone open to find a text from an unsaved number.

I just heard Paper Planes on the radio, but I can't tell what the lyrics symbolize. Do you think you could help me interpret them?

Birdy grinned.

Birdy learned a lot about Lucas that week. One day he met her at the end of her shift, and they drank milkshakes in the outdoor seating area, away from Mr. Breech's disapproving eye. His parents were St. Paul's parishioners, but after his first experience of Songs and Teens at age 13, he'd refused to ever go to it, or to church, again. "I just hated all that posing."

When she told him she'd gone to various private schools and had even spent a stretch as a homeschooler, he said it wasn't a bad idea. "I hated going to Conrad High, I just felt like I didn't fit in there," he said, adjusting his letter jacket. "The conventional education system is such a sheep factory. If you're someone who sees the world a little differently than everyone else, then it's just really constricting." Then he smirked. "Of course, the Catholic Church is totally fucked up. Especially for women. They're really trying to bring you all down. How did you turn out so cool?"

Birdy laughed. "It's been a wild ride."

Lucas leaned forward. "You know what else was a wild ride, this one time I went white water rafting in Harpers Ferry..."

Since graduating high school, Lucas had been on numerous adventures between his trips home to Conrad. He'd hiked the Appalachian Trail—not the whole thing, he conceded, but a few sections. On one trip he'd befriended a chipmunk by feeding it bits of granola. He'd eventually coaxed it into the pocket of his shirt. "Kinda goes against the whole 'leave no trace' thing," he laughed. "But it was so cute, and I could tell it wanted to play." Another time he'd gone to Miami with a friend he'd known for a week—Danielle was her name, she was short like Birdy— where he had gotten crazy, drunk, high, and almost arrested. He'd always written his own music, but that adventure inspired so many songs that he decided to start sharing them on YouTube. His channel, Lucas Sings, had just hit 30,000 subscribers and he'd started talking to a few studios, trying to cut a deal that would help him make it big without losing artistic control of his work.

Lucas used her name frequently, and it gave her a little thrill each time. Birdy, Birdy, Birdy. She'd learned in COMM103 that using someone's name was a classic method to establish a rapport, and she was irked at the power this psychological trick had on her. Nevertheless, it was intriguing to watch his handsome mouth use her name, to hear it in his rumbling voice, to read it on her screen and know he'd typed it out, capitalized it even.

Lucas was clearly enamored of how unique he was. He told all his stories with passion and gravitas, even when their content was mundane. Birdy did find him unique, as well as a bit silly. It did not escape her notice that he was far more interested in his thoughts than in hers. But Birdy was a fantastic listener who was sick of her thoughts. *This whole thing doesn't have to be a big deal,* she told herself. *I can just have fun for once.*

Two weeks after they met, Birdy got ready for another bonfire at Vince's—Flames and Friends. Vince was running out of alliterations. By the look of the Facebook invitation, not many people were attending this one. Birdy put on a red tank top, took extra time with her eyeliner, and straightened her hair carefully. Then she drove to the party.

She was talking to Vince and Kevin when Lucas walked in and greeted Birdy with an enjoyably solid hug. "Where's your girl, man?" he asked Vince.

"She's working till eleven, but she'll be here after that," Vince replied,

"Oh," said Lucas, then he turned to Birdy. "And where's your other friend?"

"Who," said Birdy, "Kelly? She went to the beach with her cousins."

"Oh, so it's just you and me huh?" he said, putting an arm around her. Birdy gestured to point out the continued existence of Vince and Kevin, but they had vanished. Lucas steered her over to the corner where some cans of Keystone Lite were warming in a cardboard box. He cracked one open and handed it to her, then got one for himself.

"That reminds me of when I was out in California and I camped on the beach. I slept out under the stars, and in the morning the sun rose up over the water. It was just gorgeous. Almost as pretty as you."

She laughed out loud. "Oh wow, must have been really pretty!" She paused. "Was that the California trip where it rained the whole time?"

Lucas looked guilty. "Okay, you got me. It did rain the whole time I was in California. I was in Ocean City the time I camped on the beach. The clouds were beautiful though, shades of mauve and ocher and fuchsia. And you're not allowed to camp on the beach there, so I had to move around a few times to avoid the cops."

They started walking out of the barn. She drank her beer and told him about one time when she stayed up with Mel, Beth, and Kelly to watch the sun rise, but when the sun finally came up the trees were blocking the way. "The whole next day we all had to work and were all miserable. That was the day I started really drinking coffee," she finished with a laugh.

"Oh, yeah, I met that Beth chick a few times. She was wasted, and then she was like crying about her dad or something."

"Well... yeah, she's had a lot going on."

"She does have some good weed though!" He burst out laughing. Birdy's face spasmed, but Lucas never noticed because he just kept talking. "After I smoked her stuff, I had the best idea for a song. I had to practically crawl to my car to get my notebook but I did write that shit down. I'll have to play it for you sometime." He turned to smile at her, but at that moment, a stray Minuteman stumbled up and beseeched them to join a game of flip cup. They accepted the mission. The party was running low on shitty beer, so the cups were sloshed with shitty vodka instead. They won neatly, and Lucas swept Birdy off the ground in a celebratory hug. Her head spun and her body felt heavy as she rested against him. Then he took her hand and led her back out of the barn.

They wandered along the trail through the woods. Trees spread sheltering arms above them, their roots popping from the dirt like veins on flexed muscles. They stopped at the edge of the creek, in a clearing Birdy knew well. They sat down and looked up at the clear night sky. A faint bass line pulsed from the direction of the barn, but otherwise, all was tranquil and secluded.

Lucas put his arm around her and took her hand, pointing her finger as he told her the constellations again. To Birdy, they remained illegible. She tried to relax her body into his, but the cheesiness of his play made her tense. He lowered her arm down again and squeezed her a little.

"What are your paradigms?" he asked.

"Uh... what?"

"You know, like, the ideas you live your life by, your paradigms."

"Uh... " Something about his delivery was annoying. It felt like he was asking only to seem impressive. Still, it was an interesting question. After a moment's thought she answered "Probably the golden rule. Treat others how you would like to be treated, you know." She waited for some sign that this resonated with him. Met only with his anticipatory silence, she asked "What are your...paradigms?"

Leaping at the opening, he crowed "Experience everything," with a relish that made her want to crawl under a rock. But he wasn't done yet. "And my other one would have to be, there is no universal truth."

Ew. Up until now, Birdy had chosen, with willful blindness, to interpret his untroubled attitude along admirable lines. Even at her happiest, worries always looked over her shoulder. She found solace in people who led with freedom and joy, like Lucas. But his confidence was not paired with kindness. She doubted that he had landed on his paradigm from an impulse of empathy or because he valued a variety of perspectives. No, she suspected it was more that he didn't want anything to be true because he didn't want anything to be wrong.

This understanding came in a flash, but she still recognized the humor in the situation. As her usual diplomacy was diluted by alcohol, she had no problem asking the first and obvious question that came to mind.

"Isn't 'there is no universal truth' a universal truth?" she said.

Lucas jerked like she'd stabbed him. "Wooooow," he said. "Wow." He recovered after a moment. "Wow, pretty girls who challenge my paradigms, doesn't get better than that." He smiled to convey how much he loved being challenged. "I've never met anyone like you before, Birdy. Trust me, I've been a lot of places and met a lot of people, and there's something different about you."

Pretty sure you left Conrad for the first time two years ago. This thought hovered in the back of her mind, but she flicked it away.

Lucas was distractingly cute. When he was smiling at her like that, it was easy to smile back. He leaned in closer and cupped a hand on her waist.

"There's something I've been wanting to do since you beat me in that thumb wrestle…"

At first, kissing Lucas was great. This wasn't like Isaac's cold mouth or Danny's wasted slobbering. He was handsome, he had an unusual mind, even if he was oddly fascinated with it. He was Very Into Her, liked her, even though she had punctured his cherished worldview just seconds ago. And he smelled good. He leaned up against a tree and pulled her onto his lap. She didn't love the guy, but making out with a football player slash singer in the woods beneath the stars wasn't a bad deal. She didn't know why she had spent so much time worrying about this type of arrangement.

Her carefree attitude didn't last. It soon became clear that of all the experiences Lucas was interested in having, the most immediate one was her.

After a few minutes, his thumb edged beneath the hem of her shirt. She couldn't figure out what to do about it at first. It felt nice. When his thumb rose a little higher she laughed because it tickled her stomach. She felt him smile in response and he advanced his hand further, but she got nervous and moved it away.

Maybe she was being silly. By all accounts, this was to be expected. People kept saying that was just the way guys were. She knew he was older, and it seemed like a given that he was more experienced. But she had no reason to trust him, and he'd said a few things this evening that really bothered her. He had bent the truth to paint a picture of his free and boundless spirit, and that was before he had laughed at her suffering friend.

Still, he knew about her sheltered background. He liked that song about treating women well, and he sang it with such feeling that it seemed like the lyrics meant something to him. They'd had fun so far. She just couldn't figure out how to deal with those red flags. Some of them were more like dealbreakers, but it was hard to deal with dealbreakers when no deal was on the table. But she could worry about that later. She didn't have to know the future to enjoy this one evening. She would just keep things at a low simmer tonight and—

His hand was back under her shirt.

She pushed it away again. The thing was, she just didn't really believe that was how guys were. Not all guys. How could all guys be one way? Was she really to believe that the half of the population that supposedly controlled the world had no control of their own hands and dicks? And—*why am I thinking about this now*—she had seen something not long ago that showed her men could be more. Men, all people, could rise above their basic operating instructions and do things that were mysterious and glorious. They could put aside a lifetime of mistakes and become something better. At least they could try. She had witnessed it happen, and now that lived in her bones. She couldn't get comfortable with someone so eager to ignore this possibility. She wanted a man with a higher estimation of his capabilities.

Birdy and Lucas had laughed together at her super Catholic name, but now she thought his scoffing came from a more self-interested place than she had foreseen. He might think she was eager to shed that identity, not knowing how it tortured her. Now here they were, alone in the woods, and he expected something from her. Was he going to be mad if she said no? To her, moving his hands *was* no, but to him, it was try again soon. But her friends had muddled through these conversations, he would have to ask for real soon. *When he asks, I'll tell him I'm done.* Until then she'd sit tight, power through, and climb inside her brain, just like always.

Lucas shifted her leg so he could put his hand on her butt. *I guess that's fine.* The swamp in her brain made it hard to focus. She didn't want him to think he'd wasted his time. So she thought *I'll just keep hanging in there,* followed immediately by *You'd never let one of your friends get away with thinking like that.* He pushed his hand under the hem of her shorts. She pulled it out. Then she understood. He wouldn't be stopping to ask. He didn't want to hear no.

Unique though he wished to appear, Lucas was just another kind of hypocrite. Taken one way, his adventurous approach to life meant he wanted to soak up all the fun and happiness their world had to offer. Taken another way, it meant he was selfish and didn't care about consequences. He lived his life without any thought to the network of his existence, and he was inviting her along, for this one evening anyway. She already knew she would make an inconvenient girlfriend for someone like that. It turned out she couldn't even make herself be a convenient hookup for someone like that.

The alarm bells in her head quieted when he kissed her neck. She was shocked by how good that felt, and she sighed without meaning to. Encouraged, he maneuvered them away from the tree and down onto the dirt. This turned out to be his fatal mistake. For though Birdy's head continued to spin, the new posture put her on alert again. He put his hands on her in a new way, feeling her side and then her ribcage and then stealing the next base as if it were just by accident, which was confusing. She reached to bat his hand away, but he'd already leapt down her torso again and then all the way up her shirt, closing in.

Birdy could now see the path before her. How eager he was to move her from step to step. Get her drunk, get in her shirt, get in her pants, get laid. He could say he was down for whatever, but judging by the way he pushed himself against her now, he obviously hoped "whatever" would involve a certain part of his body having a certain type of fun. He barely knew her, but he wanted to have her. She was supposed to be okay with this, but she wasn't. She wasn't supposed to think sex mattered, but she did. She knew that was where this would end if she didn't stop it. She did not want it here, with a rock in her back, with him.

So many times she'd tried not to rock the boat. To be so still and steady that the storms around her would calm themselves. But that only ever delayed the inevitable or invited worse storms. Mary was still gone; Beth was still gone. Sam Purcell was still dead. Birdy, in her precious pride and privacy, could take a thousand punches and never tell a soul. But she could hit back, too.

Birdy wanted respect, and she wasn't going to get that from Lucas. He didn't see her as an equal, he saw her as a nothing, a void existing for his pleasure. He thought she was a challenge, a tease, a sexy robot puzzle who if he could just touch here, here, and here, would be ready to do exactly what he wanted, of her own free will of course. She was a challenge, but not the kind he liked. She didn't believe she should just get this done to save herself some future embarrassment. She wanted better. She was not someone to be worn down. She was someone to be earned.

He won't stop pushing. No one will stop this but you. So stop it. Now.

She put her hands on his shoulders and shoved hard. He rolled off her reluctantly. She sat up and turned her face away, eyes squeezed shut. A few beats passed before he sat up beside her.

"You okay?" he said. "I thought we were having fun here."

"We were," said Birdy. "But... I'm done." She grabbed hold of the swirling thoughts in her head and forced herself to look at him. "I don't want to do more, and I think you do."

He was quiet.

"Right?" she urged.

"Yeah." He glanced over the water. "You really seemed like you were heating up for a second there."

She blinked.

"Vince said I should go slow with you. I didn't realize he meant that slow."

Something within her stirred as Lucas kept talking.

"But I guess you do come from a really strict background." He placed his hand on her thigh, fixed her with a concerned gaze. "I've met girls like you before, Birdy." He stroked her leg with his thumb. "So many people are just tied down by other people's feelings. Birdy, have you ever thought maybe you should just live your life the way you want, without worrying about what anyone else expects of you?"

"Get my name out of your mouth."

Lucas looked like his pet chipmunk had turned into a scorpion. Birdy took his hand off her for the last time. She stood up, knees wobbling. There was a lump in her throat, but she spoke through it, and it made her voice full and loud.

"I am living my life the way I want. That's why I'm walking away from you now."

And she left him and his paradigms alone on the edge of the creek.

4

THE SMOKY AROMA OF a late summer night drifted through the window screen. John looked out into the yard and smiled. Mel and her friends had set up a tent and were gathered around their anemic campfire, looking serious. After all they had been through, the innocence of this activity warmed his heart. But knowing all they'd been through, he also counted his beers and checked the shelf where they kept the wine and rum. Nothing was missing, but he realized with embarrassment that their alcohol storage system was long overdue for an update.

Lily came and stood beside him at the counter. Their family had just taken an unprecedented and much-needed trip to Ocean City, and a week on the beach had given Lily's hair an intriguing, coppery sheen. She'd also used about a gallon of sunscreen during their visit. Though she'd showered twice since their return, he still caught its light scent as she drew near.

"Where's Jessie and Bailey?" he asked.

"Playing pool," she said. "How'd it go?"

He crossed his arms and leaned back on the counter, trying to answer. John had spent months of tense discussions with his boss about how CCPD could redirect some of its resources to preventative and rehabilitative community programs. The budget just wasn't there, but his boss was shaken by the recent incident with Jude. Last week, he'd finally agreed to let John start a program if he could raise the money. John had no idea how to do that, but he thought Karen Doppelski might. Today he'd gone to the jail to talk over some ideas with a colleague, and while he was there he visited Jude.

Naturally, Jude was curious what John was up to, and he was enthusiastic at the answer. "I'm gonna turn it all around," he said, his eyes sparkling. "Last time I was in jail I was so pissed, I thought everyone was against me, but I'm ready now, I'm gonna get better in here and I'll help you once I get out there. We've gotta help people like me, before they turn into people like me." He laughed, looking nothing like a man who'd recently attacked his family.

But John had seen it all before, the way Jude could fall in love with an idea and champion it right up to the moment he abandoned it like trash. After a lifetime of games, laughter, and beers by the fire, their friendship had come down to chatting in a windowless room. He looked outside again at Mel, Birdy, and Kelly, now doubled over with laughter. That bond of friendship could carry you through the worst of times or lead you to them. It could help you become who you wanted to be. Or it could wreck you.

Their whole lives, Jude had overflowed with tall tales. Lately John had been haunted by the worst of them. They were both gutted when St. Ann's closed, to the point of sharing secret tears in John's treehouse. During their first lunch period at Conrad Primary, one of their new friends asked them why St. Ann's shut down.

John didn't know why because their parents wouldn't say, but Jude put on that signature smirk and said, "Well, people don't like to talk about it, but there was something going on between the priest and this one nun. If you know what I mean." He raised his eyebrows at the kid, who didn't even think to be skeptical.

"But how do *you* know that?" he asked, awestruck.

Jude sipped his milk with an aura of superiority. "I'm an altar boy. Sometimes you see things." He wiped off his milk mustache. "I mean, she was hot, for a nun."

John remembered watching Jude talk and thinking "No, that's not true." Not the way you do when you don't want to believe something, but the way you do when a story just doesn't add up. Sister Josephine, he had to mean, but Sister Josephine was warm and smart and funny and fierce and true, and she wouldn't, John knew it. And Jude told the story the way he did when he told the other stories John didn't believe, like when they were seven and he said his face was all messed up from jumping off the jungle gym, or when they were nine and he said he'd smoked a whole pack of cigarettes and put some of them out on his own hands and back, leaving those angry round burns behind. Jude always told those stories triumphantly, making himself the hero and not the victim, and maybe that was another reason John had stuck around him for so long. He'd known all along that someone was hurting Jude. John wanted to shield him from that secret pain, and the only way he could think to do that was to keep being Jude's friend.

Within weeks, John heard his own father repeat the rumor about Father Gerard and a nun, and soon it became Conrad's truth. John had never forgotten that moment at the lunch table, but it had been many more years before he had understood what it meant. By the time he did, he and Jude were men, with kids of their own. That childhood impulse to help Jude had kept their friendship alive all those years, but it had grown warped and troubled, just one of many things John no longer understood. So he buried the secret in his mind until the day he saw Jude sobbing on the kitchen floor.

John looked at Lily glowing in the evening sunlight and took her in his arms. She laid her head on his chest, where wisps from her bun tickled his nose. He felt the warm floorboards beneath his feet spreading through the house where his four girls lived and breathed. Sister Josephine told him every person was even more precious to God than his girls were to him now. As a child, he'd believed her, and had wanted to grow up and protect all those beloved souls. As a man, he'd felt like a fraud because he'd never known how. In the face of complex reality, he'd given up. But for the woman in his arms, the children in his home, the people in his town, he would step out from behind the shame of turning away, and do what he could.

"It was hard," he said into Lily's hair. "I don't know what's going to happen. But I know I love you."

5

"MY MOM WOULD NEVER do this," said Kelly proudly.

"That's true," said Birdy, who could not picture Mrs. Merryman choosing to sleep on dirt.

They were armed with smore's supplies, which were already half gone, Smirnoff Ices, which Peter had bought Birdy in pity and revulsion, Mr. Cleary's tent, which they had assembled with some struggle, and a fire, which Mel had started using directions she'd printed from Google.

"Voila," said Mel, tossing the balled-up instructions into the small flames. Officer Holloway had stopped by on his way into the house and nearly had a coronary at the sight of Mel trying to build a fire on the Internet's advice, but she had waved away his offers to help and eventually succeeded.

It was Monday night, a reunion and a parting. On Saturday, the Holloways had returned from their vacation. Kelly had spent the two weeks before their trip at Deep Creek Lake, during which time the Clearys had visited Patrick and Birdy had been cured of any homesickness she might otherwise have brought to UMD. In three days, Mel would head for Frostburg and Kelly for Salisbury, the extreme ends of Maryland's odd sprawl. This was to be their last sleepover before college, and they had tried to make it extra special. Hence, the setting in the great outdoors.

"Did you see who's Facebook official?" said Mel.

"Yes," said Birdy.

"No," said Kelly.

"I'm sorry to tell you this, Kelly," said Birdy.

"It's okay to cry," said Mel.

"Who?" Kelly demanded.

"Kevin and Angela!" cried Birdy.

"No way!" said Kelly.

"Honestly, they're a cute couple," said Mel.

"Or at least they kind of make sense," said Birdy.

"Apparently Kevin's been into her ever since that one Halloween party, and he told Vince like a year ago," said Mel, "and Kevin thought Vince would tell Angela, but Vince never said anything, and Kevin was too shy to say something himself."

"I can't imagine Kevin being too shy to say anything to anyone," said Birdy.

"He must really like her!" said Kelly.

"What's with all of us trying to communicate through Vince all the time?" said Birdy.

"How about we never use him as a messenger for anything ever again," said Mel. "I love him but that is just not his calling in life, it never goes well. He felt so bad when I told him about Lucas."

"Maybe there will be better guys at college," said Kelly said to Birdy.

"Maybe," said Birdy skeptically.

"Are you doing okay?" asked Mel. "After that whole thing?"

"It's fine," said Birdy. "I knew all along it wasn't going to be anything special."

"Right," said Mel, "Except you keep staring into the distance like you always do when you're wrestling with big thoughts."

"I never do that," Birdy scoffed.

"Come on," said Mel. "Do you need to chug one of these Ices, or are you going to just go ahead and say what's on your mind?"

Birdy smiled and dug her fingers in the dirt. "It's like... my whole life I had this idea that truth is real, like it's this tangible thing, that you could grab onto it, almost. Because we were Catholic, and that was supposed to mean we had the truth on our side, and on top of that we had all these books around where good versus evil was always so clear. And the last few years I've realized it's usually not that clear at all. There's not always a black and white answer for everything. And anyone who says there is is probably an asshole. But I still think some things *are* true no matter what."

"Like what?" said Kelly.

"Like—love your neighbor. Or at least don't treat people like shit. Actually do good, don't just sit around talking about who's wrong. It's just depressing to act like the truth isn't there just because I can't find it right now. I want to keep trying."

Summer freckles spiced Mel's watchful gaze as she listened to Birdy. "Well, I think it's safe to say he didn't deserve you." She leaned back on her elbows. "And I wasn't going to say anything, but Vince *did* say he sucked at running Atomic Crab."

"And *I* wasn't going to say anything, but "Daughters" is kind of a stupid song," said Kelly.

"Yeah," sighed Birdy. "That part about how you can break boys is pretty messed up."

"Twenty bucks says John Mayer turns out to be a creepy weirdo," said Mel. They all laughed, then got quiet again.

Over the past year, Beth's absence had been as distinct as her presence. Tonight, they felt it like a knife. They would love and protect her forever, but their contact had dwindled to Facebook likes and little else. Now they were on the brink of new lives, about to leave each other behind. Birdy couldn't wait to move away from Conrad and Victoria Street, but she'd made a home with the girls beside her. She prayed their roots would remain forever tangled.

"I'm gonna miss you guys," she said.

"Stop," said Mel, blinking fast. "It's too early for that. It's time to make our 'no more' list." She cleared her throat and placed a fancy hand on her heart. "I shall begin. A 'no more' list is a list of all the things you're excited to leave behind and you want no more of. So I say, no more plaid skirts."

"Hmmm. No more khakis," said Birdy.

"No more blouses," said Kelly.

"No more tights!" said Mel.

"No more polos!" said Birdy.

"No more yoga pants," said Kelly.

"Kelly! How could you!" Mel gasped.

"Because I also say no more thongs!"

"It's so early in life for that kind of statement! Take it back!" Mel smacked her shoulder.

"No more CRL," said Kelly, waving Mel away.

"No more CHOC," said Birdy.

"No more APUSH!"

"No more Songs and Teens!"

"No more Praise Night!"

"No more awkward dances!"

"No more 'dates' to 'watch movies!' said Kelly, air quoting emphatically.

"And no more guys with weak vocabularies!" said Birdy.

They would stay up till the sun went down and came back up again, even though they knew they wouldn't be able to see it rise. It was their last night together, and they wanted all of it. Birdy laid back on the grass and looked at the stars above. To the black ants scurrying beneath her, she was a giant. To the red giants millions of miles away, she was nothing more than a speck. But the ants beneath her had their own busy purpose, and so did she.

This world of specks burst with such pain and such joy. A speck could turn its injuries and yearnings into weapons, or it could nurture its tragedies into glories. Birdy had her injuries and her yearnings, her tragedies and her glories, unknown to the universe but vital to her. She hoped she would use them well. She was grateful for the chance to try. A few thousand years from now she would be nothing but dust. But even to be dust was to have once lived.

Thank you for this night.

Fall 2011

BIRDY STOOD IN A long, steamy room. The floors and two walls were padded. A third wall was covered with mirrors, and the fourth was lined with heavy bags and speed bags. The smell of sweaty hand wraps filled the air, telling Birdy it was work time. The boxing club had just returned from its run.

Birdy's first month of college had passed in a flash. Moving into her dorm was blessedly efficient, as a hurricane was barreling up the East Coast and Mom wanted to get back home before they all perished. That evening, as rain pounded the windows of their building, she'd bonded with her roommate over their love of soccer and Harry Potter. All that weekend they were subjected to various freshman indoctrination lectures, the prevailing message of which was that the administration supports whatever form your sexual journey may take this year, but please remember that Consent is Sexy. Thus armed with the powers of seduction, students could pick up sexy free condoms from the natural foods co-op.

Birdy had found to her dismay that the food the dining hall served during the school year was nowhere near as good as the food it had served during her campus visit. She liked most of her classes and had finally figured out the shortest distance between each one. She had used the enormous gym and had browsed the enormous libraries. She had been to a soccer game and a football game and had gotten five free t-shirts so far. She had figured out which guys in her dorm were definitely creepy and was withholding judgment on several more. And most importantly, she had signed up for the boxing club during the first week of classes.

Practices were always packed. Each night they ran, did calisthenics, and hit the bag and mitts. If that wasn't enough, there was the option to try the competitive team. Just this past week, the prospective fighters had started meeting at six A.M. three mornings a week to go for extra runs. The boxers were not legally allowed to hit each other on campus, but those who proved their mettle by coming to runs would soon be invited to a nearby gym where they could spar.

"Ready, girl?" Birdy turned her head to find Hadley, her usual drill partner, beside her.

"Ready," said Birdy.

"Oh, this is perfect," Hadley murmured, "It's not so crowded tonight." Birdy followed her hungry gaze. Hadley was on the prowl for boxing guys, and her primary target had just finished wrapping his hands. Jack was a junior, the team's resident heavyweight. Despite his hulking frame, he was light on his feet and led them on swift runs all over their hilly campus. Many people liked to start their weekend festivities on Thursday nights, but Jack had never missed a practice. Birdy knew because she had never missed a practice either.

"Alright everyone," called Jack, "We're about to get started with practice, but I wanted to remind you that the team is going to watch some fights at the Naval Academy this coming weekend, so if you want a chance to see a real boxing match, come along. As always, I'm here for any questions you might have."

Hadley had a question. She stepped forward, boobs first. "Jack," she said, "Do you have any recommendations for how to work your lower abs? See my upper abs are really defined—" she lifted her shirt to demonstrate her upper ab definition and also her pink sports bra "—but I just don't know how to define my lower abs." She put a thumb in her waistband and hiked her shorts down to demonstrate her allegedly weak lower abdominals and also her red panties.

Jack looked alarmed at this turn of events, but his response was professional. "Well," he said, lowering himself to the floor, "and I apologize if this looks crass, but reverse crunches are good for working your lower abs." He laid on his back, put his legs straight in the air, and lifted his hips off the ground a few times. He got back to his feet quickly, and, to Birdy's amusement, did not look back at Hadley, who was shooting him a lascivious smile of gratitude. Instead, he addressed the room at large.

"I promise you that if you keep showing up and putting work in, you'll have a rock-solid core, even if it doesn't look as defined as some P90X commercial or whatever. You have to use your core to throw those good punches, so you're always working it hard when you're in here. But we're not here to be body builders. Don't get me wrong, we'll all get in amazing shape and that feels good, but what I love most about boxing is what it does for you on the inside." He thudded his gloved fist on his powerful chest. "Life can knock the shit out of you sometimes. Boxing teaches us how to keep walking through that suffering, fight back and win the day. Shit, sometimes we don't win the day, but we still go to sleep knowing we fought back.

"When you get up and go running with me at six am and then you go to class, you've already done more that day than anyone else in that lecture hall. When you push yourself harder than you ever thought you could before at practice, you start believing you're capable of more in your personal life too. When you choose not to get wasted on Friday because you're sparring on Saturday, you're teaching yourself that there's more to life than the status quo, there's something greater you can strive to be. You bring that mental toughness to everything you do, and you start showing up for yourself. And just as important, you show up for the people around you. We compete alone, but we train as a team. We've gotta be dedicated to each other. I might hear my alarm in the morning and feel like staying in bed, but I know I've gotta get up and run because I can't let you all down. I know you won't let me down either."

The sweaty would-be fighters stood in contemplative silence. Much was made in college of doing your own thing and living like each night was the only night there would ever be, unless you were going to a networking event that could enhance your future career as a professional MBA holder. To have a peer calling them to push their minds and bodies to earn their own respect and to support their teammates, that was something new.

Jack turned to Birdy. "And speaking of dedication, I know one person in particular who's always putting in serious work. Birdy, I saw you throwing that killer jab around yesterday. Will you show us how it's done?"

Me? Birdy was already wearing her mouthguard, and she grinned so hard it almost fell out. She clenched her mouth back around it and got into her stance. Jack popped in his own mouth guard, switched out his gloves for mitts, and stood in front of her. His straight, thick eyelashes cloaked round eyes that came to sweet tapers where he smiled. He tapped her shoulder with the mitt and held it up. "Let's go!"

Birdy smiled and unleashed her left hand.

Acknowledgements

To paraphrase Pam Beesly, I have so many people to thank for this book!

To the Author of everything, thank you for music, mountains, oceans, and my life. You're never shy about the plot twists.

Thank you to the writers who shaped me, especially Harper Lee, Brian Jacques, Madeleine L'Engle, C.S. Lewis, Toni Morrison, and Gillian Flynn. Further thanks to the writers whose professional wisdom helped me get a book out of my head and into the world: Stephen King, Anne Lamott, and Ursula K. LeGuin.

Thanks to YouTube for letting me constantly listen to 2000s music so I could properly immerse myself in the vibes.

To all my ARC readers and launch team members (several of whom will also be mentioned below), thank you for helping me spread the word about my first novel.

To Elizabeth Walters for being my very first mom friend and for encouraging my writing aspirations from afar for so many years.

To Ana Padilla, for answering my ER questions in the school parking lot. Your holiday earring game is matched only by your warmth and kindness. Any errors in representing hospital protocols are my own.

To Michele Krueger, Lauren Opinion, and Jenn Koslowski, a.k.a. the Garbage Cats of Cockeysville. When I started writing this book, I had a good chuckle over the moms and their precious walking group, but just look at me now! Thank you for all the steps taken, hills conquered, stories told, and support given on our mom walks, and for sharing your delightful families.

Thank you to Courtney Gahagan of Freestyle Designs, LLC, for your beautiful cover design and beautiful friendship. It's a privilege to work with you, learn from you, and bring up our sweet kids together.

To Erin Oberrender and Shannon McIntyre: I still refer to you as "the Reilleys," but I'm pretty sure you can forgive me for not calling you by your proper names. To paraphrase C.S. Lewis, friendship is born in the moment when you realize you aren't alone. From nights in the tiki bar to hours of soccer to retreats we wanted to retreat from, from rounds of boxing to rounds of drinks, from midnight queso to midday gluten-free, dairy-free, animal-free, alcohol-free meals, from beach days to wedding days to Christmas Crafting and Baking Days, we've shared so many precious moments over the last two decades. I wouldn't be me without the two of you. Thank you for reading multiple drafts of this story, for being faithful post-likers, and for all the ways we've grown together.

To my fantastic in-laws, John and Deanna Busch, who raised a rockstar future husband and who have embraced, supported, and encouraged me since the day we met.

To my Busch side siblings: John, Katie G, Em, Matt, Katie N, Ben, Mary Shea, Betsy, and Chris. I'm so glad I gained even more siblings when I married your brother. Thanks for accepting me into the ranks.

Special thanks to Betsy for reading, critiquing, and championing this book many times over, all while becoming a Musicology Master. Who needs a fancy writing conference in a cabin when we can sit on my basement carpet that smells vaguely of the previous owner's dogs? I can't wait to see your books in print someday.

To those brave, beloved souls who became my siblings when they made the questionable choice to marry Breslins: Angela, Liz, Kevin, Rachel, and Callie. Thanks for tolerating and vastly improving our family.

To the best crew of cousins ever: Kendall, Sarah, Mary, Hannah, Ruth, Julian, Ignatius, Ben, Ellie, Edie, Bash, Theo, Toby, Gladys, Rory, Arthur, Luca, Ari, The Baby, Logan, and Jonah. I love being your aunt and I am so thankful for all the crowded family gatherings!

Mom, thank you for teaching me to read and write, and for your boundless enthusiasm and fierce love.

Dad, thank you for instilling my love of the darkly humorous with *Little Orphan Annie* and *The Spider and the Fly*, and for so many doses of kindness and breakfast through the years.

To the Opera of Death: One reason I write is to attempt to capture what all of you mean to me. The gift of your companionship makes me halfway functional, or at least halfway funny.

Thanks Mike, for leading us with strength and sarcasm, for being tough, loyal, and loving, and for answering my Marine questions.

Thanks Joey, for forging the path of authorhood, for your insight and advice, and for writing the improved version of a popular praise song found in these pages. When you consider that I'm only eleven, this book is really impressive.

Thank you Kristin, for carrying me when I was a baby, for reading an early draft of this book, and for being my long distance BFF in our "parenting journey." I see you, mama. Birdy would have been much better off with a sister like you. Don't worry, there will be a sister in the next book.

Thank you Casey, for all our journeys to Wal-Mart, for driving me to odd recesses of Maryland, and for the reels and memes you supply me with on a daily basis.

Thank you Max, for the hours we spent watching Spiderman, Smallville, and The Dark Knight, and for all our trips to Exxon and 7-Eleven for snacks.

I could never have written this book without my three kids, who encourage, motivate and delight me every day. PJ, thank you for talking about plotlines with me and for your inspiring dedication to your projects. Martin, thank you for looking at the world in such a colorful, clever way and for your inspiring confidence. Reggie, thank you for cherishing the beauty around you and for inspiring me to be committed to the details. The three of you have supercharged my creativity and shown me exactly what matters most. I'm glad I got my writing career going before Mutant Comix takes off—maybe you can buy the movie rights someday?? Also: 6/7.

And last and greatest, my husband Tom. My ideal reader, my teammate forever. Through sickness and health, through floods and freezes, through beaches and woods and through all the sleepless nights, there's no one else with whom I'd rather I'd rather take on the world. Thanks for leading those runs. I'm glad I caught you.

About the Author

Catherine Busch has a psychology degree from University of Maryland and uses her fascination with human behavior to write books and raise kids. When she is not reading, writing, or exercising, she is probably making food or cleaning it up. She lives in Maryland with her family. Follow her writing and publishing updates on Substack at catherinebusch.substack.com and on Instagram at catherine.busch.author.

Author's Note

I will never stop marveling at the way relationships have such power to hurt us, heal us, and grow us. I hope you can use *Birdy Cleary* to connect with loved ones, so I've created a free book club packet with discussion questions, menu suggestions, and more. You can find it on my newsletter site, catherinebusch.substack.com, or my publishing website, ceruleanpressllc.com. Take the ideas you like, grab some snacks and beverages, and let the good times roll.

As Kelly said on page 264, word-of-mouth is an essential part of any advertising campaign. Authors especially rely on reviews and personal recommendations from their readers. If you enjoyed *Birdy Cleary*, please leave a review online, request a copy through your local library system, and tell your friends about it. Do the same for other books you love, too! Their authors will thank you.